C000001143

CHILDREN OF

By Dee Kearney

I hope reading this book
reminds you of home.
Love always.
M x

ISBN 978-1-9163900-2-7

©Dee Kearney 2020

Published by Elsworth Creative

DEDICATION

For the family who are friends and the friends who are family and for those great characters gone before and *particularly* for the amazing **1950's women** who fight alongside me for pensions justice and their stolen pensions. This is a book about women and family and how often women set aside their personal dreams for love or family because it is innate within us.

***

We often leave it too late to ask our parents to lay down our family history before it's forgotten. This is my way of saving the little I know for the ones to come.

It is almost entirely a work of fiction, based on small memories of my wonderful family, but mostly it is to preserve their individual characters as I remember them for the generations to come.

For May, Edward, Rene, Arthur, Lillian , Doreen, Gary and Maureen and lastly Graham, who I loved like a father. Also for Paul, my cousin who we recently lost far too soon. My gratitude to his daughter Claire for helping proof read this book.

They were mostly poor, but they were proud. They fought each other and they fought for each other. That is the essence of true family.

Also for my children Alex and Sarah who, every day make me very proud for the intelligent and compassionate human beings they are ...and for my best friend and husband Duncan, who bears my manic episodes of writing with good grace and supports my fight for pensions justice.

Most of all, it is for my grandchildren Ishani Mistry, Benjamin Kearney and Liana Mistry, so that one day they may look back and be proud of their WASPI, Government challenging and creative grandmother who adored them and who refused to toe the line, even with old age approaching.

If I am lucky, my family will have some precious memories of me and that's all we can really ask.

This book is especially dedicated to the inspiring women who stand beside me in the fight for **1950s women's pension justice**, despite loss, poverty, ill-health, overwork and despair!..and for the 90,000 and counting, who have died early, pension-less and betrayed by their own country. They did what was asked of them at a time when equality wasn't even expected. Having reached an age where they should finally have had 'Equality'. It has been used against them as a means to steal from them in old age... No apologies for campaigning here. It is one of the greatest crimes of our century and perpetuated upon women by the government they had been brought up to trust. This book is for those broken, brave and fearless women who have chosen to fight this rather than let it happen. For all the women who are 'NOT GOING AWAY'

Thanks also to Michelle Collier for her proof reading and support and to Patsy Allen for her ever present belief in me.

Dee Wild Kearney

Chapter One
(Introduction)
Lancashire 1945

The sun was at its zenith as the girl surveyed her kingdom, high on the Lancashire moors above Newhey. Inhaling a long deep breath of warm spring scented grass as she lay, bare legs dangling, over the edge of the quarry. Lillian, known as Bill or 'our Billy' by the family, for her tomboyish ways, was oblivious to the danger of being so close to the edge on soft ground. It was her place for dreaming and an escape from the hundred pumps at the well she knew would be waiting for her at home.

High over the Ogden reservoirs the sky was a pure cerulean blue with the sun full and bright in an almost cloudless sky. Stretching her slender arms back over her head she anticipated the summer to come. Soon it would be time for white pleated skirts, dancing and stealing a few surreptitious kisses off some surprised, yet lucky local lad at the Hill Stores dance hall. Now that the spring was upon them and the war was over, she was eager for romance and at eighteen, it was long overdue. The memories of watching the bombings on a distant Manchester light up the sky, like a blurred hell from this high viewpoint were starting to fade and with it the terror she had once felt would never leave her, had been smothered down, but never quite erased as she would have liked.

One of seven children, that should have been ten, she was glad of the peace up here. Sadly, her mam had a habit of strangling the babies with the umbilical cord in childbirth and she accepted that as only a child born to poor parents could. Besides, mam was always pregnant and despite being ex-communicated for marrying a Protestant, she was still a good Catholic girl at heart, resulting in three boys and four girls, of which Lillian was the third eldest and the wildest.

With the exception of Arthur, who had the heart of a gypsy, the roving eye of an Italian and the fists of an Irish street fighter, which he used often, she was the toughest of her siblings. The streaks of fire through her dark hair were mirrored in her nature and she could fight better than any lad her age. Though manly stuff was kept for men and that kind of trouble was hardly ever brought home, the telling of Arthur's escapades were confined to the pub and it was Lillian's exploits, more often than not, that were the cause of the majority of hammering upon the solid oak door at Wood Mill Cottage.

"What new trouble has she brought to us now?" her mam would snarl as her dad would pull his boots on with a grimace and make his way wearily to the door. Her mam and dad had their hands full, yet it was a loving family, with varying levels of boisterousness.

Suddenly, she became aware that she was not quite alone as there was a snort of warm air that brushed the choppy fringe from her forehead and she opened her eyes to look into the nostrils of Trotter, the family's donkey, who was lovingly nuzzling her and pawing the ground beside her. Trotter was an aspiring equine escape artist, recently having learned to pull up the loop of rope on the gate that kept him in the paddock. In the distance she could hear her mam shouting his name over and over with increasing annoyance.

She rolled out from underneath him and onto her feet making a grab for the halter, but trotter wasn't having any and he pulled away with his front hooves perilously close to the edge. She scooted round to the rear and made a grab for his tail just as her mam appeared in the field beneath the cliff edge. In tow were the three youngest children who had been reluctantly enlisted in the search. Lillian gripped the tail tighter, determined to win, but hadn't bargained on a donkey with an equal determination and May, her mother, crossed herself in terror as she spotted the strange circular dance of the girl and the donkey atop the cliff edge.

"For the love of God! Lillian! Lillian! Let go of that bloody donkey before he has you off!" she screamed but by now Lillian was enjoying the battle and the adrenalin had made her fearless.

"It's all right Mam, I've got him!" she cried joyously as she spun and spun ever closer to the edge.

Just as May had lost her voice in fear and the twins and Graham gaped open mouthed at the scene, there was a piercing whistle and the donkey stopped abruptly, toppling Lillian onto the ground with the sudden halt in momentum. Having left her winded and flat on her back in the trampled grass, inches from the edge, he trotted obediently away down the path from the cliff face and straight to the hand of their dad, Edward Handley.

Scooping up the halter, Teddy (as he was known to friends) turned him round and shouted just two words. "Lillian.. Home!" Lillian knew he meant business and picked herself up and dusted off the cotton dress muttering in annoyance. Did they not know she had it sorted, bloody donkey!

Edward Handley was an amiable man, small and slight, he had passed down his wiry frame to at least two of his boys. There was no mistaking the Handley males, young or old. Gaunt bone structure and prominent eyes made for a characterful face that wasn't easily forgotten. With fine jockey's hands that indicated it was surely meant for Edward to have a natural love of horses and they, in turn, sensed that with Edward they were safe.

He saw the same nature in his youngest boy Graham, who at five had already begun bringing sick chickens into the house to nurse them by the warmth of the iron stove that was the heart of the kitchen. There they jockeyed for position beneath the washing maidens, that for a home with nine people, were a permanent fixture and whatever was cooking on the stove was the fragrance that lingered on that day's laundry.

May was often heard cursing the latest invalid for roosting on her clean washing as she struggled to maintain order in the small room, made smaller by its many occupants, but Graham was her last baby and she never shooed his birds out, although she protested loudly each day, just to let him know there was a limit.

At the other extreme, Arthur Handley used his hands to take on all-comers. Devilish humour combined with the Irish temper made him the antithesis of his younger brother, but brothers they were. Arthur was fiercely protective of his younger siblings and whilst he caused trouble, he equalled it with laughter and the majority of his siblings adored him for the devil he was.

He was also adored by his mother. As her first born son she forgave his episodes of drunken behaviour and womanising, excusing them as the high spirits of a growing young man. with half his blood running full with the blarney. He wasn't handsome by any means, but a thick head of curling black hair, piercing eyes and the gift of the gab, gave him the edge over less confident young men. He was the living spit of his father and she had first-hand experience of how persuasive that combination could be for a young woman. She was sure it wouldn't be long before he was some girl's downfall.

The only real clash he ever had was with Rene, who was the eldest child and already showing signs that she was meant for better things. It irked Arthur that she had an air of grandeur that got right up his nose and he had recently taken to calling her 'The Duchess', which had now been taken up by Lillian. Rene on the other hand just didn't approve of his behaviour and made no bones about letting him know. She spoke plainly, but intelligently, and it was clear to Arthur that she thought herself his better and it grated.

Rene at twenty-four had been blessed with a face that had an air of sophistication and personality, with a quiet yet large dose of self-esteem that could back it up. She would be nobody's fool. With satin smooth black hair scooped up in a French pleat and immaculate make up, she saved her allowance from her wages to buy clothing that would mark her as something more than the daughter of a poor Irish immigrant. You would never have guessed they had grown up with just two sets of clothes, one of which was kept for Sunday and the other washed daily.

Had you asked, you would have been shocked to learn that she worked in the cotton mill each day folding sheets. She saved determinedly and chose wisely, unlike her sisters, until she had accrued a small but select wardrobe that was the envy of her female siblings. When she pulled on a simple cut blouse and her jodhpurs and climbed on the back of Captain, (the massive shire horse that her father had walked home all the way from Appleby Fair when he had found him ill-treated and on sale for horse meat) she graced the powerful horse with the seat of a lady. She could have chosen the little pony Lady May but Rene preferred the challenge that Captain offered.

Captain, now fed and beautifully groomed with a shining dark mane, was a match indeed for the young woman on his back. They made an impressive pair. The stubborn horse and the haughty young woman, each with a fair bite if you got too close!

Edward Handley walked slowly down the hill with the errant donkey following obediently at his side. On his other side his youngest, Graham, who idolised his father, skipped to keep up, but the small boy instinctively knew now was not the time to speak. His dad had his serious face on. A consequence of fatigue after a hard day and annoyance with his wayward daughter and the fright she had given them with her recklessness.

Graham would normally wait for his dad to make his way through a steaming mug of tea and then he would squat down beside him by the fire and receive his nightly hair ruffle. After letting Gray drink the last quarter of tea, his dad would take him out to the barn and let him help with the animals.

For the small boy, this time with his dad was heaven because he felt important and needed. His dad would tell him stories of his adventures in the army and about horses and the gypsies he met at Appleby Fair. For a small boy who struggled at school with his reading and writing, it was all so exciting and was the life he saw for himself when he was grown that didn't have to involve sums.

Graham had started school but was not faring well, did they but know it, today he would have been diagnosed dyslexic and supported. Instead he was labelled as 'slow' and it did not make for happy times for a small, shy boy and so he went within, much preferring his animals to people.

His dad had pulled off his boots for a brief rest of the aching feet too long encased in cheap leather and laid his brush
and polish on the table in readiness for his nightly ritual. With woollen socks beneath that were holed and worn, he wriggled his toes into a more comfortable position to let the blood flow back into his

constricted digits. With seven kids to wash for and feed, May did not have a lot of time left for the niceties of housewifery and the mending was usually passed onto the girls, who on the whole, were not enthusiastic seamstresses. Rene would find an excuse, Lillian would stomp about until brought to heel and so usually the sewing was left to Doreen the middle child to keep the peace. Besides, she didn't seem to mind.

Doreen was the quietest of the girls and had been a sickly child, so the less physical chores were given to her and, in doing so, it served to silence the rumblings from the older children that she was spoilt.

Doreen was her mother's favourite daughter. Born early at two pounds she had been a surprise to say the least. May hadn't been feeling well and was putting on weight, but as her periods hadn't stopped, it never occurred to her that she may be pregnant. It was only a chance encounter with the local midwife that had raised the question of her weight gain and the next day the midwife had called and confirmed the pregnancy, she was about six, maybe seven months. The shock struck May to the core and she had kept the knowledge to herself, hoping secretly that it was a mistake. Another babe was far from ideal, with one still birth and three children already, another would mean eking out the little they had once more. They would need more room. What were they to do?

She only managed another week before the baby started to come and the labour was traumatic as May's body hadn't readied itself for the birth. The passage was quick and painful and there was little the midwife could do but give her a sip of whisky and wait. Both of them believed the outcome was not going to be a happy one, but the intensity of the birth gave them little time to ponder on the likely fate of the wee babe that was coming far too soon. May prayed for forgiveness of her earlier doubts and clutched her rosary more tightly with every contraction.

When finally May was delivered of the tiny little girl who looked liked nothing more than a skinned rabbit. She wasn't breathing and the midwife gathered the baby to her, wrapping her in a towel and rubbed her gently to no response. Laying her in the bottom drawer that had been traditionally the cot for the new babies whenever they arrived in this poor household, she placed her hand over May's sadly. Jesse Booth, who had delivered nearly all of May's children, quietly said "I'm sorry my love...too soon for this little one" and passing May her hanky so that she could dry the tears that were spilling from the grieving mothers eyes, she began to clean May up, so that she could rest and regain some dignity.

As Jesse moved about slowly the atmosphere in the room was sombre. The midwife worked quietly and sympathetically, understanding the need for respect at this time. Annie, May's elderly mother sat below at the kitchen table, torn between needing to watch the children and her fear at the likely loss of a new life and the need to be close to her daughter to give her comfort.

Little was heard in the house other than the ticking of the grandmother clock in the corner of the kitchen and May's cries of distress upstairs. As the longing to support her daughter fought with her role to watch the wee ones sensing they were frightened too, she had been driven outside with the need for activity where she hovered under the window, waiting for a shout that would tell her she was urgently needed.

Edward was away these last few days. He had gone up to Appleby to horse trade with the gypsies and wouldn't be back for a couple of days. He was totally unaware of the pregnancy and in March of 1930 there was no way of telling him. May pondered on the sad welcome she would have to give him on his return.

At this time May was twenty eight, but looked older. A result of several years of scraping a living on these moors with a husband whose physical ability was limited. The dose of mustard gas he had suffered in the trenches had taken its toll on his constitution. This, combined with a runaway cart a couple of years back that had pinned him to a wall crushing his ribs, had finished his prospects of any job that required hard physical labour. At the thought of telling Teddy the tears had started to spill over once more and she had just reached for Jesse's hanky again when she heard the tiniest of bleating cries coming from the drawer.

"Jesse!" she cried out, but Jesse was ahead of her and had already turned and was rummaging in the towel to uncover the tiny girl who was opening her mouth like a little fish seeking oxygen. She gathered the baby in her arms and raised her to her mouth, blowing gently to fill the infant's lungs with life-giving oxygen. Waiting a second she blew again and the little wrinkled arms and legs started to stretch and the tiny clenched fists reached out for recognition of life.

Jesse lay her down on the bed and started to rub her down once more, aware the room was cold and she would quickly deteriorate if she wasn't warm very soon. Throwing open the window she called to Annie who she spotted below. "Annie I need a warming pan NOW!".

Shutting the window quickly, she cradled the little girl to her chest she continued to rub until the little mite started to shout in protest at the manhandling she was receiving. It was a high-pitched bleat of a cry that demonstrated the immaturity of this little soul and made it all the more compelling. Oblivious to her own fragility, May swung her shaking legs off the bed and reached towards the nurse.

"Give her to me Jesse". The midwife handed her over and May cradled her to the breast she had bared and then wrapped the blankets around them. The child, as if knowing its power, latched onto the breast and proceeded to suckle gently and May, looking down at the tiny miracle, thought she was the most beautiful thing she had ever seen. "While I'll be blowed!" whispered Jesse with a huge smile of relief. Annie came in with the warming pan and more blankets to pile around them, stared in wonder at the baby feeding for a second and ran off to bring a hot water bottle for additional heat. The fire, rarely used, had burnt low and the room was cold. This babe needed coddling, she would fetch more coal.

It was the start of a journey that would see the child cosseted and pampered and protected. For Doreen would be adored and with that adoration would come consequences, but May would always love her, she was her little piece of perfect.

Chapter Two

Book One

IRELAND 1919

May had been brought up on the outskirts of Waterford in Southern Ireland. The family were not rich, but they had some assets and Great Aunt Anne, being furnished with more money than the rest, was the matriarch of the family and her own mother's namesake. It was she that had ensured that May went to a good convent school. But often good and brutal went hand in hand. Whilst May learned her subjects faithfully, there was a streak of quiet defiance in her that often ensured she was on some punishment or another.

Ireland at that time was deeply in the grip of the troubles and life wasn't peaceful for anyone. There were gentle nuns and there were tyrants and May seemed to bring out the best in some and the worst in others. Religion held them all in fear of damnation and it started its indoctrination early.

At the time her great aunt had informed her mother that she intended to fund May's education. May had thought herself badly-done by, being imprisoned in a convent and not allowed to be running wild through the fields like the poorer children. Her youth and naivety had blinkered her to the plight of Ireland after the great famine and also to the fact that, in having had a wealthy relative, she had been saved from a life of poverty. A potential escape seemed unlikely.

Even with the great famine having halved Ireland's population in earlier decades, work was scarce and times exceptionally hard for most. Kids were running wild with no food, no warmth to come home to and no hope of employment, so run wild they did. It was a harsh existence that ended, at best, in near slave labour to earn a crust, or married and dying early through the trauma of too many births.

Young as she was, she looked only to the present and couldn't see its relevance to a bleak future for those very children she envied. May was unaware of the protection that the bubble she inhabited gave.

It was expected that she would become a nun, but Great Aunt Anne had made a stipulation that, in order for her to provide the two hundred to four hundred pounds (which in those times was a small fortune) for the dowry, then she had best demonstrate that her elderly Aunt's faith in her intelligence was well-founded. Otherwise, the only way she would enter the convent would be as a lay sister.

The lay sisters were colloquially known as 'skivvies' and in fact were little more than servants to the wealthier 'dowried' nuns. May had no option but to comply, for Ireland in the early twentieth century had but three routes for women. Emigration, which was a fearful thought, as many young women were going alone with only the price of the ticket and knew not what fate may befall them when they stepped off the boat in New York. Marriage to a likely much older man was more the norm, or the Convent. A very limited choice.

As she didn't feel much like falling into the hands of some lecherous old mammy's boy, she kept quiet and conformed. Whilst women tended to be the leader of the family and she may well marry well with her aunt's influence, the thought of being bedded by some greying middle-aged and soft-bellied farmer's son was far too much for the girl whose head was full of dreams and handsome young lads. No, reluctantly she acknowledged that she was where she should be.

Whilst she hated the convent regime, she relished the learning and her need for knowledge and likely escape when she had an education was strong, it would aid her journey forward.

In the beginning of the twentieth century nuns made up a large proportion of working women in Ireland and, faced with either marriage or emigration, the convent had seemed a place where a woman could have respect and status. The consequence of this was that between the years of 1841 and 1901 the number of nuns had increased eightfold.

May knew how lucky she was to have the education and possible dowry, but she would have much rather have had the dowry for other things, like a dress shop in Dublin! That bright idea had been quickly quashed by her mother before her aunt got wind of her flights of fancy and she was threatened that God Almighty would be frowning heavily upon her if he got wind of her flighty ungrateful talk, let alone her aunt!

The threat of God's wrath brought the young girl to heel and she returned to her studies and confessed her sins of selfishness as soon as she could get through the church doors.

In rural Ireland everything was somebody else's business, unless you headed to Cork or Dublin, there was no anonymity to be had. Hard times were upon them and people judged harshly and were judged equally so in return. Southern Ireland was strong in its Catholicism and no one dared fall under the keen eye of the church and its representatives, except perhaps for charitable works and devotion to God. After the 'Great Calamity' around two percent of men became priests and, good or bad, there was no getting away from religion and all its repression and with it, the political division that devotion to any faith encouraged.

Yet in the spring of 1920 an early thaw was encouraging the warming earth to push the first primroses through their winter bed and their pretty garb moved even the hardest heart to a sense of new promise. Being isolated as they were out here in the countryside from the troubles, it was easy to feel renewed hope that this year would be better.

May was sixteen and whilst not pretty, she had a strong boned face and a thick head of wavy hair. It managed to bring her attention from some of the young men as she walked the streets from the convent to her aunt's house with a skip in her step. She was always eager to be free of the constraints of the day's devotion to God and her education.

Despite the nuns' best attempts to bring her hair under control, she always had tendrils breaking free and that, added to her large sparkling, mischievous blue eyes, gave the nuns cause to worry that they had a strong willed wanton on their hands. Strong willed she was, wanton was the furthest from the truth. May had no concept of her attraction and at sixteen and a half the horrors of bringing 'trouble' home had been drilled into her by her mother. The only problem she had was that no one had ever explained to her what that 'trouble' was. She blithely went about her business with no knowledge of the ways of women and men. Except for the knowledge that you married and something the man did gave you babies, May was a complete innocent.

In early twentieth century Ireland, that was how it was for young girls and how the generation before wished it to continue. Abstinence in a Catholic society was the only way to guarantee fewer mouths to feed. As a result it produced strong-willed matriarchs on the whole, determined to dictate when their favours would be received. It was all hush-hush and rarely talked about freely. But it was a knowledge that women in that society had come to know through painful experience and bereavement. Breed less, survive longer. This was the unspoken secret they kept. No room for foolish ideas of love and passion. Mothers ignored the needs of their daughters and smothered down any likely catastrophes by threatening them with the wrath of God for a sin that couldn't even be hinted at, let alone explained to give the poor unfortunate girls any kind of idea of what it was that would likely take them straight to the path of the Devil.

The consequence of this ignorance was the number of 'fallen' women that disappeared from home and straight to the purgatory of the Magdalene Laundries, which were little more than workhouses for women unfortunate enough to have found themselves with child for a moment's pleasure and without any idea of the likely consequences.

Most of these poor unfortunates were forced into these institutions by the power of the church and often by family members who could not live with the shame of having a baby born out of wedlock. Many of these 'laundries' were worse than prisons and contradicted the perception that they were there to treat women instead of punishing them.

Named after Mary Magdalene, the prostitute who Jesus tended, these hellholes continued on into the late 20th century. For any young woman with enough knowledge to understand, the mere name was enough to strike fear to the heart and a renewed determination to lead a godly life.

May waved to Francis O'Neill's eldest girl as she passed, drawing a limited response. The more unfortunate children of the parish envied her strength of character and the clothes that whilst simple, were clean and free from tears and patches. She shrugged it off with a muttered "miserable bitch", the favourite curse she had heard one of the men say whilst complaining about his wife outside the pub. She dared not voice it aloud but it always gave her a thrill to whisper it and she smiled continuing up the small lane to her aunt's house. She'd say a Hail Mary later and might omit it from her confession.. less guilt that way.

Her aunt's six bedroomed house was on the edge of a grand estate, now largely abandoned by its British owners in the great famine and gone to virtual ruin many years since. With only the occasional visit by an estates man to ensure the house remained standing and secure. It had deteriorated from its great beauty to a haunting shell. The house and gardens were overgrown and boarded up and as the garden came up to the rear of the aunt's property giving them an uninterrupted view of the land, it was as though it was their own. It had a haunting beauty that always intrigued May.

The aunt's house, small by comparison but still quite stately, was too large really to be solely used for housing a lone elderly Irish woman and her housekeeper. By many standards it was grand itself.

Her great aunt's father had made many lucrative business investments had gone from a small farmer to a wealthy Irish statesman in just a few years. Having no son and after disowning his eldest daughter for marrying an Englishman and a non-Catholic, and following the death of Bethany, May's grandmother, his other daughter, had left his entire estate to May's Great Aunt Anne, overlooking his grandchild and May's mother entirely, for what reason they knew not.

May could only think that perhaps it was his dislike of her father as a husband for his quieter daughter and his apparent inability to maintain employment, that he had perhaps felt safer leaving the keeping of the family wealth intact in the hands of his strong and most sensible daughter. He needn't have worried, for her Da followed him shortly after his death and her mam had always felt they would have received an inheritance if Da had gone first. Deep down it must have angered her mother, but if it did she never let it show.

They would never know why he had willed it this way, but Great Aunt Anne, as frugal as she was, saw they never went without. May's widowed mother and herself were the only close family members left and they lived in a small estate manager's cottage nearby. Her aunt had rented out the majority of the land to local farmers but held onto the house and the cottage as her father had had them built at the zenith of his influence. Both he and she had loved it so.

Valuing her privacy, but needing to at least house the small family that had been overlooked by her father, she had moved them into the cottage when May's mother Annie had been widowed. She was a godly woman, stern, but with a heart of measured kindness and certainly very astute. The house she had given to them to live in rent-free was small and basic, but by most people's measure they were lucky to have a sound roof over their heads.

Annie Dearden, her mother, took in the occasional lodger to help make ends meet and when that occurred, May would have to share a bed with her mother as there was only two upstairs rooms. Over the winter time they had the house to themselves as usually the lodgers were seasonal workers coming to help with the local crops. May often wished there was a need for her to share her mother's bed in the bitter winters instead of having to pile every coat they owned atop of the bed to keep off the cold from the ice- laden windows.

Despite its comforting warmth May never liked the summer, as you never knew who you'd get and a stranger in the house made for uneasy company sometimes. Still, that and a little sewing were her mother's only source of income above the allowance that Aunt Anne had placed on them, but it made her feel she had at least paid her way in some small way.

May had to put up with it as it was their only independence from the aunt and brought them the little luxuries that most of the families thereabouts couldn't even dream of.

Coming into a great fortune would have turned most women's heads, but Aunt Anne was having none of it. She managed the estate efficiently, quickly learning how to maintain the investments and lived quietly.

Finding no use for a husband, she never married, but she ensured her niece had enough of an allowance to keep her and her daughter from poverty. Having been born at the time of the Great Hunger, her young eyes had seen too many horrors to be frivolous with money. As head of the family, she had felt duty-bound to care for her poorer dependent relatives. Her investments held and she was said to be comfortably off. Living in this quiet way would allow her security for her lifetime.

May swung open the gate and made her way around the side of the house to the back kitchen door. Aunt Anne, who was not one to have many staff, had only the elderly housekeeper Ada and a young mother Susan from the village who was brought in twice a week to clean They were in the kitchen sitting at the large wooden table and about to have a pot of black tea they had made from the saved used leaves and dried for later use. The day's washing had been brought in damp and was steaming in front of the iron fireplace which housed the black oven and water boiler.

"Evening young May." Ada paused in her stirring of the pot and smiled quietly at the young woman as she turned from closing the door.

"Good evening Ada. Evening Susan. Where's my aunt?" May sniffed in the aroma of the stew as she passed the stove and knew there would be a bowl waiting when she came back from spending some time with her aunt. She was too engaged in the aroma of the food to notice the quiet look between the two women.

"Front parlour and not on her own either." came the response.

"Oh, who's visiting this time of day?" asked May, curiosity aroused. The aunt rarely had visitors unless it was business and they usually paid their respects earlier in the day.

"Said he was family." Susan leaned forward to take a mug of the black tea as she spoke.

Now that raised May's curiosity even further. As far as she knew there was no family hereabouts. Certainly no family had been by in years…and in the front parlour too. That was a room for serious occasions.

She headed for the front of the house and along the wide hallway with its muted light streaming delicately through the leaded glass window at the sides of the mahogany door. The light trickled further across the wooden floor that was graced with a deep red Turkish carpet runner. It was a truly imposing hall and the valuable carpet with its rich hues that no one was allowed to walk on with outdoor shoes, echoed the wealth of past times prior to "The Great Catastrophe".

She tiptoed down the sides of it avoiding the edges and paused on hearing muffled voices coming from the large room at the front of the house that, whilst grand in its attire and clean, always had the smell of age, and a mustiness that almost left a taste in the mouth. Not at all like the cosy snug overlooking the back fields where she and her aunt normally did their usual early evening ritual of discussing her experience of the day's education.

Failing to grasp any of the conversation through the heavy door and curiosity overcoming her reticence to interrupt, she knocked and slowly pushed open the door gingerly peering around it into the room. It was a busy room, full of brocade and Hepplewhite curves and heavy velvet curtains. There were many ornaments and May particularly loved the ruby lustres that graced the upright walnut piano that was inlaid with mother of pearl. The walls were lined with books and May often when sent in here to find a certain book, would carefully lift the piano lid and press the keys as quietly as she could revelling in the sound as the note vibrated quietly and slowly away. How she longed to have been able to play, but never dared ask her aunt if she could teach her and so the piano stayed silent and unloved. She certainly never heard or witnessed her aunt playing it, which seemed strange.

May took several seconds to focus on the two occupants sat either side of a small fire. It was the one thing her aunt wouldn't stint on and the warmth of the room wherever her aunt chose to inhabit was always welcome in the cold of winter. She would complain that the damp was 'in her old bones' and she insisted the house was kept as warm as possible to fend off the rheumatics.

"Aunt Anne?" she questioned, casting a glance at the occupant of the other chair and struggling to see anything other than a mop of black hair in a slight young man's frame.

"Come in May. You will be interested to know you have a cousin over to visit from England."

May was struck dumb, she didn't even know she had family still alive in England, let alone a cousin! And English to boot, hardly a popular origin in these parts. She came hesitantly forward and the young man rose and held out his hand and in politeness she took it quickly before raising her eyes to the newcomer's face.

When she did the shock of black waves above deep-set eyes took her aback. He looked like a gypsy and though his skin was pale and he appeared slight in build, there was a quiet strength about his demeanour. She flushed as he smiled shyly.

"Good afternoon Miss."

"May," added her aunt, "This is Edward Handley" he is the son of my elder sister, who I had not seen for many years. Edward has come to tell me she has recently passed on, may God preserve her soul."

There was something in the words that gave May the feeling there was a deeper story here. Her aunt, not normally given to emotion, clearly was feeling the loss and her normally sharp eyes had misted over with unshed tears and it was clear she was struggling to maintain her decorum.

"I'm so sorry Aunt... for you both." She stumbled over her words, having been thrown into a situation she had not expected and it left her devoid of the appropriate response.

"Perhaps you would go and ask Ada to make some dinner for all three of us May whilst I talk to your cousin. This young man has come a long way and I'm sure he will appreciate a warm meal after his trouble."

"Yes ma'am." May scurried away, conscious that she might have picked the wrong moment to arrive and went to do her aunt's bidding. She then accompanied Susan to open up the small dining room and started to set the table ready for the evening's meal. It was rather exciting really, to have a mystery cousin arrive out of the blue. She couldn't wait to scurry home to her mother to question her about the English end of the family.

May busied herself by tidying the room and lighting the lamps as the sun was swiftly setting. She loved the chance to look around this great house without being watched over. She polished the silver and bone cutlery as she laid each individual piece in the manner her aunt had taught her. She buffed the delicately engraved tall glasses for water. They had nothing more than earthenware at home and the beauty of these precious things always fired her imagination and a longing for a better life than she had.

Every couple of minutes she paused by the door that adjoined her aunt's front parlour in a vain attempt to hear the conversation, but the walls were too thick and the conversation low and muted. She eventually gave up irritated and worried she'd be discovered with her ear to the door by the servants.

Her own mother, whilst the niece of Great Aunt Anne, never seemed to have much more than basic dealings with the old lady. It seemed the rapport had missed a generation and fallen to the young girl to embrace. Whilst at times it was tedious, embrace it she did and she had come to realise that she had indeed a fascination and fondness for the matriarch that her own mother had not, and that was perhaps why she had received the majority of the nurturing in her stead.

May stayed away as long as she could bear. She was not the only curious member of the household, as both Ada and Susan were virtually afire with it. "Now off you go darlin', I'll finish this, go help Ada," instructed Susan as she brought more crockery in. They both knew the cleaner would be hoping to eavesdrop on a juicy bit of gossip the minute she left the room, but she complied regardless.

The meal was ready and Ada sent May to call her aunt and the visitor into dinner. May straightened her skirt and brushed her hair in readiness for the announcement and as she did the thought came in her head that here could be a threat to her future. What if Aunt Anne passed her favours onto this newcomer? He was family after all.

The thought lifted her chin into what would have been described by the nuns as her 'stubborn face' and she gripped the handle and decided to forgo the polite knock that would normally announce her entrance to her aunt, determined to show 'him' she was of standing in the house.

If he saw her displeasure, he never acknowledged it and instead rose politely as she entered with a reserved smile. It was clear he wasn't a sophisticated man, but he had obviously been taught some manners. She swept him a haughty look and bestowed her best smile on her aunt.

"Dinner is ready Auntie." She tried to sound the least servant-like she could and the endearment was not lost on her aunt, who hid a quiet smile of amusement.

The older lady rose also and beckoned them both through to the dining room where Susan had brought warm bread and a hearty stew to the table. They made their way to the table and he politely drew out a chair for her aunt and would have done the same for her, but she beat him to it and sat herself down.

Their visitor hovered, allowing them to be seated comfortably, obviously a little overwhelmed by his surroundings, before seating himself. May realised she quite liked his deferential manner and she suddenly felt quite the grown-up.

This new-found confidence crumbled quickly as Aunt Anne asked her to serve. Whilst an honour, it was effective in making her very self-conscious. There was an uneasy silence as she did her best to act the lady as the ladle trembled in her hand. She managed to save herself the humiliation of spilling on the pristine white cloth.

Aunt Anne was first to break the moment. "So Edward," she said, "What will you do for employment now you are no longer with your regiment?" May's ears pricked up. It appeared this young man was fresh out of the army.

He shuffled uncomfortably in his chair. "I'm afraid it's been difficult since the war ended Aunt Anne. My health hasn't been good since I was gassed in the trenches. There are a lot of us all trying to find work, so its looks like my only option is to join the Royal Constabulary Special Reserves, they have been recruiting from ex-army forces. It's not what I wished, but there are little other options." He looked down almost afraid to meet the old lady's eyes anticipating her likely response and expecting to be shown the door. This was Cork after all.

She straightened in her seat and quietly surveyed him across the table. He glanced up nervously, preparing for the way the conversation was about to go.

"You'll be meaning the Black and Tans then young man?...Are you aware of what they are saying about them?"

"I'm not sure what you mean Aunt." he replied.

"Well I'm sure you will have heard why they are being recruited." This was a woman, whilst out in the wilds of Southern Ireland, still maintained a grip on current affairs and it was clear she wasn't behind the door when it came to business and politics.

"They are being recruited to back up the police, but it's widely known they are here to seek out and destroy any IRA or Sinn Fein activity. You may have come with honest intentions lad, but their brutality is already becoming known and they've only just started up. Tudor's men have the hatred of anyone in possession of a true Irish heart. I wouldn't be advertising the fact around here... So I can take it you're not of the faith then?"

"I'm not a Catholic Ma'am. I was brought up in the Church of England, but my mother still held her faith to the end. It broke her heart." He paused to swallow down words that he knew would offend and replaced them with "So if you'll forgive me, I haven't much truck with religion."

May crossed herself internally, a protestant and an atheist to boot, how exciting! There'd be hell to pay if word got out. She had no idea who the Black and Tans were, but it was enough to see her aunt's stern face to know he wasn't imparting any happy news.

"When do you join them?" asked her aunt.

"Three weeks hence...first of the month." May noted that that was actually two and a half weeks away.

"What will you do till then?"

"I was hoping to come here and then work my way to Cork till I'm due to start. I thought I'd try and pick up some casual work and lodgings on the journey".

He shuffled uncomfortably in his seat and May realised he probably hadn't two halfpennies to rub together, her aunt became pensive for a few moments before replying.

"I think I can help you there. I have some maintenance work on the house and gardens that will give you at least two weeks' work. I will give you room and board and 11 shillings a week if you have a mind to take my offer, but you will earn it".

Aunt Anne's tone brooked no argument and May knew it was a fair wage in today's times. Most labourers were on that wage without free board and lodgings thrown in. She must have been feeling sorry for him at the loss of his mother and his courtesy in coming this way to impart the news. As long as he hadn't any other motives for coming. Regardless, Aunt Anne would soon put him to rights if he tried any funny business.

The young man smiled, knowing his wage would be ten shillings a day in the Black and Tans, but for labouring it was a good amount to a man who had currently only two shillings to his name.

"That's very kind of you Aunt Anne, if it's not too much trouble I'd like to accept. I will work hard, I'm no shirker and it will allow me to travel directly there at the end of my time with you...my thanks." He shot a sideways glance at May as if to demonstrate he knew she did not trust him. She in turn had been noting his thick accent, but couldn't place it and also his attempts to speak like a gentlemen for his aunt's sake. He was certainly no Prince Charming, but she could see he had been brought up to mind his manners.

"That's as well, because there's much to do," came the response.

Susan broke the moment by entering to take their dishes, and bringing in a large bread pudding, the best Ada could do at short notice and placing it in the centre of the table. She then collected the dirty dishes.

May realised the cleaner wasn't aware of serving etiquette, but the young man was obviously unaware and this made May feel slightly superior as she surveyed the steaming pudding, which for them was a treat. Susan's eyes had been darting from one to the other, trying to assess the scene before her for an inkling of undercurrents. They opened wide like two saucers when the old lady asked that she prepare the small bedroom at the back of the house for the young man after she had served dessert.

"Yes ma'am" The girl scurried away to impart the news to Ada that the old woman was taking the young man in. What a turn up!

When the young girl had left, Aunt Anne turned to May and the look she gave her was enough to know serious words were to follow.

"May, I must insist that you speak nothing of the conversation you have heard over this table, not even to your mother, do you understand?" May didn't, but nodded anyway. She then turned to Edward. "If anyone asks, you are just visiting Edward, it wouldn't be wise to let anyone know your future work intentions."

She was not privy to politics at her young age and so she could not know the trouble that the mention of a member the Black and Tans under their roof could bring. They finished the pudding, drizzled in preserve, in silence.

When he had finished, Edward cleared his throat and straightened up in his chair in his nervousness.

"May I ask a question Aunt?"

"Please do Edward," his great aunt replied and settled in her seat to give him her shrewd attention, laying her spoon down.

"I never knew my Grandfather. Why did he never allow my mother to return?" It was clear to May that there was much pain behind the question and her interest was engaged once more. She finished her pudding in silence whilst they spoke, relishing the luxury. Her Aunt thought for a moment on her answer, as though there was much to say and it had to be put with some forethought.

"This is not a country for middle ground Edward. My father had strong opinions and he lived his life by them, but had he not, there would have been much trouble and shame brought upon us. This country does not look kindly on interfaith marriage. The lines have been drawn for many years and it will take many more before the people of this country will be able to set aside their feelings and move in each other's company peacefully. We are in dangerous times." She paused as though she had said too much and turned to May.

"May, my dear, would you go and check Susan has set a fire in Edward's room and everything is made up in readiness...and tell them to prepare a wash bowl for him. I would like to have a few minutes to talk privately with your cousin."

"Yes Aunt." It was dark by now and May lit a candle from the lamp to take with her.

"Oh and then get yourself home girl, it's getting dark already."

"I will Aunt, goodnight". With a quiet "Goodnight Cousin Edward." She left with a swish of her skirt to demonstrate she was not happy at the dismissal and thought she caught a glimmer of amusement in the grey eyes of her cousin.

Chapter Three

May kept her head down at the convent the next day, eager to be free without detention for some misdemeanour. That way she could be swiftly to her aunt's to check on the cousin and ensure he was earning his wages. She came up the drive to find it quiet and so made her way round to the back of the house to discover that all the lawns had been cut and the overgrowing pathways had been cleared. Of Edward there was no sign.

She followed the garden round to the work sheds at the side of the house to find him mending the roof on the old grain store. He was looking cold and weary. Obviously he had thrown himself into the list her aunt had given him and that raised him up slightly in her esteem. At least he was repaying the kindness shown him.

She noticed his hands were red with the cold , whilst it wasn't hard labour, there was a chill breeze in the air. As she stood at the corner of the house, he raised his head from his labours sensing he was not alone and saluted her with a solemn, "May... afternoon," through a mouth full of nails.

She came a little closer and smoothed her skirts unaware that she was preening and peered up at him through her fingers to shield her eyes from the low afternoon sun that was streaming through the bare trees above. It wouldn't be long before the light faded and his day would be thankfully over for him. His slow movements showed that he ached with the day's labour and it would be a relief to finish.

"Have they fed you Edward?" she asked with a young Irish girl's coquettish lilt. Edward paused and looked back at her and then his mouth widened and he spat the nails into his hand with a devilish smile which changed his quiet persona entirely and May felt herself flush.

"Aye Cousin they have, and well too, thank you."

"Very good. I'll leave you then." She went to turn but his voice called her back.

"But May, it was lunchtime then and I could murder a brew!" May was a little perplexed by his colloquialism and accent but she got the gist. She couldn't help but smile at his cheek. Still, it was cold and Ada would hardly think to fetch him anything as she didn't like venturing outside on winter days, preferring the warmth of the house and kitchen.

"I will ask Ada to make you something". She left him on the roof and made her way round to the kitchen.

Ada was baking bread and the room was a delight to enter. Her aunt was alongside and making cakes, which were always an experiment but nonetheless a treat. It was a strange companionship, the servant and the lady of the house working side by side, but over the years it had become the norm and whilst Ada maintained the respect required between them, it was an easy relationship.

"May I make Edward a mug of tea aunt? He looks perished and he seems to have done a lot out there".

"That he has my dear. You could take him some of this slab cake also, it will tide him on to dinner. Tell him to finish up now and come take his ease in the parlour"

May nodded, but was a little taken aback that she would have to share her time in the parlour with her cousin. Hopefully, it would distract her aunt from her usual questions on the lessons of the day, which had almost sent her to sleep at times.

She looked forward to warmer evenings when her aunt would walk round the garden with her and point out all the different shrubs and flowers, teaching her their names. She liked that much better than having to repeat the content of all the boring lessons she had just escaped.

Carrying the mug and cake carefully round the corner, she found him washing his hands in the trough by the stable door. He cocked his head to one side and smiled his thanks. May thought, for a slight young man he had a charm, despite his lack of education.

She balanced the food on the wall nearby and surveyed his work. He had made good the roof in the grain store, which was no easy feat, as unused for several years now, it had been passed over as a non-vital job. Recently the house was starting to look a little unloved, a probable fact that Aunt Anne was getting older and weary of the day-to-day management of a large house and its adjoining buildings and land. It was nice to have someone to do the more labour intensive work. It was certainly good to see the garden under more control. Only the wealthy had the luxury of a garden hereabouts and as she loved the tranquillity of the wooded area within it, in this at least she counted herself lucky to be allowed to share it.

"Aunt says you're to finish up and come in for a warm before dinner Edward. This is to tide you on till then." She went to move off and his words halted her. She had an inkling it was a pointed rebuke of her reticence to speak more than a few words to him, or compliment his work.

"And how was your day lass?" He grinned as he rolled his sleeves back down and rubbed his hands vigorously to revive them from the cold.

"Latin!" her raised eyes said it all. "Amo, Amas, Amat!" she replied and he looked puzzled.

"Meaning?" He gathered up his jacket and swung his arms into it and as she answered she noticed that, despite his build his back was strong. The jacket was a clean as could be expected for a man who had travelled from England in it, but the weave was cheap.

"I love, you loves, we love, and so on..." For some reason the words spoken so naturally caused her to flush and in her confusion she turned away with an abrupt "Don't be dallying, Aunt likes to sit and chat before dinner."

"Aye... I'll be in shortly, just putting my tools away." He smiled as he gathered the small pile of tools together and stashed them in a canvas bag that he'd found in the stables.

"Good Catholic girl..learning her devotions.. what a waste." he muttered with a smile as he watched her round the corner of the house and out of sight. Picking up the steaming mug, he paused to look at the countryside and thought himself lucky to be here right now in this beautiful piece of countryside.

***

May was already sitting with her aunt as Edward politely knocked and put his head round the door. He was summoned to pull up a chair by the fire to stir a little more warmth in his bones and he stretched out his hand for the comfort of the flames that were starting to flicker upwards from the newly stoked fire.

"How have you managed Edward?... My tools here are a little limited I'm afraid." Aunt Anne questioned.

"Quite alright thank you, I've sharpened the scythe and I found a few more items in the grain store and some wood which I used to mend the roof struts. The whole thing was about to come down as the supports had rotted, its lucky I spotted it as it could have been dangerous. I could do with some nails and a good saw though."

He placed his hands palms down on his knees to transfer the heat and looked across to May's aunt as she sat with a book at her side.

"Very good, you shall have it, I'm pleased. Do you think you will achieve everything I've asked before you leave us?"

"I hope so ma'am, I'll certainly try my best." He smiled and glanced quickly at May, who looked back down at the book she was holding for something to distract her.

"Good man...Now how's your room? Did Ada and Susan make you comfortable?" replied the older woman.

"Excellent thank you, I was very comfortable". He smiled once more and May had to admit he was a very likeable character and not at all the rogue she had initially suspected he might be.

"If you wish to borrow a book, you may take one from the front parlour, as long as you put it back when you are done." The aunt was being very generous to him. Previously it had taken her some time to offer May that privilege.

"Thank you Aunt Anne, but I'm afraid I struggle with my reading and writing." He looked embarrassed at the admission but Aunt Anne was having none of it.

"Then you must sit with May for an hour in the evening and she will help you, won't you May? A young man nowadays needs to be able to read and write well. You must address it… Now where's that coal Ada promised?" She didn't allow either of them an excuse and had moved on in the conversation expecting their compliance. Edward stood up and picked up the empty scuttle.

"Let me Aunt." He moved to the door and her aunt smiled beatifically. It seemed even she was not immune to the quiet young man's charms. May bristled at her time being taken without a thought for her. Yet in another way it would be interesting and better than reciting her lessons every evening. Her aunt, sensing May's reluctance looked her squarely in the eye as the door closed behind Edward.

"May," she said. "Your cousin has not been as fortunate as you and is trying to find his way as best as he can in this life, misguidedly or otherwise. It is our duty to try and help him in any way we can. Don't forget how he fought to defend his country and suffered for his bravery. These poor young men have been given a very raw deal after leaving the army and life is very hard for them. As his only family, what we are offering him is nothing by comparison and he has so recently lost his mother, a terrible blow...Will you help him May? It's the least we can do, don't you think?"

Her words were sobering and May felt a little shamed by them so she nodded her agreement as Edward returned with a full scuttle.

"Put some coal on that fire young man, we have enough cold outside without having it within. May will help you read, it's decided, so tomorrow at this time you will light a fire in the front parlour and use the time wisely". She smiled and rested back in her chair satisfied with the outcome. If May or Edward had other ideas, now was not the time to voice them and so they complied.

Each evening for the next few days Edward would light the fire and May would set out the book of the day, secretly relishing the chance to be the teacher. Her young heart didn't even consider the mortification that he would be feeling at having to go back to school at the age of twenty and be taught by a girl some years his junior. So May taught him enthusiastically and as the days passed an easy companionship was born and they settled into the study as his embarrassment lifted and interest in the books took over.

By the end of the first week, May was skipping home from the convent school and Edward would be waiting washed and eager to start again where they left off. He liked the books on animal husbandry the best, so she started to allow him this boon, as it kept him more engaged.

They would sit at the table drawn closer to the fire with a steaming mug of tea and read by candlelight until called in for dinner. When the meal would finish, Aunt May would ask Edward to ensure

May got home safely and they spent this time in easy companionship for the five minutes or so it took.

During the day Edward would work hard and tired or otherwise, he had begun to show a definite improvement in the standard of his reading. Even if his writing was quite uncertain and his spelling appalling. Still he appreciated the help he was being given and worked hard. It was an easy time and as they chatted, May started to get to know the hardships this young man and his family had endured in their exile to Manchester from snippets that he let slip in their evening conversations.

He was an only child it appeared, like herself, and his mother had been widowed about four years ago. He spoke little of his father and so May assumed it had not been an easy relationship. It transpired that his mother had written to Anne telling her of her circumstances and she had sent them thirty pounds to help get them on their feet and five pounds a month thereafter.

Edward had enlisted in the army and although he sent home pay, most of it was deferred until discharge and so his mother in reality had little financial support.

He was particularly unhappy and voiced it to May that, when he had been injured and in hospital as the war was coming to an end, they had reduced his pay to one shilling and sixpence a day whilst injured. They had the audacity to dock them a week's wage when a tent had caught fire in the Armistice Day celebrations, even though he hadn't even left his bed! A blatant sign of the disregard the enlisted men where shown for their sacrifice.

Edward had been a cavalry man and loved horses. Having seen the horror and suffering they had endured, he told May that he only ever wanted to see horses canter and play in a field of green grass from now on. If he ever made enough money, he would have horses and he would ensure they were well looked after. May had seen Edward shudder at the memory and she could see it was something that had burned into the young man's soul, never to be forgotten.

When his mother had died he had felt it was only right that he came personally to thank Aunt Anne and to tell her his mother had passed in far more comfort that she would have done without her sister's help. She could now stop the financial support as he was old enough now to pay his own way.

'What a dark horse Aunt Anne was,' thought May, and how generous! You would never have known that she had been secretly doing all this and it put her quiet, stern faced aunt in quite another light for May. She knew she didn't entirely conform to what was considered 'an Irish lady' but it seemed she was quite a rebel on the quiet, funding her exiled sister's family against her father's wishes. May couldn't remember the old man, but he was apparently a bit of a tartar from all accounts and not someone to cross swords with if you knew what was best for you. The fact he had amassed and kept his wealth throughout the famine and a fortune to leave his daughter sufficiently cared for in the future, was enough to demonstrate his business acumen and ruthlessness.

Sad that it had left him hardened to such an extent that he could behave so coldly to his own flesh and blood the way he had. Only Anne had kept his favour and May wondered whether it was a case of her aunt's spinsterhood and only having her father for company that had brought them so close. It looked like she would never know. Her aunt certainly was very closed on the subject. All she would ever say was that it was a very sad time and not something she wanted to remember and with that, May had had it made clear it was not a topic for discussion.

The days passed easily until the time for Edward's departure was imminent and May felt quite sad that her newfound friend was about to leave them. Company in this village was limited and despite his problems with spelling, Edward had a quick mind and was equally quick to humour. As he brought his bag downstairs to say his last goodbyes, May pressed her address into his hand with a request that he write to them both.

"Is it a test to see if I'm keeping my studies up?" he quipped and May laughed.

"Silly!" she said. "No...You are family and family is important, especially when we are such a small one." She hugged him as only an innocent girl could, oblivious of any effect she had and it was only when she noticed him redden that she realised she might have overstepped the bounds of propriety and she coloured up also.

Edward stepped into the back parlour to give his thanks and say goodbye to their aunt and May ran to the mirror to check if her flushed cheeks had subsided whilst he was within.

He came back out with the aunt behind him and as he walked to the door she followed and also hugged him gently to her, placing a kiss on his cheek.

"You're a nice young man Edward. You see this posting doesn't change that." she warned with a solemn smile.

"I will try Aunt and besides, if it's so bad, I can give a month's notice." he smiled back.

"See you don't change... and come and visit with us when you can, you are always welcome."

He stepped back and glanced to May. "Goodbye May, thank you for all your help, I'll try my best to keep my reading up." He reached out his hand and she took it and held it gently.

"Goodbye Edward... You take care of yourself and we'll hopefully see you when you get some leave," she smiled shyly.

"That you will lass," was his answer and with that he placed his cap on his head, swung his bag over his shoulder and was gone. It was a Saturday in March and neither of them knew it would be twelve months before they would see him again and that, in that last, delicate touch of hands, something irreversible had been set in place.

Chapter Four

May had just had her seventeenth birthday and had left the convent school, starting working as her aunt's assistant in all things business. She found she liked living in the knowledge that she was overseeing the running of the small estate. It interested her and she was an intelligent young woman and a quick learner to boot.

She had agreed with her aunt that she would assist her for one year and decide then if she wanted to enter the convent as a novice. May found she liked the freedom of working for her aunt and, although she never slacked, it was much more enjoyable than being under the regime of the nuns at school.

She was paid the grand sum of fifteen shillings which, for a girl with no money of her own previously, was a fortune. She tipped up half to her mother and kept the rest gathering for something precious, in a tin just inside the loft door for safety. There had been a theft by a previous lodger, so now they saw the wisdom of ensuring anything precious was stowed away safely.

She had filled out this last few months and even had her hair cut into the latest flapper style with a wavy bob. She wasn't quite as pleased with her breasts' development however, as the latest fashion required you to be flat chested. She had started to make her own clothes in the flapper styles she found in the papers and she cut out the photos of the latest designs. They lent themselves to being copied quite simply. Her aunt had let her use the trestle sewing machine, which thrilled her. She was quite pleased with her new look generally and walked to do her aunt's bidding with a new air of superiority. Unfortunately, this didn't go down well with the poorer girls of the village, and as being poor there was the norm, she was somewhat isolated from any chance of friendship. Aware they called her unkind names behind her back, she kept her distance. For a young naturally sociable woman it was a quite lonely existence.

Any other girl of her age and standing would have probably made for the city, but May was fully aware that her aunt was grooming her and offering her a choice other than the convent. The chances of being her aunt's beneficiary and its eventual wealth swayed her from pursuing previous goals. After all she was not stupid! Having grown fond of the old lady, she was loath to leave her at a time where she was growing frailer and perhaps now she could help repay the kindness they had been shown.

If she carried on in this way she would soon have the confidence and knowledge to take over the running of the estate. Her aunt made her take note of business as well as teaching her the etiquette of being a young lady. This area she was more resistant to, as she was a tomboy at heart, but she saw the value of having certain social skills.

Edward had written religiously once a week. He wasn't based too far away, but they were only allowed one month's leave every twelve months and she eagerly awaited his return. His letters were very limited, keeping his news mainly to what he had done in the evening and enquiring after her aunt's welfare. She in turn told him of all she was learning under her aunt's guidance and how interesting it had been. How she had tried to keep on top of the garden where he had cleared it and any local gossip, which in the village for her with so few real contacts, was minimal.

Towards the end of his twelve months absence, his letters had been a little more guarded and he spoke more and more of how he was so looking forward to seeing them both soon. She guessed he was deeply unhappy where he was and when questioned if that was the case, he would only answer, 'Its no bed of roses here' and that would be as forthcoming as it got.

Older now, and slightly less naive, May had heard the rumblings in the village about the atrocities carried out by the Black and Tans, but she could not see how Edward would have anything to do with any such thing. It just wasn't his nature and his uneasy letters clearly demonstrated his lack of love for his present occupation.

She decided to ask her aunt about them, having been isolated in her fortunate bubble from politics most of her life. She did so as she sat for afternoon tea in the parlour on a cold and blustery February day.

"Why do people hate the Black and Tans so much Aunt? Edward is a kind young man, he would never do anything wrong." She asked eager for reassurance that her friend and cousin was misjudged in being a member of this force.

Her aunt sipped her tea as she gathered her thoughts. "My dear, men often have to become what they are not in order to survive. Yes Edward is a nice young man, but he has seen much during the war like many other unfortunate young men and it hardens them. I'll tell you what I know of the Black and Tans and then perhaps you will understand why you must never tell anyone where he is or his occupation. It would be the death of him, especially around these parts and would bring us great trouble."

Aunt Anne took another sip of tea and looked May squarely in the eye and she began to educate her on adult things that as a child, she had previously been protected from.

She started to tell her about how the Republican campaign against the Royal Irish Constabulary had become more violent in recent years. How the police had been forced to abandon rural stations to consolidate what strength they had into fewer, more fortified stations. The campaigns from Republicans had exerted so much pressure on the RIC men, their families and anyone who befriended them. Or indeed anyone who did business with them. That it resulted in unfilled vacancies and a serious weakening of the force.

Lloyd George's government would not recognise the IRA and had placed the responsibility for control largely on the community based force of the RIC. This police force had been steadily chipped away at and compromised since 1916 and this caused them now to have a heavier reliance on the military to keep control over a largely Republican population. It was not so much a religious war as protestants were indeed members of the IRA. It was a war for Irish independence from the British.

How, in order to augment their numbers and capabilities, they had started recruiting war veterans throughout the UK to supplement the ten thousand force of the RIC to about half as much again. The young British war veterans finding no 'heroes welcome' on their return and little work back home, had succumbed to the lure of using their hard learned skills once more in Ireland.

Many thinking that they were joining the police force and would be earning an honest wage, would soon be disabused of that idea. They were expected to stand fast and dish out swift retribution for any show of dissent. They operated a shoot to kill policy and woe unto he who walked towards them with his hands in his pockets.

The name had come about because uniforms were in short supply and they had to employ a mixture of military khaki issue and the bottle green of the constabulary uniform. That name very soon started to strike equal amounts of hatred and fear into the local population. County Cork had recently been the centre of much of this activity and here feelings ran particularly high and violently.

The Black and Tans were introduced to reinforce county stations and support the police on major events and their experience with weapons and tactics gave them a tougher edge. They were never regarded by the communities they served or even by the existing police as ordinary constables. Instead they were becoming hated for their brutality and the subsequent militarisation of the police.

This was why on no account was she to tell anyone of Edward's secret, not even her own mother. It would be his undoing and their own with it as his relatives. May found that she had a frisson of anxiety stirring in her belly and realised that being considered 'old enough to know' wasn't always a good thing. She was determined no one would find out from her, but now knowing the danger of the knowledge she held, made for an uneasy feeling. She realised that she would have to watch her words, even in the house where Ada or Susan might overhear.

***

The days went by and February turned to March and March this year had been particularly cold and long. Thankfully the month was almost at an end and the first mild days were starting to appear. May had all the books of the estate out on the table of the front parlour but her attention had drifted off through the large window as she surveyed the first golden yellow heads of the crocus and primrose pushing up through the softening soil to greet the early spring.

Her aunt was now letting her deal with some of the tenant farmers as a start to giving her the reins and she relished the work and the figures she was required to do. She liked having the ability to add up accurately and was even learning by discussion with the tenants. She had begun to understand how they worked the land and some of their methods. Men were always happy to show off to a pretty girl and so she was learning fast.

Today, her aunt had hired a cart to take her to the local town to buy supplies and see an old acquaintance. Ada had been doing the washing, Susan wasn't due today and so she virtually had the house to herself for most of the day. As she got older, she had exhausted all the exploration of the house that she had been allowed. She now wandered quietly along the bookshelves looking for a volume that would entertain her later. The years had limited her choice and she was running short of material that interested her.

Wandering over to the window once more, she noticed the aunt's cart pulling up and so she ran to the front door and down the path to see what help was needed. As she reached the end of the drive, the carter was helping her aunt down and another man was lifting down the baskets of groceries. Days like this were always a treat, when all the new little luxuries and preserves were brought home and the meals over the next few days were always extra special. She went to take some of the bags off the man and as he straightened up and raised his head she was shocked to see Edward, much earlier than they had expected him to arrive.

"Edward, it's you!" she cried and stood back amazed and her smile grew wide. He returned the smile as he juggled the goods in his arms.

"That it is lass! You're aunt picked me up on the road." He turned to the aunt to ensure she had alighted safely and then looked back to May. "You've cut your hair..." He sounded disappointed and May self-consciously put her hands to the waves.

"Don't you like it?" Her face fell and Edward moved forwards but couldn't do anything with his hands.

"No lass, its lovely, just different, very modern." His smiling reassurance made her feel better and she took one of the sacks of groceries from him. Her aunt drew close and smiled.

"That was a nice surprise wasn't it? Come along you two, I'm frozen to the bone!"

She walked along the pathway to the house and turned back to May. "May will you take the driver into the kitchen and give him something warm.. and Edward too. Tell Ada to bring me a pot of tea... oh and tell her there's one extra for dinner tonight and she needs to make the bed up in the back bedroom. Edward will be staying awhile." May thought she'd rather not be the one giving Ada a list of chores after a heavy day's washing, but it looked like she'd no option and so she put on her most confident face and went to do the deed. Edward was back, how exciting to have good company again.

"Aye I will Aunt," she said as she made her way back with the groceries.

"Good girl," came her aunt's reply.

***

The house seemed somehow to come alive again that evening as she lit the lamps and scurried round, setting fires and helping Ada who had been most put out with the lack of warning for visitors. The kitchen was a hive of activity as they stowed all the goods in the pantry. As May took that task from her Ada was adding to the rabbit stew she had prepared, to stretch it out. Luckily the apple pie, already prepared, was large enough to cope with three peoples' appetites and May added some cornflower, sugar cane and egg to milk to make a sweet sauce.

Chatting companionably, Edward and the driver sat at the table with a steaming mug of tea as the women scurried around them getting the kitchen back to rights. Companionably Edward talked as though he had just come across from England and May realised that he had made a wise decision. The cart driver, whilst a pleasant enough man, usually had a snippet of juicy gossip for his passengers. They were best sticking to that story, even to Ada.

The evening closed in and they all gathered round the candlelit table, relishing the food that would comfort any belly on a cold evening such as this. The talk, deliberately or otherwise, was focused on May and her new role and Edward, either cautious or reluctant to talk for other reasons, stayed well away from the subject of his employment. It was probably for the best as Ada was in and out the whole time.

"How long do you think you'll be staying with us Edward?" asked the Aunt.

"As long as you're happy to employ me Aunt Anne, I'm very happy to be here." May's ears pricked up as she realised there must have been some discussion on the final stages of the journey about Edward working his leave.

"Indefinitely Edward for now..if you're game of course. We are short of a trustworthy man around here and there's much needs addressing that requires a man's strength and skills." May was puzzled and she looked to Edward.

"But what about…?" May started to ask, but he pre-empted her.

"Gave my month's notice before my leave, effective immediately." His voice was quiet and it was clear he didn't want to discuss the subject any more.

"Well, all the better for us to have your company cousin Edward." she smiled and was unaware of the pretty picture she made in the light from the lamp, her new curls spiralling softly around the edges of her face.

It was eight thirty before Edward saw her safely home. She knocked on the door and entered beckoning Edward in. After all he had to meet his remaining family member sometime. Her mother was sat by the fire in the kitchen and was sewing by candlelight. She glanced up as May came in and cast a curious glance at Edward.

"Mammy, this is your cousin Edward who I've told you about. He's over again from Manchester." Her mother gave Edward a good looking over and it was clear she was taken aback at his youth.

"Your mammy had you late then?" she questioned.

"Aye, she did. She didn't keep babies well, so I was the only one survived to be born."

Annie, her mother, was not one for much talking, but she smiled and patted a chair beside her for Edward to sit.

"I expect Aunt Anne will be pleased to see you, she needs the help nowadays. When she was younger she took on a fair bit herself, but we all get old in the end.. I was never that kind of constitution. May's more like her..." she glanced over to where May stood.

"May darlin', put the kettle on and give Edward some of that oatmeal cake. A young lad needs his food.. Now Edward, tell me all about yourself." May flashed him a warning 'no' and Edward grimaced and found himself having to cover the truth once more. When he had finished his tea he made his excuses to leave. It was clear lies did not sit easily with him and he rather be out of an environment where he was under scrutiny.

As she saw him out the door she whispered "Sorry, least known best served." He doffed his hat and turned to leave.

"See you in the morning Edward," she called.

"'S'pect so lass, goodnight to you both and thank you kindly for the tea."

He walked off into the night and May closed the door, turning towards her mother who had taken up her sewing once more. She didn't look up, but the meaning was perfectly clear.

"Don't be getting foolish now girl..." Was all she offered and May scurried away to her room, full of young girls' fancies and a heightened flush on her cheeks with a cry of "Ma! He's family!"

"Mmn..." came the response.

The morning sun was just filtering through the heavy curtains in her room when May awoke. The night had been cold and the frost on the window was just starting to melt under the sun's warmth.

She stretched and drew her legs back to where the sheets were warm. Getting up in winter was never pleasant, so when she arose, it was a quick grab for a heavy dressing gown and she slipped her feet into some old clogs that she used for slippers over her bed socks.

Glancing in the mirror she notice her hair was awry and the first thought that came in was 'What would Edward think?' She flattened down the waves and took a long look at herself in the mirror. 'Was she pretty?' She thought so, but it was considered flighty to ask and so she never did. Vanity was frowned upon in the church and she really didn't want to have to list any more sins than was necessary in confession. She opened the gown and cinched in the waist of the nightgown to inspect the shape of her breast and hips. On an eighteen inch waist, she knew she had what they called an hourglass figure without really knowing what that meant. She had bemoaned the fact that her breasts were nfashionable to Ada one day, to be told that she was 'nothing but a snip of a girl and besides, men liked a bit of meat on the bones.'

At the time she wasn't bothered about what men thought, but this morning she wondered if that was really the case. Did men like to look at girls' breasts? The thought shocked her and she knelt down and asked for forgiveness for impure thoughts, crossed herself and went downstairs to light a fire, busying herself until she had erased all thoughts of Edward and what he might like, from her head.

By the time she reached her aunt's house, Edward was away to the back of the gardens, starting the list of chores set before him. Prepare a vegetable garden, mend the fences, paint the outbuildings and any repairs. He whistled his way round to the back of the grain stores where he had stashed his tools, happy to be free of worry for the moment and thinking that he had a good few weeks work on the list alone, never mind when his aunt started adding to it. He liked being outdoors so it was no bother to him, in fact he relished it. At least here he was creating something, not destroying it.

He mused on whether he could make himself a little workshop area in here and thought he would ask the old lady if she would allow him to do that when he reported back to her later. First thing was the vegetable garden and a cold frame if they were going to have vegetables by summer. He grabbed the garden tools, an old wooden barrow and wheeled it to the spot his aunt had decided she would like her kitchen garden and commenced the marking out with a ball of twine and pegs until he was satisfied. The local grain suppliers nearby would have some of the seeds he requested, if the aunt hadn't.

He couldn't help but think how bad it had felt last night to deceive a member of his own family, but he was just grateful to be away from his role in the Black and Tans and it wasn't something he was proud to speak of, knowing what he knew now. He had seen too many atrocities in the war without having to endure more in the name of keeping the peace. He was determined to block out the last year and all he had witnessed from his mind. Hopefully, then the gnawing anxiety in his belly might shift and allow him some peace.

The war, followed by losing his mother and then a year posting to Ireland had left him bereft of any happiness. He had endured it only by waiting religiously every week for word from May. The arrival of the post was always successful at lightening his mood for a while and he was grateful for his improved reading ability.

Filled with trivia about the aunt and Ada and herself, her letters had transported him back to this lovely garden with its peace, fresh air and no one to trouble him. Now he was actually back here with the sweet smell of the grass and earth and the wind playing a gentle lullaby through the branches of the trees, he felt a true lifting of the spirit that had been a long time coming.

He commenced the digging with vigour, eager to make a difference on this long-neglected garden. The little he had done the previous year had already been eclipsed with new growth. It would be good to get it back to its former glory.

May brought him a mug of tea around ten am and he was relieved to take a break. His bones were screaming in protest after two hours of hard labour. She approached shyly and laid a cloth with food in down on a nearby wall with the tea and turned to leave him to it.

"Aren't you going to sit awhile May? We haven't had much chance to catch up yet?" He leant his spade against the wall and wiped his hands on a rag giving her an endearing smile. May found herself flushing violently, a good catholic girl, the memory of her impure thoughts earlier were all too fresh in her head.

If he noticed her flush, he didn't draw attention to it and instead picked up the cloth and started to unfold it.

"What's in here then?" he asked.

"Currant bread…Aunt Anne's been stocking up on preserved fruit, it's a treat." she quipped, hoping to cover her embarrassment. Edward took a bite and his face took on a look of deep pleasure.

"Wonderful!" he beamed as the butter encased fruit crumbled away and took a mouthful of tea. May had recovered her equilibrium and was eager to fire a number of questions at him whilst out of earshot of Ada and Susan. She hoisted herself in a rather unladylike fashion onto the wall close to where he was leaning.

"What made you come out of the police Edward?" She looked at the side of his face and she saw the food he was chewing with gusto, struggle to be swallowed and his smile failed as he turned to her.

"I wasn't really in the police May.. That's what they led us to believe, but they only brought us in as the bully boys. It wasn't what I signed up for... Just take my word for it and let's leave it at that." He took another bite of the currant slab, but it was clear he had lost all pleasure in it.

"But Edward why…?" He held up a hand to silence her abruptly.

"May...Enough please lass, it's not something I want to talk about. There are just some things a person would rather forget, so let it be, all right?"

"All right," she said quietly, feeling reprimanded and seeing his sad face she felt sorry for his discomfort and continued "So what has Aunt Anne got planned for you?"

This was a safer subject, so he launched into his intentions for the garden and she listened interested.

"Do you think I can have a small space for myself Edward? I'd like to try growing some things." She looked down at his face, animated once more and thought that here was a man that loved the land.

She always thought she had a yen to work in a big city like New York and she had listened to others talk about it fascinated, but somehow she instinctively now knew, that despite all her girlish dreams, she was meant for the life she had. Walking the fields with the sun on her face and a fresh scented breeze flavoured with bluebells to be breathed in and almost tasted.

It seemed to her that she and Edward were much the same in this respect and it made her feel closer to this quiet young man with the ghost of a twinkle in his sad eyes. She jumped down from the wall and pointed to a corner of the garden facing out over the nearby estate.

"See there! I could plant flowers and gooseberries and blackcurrants.. how grand would that be?"

"Aye lass it would...I'll see what I can do". He smiled, passed her his mug and the linen cloth, picked up his spade and commenced digging once more. She was dismissed as he returned to his task and she made her way back to the house with a happy smile.

The days melted into each other and they fell into an easy friendship. May, in her innocence, had no idea how her flirtatious nature and easy Irish charm had beguiled the young man. The aunt was very pleased with how the garden was coming to life and often now the three of them would walk through the woodland garden, remarking on the changes and planning for more. It seemed Edward's arrival had sparked new enthusiasm in her aunt also. It was lovely to see.

Edward now had his workshop and had cleared out the stables and outbuildings and everything was starting to look loved once more. May would often take the gardening off his hands and they had bought some chickens and had fresh eggs each day. Life was good and in the cocoon of this quiet countryside it was easy to forget the trouble going on around them.

Occasionally Edward would venture to the local inn, but he never stayed long and May guessed that probably, whilst he went in search of male company, an Englishman - related or otherwise - was never well received around these parts and he had come back to the house, after a fruitless search for amicable company, a little sadder.

It was a Saturday evening when May had come across Edward strolling back up the lane after one such occasion. Edward had had a couple of pints and for once was just getting more jovial with one of the locals who was into his horses, when a young man and obviously republican had joined in the conversation and turned it onto Edward's background in a none too friendly way.

Worrying that he might let something slip with the alcohol he had consumed, Edward drank up and decided it was time to make his way home, thinking that he would never be able to be at ease here, yet how he wished he could. In every other way his life was taking a turn for the good and it frustrated him that whilst he was half-Irish, he would never be good enough for these folks tied up in politics and hatred and bound by the damn beads on their rosaries.

May had been to the local town with her mother that day and returned with some material for summer dresses. She was in high spirits and eager to be at her aunt's on the Monday to start the new creation, that she had in her mind's eye on the sewing machine. With a skip in her step and mischief in her eyes, she had linked Edward's arm as she caught him up. Oblivious to Edward's mood, she had started to chatter on about her day. When he remained unresponsive she rebuked him.

"Well you'll be in a fine mood I dare say Edward Handley. Here's me telling you all my day and you can barely speak.. and you've been to the inn no doubt, with the smell of the ale on your breath now!" She pulled her arm from out of his and pretended to flounce.

"I'll be going then, perhaps you'll be better company when you've sobered up!"

"I'm not drunk May, just tired of these bloody Irish and their miserable faces". He realised as soon as he said it, that it was an unkind remark to make to one who had showed him such kindness and her stricken face couldn't have made him feel worse.

Whilst it was the furthest thing from the truth, May had taken it as a sign he was getting ready to move on and her stomach lurched with the fear that Edward, who she had come to see as her only real friend, was about to desert her. Her oval blue eyes pooled with tears that were rising fast and he reached out a hand to pull her back to him, trying to find a way to show he was sorry. She stopped dead in her tracks as she blinked away the unshed tears.

"Aw May, I'm sorry lass," he said quietly, I didn't mean that how it sounded. I just had a bit of a set to in the pub, I didn't mean you."

She stood with her head slightly turned away trying to hide her embarrassment at being so upset, she was usually stronger than this and hardly ever cried. 'May', she thought, 'you've had nothing to cry for before now'. Edward's hand cupped her chin and he turned her face towards him with a tender smile.

"Nay lass, don't shed tears over something I've said, I'm an idiot." He gave her a little shake with his hand to make light of it and as she smiled in return, the wobble encouraged a single tear to spill over and roll down her cheeks to her lips, where she instinctively licked it away. It was the undoing of him and all his promises he had made to keep his distance from this young girl, melted away with it. He drew her mouth to his and placed a gentle kiss on her lips...the moment seemed endless to him and to her, the most perfect thing she had ever experienced. It seemed they were frozen in time, the sad young man and the innocent young girl.

Feeling he had overstepped the mark, Edward stepped back and in an anxious gesture, pulled the flat cap from his head and wrung it in his hands. May's eyes opened slowly and her look almost caused him to lose his resolve once more.

"Best get home May… or I can't promise I won't kiss you again," he grinned in embarrassment and suddenly, quite overcome with some urge to laugh out loud. May's eyes flew wide.

"You wouldn't dare!" she teased, her voice lowering seductively as she acknowledged the realisation of some secret power she had. For safety's sake, she was already taking one step backwards, just in case.

"Then don't be turning those big blue eyes on me girl...Go on now, off home to your mam, before I get me-self in trouble!"

The laughter came and May wasn't sure whether to laugh with him or be mortified. Her stomach was doing the most incredible lurches and so she did the best a young girl could and walked towards her aunt's ahead of him with as much dignity as she could muster.

"You have the devil in you Edward Handley!" was her parting shot as she glanced back from a safe distance.

"Aye, that I have and I know her name," he muttered with a wry smile as he pulled his cap back on and made for his lodgings at the aunt's at a slower pace, letting her be.

Chapter Five

The day seemed endless to May as she sat in the drawing room in front of the window and added up the month's household income for her aunt. She added well, but today, every time she got halfway down the list, she found her eyes drifting to the window in the hope of seeing Edward.

Having never been kissed by even a boy before, let alone a young man, her belly leaped and churned in the most nervous but joyous way at the memory. What would she do when he came in later? And how would she cope if Ada summoned her to take him some lunch as was her habit?

Fortunately for her Edward had been despatched on a mission for the aunt and it gave her a little peace to know that she had a chance to gather herself before his return. Still, she couldn't help but wonder if he was as nervous as her and if he had been serious kissing her or just enjoying a little dalliance.

She needn't have worried about encountering Edward because he had been given a task that was currently giving him greater pleasure than the memory of the innocent kiss he had pondered on all night, keeping him far from sleep. Aunt Anne had dispatched him to look at a horse and cart for sale at one of the local farms and trusted him to buy if the price was right. His heart was full of joy that he may soon have animal company to inhabit the stable he had refurbished so well and to lavish his care upon.

Aunt Anne had been quite taken with the thought of having someone to drive her to town rather than having to rely on the local carter. Now Edward was here, it was good to have a capable young man for the things that her age and impending frailty would soon prevent her from doing. Growing older was a worry and it was a comfort to know she had the two young people to nurture and in return, rely upon.

As he walked along the lanes, Edward had more of a spring in his step than on his walk home the previous evening. He couldn't wait to get there and he sped up instinctively in his anticipation of the new acquisition.

Arriving at the old farm, he could see by the run down nature of the buildings and yard that the farmer was either old, uncaring or both. The cart stood at one end and hadn't had any attempt to make its appearance inviting and his heart fell. The farmer, seeing Edward approach, was out of his door and obviously eager to make a sale. Looking now Edward wasn't so sure he wanted to buy anything, but on being taken to see the little brown mare stood forlornly in the field and obviously in need of some kindness, his heart melted and he knew this neglected horse would likely be the undoing of him.

An hour later and after ensuring the cart could be refurbished and sturdy enough to be useful, he had haggled the farmer down to enough of a price to feel that he wouldn't be doing his aunt a disservice. He hooked the horse into the shafts and led her out of the yard towards home. He kept his pace slow and steady and his voice low and even as he helped guide her forward.

The little mare responded well to his voice and reckoning she was in need of some friendly company, he chatted quietly to her all the way home. She needed to know his voice and that she was safe, so he confided all his thoughts to her about his shameful past in the Black and Tans and how he was being given a second chance, just like her.

The arrival of the horse was somewhat of a distraction for the household. It was many years since they last had horses and the little mare, though wary, received the pats and attention from everyone with good grace. It allowed May and Edward to come together in something other than embarrassment and the day ended well with her helping Edward to bed the little horse down in the stable for the night.

A much warmer home than the exposed field she had inhabited all year round, she happily munched on the hay he had bought on the way home as Edward brushed the mud away and washed her down. Soon she resembled more of the horse she was meant to be. It was clear she was undernourished and he filled the bucket with a few handfuls of oats to fill her belly, but not too much as to overfeed. Horses were temperamental creatures health-wise and a change in diet from poor to rich suddenly could cause as much of a problem as neglect.

The talk was light-hearted and equine and for the moment all other thoughts of kisses and temptation were banished. Edward crooned to the mare, brushed her over and over again until she ceased to shiver at his touch. 'He had a way with horses', thought May and a kindness that they both sensed. He was a good man, despite his seriousness that much was clear.

Here was no flash Charlie, but nevertheless May found herself starting to admire his finer qualities. The stall smelt of wood, hay and freshly polished leather. Soon he would work on the cart and would produce something both she and her aunt would be happy to ride upon. She knew it instinctively. He was just that kind of man. True to his nature, the next morning bright and early he led the little horse to a nearby paddock and let her run around and return to him for handfuls of oats when he called and, sure enough, the effect was nigh on immediate.

As the mare snuffled in his hand for the treat he asked her what she should be called and she told him with a snort that she wanted to be called Lady May. Laughing at his own nonsense he walked close to the horse's head, stroked the long nose and whispered.

"I think we'll just call you Lady for short, the rest can be our secret." The horse pawed at the ground and snuffled at his pocket smelling more oats and he smiled.

"Demanding already, just like your namesake." He chuckled to himself and with a pat on her rump, he turned and walked back to the stable to commence work on the carriage, leaving the horse to enjoy her new environment.

As May brought him oat biscuits and cheese for lunch, he was hard at work varnishing the wood and reconditioning the leather seat. She watched him working as she approached and thought that the old cart that had looked a wreck would very soon be quite pretty under his attention.

"Lunch Edward!" she called and he stretched up straightening his back slowly as the varnishing had him in a strange posture and he ached to the bone. May laid the wrapped food on a nearby trestle table he was using for his tools and peered over the wall at the horse grazing nearby.

"Have you had yours May?" he enquired unwrapping the linen with anticipation. He had worked up an appetite. For a small framed man he could put some food away and May smiled.

"Aye I have Edward...The cart's looking good."

"Sprucing up nicely I think, almost worth the money I had to pay for it to give the nag a home," he quipped.

"No! She's not a nag, she's lovely...At least she will be when her ribs aren't sticking out so much."

"Indeed. I've renamed her Lady," he smiled quietly, reliving his little joke.

"Suits her," she paused and looked around before posing her question. "Can we work on my garden soon Edward?"

"Can't see why not. Give me a couple of days and we'll make a start, but you'll have to help," he reminded her.

"I had every intention of helping!" Her nose lifted ever so slightly.

"Aye 'appen." His reply said he doubted that. "You'd best come dressed for working then".

"I will!" she laughed and skipped away, leaving Edward wondering why this slip of a girl held his fancy so much. One minute child and the next a capable young woman, she was a mystery to him.

True to her word on the appointed day she arrived in work clothes. As most people had little in their wardrobe, work clothes consisted of the oldest, outdated dress and as she had only recently started making her own clothes, it was heavier than the current shorter fashions, so she didn't add the petticoats and hitched it up into a belt to keep it from dragging in the soil and wore clogs. Clogs were for poorer people so this particular pair had been pushed to the back of the wardrobe and all but forgotten. Her wavy hair being shorter now was easily kept under control in a headscarf. Showing ankles and slim calves was still rather risqué for a young Irish woman, but she now considered herself to be a woman of the world and no longer some timid convent mouse and whilst the dress was outdated, she kind of liked the feel of the full skirt swishing against her bare legs below the knee and no stockings... shameless!

She noticed that Edward's eyes couldn't help but fall to her legs as she walked towards him and she got the strangest of thrills that ran through her core as his eyes raised upwards once more. She caught a look that no well brought up Irish maid should have seen. He covered it well, but she noticed that the colour in his cheeks had raised and she felt quietly pleased with the effect it had on him.

"Good morning to you Edward," she smiled as he busied himself with the garden implements to hide his discomfort.

"Aye, it is indeed lass, I hope you're ready to work?" he replied, his back to her.

"That I am. It's a darlin' day for it don't you think?" Her words held a flirtation and sensing the challenge and recovering his wits rendered senseless by the sight of bare legs, he turned and handed her a spade.

"You'll be needing to start over there first and we'll take turns working this way, you need to dig deep and turn over the sod, this grounds been laid undisturbed too long. I'll be back in a moment with the barrow."

It was clear she was expected to be fully participating in the day's labour, but May was made of stronger stuff and she dug in with gusto, relishing the start of her new project.

Very soon, they were working side by side and chatting happily. There was an ease between them and it made for a good working partnership. The garden area she had chosen was turned over and hoed very quickly. Next they would be able to mark out the rows for her vegetable and flower seeds. The rest they would plant in boxes and put in the cold frame Edward had fashioned from stone and an old window that had been stacked at the side of the stable.

Even Aunt Anne had strolled down with Ada, curious to see the progress and it made for a happy companionable morning. The Aunt sat on a bench nearby to watch them work on her garden. Life felt good. The spring was turning warmer and it was a joy to sit below the trees and watch the sun filtering through. Every so often the old lady would exclaim at the sight of some new plant poking its first tendrils upwards to the light. Eventually she tired and took herself in, leaving the younger, stronger ones to carry on without her supervision.

Later that day and mug of black tea in hand, May and Edward stood side by side aching but happy as they surveyed the fruits of their labours. There was something about a newly edged and planted garden that gave a deep satisfaction. May brushed her escaping hair back off her forehead and turned to Edward with a deep smile of pride. She pushed the hair back under the scarf with a muddy hand, unaware of the dirt she wiped across her face that gave her the appearance of a street urchin and, as she folded her fingers around the top of the hoe and rested her chin on it with a sigh of, "Oh Edward, its grand!," she was completely unaware of how beguiling she was.

Edward put down his shovel and laughed as he came towards her.

"Look at the state of ye girl, you've half the garden on yer face!" He pulled the headscarf off her head and licked it, proceeding to wipe the mud from her nose and forehead.

The action, though innocent enough, seemed intimate somehow and May coloured and looked down.

"Goodness, I'm not fit to be seen!" she said flustered. Edward had realised by now that this young slip of a girl, innocent as she was, already had his heart in her slender fingers. He wiped the last bit of dirt from her face and, as she raised her eyes to his, still clinging to the hoe and lips trembling with a sudden onslaught of emotions she had never experienced before, it was his undoing.

"Not fit to be seen, right enough, but fit to be kissed lass!" he muttered and with that he dropped his mouth to her upturned face and kissed her in a way that demonstrated his passion.

She froze at first and then, as if some deep buried instinct had come to the surface, she opened her mouth to receive his kiss. Edward groaned with something that was alien to her and pulled the hoe from where her hands limply held it and throwing it to one side, he gathered her in. The kiss lasted for seconds only, but when May pulled away she was flushed and breathless. Her mouth opened like she wanted to say something but nothing came and as Edward reached for her once more, she turned and fled for the house as only a young girl could.

Chapter Six

Supper that evening was a constrained affair. Aunt Anne, eager to talk of the day's activity carried the conversation forward when it would have lagged and spared them having to converse normally. May hardly dared look at Edward for fear of giving her longing away. Since that kiss a few short hours ago, she had felt the most incredible sensations in parts of her that no good catholic girl should know about and the shame and joy of it painted her pale complexion with a permanent blush.

Edward himself had little experience with women. Being drafted into the army and then, soon after mourning his mother's death, signing on with the Black and Tans. It had pretty much ruined his chances of finding a decent girl to court. The months spent in Cork were lonely ones. No self-respecting catholic girl would be seen with a member of the unit, let alone bestow any favours on one.

It wasn't safe to be out alone and so the soldiers kept each others' company in a safe pub, but the limited women they found there were not for him, too brassy and loud. No, May with her dark waves and oval blue eyes that seared into you with whatever mood was upon her had held him fast. The thoughts that nothing good could come of it filled his head and he felt ashamed that he might be considering anything that would hurt the very family that had took him in without passing judgement. Let alone considering the risk if they were found to be harbouring an ex-member of the Black and Tans in the heart of IRA territory.

Casting a sidelong glance at her as he conversed with the aunt, sent shivers down his solar plexus to his belly and below and he realised that he was on a route to this young woman that nothing could stop. Never had he felt desire like this. Yet it was tempered with real emotion that he also found hard to restrain and he shook slightly with the realisation that he was experiencing the first awareness of real love.

After the evening meal the Aunt had seated herself comfortably in an armchair with a book, May started to gather her things nervously, hoping to make her escape without further embarrassment. The aunt had other ideas and seeing that May was preparing to leave, she tapped Edward on the shoulder as he stooped to stoke the fire for her and waved her book towards her niece.

"Would you see May home safe Edward? There's a good man," she said.

"I'm fine Aunt, the nights are much lighter now." May answered before Edward had chance and scuttled towards the door, but the aunt was having none of it.

"Nevertheless, best safer than sorry," she said in a voice, though quiet and pleasant, was expecting compliance. May started to tremble with something akin to a fever as Edward held the door open and looked her full in the eye. She made her escape before anyone noticed her scarlet cheeks.

Before Edward had said his goodnights to the Aunt, she had already retrieved her shawl from the coat rack and had the front door open.

"Wait up May lass!" called Edward, but by the time he closed the front door she was away down the path and already at the front gate. Striding fast to catch her he put his hand out to still the opening of the gate.

"May, wait, be still!" May drew a deep breath and stood awaiting his release and her feelings clearly showed on her young face.

"Let me be Edward! Do you really want to shame me further?" Edward slowly opened the gate to let her through.

"Be still lass." he said quietly. "No one wants to shame or embarrass you."

She walked quickly on and seeing her flushed cheeks, he kept his pace just a step behind hers so as not to put her under further scrutiny and gradually she slowed her pace.

"Do you have any feelings for me Edward or is this just some game?" Her voice quivered with emotion and Edward felt his heart do a flip and reaching out, he caught her arm to bring her to a halt.

"Look lass, I'm near bursting with feelings for ye!". He let out a heartfelt sigh "..But your aunt trusts me to look after ye and she's been so good to me.."

"..and to me Edward," said May quietly.

"..There then, what am I supposed to do? What are we supposed to do? We're also family, no one would expect this to be upon us because of that, but it is and I'm so full of love for ye lass, but it would drive a wedge through the family if we pursued this."

May's blush deepened and as she looked up, her eyes were filled with tears.

"Aye, there's that, no doubt.. but my heart feels full with this feeling for you Edward, what should we do?"

"We do nothing for now my sweet, but know this, my feelings are true lass, time will likely tell, but right now we have obligations and expectations to meet, so as much as I want you, we will be friends first, eh?"

"Aye, I expect so," she complied, but her heart was speaking other words, none of which were wise. Edward let her arm go and it dropped forlornly to her side.

"Right then!" he said in an effort to lighten the mood. "Let's get you home girl, tomorrow's a new day!" His words were chipper but his mood was less so and he didn't want to take her spirits down any lower.

They walked home in silence until they reached the gate of her cottage. Edward planted a gentle kiss on her forehead and pushed open her gate with a smile.

"Get theself in lass..and give your mum my best." He doffed his cap to her and turned away before she had time to reply.

Walking slowly in, her mother raised her eyes from her sewing. The light was going now and candlelight didn't make for accuracy and so she set the piece she was working on aside.

"Good day?" Her mother didn't often have a lot to say, but she saw much. Her daughter clearly wasn't herself and despite that there had never been a close mother/daughter relationship, she knew something was amiss..

"Aye, we dug my garden, it looks grand.. oh and Edward sends his best". The words should have been animated as Annie knew her daughter had been excited about it, but there was a sadness in her voice that set the first thoughts of worry to seed in her mother's mind.

"Does he?.. that's nice," she replied. "Best put that water on for the warming pan May, it's getting chilly."

Her mother quietly watched her daughter move to the stove and pour water from the jug into a pan. She'd best keep a closer eye on her from now on. The easy years of childhood were over and this strong-willed young woman was now at an age where she could so easily go one way or another. May was a determined soul and she and her mother were not made of the same stuff. Annie was mild-mannered and had little expectations of life.

Being widowed young had taken all joy from her and she well knew without the Aunt's indulgence, they would have been in a sorry state and might not have survived and for her it cast a permanent shadow. For Annie the challenge of a headstrong daughter to bring up for many years alone had been a harder task that Annie was made for. She sensed her daughter was in need of a mother's care more than ever at this moment and wondered whether she would be up to it.

Later that evening she quietly opened the door to May's room thinking to speak to her about what might be troubling her. She paused as she saw May apparently asleep and crossing to the bed, she blew out the candle and looked down at her lovely daughter's sleeping face. She was a child still in some ways, but she had the brains and ambition of a far more mature woman. Womanhood was beckoning and Annie worried that life would not be up to her daughter's expectations and she feared for her in this tightly controlled and insular community.

She closed the door with a click and only then did May open her eyes. Now was not the time for sleeping. Her head was too full of Edward. It was some time before Edward left her in peace and her eyes finally faltered and closed in fatigue.

***

The next couple of weeks went by in a flourish of activity. The mornings greeted them warm and bright and fresh green growth was painting the countryside with the promise of summer to come.

Much was being done in and about the house and both Edward and May had little time to spare for each other. Edward was busy bringing the long-neglected garden to its full promise and short of occasional visits to her garden patch, May was enlisted to supervise a spring clean of the house.

The windows were thrown wide to greet the day and the sweet smell of the countryside aired the rooms with its breeze.

Ada could be heard loudly chivvying Susan up in her chores as she had '..a list as long as her arm!' from the aunt.

Despite only coming together briefly other than for the evening meal, Edward and May managed to grow ever closer and there was much laughter about the house. The atmosphere was as bright as the daffodils that waved in the breeze like a fond farewell as they walked the garden paths in the sunshine. Gone was the chill of early spring and the nights were staying light until eight now. 'Oh the glory of it swells the heart.' May thought as she threw curtains wide and opened the windows in rooms that were seldom seen. Each room revealed some new fascination in the old house.

The aunt seemed to have a second lease of life and it was obviously doing her good to have young people around the house. She busied herself sorting books and even joined in the cleaning, talking to May as they worked about the antiques in the house and their origins. May loved the ruby glass lustres that graced the piano and Aunt Anne told them her father had once taken them to Dublin and found them in a small shop there. Anne's mother had loved them so much that he had bought them and they had a very cautious journey home ensuring the delicate crystals survived. May always loved how they cast a rainbow around the room early in the evening when the sun came low through the window. As a child she thought it magical and when she told her aunt, she smiled and answered, "So did I, you shall have these one day."

The promise unspoken from her benefactor brought home the thought that her aunt was getting quite old and she may one day soon lose her. It was a thought she didn't want to acknowledge and it brought home to her just how much she cared for the slightly eccentric old lady who had given them so much encouragement and support.

If Edward felt anything for May, he never showed it in public, but occasionally, when they encountered each other privately, his eyes upon her told a story of their own and she always found herself short of words under his gaze.

She had come on in leaps and bounds in knowledge and confidence since taking over the accounting for her aunt's estate. Yet every time she went to confession she felt like a child once more, guilty in the knowledge that she hadn't owned up to some dark sin.

'She hadn't done anything.' she would tell herself, but deep down, she knew the unclean thoughts that always came to her after a shared moment with Edward should be punished. Yet she felt they were not for the confessional. The stuffy old priest in the village could go boil his head, she wouldn't give him something of hers that was precious. Still, the thoughts held heavy on her conscience. An effect of living within a religion that ruled by penance and guilt.

When the glory of summer was finally upon them, May spent many early evenings after work in the garden tending her plants and the knowledge that she was nurturing these to fruition gave her a thrill. Her early vegetables were now starting to show the promise of fruit.

No one in Ireland ever took food for granted after the Great Famine. The fact that the wealthy English landlords had left many to starve and die by the roadsides without intervening, still burned in the hearts of many who had seen it first-hand. The English gentry would not be welcomed in these parts for many generations to come and even without the Republican's agenda, that on its own served to strengthen the divisions.

On these evenings, not feeling comfortable to venture to the local tavern, Edward had taken to training the horse in a fallow field nearby. When May had finished her task, she would walk to where they worked and watch the progress. Edward had a definite way with horses and the little mare, now well-groomed and loved, showed the benefits of living under a kinder regime.

May leaned on the gate and watched him gather the horse to him, whispering his magic and the horse stilled as though she heard.

"Are you ready to ride her May?" he enquired.

"Me?" she gasped taken by surprise.

"Aye, come on lass, shap thesen." He used a northern colloquialism and she faltered as she walked towards him.

"Hurry up shape yourself girl, I'll give you a boost up and lead her. Ye'll be fine."

True to his word. Edward boosted her lightly onto the horse's back and the little mare waited quietly as May settled herself, only moving when Edward called, 'Walk on Lady'.

May couldn't remember ever being on a horse, let alone bareback, but she loved it. The freedom of it and the feel of the horse beneath her was seductive in its power. She would love to ride like she had seen Edward do and the feeling of being high up there, in control of the animal was intoxicating and she breathed the evening in, feeling life was perfection. Edward led the mare across the field and towards the old mansion that lay empty.

"We shouldn't go in here Edward, it's not allowed!" She looked anxiously to him and he smiled quietly.

"There's never a soul here to find you girl, we're only having a look in the grounds. Do you never wonder what's in there?" He asked as they walked towards the gate that bordered the grounds and he opened it, the chain having long since rusted away. She had no choice but to keep her seat and be led.

The summer sun was low in the sky and the colours of the evening filtered through the overhead canopy of the trees and dappled the ground in golden light. May relaxed onto the back of the horse and moved with its gait, revelling in the warmth of the delightful summer evening and all its scents and sounds.

The house loomed and, true enough, there was no sign of any occupation. It's windows boarded and doors barred, it was a sad but romantic sight to see such faded glory so deserted and quiet. Edward stopped the horse to the side of the house and tied her to an old fence where she happily chomped on the sweet woodland grass.

"Come on, where's your spirit girl? Let's have a gander, we're not doing any harm." He held out his hands and she slid from the horse safely to the ground.

She noted his hands lingered on her waist a little too long and it made her far too aware of him as she walked by his side to look at the beautiful old building. Around the back there was a walled garden and curiosity led them to the door. Inside was deserted and overgrown where once had been order and industry.

"Look, the plums have gone wild, we'll have to come back later in the year and do us some picking," said Edward has he pointed to the orchard end.

It certainly was a thrilling place and she wondered why she had never had the courage to explore it before. Still she was here now and the overgrown paths felt like an adventure to be had. She led him onward, winding round shrubs and trees exclaiming at new treasures found.

For this moment she forgot she was trespassing and imagined this abandoned place as her own. How wonderful to own all this and how selfish to abandon it to nothingness. It was a joy to the senses.

"Oh look Edward!" she pointed to an old folly with faded doors. "I would have loved this as a child," she exclaimed.

"I think your loving it now lass!" he laughed as they walked towards it. The hinges had rotted and one of the doors was hanging diagonally on its hinges affording them a tantalising glimpse of the interior. They pushed the door and it gave, allowing them enough space to squeeze in to the darkened depths beyond.

The dust they had loosed into the atmosphere hovered in the air and danced like fireflies in the sun's muted rays. Once their eyes became accustomed to the gloom they could see an old lace curtain shading the room. Edward walked over and scooped it to one side flooding the room with the golden light of sundown.

As they cast their eyes about, it was like stepping back to some grand age, long forgotten. There was still some of the furniture left behind and a chaise longue covered in faded satin, but largely unscathed, that would have still graced any of the houses around here, had anyone had the nerve to take it and hang the consequences. A small hexagonal table stood close by and beside it, a large easel hung with cobwebs and a sideboard with jars of brushes and rags had been abandoned like a fad that no longer suited the painter.

Edward had the devil in him today and he picked up a brush and posed before the easel with an imaginary palette.

"Would 'modom' like to model for me?" He grinned and struck a pose and May, in the moment, launched herself like a grand lady onto the chaise and struck an equally ridiculous pose holding an imaginary cigarette holder.

"Oh dahling," she said "...I'm not sure I can be bothered, I have to go beat the servants and discuss important things with the butler!" She lay back and smoked the imaginary cigarette.

"I really must get the servants to work harder, they've really done a poor job dusting in here," she continued drolly and wiped a disgusted finger across the table top, drawing a line in the dust.

Edward stood and smiled and his face was obscured in a halo of sunlight as she babbled on, thinking all the while that she could probably, with a little practice, pull off the lady of the manor role. Her slim ankles dangled off the edge of the chaise and he couldn't help but be drawn to them. She was oblivious to his scrutiny as she continued to play the role with enthusiasm.

Before she could understand what he was about, Edward had crossed the space between them and gone down on his knees to draw her into his arms and the kiss left her in no doubts that his feelings, though controlled, were very much in evidence.

"Oh Edward, you're a darlin' man," she whispered and pulled his face to hers once more.

May had been kissed by her mother, that's all she had ever experienced until Edward, but this was something so far removed and hedonistic that she lost all sense of being anything other than in the moment. Her arms wrapped around his neck and he pulled her upwards so that she sat perched on the edge of the sofa with her legs around his waist and all decorum lost in the eroticism of it. Mouths opened and tongues explored and with a groan Edward knelt up and hands on her buttocks, he pulled her close towards him and a shock of sensations pulsed through her as their bodies searched for each other unsatisfied through the barrier of clothing.

They spent an hour like this until the sun was almost gone and there was no excuse to stay and, almost in a daze, they made their way back. The girl sat high on the horse and the young man quietly leading her with his shoulder brushing her leg occasionally. To see them, you would not have known they were anything other than friends, making their way home across the fields, but within them there was every new sensation that came with first love and a building of intimacy.

It was dusk when Edward lifted her down from the horse and led the mare into the stable. Edward was all business now he was home and May had just started to feel he was regretting his earlier weakness when he came from the stall, pulled her to him and kissed her once more with passion.

"Just so you know," he said and let her go as swiftly as he had held her. "Your mam will be worrying if we don't get you home soon," he said and he stepped aside to allow her to walk from the stable and then followed politely. Only when he reached her gate did he let his fingers graze hers in a silent goodbye and it was all she could do not to throw herself back into his arms.

"Night May" he smiled with his eyes and she knew she would be his forever.

This nightly ride continued into July, each time ending at the old folly and the knowledge they would come here at dusk was the only thing that kept them able to function normally within the household each day.

Kisses became caresses and they spent the time exploring each other's body in a gradual awakening within that they knew was foolhardy but inevitable.

Just Edward's hand on her breast and caressing the nipple that had raised to meet his fingers through her bodice was enough to send her quivering with sensation that, in her innocence, she did not recognise as the beginnings of an orgasm. All she knew was that she needed him closer and there was an ache for something she craved but couldn't explain.

Each day they risked more, until clothes started to be pushed aside and hands and mouths sought deeper places that caused them both to cry out with frustration. Finally one evening Edward couldn't hold back any longer and as she writhed against him, he laid her back against the faded satin and raising her skirts and pulling down her undergarments, he unbuttoned his pants and rubbed himself against her until she could stand no more and with a scream of joy she drew him to her and he entered her with an equal cry. His lovemaking was over too soon and messy as he pulled away at his climax, returning to her several minutes later to make love to her once more with more control. Each time he pulled out and in her innocence she thought that would be enough.

The following weeks she was eager to have him close and they were risking all to satisfy this new desire. They took many risks to meet for a few snatched kisses in the work shed, the stable and in the evenings at their private triste, where they would make love with ever-mounting passion. It was true love indeed and Edward was as besotted as she and just as foolhardy.

Ada caught the odd exchanged glance and raised an eyebrow occasionally, but the aunt was oblivious to the charged atmosphere whenever they were together at mealtimes. In truth, it became tantalising to tempt each other in company, without doing anything obvious to the eye.

Only May's mother sensed the change in her daughter, but being the introverted character she was, she never found the words to question her daughter on a subject that for most Catholics was taboo. Frozen in her own fear of facing the situation she suspected was upon them, she chose to do nothing.

In her own heart she could be forgiven for thinking they were just innocents who had feelings for each other. She trusted that May's fear of God and convent education had kept her from further temptation with the threat of damnation and falling into sin. Anne's own marriage had been one of duty and so she was completely ignorant of desire, being used only to submission. Her daughter was headstrong, she would stand fast. It never occurred to her that it would be that same strong will that would make her daughter actively seek temptation rather than resist it.

For Edward and May, they were so caught in the moment that they never even dared consider anything in the future. It was something they could not even conceive of, such was the unlikely pairing of the educated young woman and the uneducated manual labourer.

The fact that one was protestant and the other catholic in troubled times, only served to convince them that the present moment was where they should remain for now and that any attempt to bring their love out into the open would be disastrous.

It made it all the more dramatic and exciting and so it continued until the sun was high in the August sky and May awoke one day to realise she was a week late on her bleed.

Chapter Seven

Ten days further from this May started the sickness and the dawning realisation that she could be with child almost paralysed her with fear. Her pale features hadn't gone unnoticed and she was aware her mother was watching her with a concerned eye.

She couldn't find the words to tell her mother that she was about to bring this great shame upon them. She couldn't tell anyone, such was her distress and even Edward couldn't understand why she had suddenly found reasons not to come to the folly at dusk any longer.

Assuming she had waned in her affections he had withdrawn and concentrated on his work. Yet deep within he burned with pain thinking she was no longer in love with him, as she had sworn to be so forever in their lovemaking. He was too proud to ask why her feelings had so suddenly changed towards him. He had no idea that, thinking herself already pregnant, she had decided to abstain just in case a miracle made it not so. She didn't dare risk giving herself to him again as she could barely stand up with the terror that radiated through her body. Every night she prayed over her rosary that this could be something else other than what, deep down, she knew it to be.

Her eyes were red with crying each morning and she moved wanly about the house trying not to disgrace herself by vomiting in public. It was one such morning when Edward, at a loss as to why she had been avoiding him came across her retching in the chicken pen as she gathered eggs. Looking at her hanging wanly on the fence the penny dropped.

He came behind her and put his hand on her back as she sobbed and threw up her breakfast and rubbed her gently.

"May..." he asked solemnly, "Are you pregnant?"

"I don't know, I think so! Oh, what am I to do Edward?" She cried and cried and retched some more and when she had gained some control over her stomach, she stood stooped over the fence in abject despair. He gathered her to him and hugged her like a child.

"We will do something May. We'll be married and I'll come with you to tell your mother and Aunt Anne. This is my responsibility. I was a fool to think we were safe as we were. Come on now lovely, dry your eyes."

She sobbed all the more as the words came brokenly that the priest would never sanction a marriage with someone outside of the catholic faith.

"Then we'll go where they will, come now dry your eyes, this won't do. May! Calm yourself... Do you love me?"

"Yes!" she sobbed, wiping her eyes on her skirts. Thinking all the time of the damnation that was coming her way for even considering defying the strictures of her faith.

"Then that's all we need to know, because I love you more than you can imagine." His words had the desired effect and she slowly hiccoughed her way back to silence, too drained to cry any longer.

"Come now, go about your business for today and give me time to think and I'll come up with something. We'll speak later."

May finished drying her eyes and continued gathering her eggs whilst her red face calmed itself, so as not to draw unwanted attention from members of the household, but her thoughts were a jumble of contradicting emotions. She would be shamed for sure, but Edward had said he would look after her. What if he left her? She would be for the Magdalene Laundry if her mother and aunt turned their backs. The thought filled her with horror.

One part of her gloried that Edward had spoken his love yet again, but another part of her knew that she had just lain forfeit all her future prospects here with her aunt as benefactor. What a fool she was to be carried away by this wantonness. God would surely punish her for her stupidity.

She threw herself into the day's work in order to block out all the fears and questions that screamed behind her eyes. After a strained evening meal she made her way to their meeting place to find Edward sombre and quiet sitting on a fallen log awaiting her arrival. She sat beside him and took a deep breath to calm herself. Taking her hand in his he cupped the other over it and held it tight in his lap.

"Right now.. we say nothing yet," he said. "That will give me time to save more money and then in a few months, we will go to Manchester and be married. You must not say anything yet because if it goes badly for us we will have nothing saved to start a life, do you see? You must save every penny May, every penny! Then, when we are ready we will have at least something set aside to get us a roof over our head. My mother left me a small amount which I have saved and most of the wages I've earned here, but there is no guarantee how long that will last. Work is not easy to find and you with the babe will have nothing to bring to the table. Do you understand?" He looked at her earnestly and clasped her hand to his chest. She nodded her assent.

"I do Edward, but this will bring so much shame on my mother and aunt, what will they do?" Her mouth trembled fearfully.

"I know lass, but they will bear it. It is you and the child I am worried about most of all. How far on do you think you are?"

"About six weeks maybe, I don't know about these things, mother never..."

"It's alright May. Neither of us had brothers or sisters to learn from, so we will have to do the best we can. If it's early days you'll be awhile before you show. That gives us about three months to save. Can you bear not to tell for that long? I know I am asking much of you."

He gripped her hands tightly and kissed her forehead like a child and she found his care comforting.

"I will do my best, but I'll not be proud of the deceit Edward," she said quietly.

"Nevertheless, it needs to be so lass, be strong eh?"

"Yes I will." May quietly sent up a prayer for forgiveness and then thanks that she had followed the new fashion for shapeless 'flapper' dresses for some time now and that at least she would have more chance of disguising her condition for the moment.

"Home now and rest," he said seriously.

"Aye I will." He gave her one last embrace and then he pulled her to her feet and walked her to her gate as was the norm.

Watching her face as she waved him off Edward saw her pain and fear and he walked home with a very heavy heart.

What possessed him to bring this hell down upon them just as life was good. He questioned himself as to the rights and wrongs of the situation and with foresight would he have done the same again? He instinctively knew that the answer would have been yes...wholeheartedly. For he loved May with all his heart... So they would have to endure all that was to come and hopefully one day in the not-too-distant future they would look back, at peace and with a resolution found. The warm summer night had suddenly lost its smells and wonder. It had been a brief, but glorious interlude for which they now must pay the price.

The weeks that followed were an unhappy trial for both May and Edward. For May just keeping on her feet, with the fatigue of early pregnancy alone was enough, but to be carrying the burden of all she might bring down upon the very people she loved most, was the heaviest of all.

Fortunately for them both, whilst May felt sick nearly all the time for the next few weeks, she rarely was and that at least served to keep her from her mother's scrutiny. The fact that she and Edward had also pledged to keep as much distance from each other as possible, other than in daily routines served to keep a kind of normality and made for less fear of being discovered.

Occasionally they would sit on a bench in the garden and, whilst no one was looking, they would pour out their worries, or at least May would and Edward would do his best to reassure her. In truth, his heart was low and having swallowed down his pride and gone to the next town to seek advice from the priest as to whether they could marry, he had come away angry and disillusioned once more with religion.

He had been disapprovingly told that 'If there was a priest happy to marry them, then the children... (and he used the word pointedly, leaving Edward in no doubt that he had guessed the at reason for his visit) would be brought up in the catholic faith and he personally would have to make an undertaking that to that effect.

He had seen too much unhappiness caused in his family through the pressures of religion and no child of his was going to be subjected to it. Despite May's pleas and quiet tears as they sat side by side, he was truly adamant on that point. It was a bone of contention between them, but Edward knew that back home in England she would be less under the scrutiny of other Catholics and more able to choose the future of the child without having to adhere to the dictates of the church.

Animosity was still running high in the wake of the papal decree (Ne Temere in 1907) and it had strengthened the resolve of the church that children born from interfaith marriages should be brought up within the Catholic faith. The sectarian tensions only served to strengthen the divide and the frequency of interfaith marriages was falling due to these conditions, combined with a lack of females through immigration, that further reduced the number of available women.

The church was holding up the Virgin Mary as the model for all women. They were taught to pass on, as the transmitters of the Catholic teaching, the message that all sexual activity outside of marriage and within marriage, not aimed at conceiving children, was evil. For May it was a double sin, she knew now that the beauty of their lovemaking would be forever tarnished by the fact she had fallen on both counts. She hadn't wanted a child, she had revelled in the desire and worst of all, she had committed the sin of sex outside of wedlock. Each night she prayed over her rosary for forgiveness and each morning she woke to the knowledge she would have to continue with this deceit for another day. It was draining her spirit.

Women in the post famine period had been offered (and this was taken up by many) the role of bringing the children up in the faith. In return for embracing this new 'morality' they were given a level of respect. In truth, they didn't have much choice in the matter, but many took to it with a vengeance and the practice of praying to the Virgin Mary by reciting the rosary came to the fore. Life became more judgemental for this and women found wanting were judged, not only by God, but by their own peers as his disciples.

May, whilst brought up Catholic and subject to all its restraints, had lived an isolated life. Being an only child and due to her mother's reluctance to socialise with the more common families in the village, she had lived on the outskirts of this judgemental society. Whilst she had escaped much of it's indoctrination via normal social circles, the convent education and church as a child, had been enough to instil the fear of retribution for her sins to her core.

Whilst in many ways she was a free thinker, the constraints of the society around her were at odds with her own natural leanings. Had she been brought up in a less judgemental society who knows what ambitions she may have had. For now the abject shame that she would bring humiliation upon her family kept her quiet and fearful and

Edward could see her daily losing the spirit that he had so admired in her. He would have to get her away from this place, and fast.

The weeks ticked by like an old clock that was loud and echoing on a dusty mantle. Both May and Edward felt they were dragging the heaviest of burdens behind them.

May sat tearfully at night saying her Rosary and then, in complete deviation from her guilt-ridden devotions, would sit counting the money she had saved and hidden under the floor of her room. She had twelve pounds, six shillings and sixpence accrued.

For someone single and living at home it was a small fortune. Yet for someone who was to make a journey to England, find somewhere to live and bring a babe into the world, it counted for just a few weeks' safety.

The knot of anxiety was tightening in her stomach and she chastised herself for her own foolhardiness for this situation. Babies should be welcomed into the world and anticipated with joy. She could only dread the thought of being somewhere ugly and cold without her mother to rely on, bringing forth a child that was unplanned and that she was totally unprepared for.

She had started to gather things she would need for the journey and had hidden them under the base of her wardrobe in a canvas bag, just in case they were discovered and had to leave quickly. She allowed herself a few small mementoes of home to carry her through lonely times, but she knew they would have little space to take anything other than the basics.

Edward meanwhile was working as hard as he could to ensure the aunt had as much done for the paying of his wages as he could give her. This was the only way he could salve his conscience and he fell into bed each night exhausted and drained of every thought but how he would make a life for them back in England. How would he put into words the explanation that would even warrant a fair hearing with Aunt Anne and Annie? He felt like a rogue, who had been given their trust and defiled it in the most terrible of ways. All he would be able to do was assure them that he would do his utmost to give May a happy life and his love.

Not much given to words, he decided to use his new-found skills and write the Aunt and May's mother a letter. Hopefully, the Aunt at least would recognise the effort he had gone to and he spent many nights writing and re-writing the words that he knew didn't come close to describing his gratitude and his shame. It made for many a sleepless night until he felt he had the letter to a passable standard and he slipped it into an envelope and sealed it, awaiting the sad day it would have to be delivered.

Chapter Eight

November came and the nights were dark and cold and so May and Edward had little chance to snatch any time alone together. For sure now May was pregnant and the sickness had settled down. She had no real idea of where exactly she was in the pregnancy, but pregnant she was and her very core felt the babe growing within her, even though it wasn't visible to anyone other than herself.

Her breasts were tender and her belly rounder. It was like a time bomb ticking down to disaster and so she felt none of the joy a mother-to-be would have in watching the changes the baby was making upon her. Instead each new development was an indication of the little time she would have left with her mother and the aunt and she treasured each moment, knowing them to be all the more precious to her as they dwindled. Her heart was close to breaking.

In reality she had no idea what to expect. Never having seen her own mother pregnant and being an only child, she panicked over the slightest thing and would go running to Edward for comfort. When he could, he would cradle her to him and whispered reassurances would ease the fear for a moment until she was once more on her own and the thoughts would come flooding in once more.

The long days of summer were over and it was a case of rising early to ensure all was done before the evening was swiftly upon them. May hated dark days and Edward loathed them more. An outdoor man, he didn't take well to being confined in the house and after taking May home safely to her mother's cottage he would have the choice to go back to the house and read by candlelight or sleep. As sleeping didn't come easy, he would sit by the failing fire after the others were abed, his thoughts churning around, just like his belly, with anxiety.

Just occasionally and in search of male company, he would walk to the pub and order a pint of ale. It was his only vice and an excuse to stay outdoors a little longer. The publican, knowing him to be related to one of their own had grudgingly served him, despite him being English and probably Protestant. Over the months he had struck up a conversation with a couple of the occupants who were more disposed to integrate and it certainly eased the monotony of women's conversation for a short while.

May was about four and a half months they calculated and would soon be showing and so he knew the time was growing short for saving, so he religiously would stop at two pints, once a week.

This particular evening the local carter was in and Edward greeted him as he entered. The pub though small was usually quite full, being the only place other than the church to meet and seek diversion from everyday life. It was the lot of the poor, drink and religion. Only Edward had no time for one and the sense not to engage too much in the other.

Some of tonight's occupants, though living hand to mouth, managed to find enough to get themselves well-oiled he thought and probably leaving a few empty bellies at home whilst the food money went down their necks. All for a moment's release from the daily toil.

His child wouldn't be waiting for food whilst he drank in the pub he thought grimly. He had no patience for those types. Taking himself to the quieter end of the bar where two men stood that he hadn't seen previously, he nodded, seeking intelligent conversation rather than drunken banter.

"Owdo," he said, forgetting his northern greeting would confuse some people. The two men looked up from their drinks and nodded in response. Something in the eyes made Edward wary.

"Not from round here then?" the first enquired. Edward circumspect as always replied.

"Not previously, but for some time now." He accompanied it with a smile to show friendship.

The second man managed a half smile as he raised his glass to his lips, took a sip and spoke quietly.

"Farming then?"

"Of sorts, and you?" said Edward, but within something unnerved him slightly. It should have been small talk, but somehow it felt like an interrogation.

"Oh this and that, I have family here but just came back from working in Dublin, not the best there with all the strikes. Where do you come from?"

Edward wanted to leave the conversation, these were no ordinary men, that much was obvious, they were too cocksure of themselves, but leaving now might draw them to question more, so he stayed in the conversation and kept as near to his truth as possible. These two were IRA as ever there was, so he calmed his breathing and tipped his glass to his mouth, giving him time to think.

"Manchester."

"Mucky place, can't breathe in the air there."

"That's right enough," replied Edward attempting to keep the conversation light. "Prefer up in the lakes meself, Appleby, I go whenever I can, plenty horse trading to be had with the gypsies. I've had many a good night round their camp fires."

The first man looked at the other and then turned back to Edward whose hand gripped his ale just a little too tightly and maybe the tension showed.

"What brings you here, not a place for the British right now," he said.

"I'm half-Irish and I'm helping out family for a while farming." To Edward it seemed a lame comment, so he took another swig to clear his glass quicker, so that he could be gone without trouble.

"You've a look of the military about yer," came the pointed response.

"For my pains.. gassed in the trenches, not much for me to do now but find fresh air, not up to much else." Edward hoped it would be enough to make them think he was completely unfit for any other service since the first world war and dissuade them from probing further.

"Well you'd best keep close to home man... there's things afoot that will make life for a 'half-English' none too good around here." He stared into Edward's eyes and Edward saw his meaning was clear. This was now an IRA pub and he'd best make himself scarce. He'd heard that trouble was on the rise in Dublin with the IRA guerillas steeping up action against the RIC and his old Auxiliary Division of the Black and Tans. Cork, nearby, was also rife with trouble.

Fortunately, Edward's past had been kept safe by May and the Aunt, but the Irish were a curious nation. It wouldn't take much of a slip to draw unwanted attention. He pulled on his cap and smiled.

"I'll be bidding you goodnight then," he said quietly, not to draw aggression.

"Aye, you do that," said the second.

Edward closed the door and quickly strode around the corner of the pub then ducked down an alley to see if he was being followed. When he was happy it was safe, he made quickly for home and it was not an easy stroll. Time for moving he thought. If only he had thought it a week sooner. It wouldn't take much for those two to find an excuse to come after him just for the hell of it and he knew that, isolated and alone, he would be an easy target with no one coming forward to help him should they choose to do so.

Chapter Nine

The morning of the 21st November 1920 dawned crisp and fresh as many others and Edward had not had any further trouble, mainly by keeping his distance from village life. When, however, he ventured into the village this particular week to buy provisions, there was much talk of Michael Collins and the troubles building in Dublin. A culmination of strikes and incidents where force had been used with a little too much enthusiasm, combined with the IRA activity all conspired to bring about an explosive situation.

Divisions were widening. The IRA had stepped up its game in the war of independence. Snippets of news were filtered down and had been embellished from the Irish Bulletin in each new telling. It served only to raise further ill-feeling in the rural communities who had no way of knowing what was really going on in the larger cities, except by word of mouth and therefore they believed the worst.

Local people were being continually fed some atrocity or other to fire them up and who was to say they weren't right to be angry. Edward had seen both sides. There were no winners in the power game. Only pawns and the power hungry. Sensing some local animosity towards the fact he was half-British, Edward kept his head down and only went where he needed to go to buy provisions for the horse. Other than the usual republican gossip, all seemed normal.

This next morning Edward had started as usual, feeding the horse and turning her out into the field whilst he cleaned the stable. May had arrived and was working in the kitchen with her aunt making a list of things they needed for the pantry.

Ada was grumbling about the arthritis in her hands and having to hang the washing out in such cold to drip until Edward, coming in for his morning mug of tea, took it from her to save her the trouble and his ears no doubt, more pain.

Shortly after they were all sitting around the table in quiet conversation on the day's chores to be done, when Susan burst through the back door, hair awry with the wind and eager to impart bad news.

"Jesus, Mary and Joseph save us all, we're all for it now. Have you not heard the news. Lord love us, tis a terrible thing!"

Aunt Anne stood up and beckoned the woman over. Susan complied, revelling in being centre of attention rather than just the hired help for once.

"Sit down and calm yourself Susan." Susan was not the most intelligent of women, but it was clear something had deeply upset her. Ada poured a mug of tea and Aunt Anne spooned sugar in and set it in the woman's hands.

"The bastards!...Sorry ma'am. Them divils in the black and tans and the RIC. They've opened fire for no reason on the poor innocent souls watching the game at Croke Park. Women, children everyone! God bless, they didn't stand a chance! May those evil swine burn in hell! Me Da said there's been many killed and more injured in the stampede to get away from the guns. All hell is breaking loose."

The words registered with Edward first and foremost and his eyes flew open in shock, first looking to the aunt and then unintentionally to May. Both the subjects of his attention sat in stunned silence as Susan recounted all she knew. Facts were hazy and distorted but sure as she knew, it had happened just as her da had told her. Men in the villages were already getting ready to journey to Dublin to make retribution for the atrocity.

In reality it appeared that Michael Collins, leader of the IRA, believing himself about to be the subject of an assassination attempt by undercover agents, had sent his squad out to assassinate members of the 'Cairo gang' on the morning of the Croke Park Gaelic Football match. Tipperary v Dublin. These were British intelligence agents, working and living in Dublin. The IRA had shot dead fourteen alleged members of the Cairo gang at different addresses that morning. Blood was running high.

The Royal Irish Constabulary and their cadets, who were mostly untrained, combined with RIC Auxiliaries, more commonly known as the Black and Tans, were sent to police the match. Having had intelligence that Collins and his squad members may be there, they had decided to conduct a search of the ground.

What happened after that is unclear. There are several versions of the events that followed, but it is thought that the general security of the ground were asked to cancel the match whilst the search was conducted, but refused, saying it would cause a stampede and danger to life. The game was due to commence at two forty five, but the police took the decision to search anyway and as they began, three shots were fired, which was thought to be a warning to IRA members within that something was afoot. After that the RIC and Black and Tans started firing indiscriminately into the crowd. It was thought that untrained RIC cadets who were mainly unionists, had rushed across from Phoenix Park to Croke Park when the disturbances broke out and started shooting recklessly and this, unlike the main RIC and Black and Tans fire, was thought unplanned and happened through a breakdown of discipline, yet was the most destructive. The shame brought down upon the British Government for the resulting massacre was a key factor to the Irish winning independence and Croke Park remains to this day a key symbol of Irish nationalism and named Bloody Sunday. It would be the first of many.

Yet sitting around this table with the horror and hate spewing forth from Susan's mouth, far away from the trouble as it was, it still served to run the blood cold with the individual visions it painted in each listeners mind.

For Edward it was shame initially, followed by anger and then a sense of uselessness in facing the inevitable where two sides were so divided.

For Ada, as old as she was, it was the burning anger and need for retribution for all the British Government had brought upon them that coursed through her veins.

Susan, younger and not as intelligent, was high on the anger and the thrill of a terrible tale and the chance to be central to the telling of it.

To Aunt Anne it was a sickening realization that their life was about to change for the worst and she looked to Edward with eyes full with sorrow.

For May, from the moment children in the crowd had been mentioned, the bile rose in her throat and she knew the first feelings and fear of a mother for her unborn child. The dawning that the very person who had put the child in her belly had actually been part of the hated enemy of her people who had done this terrible thing, filled her with dread. Her legs went to jelly and she slumped from the chair onto the floor.

Edward was first to her, "May, my love.. are you all right?" He shook her gently and she started to come round. Opening her eyes and not yet fully aware, her eyes flew wide as she encountered Edward and she filled up with tears.

"Oh Edward, how could you be involved with such monsters?" Edward held his breath and put his finger to her lips to silence her, but he feared the damage was done. The look that passed between Ada and Susan was enough to know they had heard and drawn conclusions of their own. There was a heavy silence in the room as the seconds ticked by.

"Get her some water Ada," he ordered and lifted May up in his arms, all thoughts of giving himself away now gone in his care for her.

Carrying her into the parlour he laid her on a sofa and surrounded by the others in that room was where she fully regained her senses as the tears spilled over.

"Are you ill child?" asked the Aunt, full of concern. Ada brought her the water and Edward took it from her to put the glass to her mouth, his attention clearly showing his feelings for May.

"I'm all right" she replied weakly, clasping the glass "I feel sick, oh dear, get me something." she moaned as she started to retch once more.

Susan grabbed the empty coal scuttle and pushed it under her chin just as she gave way and vomited all her recently drunk tea.

"Go get a wash basin and cloth please Ada and Susan...go get her mother, straight away!" said the aunt with a discipline that brooked any defiance. The two scuttled out and Aunt Anne turned back to Edward and May.

"I think you and I need to speak Edward.. immediately!" Edward felt his stomach lurch. The moment they had dreaded was upon them.

Ada and Susan closed the kitchen door behind them and looked at each other in consternation.

"That one's got a babe in her belly sure as eggs is eggs," said Susan, "and there's more to him than he's after lettin' on, that's a fact!"

"Hush your mouth now girl and go and do as she says if you know what's good for ye." Ada dismissed Susan, who quickly was out the door and scurried off down the lane.

The day had gone on with its twists and turns she thought, and she was hoping to find someone en route to impart her news to, but luckily for the others she didn't encounter anyone on the journey to May's home. 'Seems these posh ones could lay down just as easily as some of the other harlots around here and looks like we're harbouring a bastard black and tanner to boot,' she thought grimly as she marched up to the cottage's small wooden door and knocked hard.

Ada had the sense to stay quiet, knowing what was best for them all, but Susan was a true gossip and would not be one to be forgiving when there was a juicy piece of a tale to be told.

Aunt Anne opened the door and checked there was no one eavesdropping behind it and then came back with a face that was stern at best.

"Edward, what has been going on here?.. and don't even try lying to me." Edward and May looked guiltily to each other and Edward was first to speak.

"Aunt Anne, I am so very sorry.. we fell in love.. I love her so much and we've been saving to get married." The Aunt silenced him with the flat of her hand raised.

"So you've got her with child then, I take it from that?" May started to cry and the Aunt turned her anger on her.

"Be quiet stupid girl! I thought I had taught you better than this and this is how you repay me?.. I haven't time for your tears of self-pity. You know what this means Edward?.. Susan will be down the pub as fast as she the gets chance and if that happens you'll have minutes, not hours, before the lynch mob comes here. We must act fast!"

"I never meant this to happen Aunt" sobbed May.

The Aunt looked at them both and then addressed her next words mainly to Edward.

"You know what they'll do to her for being with you? And they'll kill you for sure. So there is no time now for explanations or apologies. You must get the horse hitched to the cart and get your things and hers together now and be gone before the hour is out..do you understand? Go, do it NOW!". Her voice was low but desperate and it cracked with anger and sorrow.

"Yes, Aunt." Came Edward's solemn reply with tears in his own eyes. Knowing that the shrewd old lady was absolutely right, he departed to do her bidding as she turned to May.

"How far gone are you?" she asked May.

"Four months..maybe," May answered trembling with fear and shame."Right. Far enough to travel. Stop whimpering girl and get up and come with me."

May followed the aunt upstairs and into her private chambers where the old lady pulled aside a picture and to May's surprise there was a hidden safe behind. Taking out several notes she placed £100 in her hand.

"This is for you, not Edward. You hide it and use it when you must to keep you and the babe safe. You write to me when you can. I'd hoped to give you much more but you have let me down girl! This is your inheritance and it will be all you have from me now. That and the horse and cart." Momentarily the old lady broke down but quickly brushed her tears away.

"Right you will need food and blankets for the journey. Come now, we've not a moment to lose."

She hurried down with May to the kitchen tears streaming down May's face. Ada was frozen at the kitchen table, not knowing what to do. Half of her wanted to rail at the frightened young girl and the other half to comfort her. But in doing so, she made herself a collaborator. It was a desperate moment and one that would stand a person apart from another for their integrity.

"Ada... can I trust you?" Anne asked quietly. Ada looked from the older woman to the terrified girl and made up her mind.

"Aye ma'am you can, but not Susan. She's a blabber mouth!"

"I know.. Right Ada. They need food for the journey, anything and quick, don't be fussy... and May run home to your mother's and if she is coming back with Susan tell Susan I am not well and I need her services urgently and she must come straight away! Don't let her give you excuses, threaten her with her job from me if you must. Then take your mother home and tell her to pack as well. If she doesn't leave with you then on her head be it. They will think she knew also."

"I will Aunt." May turned and hurried for her coat and was out the door, fear and adrenalin propelling her forward and drying the tear tracks upon her face.

True enough her mother was at the gate of the house with Susan. Both their faces were strained, Annie's with fear and Susan's with malice. May sprang to action before Susan had a chance to be away.

"Aunt Anne needs you urgently Susan, she is ill and she says she needs you to go straight away! I need to speak to my mother.. go on quickly!". May wondered where the strength came from, but it did.

It was clear Susan had other ideas, but uncertain of what she knew, she valued her wages more at this moment and though she complied reluctantly, the look she threw May was one of thinly concealed disgust and May felt the first inkling of what it was to be a fallen woman in another's eyes. It was clear the Aunt was stalling for time for them and she must put that time to good use. Her mother could not delay them with hysterics now.

Her mother was bemused at the goings on initially but once May frantically recounted everything in five minutes, her mother sobbing and terrified, but not stupid, was flinging anything valuable into a bag with a few clothes. She would ask the Aunt to have the rest of their things packed away and sent on when it was safe to do so.

May was quite shocked that her mother, normally quiet and circumspect, could react with such tenacity. She ran to her room and pulled out the prepared bag, stashed her money in a pocket bag about her waist for safety and added the hundred pounds her aunt had given her. By the time she ran back down the stairs her mother had gathered a tidy pile of useful things to start a new life with. There was more to the quiet woman than May had given her credit for. Running back to her aunt's, she met Edward bringing a bag from the house and pulled her to him. She resisted his embrace and he let her go.

"Please May, save your accusations for later, we haven't time. Aunt Anne's playing a blinder for us May, don't let her down. If she screams at you or anything, it's for Susan's sake. She's buying us time, do you hear. Susan thinks she's throwing me out, so just go with anything she says, right?... Say your goodbyes quietly and don't let Susan or Ada hear and meet me back at your mother's in fifteen minutes. No later! I'll load the cart whilst you get there. They will think we've stolen it, so we will have to move fast. Go!"

Once more May's legs carried her forward on adrenalin only, for there was almost nothing left in her to stand. She made her way to the parlour where Ada told her that her aunt was resting. Susan tucking a blanket around the aunt's knees, was being given the performance of a lifetime and she couldn't help but have total admiration for this woman who was quite within her rights to throw them out on the street without a second thought.

"Susan," the Aunt said weakly. "Go make me a cup of tea the way I like it please. I am feeling most unwell and I have pains in my chest".

"Shouldn't I fetch the doctor ma'am," said Susan, but the Aunt was having none of it, as it would involve the woman going into the village.

"Not for now, if I don't feel better soon I will send for you shortly. You can put a warming pan in my bed just in case I need to lie down." May knew she was keeping her close, but busy, to give them a chance to get away and her eyes spilled with tears once more as the door closed.

"Auntie?" She searched for forgiveness and the aunt filled with tears also at the use of the endearment.

"You must go now.. no time for tears girl. Get as far away as you can and write to me when you are safe. I will manage the rest of your mother's things and tell them I have thrown you all out. It is the only way they will not take retribution on me. Do you understand?"

"I do." May sobbed and for the first time in her life, the old woman gathered her close and she clung to her.

"You are like a daughter to me and you have broken my heart with this, but I will not see you struggle. Edward is a good man, not the man I would have chosen for you but kind and good in his heart. Be sure you are happy. I cannot forgive this child, but I will pray for you and you future and I will certainly not see you beaten and shamed.. So now you must go. Every moment you linger is a risk to you all.. Just do this one thing for me.. tell your mother I love her and to be brave."

She pushed a sobbing May from her and as May ran from the room the old lady broke down and cried as she had never cried in her life. In her old age she would now have to be resigned to loneliness and the light had just left her life with the departure of the child she had truly loved as her own.

May crept out of the front door and ran back to her mother's house where Edward, with her mother, were packing the last things on the cart. She had bundled pots pans and all sorts hastily in bedsheets utilising everything they had. One last look around the little cottage and they climbed aboard. Her mother sat silent and traumatised in the front and May sobbing in the back, huddled down amongst the hastily packed belongings. Her mother would not speak again until they eventually boarded the ferry to England, where she would break down and cry for all she had lost and gratitude that they had made it safely away.

Edward cracked the reins and the little horse pulled forward. Skirting the village as best they could and trying to look normal to those they passed, was the worst moment of their escape.

The people they did encounter were curious, but as they knew nothing they reserved their curiosity for later and didn't enquire as to where the three were going so heavily laden.

May kept her head down the whole time so as not to have her bloated face seen. Her last abiding memory of this place would be her own aunt's stricken face engraved on her conscience forever.

The cart made its way through the lanes until they reached a safe distance and then Edward increased the pace to get them away as fast as he could without harming the little mare. It was only then that May looked up. The trees were as bare as May's dreams and the backwards view of her home, now in the distance, would be all she had to remember for the rest of her life. She was leaving her beloved Ireland for the unknown and she had dragged her poor mother down with her.

Her mother stared straight ahead and the pain was a physical thing in May's chest as she carried the shame of what they had done to her in their recklessness. Winter was settling its chill deep within her heart as the babe in her belly chose that moment to give its first kick.

Chapter Ten

Two days later they boarded a B&I ferry to Liverpool from Dublin. Edward was below deck keeping the horse calm and watching their belongings. Ferry crossings were not good on horses and they needed Lady to get them safely to their destination.

The weather was cold and the journey to Dublin had been horrendous for the young mother to be, with its ruts and cobbles that jolted her about in the back of the cart.

There was nothing she could do but to bury herself deep in the baggage and blankets and try to sleep her misery away. Not daring to attempt speaking to her mother, she stayed quiet. It would have been impossible to have any conversation at the pace they were going regardless.

The journey for Edward was equally miserable. Annie sat silently beside him, her stony expression only occasionally broken by tears streaming down her pale cheeks, made all the more poignant by the lack of sobs accompanying them.

His heart was very low and the first night away they stopped at a small lodgings on the outside of Dublin, as the horse was exhausted and Edward, feeling safely at a distance enough to allow a stop, paid for a room for the mother and May to get their rest.

Ensuring the women were safely fed and abed, he returned to sleep on the cart, and finally allowed himself to succumb to his own grief before falling into an uncomfortable sleep.

May's attempts to speak to her mother had been silenced with a raised hand and a negative nod accompanied by a look that silenced the young woman on every attempt. From the stony expression on her face it was clear there were many thoughts going through her head.

It was only when the ferry had pulled away from Ireland and after Annie had given way to all her emotions, clinging onto deck rail, that she finally allowed May to speak.

"Mother… Please speak to me.. I don't know what I'd do if you didn't forgive me. Please…" May hung her head for what seemed like an age and cried out her grief quietly alongside her mother, who leaned wearily on the rails looking down at the grey, swirling water below. After a while she spoke.

"Did your aunt give you anything?" she asked quietly, but with a harshness to the edge of the words.

"Aye, she did, one hundred pounds" replied May.

"Least she could do, it's yours by right anyway" came the response.

"But it's not her fault, she was so upset and she really risked herself to help us."

"That's as maybe, but it's the least we deserve!" It was quite obvious from the delivery of her words that her mother had quietly held some form of ill feeling towards the aunt all these years and May was seeing it clearly for the first time.

"But she was always so kind to us!" remarked May with surprise and admonishment coming into her voice.

"Guilt maybe, she thought a lot of you no doubt, but there's nothing I've had from her that I can thank her for."

Her eyes grew steely and it was clear now that there was far more to this.

"But Mam, she told me to tell you that she loved you and to be brave!" May couldn't believe her mother, who had always been so passive, could harbour such venom.

"Brave!" gasped Annie "She's got no room to preach to others...Where was she when I needed her to be brave for me?" The words were wrenched from deep within accompanied by a sob. May was at a loss.

"I don't understand, Mam?"

"She's your grandmother! She was no better than you and got herself tangled up with the son of some fancy neighbour her father did business with. Got herself with child and then his family bundled him off to India and left her unmarried. They sent her away and then when I was born they passed me off as her married sister's child. The one you think was your grandmother was actually your Great Aunt. They even gave me her name but that was all she gave me. I didn't see her till I was six and I didn't know she was my mother till I was nineteen. Never once in all those years did she ever put her arms round me, even to treat me as an aunt would.. I never let her know I knew." Reaching for a handkerchief, she blew her nose loudly whilst she composed herself. When at last she had calmed her breathing, she turned towards May and eyes were full of pain.

"So I kept quiet and let her help us.. as she damn well should have! So.. like it or lump it, I am with you and you and he will look after this babe.. None shall say that you didn't have your family behind you and that you were forced to leave the babe as she did. I'll not have your children not knowing who their real mother is OR their grandmother. As for Edward, I'll keep my mouth shut for your sake and he'd best make an honest woman of you, God forgive us!"

May found herself clinging to the rail as all the realisations of events in her past came flooding in and clicked into place. How lucky she thought to have had a great aunt who wished to be her benefactor and who had spent, not just time and money to educate her, but in the only way she knew how, by showing her the garden and how to bake and spending little moments of togetherness with her, she had perhaps been trying to be a grandmother.

All the years her mother had kept herself distant from the woman May had thought her aunt, was now made entirely clear. Whereas she would have loved the old woman as only a child naturally could, the strain between the two older women had always been bubbling under the surface and kept them apart.

How could her mother have ever acknowledged that she knew her true mother for fear of losing her support if rejected. How much must it also have burned deep within her that the old lady had not had the courage to tell her the truth and bring her close.

She saw her mother and aunt in a whole new light and Annie's slightly distant behaviour as a mother to herself, she could now understand. Annie had probably been adopted to save the family's face and perhaps she had never known true maternal love.

She wondered if Aunt Anne had realised her mother knew and that was why she had been so keen to help them. She must have carried a great burden all these years.

Loving her aunt as she did, she could not condemn her now that she knew she was in fact, her grandmother. If, all those years ago, the pregnancy had been discovered, she would have likely been subjected to much more than May was currently experiencing in terms of shame and fear. It would have been far worse back then. Yet her mother had also borne a burden all these years and the pain she must have endured at being denied by her own mother, must have pierced her to the core.

How she must have had to smother down the bitterness and envy at all the affection Aunt Anne had lavished on May, Secrets always created distance in relationships and May couldn't help but wonder if her life with her mother would have been different had she been loved by her own mother as a child.

May reached for her mother's hand and this time Annie did not shake it off. Side by side was how Edward found them as he came up briefly to check on them. With a small amount of the food they had left in a muslin from Ada in his hand, he handed it to them solemnly and returned to guard their horse and belongings, telling them to, "Keep warm and come to the cart below when they reached Liverpool." It didn't go unnoticed that he hadn't saved any of the food for himself and May started to thaw slightly towards him once more. Edward was not an unkind man, he couldn't be capable of the type of atrocities the Black and Tans had been recently labelled with. She watched him head for the stairs to go below decks and for the first time the fear in her heart subsided a little.

Chapter Eleven –   Book Two

ENGLAND

Lancashire 1921

So, this was what had brought May to this valley, with her belly full and her heart half empty.

They had married quietly in Liverpool whilst they stopped for a few days to sort their plans, so as not to cause any gossip and carried on the next day as normal. Nothing was mentioned and as May had assumed the name Handley before they arrived, it just continued as though they had married before the baby was conceived. No one asked, so no lies had to be told. It was not the wedding a young girl in love would have imagined, but in her case 'the devil had driven and needs must'. She considered it her penance for all she had brought upon herself and she bore it, hoping that it would be all the retribution required for her sins.

After a few days of searching Edward came back to their lodgings to say he had found a place to rent and eager to have somewhere to end the horrendous journey, they had quickly loaded the cart once more and made for this valley.

He had rented a small cottage on the other side of the river beneath Wood Mill. Untrue to its name, Wood Mill was a cotton mill and you were never far from the noise of the machinery and the shouts of the workers to be heard above the clatter of the looms. Still, it was a pretty spot at the bottom of the valley and although tiny, its outlook was far better than some of the back to backs in the nearby towns they had passed on the way from Liverpool.

There, suffocating smoke and ash had spewed from the density of mill chimneys and May wondered how the people living near these mills ever survived in such an atmosphere. She couldn't have been more relieved when Edward had said that they would not be living somewhere like this. He needed clear, clean air with his chest.

As soon as the cart inched its way across the narrow Peppermint Bridge, its wheels all but skimming the un-walled edges and threatening a nasty spill into the river below. May, walking with her mother behind the cart for safety, breathed in the cold crisp air and thought, 'This will do, I will be content with this'.

The small cottage that Edward had taken on was built into the valley walls beneath the Huddersfield road. It had steps leading up to the road above at its side and was in a sheltered position. With sun early morning and late afternoon. In some ways it was fortunate to be huddled where it was for in summer the sun would blaze down and they would make for the shelter of the cooler kitchen in the shade.

On their arrival that first day, Edward, turning the key in the lock on the door, held his breath. The door creaked open onto a small kitchen/living room and as the gloom and dust subsided May's heart fell, but she hid it well. Life here wasn't going to be as comfortable as she had previously been used to. There was a parlour that had seen better times and three small bedrooms and they would need three with a child on the way and her mother to house.

Annie apparently was made of stronger stuff than they had thought and taking a long deep breath, she took off her outdoor coat, rolled up her sleeves and with a brisk.. "Well, we'd best get cracking if we're to have a bed by dark.. Edward, where's the bag of coal, we'll have that for a start and find me some kindling...May go find the well and take the bucket and big pan off the cart with you".. she started firing orders to the two who stood looking dejected at the state of their new home. She picked up a nearby broom that had seen better days and commenced a transformation. By dusk the rooms were passable to sleep in and the stove cleaned and warming the kitchen and as they sat down wearily and looked at each other across the newly scrubbed table. She surprised them by saying, "Tomorrow will be better, wait and see".

With that, she retrieved a potato pie from the oven and placed it before them. The sight and smell of it unleashed a new optimism. There was cheap meat in the pie and little of it, but to them it was a feast. It seemed her mother had kept her light quietly hidden under a bushel.

***

It had taken some time for them to be accepted in the community, being 'comer inners' and not born on the moors, but gradually through Edward's efforts and engaging nature, they started to be recognised and greeted as people passed through the mill yard on the way down to Milnrow village, where the majority of them lived.

Edward had discovered two local pubs known affectionately as the 'Top Bird' and 'Bottom Bird', as they were both named 'The Bird in the Hand'. He made a point of going twice a week to seek out contacts for work and soon enough, he was being passed the odd carting job for one or two of the local farmers. His time and investment was paying off and not to mention that being back amongst his own, the atmosphere was much friendlier than he had been used to in Ireland. Before long people were saying 'If you want something done, see Teddy Handley, he's a good man.'

Being poor was not something May relished, but the core of steel that ran through her blood made her determined that they would lay down roots in this quiet place with its bleak but majestic moors and reservoirs below. The pretty Piethorne Valley with its trickling streams, birdsong and woods full of bluebells in the spring to come, was a place for the soul and would very quickly weave itself irrevocably around their hearts.

The nearby mill meant there was always someone to shout hello to and it didn't feel as isolated as they had in Ireland. Here the locals didn't see her as the posh girl down the road and keep their distance. She was just the girl from Ireland. No, Lancashire would do and although they arrived at the coldest, bleakest time of the year, it had a beauty all of its own. The winter ensured they hunkered down and kept warm and May had little to do in her late pregnancy but sit in the rocking chair Edward had brought home with a blanket over her knees by the kitchen stove and crochet for the babe. It gave her a measure of peace. She shared the cooking and cleaning with Annie and it brought them closer as mother and daughter. The woods nearby meant a ready supply of free wood and Edward made sure they were never cold.

Christmas came and went quietly as May was tired all the time and they knew few people to celebrate with. May wondered how her aunt had fared with the inevitable mob that would have come to seek them out for retribution. She dared not write a letter straight away lest someone took it upon themselves to intercept it and when she eventually plucked up the courage, she was careful not to put anything incriminating in it other than profuse apologies and her address. A few weeks after they had settled in their home May went into labour and twenty hours later Rene was born. From the minute she held the babe her heart opened and she poured all her stifled love into the child, vowing siletly that her children would always be loved and would know it.

Annie had worked hard sewing and making clothes for the baby and put all her energies into making the house fit for them to call home. Gradually May's heart lifted as she sensed that her mother, set free from the constraints of religious obedience and the personal issues that life in Ireland had brought, had started to quietly enjoy this new life. They fell into an easy routine of looking after each other each day. The bleakness of winter was fading fast and in its place the spring was burgeoning the trees into fresh green life. Every week Edward tipped up all his earnings bar a shilling and life settled into a pattern.

The mud in the yard was turning to grass on either side of the cobbled road and primroses were donning their Easter bonnets. Edward had bought an old perambulator and the women had scrubbed and dressed it as best they could for Rene to sit outside in the sun. The baby was happy and it gave time for Annie and May to work on the garden and outhouses.

There was a pen and a stable for Lady which, in truth, had been the attraction for Edward over the requirements for the house. Still, they had been fortunate in finding this place so close to the mills as it brought them close to a source of work. The good thing was they were never short of linen as there were always off-cuts of cotton and wool rolls to be had cheaply or for 'nowt', if they were lucky.

Edward was now working as a carter, transporting the wool from the mill and May never had to break into the hundred pounds she had secreted for a rainy day as he continued placing his wages on the table each week, keeping little for himself. He was a good husband and a better father. The agent called for the rent once a month and they never had to know the shame of hiding behind the sofa as some of the more unfortunate families did.

The first few weeks had been strained, but after the birth of Rene Edward had showed so much joy in the birth of his daughter that even Annie warmed towards him and the evenings were spent in easy companionship as they passed the baby around the kitchen table.

Edward finally felt able to talk about his year in Ireland with the Black and Tans. His face held barely contained shame as he recounted that on taking up his post, he had quickly learned that it had not been the role he had been led to expect. As the 'policing' became more and more ruthless, he knew he could not continue to fight against people he considered his own and actively but quietly went against orders to avoid doing anything that went against his own moral code.

The trenches had taught him that they were just cannon fodder and whilst the occasional officer had true regard for his men, the good ones were few and far between. The death had been endless and the fear constant. He was not going to pursue glory in Ireland in the naive way he had gone to war with Germany.

Whilst he had been fortunate to have avoided being part of any of the more notorious operations of the unit, daily orders made it quite clear that this was a military operation rather than a policing and events marshalling role. A 'shoot to kill' policy was in place and if anyone approaching didn't observe the sentry's challenge, they were to shoot or possibly be killed themselves. This wasn't 'the troubles' he had read about in the newspapers, but a war for Irish Independence. He certainly hadn't been prepared for the hatred the uniform aroused and in his heart he couldn't say the fight for independence was entirely wrong.

What he had seen in the trenches of the world war had sickened him to his stomach. So much so, that he was not now ready to kill another man on someone's say so, just because it was expected of him. As soon as he was able, he had extricated himself and made his way back to May and her Aunt in the hope of a better and more peaceful way of living, having earned a little money to tide him over. It was enough of an explanation and spoken truthfully, for May to forgive him.

As soon as was possible after the last deep snows had melted, May had made the journey down the valley, to the nearest catholic church. After a long walk she came away furious, as the priest, being old school, for her great sin of marrying a non Catholic and not prepared to defy her husband by raising her children in the Catholic faith, had virtually shown her the door saying she was not welcome there. She had come home in floods of tears, mainly of anger and vowed she would never set foot in that church again.

Free now of the burden of her religion and her mother's own apparent lack of regard for the Catholic faith now that she was out of Ireland, she gradually fretted less and started to get on with her life without the need to ask for forgiveness each day. When Edward got a second job at Ogden Chapel as a grave-digger and gardener, she started to occasionally venture in there, sensing God would forgive her as long as she said the odd prayer somewhere at least. In her heart she would always be Catholic, despite her absence from her own church.

The baby was two months old when Edward respectfully asked to be allowed to lie once more with his new wife and it was a less naive and wiser young mother that took him into her arms, their love rekindled and burning brightly once more. Yet now, it was a quieter more intense love borne of adversity and family ties that replaced the passion of their youth. They were a new family.

The worry and shame of becoming pregnant was gone and they made up for time lost. Words of love were whispered under the covers quietly, so as not to disturb Annie across the small landing. The movements of lovemaking were constrained and moans of passion were smothered as best they could but occasionally couldn't be controlled. It made for their embarrassed amusement afterwards and truth be known, on the other side of the wall, brought forth the odd smile from Annie when their antics disturbed her. She was happy for them. She hadn't been so fortunate in her marriage.

Edward's appetite for his wife made sure that she kept adding to her brood yearly and, short of bolting herself in the girl's room..which she often threatened, what was a good but, excommunicated catholic girl to do? So she bore him ten children in twelve years, three of which she sadly lost at birth, leaving seven remaining. Each new child brought with it joy and worry in equal amounts and the number of children made it difficult to be anything other than a housewife. She took to most chores naturally, but she certainly wasn't a fan of darning and often Edward toes pushing through his holey socks would be a source of humour. Without Annie's help, it would have been a hard existence, but between them they managed to keep on top of all that was required for a large young family.

Years on, her body now, with its toils and heartbreak at lost babes, was that of a woman much older. But still, hidden behind the matter-of-fact façade crept the girl with the dreams in her eyes... and if hers had passed her by, then she would make damn sure her children would have her best endeavours to help them achieve theirs. She read the papers and any books she could get access to and was determined that the education she had been given would be put to good use. Her life with Edward had been hard and poor but when their eyes met across the table, he would wink and she knew she was loved.

As a mother she was kind but fierce. She pushed them to always expect better and learn as much as they could and in most of them there was a confidence borne of this. Graham was a worry, far too gentle, but prone to temper outbursts when his emotions overwhelmed him. Doreen needed cosseting and had a similar emotional nature, but the others were strong and not to be crossed. You didn't tamper with the Handleys. They held close, they squabbled, fought, cried and made up, they were a family and as a family there was no keeping them down.

Chapter Twelve 1945 - April

Lillian flung herself down on the battered old sofa with a snort, aggrieved that once again she had managed to get herself in trouble. This time over a 'bloody donkey.' Doreen looked up from her sewing and sensing that something was afoot looked as quickly down again, knowing it was wise to keep out of what was likely coming where Lillian was involved.

Sure enough mam followed through the door seconds later with the twins in tow, Graham had gone with his dad to feed the horse and pen the donkey back up. Mam was flushed and angry, a result of the shock she had experienced at the sight of her daughter dicing with death on the quarry's edge.

"What is wrong with you girl? Are you trying to send me to an early grave? You're not a child, you should know better!" shouted her mum as she pushed the little ones out of the way and started to gather up the washing. "That quarry is unstable and you're prancing about on the edge of it with not a care in the world!"

Lillian's chin went up to argue but she thought better of it and instead she muttered, "I just didn't think."

Her mother, still in full flow, was not for back peddling. "No you don't ever think Lillian!..I don't know why I bother… Go get me some water to fill the stove tank and lets have done with it. I'm sick of trying to knock some sense into you!" Lillian's mouth dropped open in indignation as she registered the chore slipped in between the reprimand.

".. But it's not my turn, it's hers!" accused Lillian, pointing at Doreen who still had her head down. Knowing when she was onto a good thing she 'cocked a deaf un' and pretended to be engrossed in her sewing. A hundred pumps to fill the water buckets was not an easy task and besides, Lillian had the strength for it and Doreen was recovering from her illness.

"She's doing the mending," her mother exaggerated the 'she' to express her displeasure at the rudeness. "So you can shift your backside and do it for her... and whilst your about it, you'd best go and apologise to your dad for nearly killing yourself and his bloody donkey!" May had never sworn in Ireland, but the years and the rougher life had loosened her tongue and it was the norm hereabouts and hardly noticed.

Lillian flounced out as best she could. She wasn't really built for flouncing, more for rough and tumble. Not being tall and elegant like Doreen and Rene, she envied them their looks, but she was strong-boned and loud, fearing no one and that was the way she liked it.

"She always gets her own way!" Lillian was not complying without a fight.

"She's been ill and she's doing the best she can. You, on the other hand have given me nothing but trouble this last week so it looks like you could do with using a bit more energy for the good. Off you go... and don't forget your da!"

Lillian slammed the door with as much defiance as she could muster. You didn't argue with mam, she was fierce when roused. However Lillian was bordering on the age where she would be looking to be independent soon and the challenges kept coming from her. May knew she had a firebrand for her middle daughter who needed a strong hand or she'd likely go off the rails. 'Just like herself', she thought and sighed.

Doreen was the younger of the two of them and at sixteen had a much quieter temperament than Lillian. Unless she had one of her 'moments' as they called it, when all hell would break loose and there would be tears first and if that didn't work a sobbing tantrum which would usually end in her fainting. Some of the older children were clearly sceptical of the fainting.

May had had high hopes for Doreen but when she got her a scholarship for the local grammar school, Doreen had demonstrated her lack of enthusiasm by getting herself admitted to hospital with a mystery illness where she kept passing out.

The hospital had kept her in for over a week, but thrown their hands in the air after no positive results for any likely cause and labelled it a 'hysterical illness'. Despite her older sister Lillian's scepticism, whispered to her other brothers and sisters that her sister had 'bugger all wrong with her!' May had continued to mollycoddle her, which didn't go down well with the other older children.

May had always been far too protective of Doreen, even Teddy had said so and he was caring and loving to all his children. She knew it, but it had just become habit after so nearly losing her at birth and then trying to keep the underweight child healthy. By the time she had caught up the die was cast and Doreen by then, was used to getting her own way through ill health and was not averse to using it as a mechanism. May also knew this and realised there would come a time when her daughter would have to learn to contribute more to the family or be a burden for ever and that time was well overdue.

None of the children were privy to the fact that May had spoken to the foreman at the mill and, like it or not, Doreen would be starting a job in the cutting room come the first of the month. Close enough for May to keep an eye on her and far enough to set her on a path to independence. She had long since been overdue employment and would have to pay her way as the other older ones did.

May was not relishing telling her but it needed to be done. Had she gone to the grammar school her prospects might have been better, but as it now stood, this was the only job available to her without too much hard labour involved. It was a great pity as Doreen had a lively and creative mind and was always with her head in a book or some small project that required imagination and little effort. 'Yes, she had it right that one,' thought May and wished with all her heart her daughter would rise to the challenge. She needed her to be a fighter, life was hard fought and there was no room for shilly-shalliers.

Lillian stomped out to the hand pump and was unhappily grumbling to herself with every pump. The sun was beating down on her back and as she stopped and stretched to ease the ache, looking about her, she took in the beauty of their home. Beyond the great mill the valley sides were rising up and the woodlands gracing them were coming into the first sweet green of spring. The mill was quieter today, as it was Saturday and few people worked unless there was a rush job on. The river bubbled nearby and the birds were singing their hearts outs, so all in all, it wasn't such a bad punishment. She much preferred to be outdoors anyway.

Grazing nearby were Lady, Captain, (Edward's latest horse rescue) and the errant donkey behind the newly secured gate. Somewhere in the small barn she could hear her dad hammering. In between bouts of hammering, she could hear the voice of her youngest brother asking questions and receiving patient answers from Edward. He had obviously calmed down, perhaps now was the best time to make the apology. She knew her mother wouldn't let up until she did.

"Ay up our Billy..no slacking now!" came a shout from behind her and she turned swiftly to see her elder brother Arthur striding up the lane towards her.

She grimaced as she picked up the next bucket to fill. "On pump duty, instead of Doreen..of course!" Arthur affectionately pushed her out of the way and with a reply of, "Of course" he started to quickly pump the handle until the bucket was filled. Despite the loss of an eye in a mystery 'fight' when he was nineteen, leaving him with a glass one staring boldly ahead, his roguish gypsy looks and dark hair gave him a rough charm. The loss of an eye had prevented him from being called up in the latter years of the war and possibly saved his life, so he considered it a fair exchange.

"So what did you do then?" he grinned.

"Slight altercation with the donkey on the quarry edge." She couldn't help but grin back and they both started to laugh.

May found them there laughing and flicking water at each other and she stood behind them hands on hips watching the horseplay and concealing a smile.

"So this is where you are Arthur Handley!... and where have you been since yesterday? as if I didn't know! You can just stop that messing about with Lillian, she's in enough hot water without you leading her astray!"

Arthur picked up the smaller bucket and started filling it, mischief on his mind.

"Aw Mam, give the girl a break he laughed. Besides it's Saturday, the sun is out and you look as though you need cooling down..." and with this he swung the bucket and flipped a bit of the water at his mother's feet.

"You bugger you! Put that bucket down if you know what's best for you!" Arthur flipped a little more with a devilish grin and his mother had to dance on the spot to avoid the water. She gave him a look that meant retaliation was on the way.

"Right, you've asked for it!" she cried and grabbed another bucket that Lillian had filled before. Arthur laughed and taking what was left in his bucket, he ran off round the back of the barn with his mother in hot pursuit, taunting her to keep up as he skipped in front. Lillian stood agog, but not displeased that her brother's return had seemed to snap their mother out of her temper. Her only regret was that her hard work was currently slopping out of the bucket as her mother ran after Arthur and it would require a refill.

By now Edward and Graham had come to the barn door to see what the noise was, just as Arthur and May were making the third circuit. May was panting and slowing fast and decided to set the bucket down as Arthur disappeared round the back of the barn once more. Giving it up as a bad job she stopped for breath,, bending over the bucket laughing. Graham seeing water, washed his hands in the bucket before his mother could stop him and picking up the bucket she launched it to one side with a, "That's no good for drinking now Graham!" just as Arthur was creeping up to drench her. He caught the water full in the face and to the onlookers it was a toss-up as to who was the most surprised. May or Arthur as he stood there dripping, his curly fringe hanging over his eyes.

"Mother!" he cried, "That's me best jacket!"

The surprise left May's face and she started to laugh out-loud.

"Serves you right," she laughed and Lillian, Teddy, and a shy Graham and May were eventually joined by Arthur as they laughed until they cried. Generations later the story of his come uppence would still be told and the telling would always bring a smile.

That evening the family sat around the table as best they could in the house which was not really built for ten and May served up rag pudding, which was always a treat. Her face red and shiny from the steam she sat down after serving and said grace. Everyone complied as she would not allow a fork to be picked up until it was done. There was ginger ale on the table for a Saturday treat and a bottle of stout for Edward and Arthur, May and an elderly Annie, compliments of Arthur who, having dried off from the earlier games, plonked them down on the table along with himself.

Jam roly-poly followed and when everyone had near enough finished, May sat up straight and surveyed her children, halting Rene, who would have risen to clear the dishes, with a raised hand. She was not relishing this moment and hoped the food had served to sweeten the pill.

"I have something to say that you all need to hear." She turned to Doreen who, sensing the focus was on her for some reason, shrunk down in her seat. May continued, "I have spoken to the mill foreman and he has a place for Doreen starting a week Monday in the cutting room. I know it will be daunting for her at first, so I want you all to help her as much as possible. May perhaps should have thought to tell Doreen privately, but it was done now and all eyes went to the object of the announcement.

Doreen herself sat white-faced and stricken, her belly turning over with fear. She couldn't possibly go to work in that loud place, what would she do? No..it couldn't happen, she wasn't well enough to stand all day in the mill. Especially at the rate they had to work.

Edward, having watched the horror dawn on his daughter's face, spoke quietly.

"You'll be fine lass and it will make you some new friends and you'll have a bit of brass," He smiled and spoke reassuringly.

"She'll cough up her wage packet like all the rest and I'll decide what brass she gets." May was more firm than normal, sensing that any weakness seen would set Doreen off. They need not have worried as the girl swallowed down the huge lump in her throat and nodded agreement silently. She was too genuinely shocked to do otherwise.

"We'll talk later love," May tempered the news with a softer voice. "It'll be all right, you wait and see..."

Doreen was quivering inside, her head a jumble of different thoughts. The thought of being out there on her own without her mother's protective eye, ever watchful was daunting. Yet with it there were the first inklings of adulthood beckoning and money of her own to spend. The initial horror started to subside.

The sobering thought then came in that mam made all the older ones tip up their wages every month and then distributed what she thought was theirs after keep had been taken out. It usually brought much grumbling and only a small return for their labour. There were a lot of bellies to feed in this house and dad was struggling with his chest at the moment and not up to full time, so it fell to the rest to fill the hole in their weekly finances. Doreen had used her times sat with her sewing to dream big. One day she would be a stylish lady with beautiful clothes like Rene, her eldest sister.

***

Rene, at twenty four and nine years her senior, seemed very glamorous to the younger girl. The most the younger ones got, was one set of clothes that had to last the week. If they got dirty the clothes had to be washed and dried overnight whilst the owner of the clothes sat in nightclothes and a cardigan. White pleated skirts and a blouse for Sundays were the norm and were not allowed except for special occasions. Lillian got the occasional hand me down from Rene, but that didn't happen often as Rene chose well and looked after her clothes.

Clothing seven children had been a stretch for May. Cardigans were knitted and May had also become quite talented at crochet. Crocheted clothes were not for Rene and she would refuse any offers from their mother politely, to which Arthur had ribbed in a high-pitched voice "Ooh... not for the Duchess, Mam! Too peasant like!"

"Shut up, Arthur!" Rene had snarled, "They're lovely, just not my style mum," Rene would reassure her mother.

Arthur and Rene were never far from a spat. Of all the family they were the two that got on the least. She certainly was the most clever and with a dry wit she could put Arthur's more earthy jibes down quickly. Doreen thought it might be that Arthur resented Rene being the eldest, but despite her admiration of Rene, she couldn't help but like the lovable rogue that was her eldest brother. A rogue he was all the same and it was apparent in his manner. Brought up on these moors his local dialect was broad. Here was no smooth mover, but his cheek got him far.

Doreen had drifted from the conversation around the table in her reverie and it was only Mam's raised voice that brought her back to the present.

"What do you mean, you're getting married?!" The table went silent once more. Arthur tipped his chair back onto two legs and raised the bottle of beer to his lips.

"Just as I said mam, I'm getting married next week." His one good eye focused on their mam and whilst there was a battle line drawn, there was also a hint of a plea as he returned her gaze that he hoped she wouldn't give him a hard time.

"To that May you've been seeing?...Why she's just a bit of brass you've rubbed up. Why on earth would you want to marry her?," Edward coughed a signal to May that now was not the time, but May was still reeling from the news. Edward was clearly privvy to something that May was not and May's eyes shot to her husband for confirmation and he nodded his head almost imperceptibly to rein her in. "...and why so soon?. oh no.. don't tell me you've got her pregnant?."

The swallow barely concealed in Arthur's throat belied his bravado and it was enough to give him away to his shrewd mother. May's heart sank as she had no argument for this. Edward had stood by her and Arthur must do the same by this woman, regardless of whether the girl was considered suitable. It was only right. Her eyes filled with tears, for she knew with that step that his youth and freedom was gone forever and like her, he would always wonder what life could have been without that first life-changing leap into parental responsibility far too soon.

"We've no money to help you," she said. "You've made your bed and you'll have to lie in it. I take it that it's that May you've been knocking about with?"

"Aye it is mam and I don't need any money, I've got a bit put by."

"..and how's that then... gambling I take it?"

"I've been lucky recently." Arthur had more going on in his life than he made his family privy to and it was best not to ask. She had tried taking a regular amount of keep from him but as he didn't have a wage packet as such, he was hard to keep track of. He kept company that May would rather not know about.

Arthur had first got in with the gypsies as a teenage boy on one of his dad's trips up to Appleby and then from that liaison into horse racing at Liverpool. Some of the people his dad had witnessed his dealings with were less than savoury and he worried, but Arthur, with the exception of the mysterious loss of an eye, had always seemed to thrive in their company.

His disappearances for days at a time were put down to this liaison. With his mother's Irish blood and dark brooding looks, in combination with his father's love of horses that had passed naturally on to the children, it allowed him to fit right in. He was definitely a gypsy in spirit and it really hadn't helped him work- wise as his wanderlust had seen him fired from a couple of normal jobs. So now Arthur worked for a bookie in Rochdale and it gave him the freedom and life he required. He was lucky Milnrow had a station to get him about, cars were few and far between in this rural area.

"Where will you live?" asked Edward quietly. His disappointment for his son was evident, but more for how he had now got himself in a situation where his future path would be dictated by mother nature rather than choice.

Edward thought on his own journey with May and always felt that she could have done better and in fact, deserved better than he had offered. Still he loved her dearly and could never regret how Rene's conception had forced their hand, but often he wondered if she had wished for another life than the one he had provided for her. He wanted his children to live full lives, without that doubt in their hearts. Arthur now, deliberate or otherwise, had set his course and was honour bound to follow it.

"I've found us a house in the village Dad, will you help me sort it out? It's a bit of a mess, but it's all I can afford."

"Aye, tha knows I will lad, just tell me when." The day had suddenly become a little cloudier, but Edward knew there would be more sunshine. His only worry was his eldest son's roving eye and

Edward wondered if he was up to keeping faith with just one woman. Time would tell.

"Where's the wedding?" he asked.

"Rochdale registry," came the response he expected.

"Will her mother and father be there?" asked May curtly.

"No," said Arthur and he looked down taking a final swig of his beer for distraction.

"We'd best do a meal here then if it's like that," said May rising. She gathered the plates with the girls scuttling around her trying to ease the atmosphere. Nothing more was mentioned.

Later, when May sat near the range in a subdued mood, she couldn't help but think on the irony that her son had got himself with child with a woman called May. Edward sat opposite, she said little, but he could see her thoughts were running wild and he left her to sort them out herself.

For May, it was the realisation that the first of her children was leaving her and she wasn't quite sure how she felt about it. All she knew was that today she felt a little older. She rose from her chair with a sigh and went over to Annie's chair, where her mother, now frail, was dozing.

"Come on mother, let's get you to bed. Looks like we have a busy week before us."

***

The day of the wedding was soon upon them and on the Saturday morning the day dawned bright and clear. May had been pretty subdued the last few days, but this morning she was taking out her frustrations on her domestic duties. Pans were clattering, doors were slamming and, before the family were reluctantly raised from sleep with the noise, May had all the younger children's best outfits hung in a line over the fire airing and newly pressed. Pleated skirts were a bugger to iron, she thought grumpily, but they looked so nice.

Breakfast plates were set ready to eat on the table and porridge was bubbling in a pan when Gary, the first of the kids, dared to venture in, smelling food. She turned him back round and sent him to wake everyone with no exceptions and get them down to breakfast straight away as she had too much to do to keep shouting them.

Two hours later they lined up for final inspection, including Edward and were passed fit to be seen. May had a little 'chapeau' trimmed with net she had fashioned herself. She was quite pleased with it combined with a dark blue cotton dress and Edward and Arthur had had their best suits pressed as best she could to bring them up to scratch for a wedding.

The table was set with the best cloth ready for the wedding breakfast. Daffodils and greenery sat cheerfully in a vase and the cheap cutlery was polished to the best shine she could manage. No one would be saying they hadn't made an effort for the new family member, regardless of whether the circumstances were unfortunate.

The parents of Arthur's girl had thrown her out when they had found she was pregnant and she was going to be married without their blessing. She had been staying in the village since then with a friend and keeping her head down until things were resolved. She would be meeting them at the station in Milnrow for the journey to Rochdale and then they would be staying the night in the newly rented house that Arthur and his father had been trying to make something of for the last week. That was all the honeymoon she could expect. It saddened May that her son and his girl would not have the excitement of a spring wedding in the chapel and all the happy expectations of those who followed the 'unsullied' route to marriage. As for the gossips, well they could all go to hell!

'Now was not the time to be maudlin 'she thought'and ushering them all out in the sunlight, they commenced the twenty minute brisk walk down the hill to the station. As they crossed the Peppermint Bridge she couldn't help but cast her mind back to the day she had crossed this bridge as a new bride. She cast a glance to Edward who was holding his youngest son's hand and swinging him playfully back and forth as Graham laughed. She loved him still, but it had been a task to keep his house, bear his children and commit herself to a life where she would never really achieve her full potential.

She looked then to her children and she marked the ones she thought would do well with an invisible tick. Rene definitely, Lillian had too much energy to refine her into something she was not. Doreen had the ability and the looks, but would she use them? The twins were full of youthful energy and she could see them making good with the right guidance... and her baby Graham, she didn't ever want to think of him growing up and leaving her. In truth she doubted he ever would, far too shy for his own good and not showing any academic skills so far, it was likely he would stay close to home and safety.

Four hours later and the deed done, the family were seated around the table with space made for the new addition. The bride, May was a pretty girl with dark wavy hair and could have been one of her own. The girl, wisely, was on her best behaviour and subdued, but May knew Arthur wasn't the type for milksops and no doubt this girl would soon step up and show her full nature. May hoped it wouldn't be a troublesome one.

Edward made the obligatory speech as the father of the bride was absent. Glasses were chinked and, for the children dandelion and burdock was a rare treat and the atmosphere became party-like.

It was almost sundown when May stood at last alone by the millstream. She breathed in a long calming breath and inhaled the smell of vegetation mixed with the warm earth as she fumbled for a hanky in her apron pocket. As the rush of the water covered her quiet sobs, she cried out something, she knew not what. Maybe the leaving of her first child to start his own life had suddenly brought home to her how quickly the years had passed and with them all she had dreamed she would be. She was a middle-aged woman, left here with a loving family but a sense of loss she could not explain.

Drying her eyes she sensed she was not alone and she turned to see Edward leaning against the wall, a sad but sympathetic smile on his sun-worn face.

"Aye lass," he sighed, "I expect you wanted better for them than we had... but no mind love. This family is rich in love. No fancy wedding would make it any better than it is or was for us... Now dry your eyes, there's another glass of beer waiting for you and a family that loves you."

Chapter Thirteen

It was a subdued and inwardly shaking Doreen that crossed the Bridge to Wood Mill a few days later. May walked alongside her to make sure that her daughter would make it through the door without drama and as she introduced her to the foreman she patted her on the back to reassure her. Doreen shrunk back against her hand and May had to steady her daughter as her feet faltered.

Burt Thomas smiled sympathetically at the quaking girl, knowing that it wouldn't be long before she would be chatting happily with the other women as they worked and this first frightening day would be soon forgotten. He took her round the mill after giving May a friendly dismissal and settled her in the cutting room with a bonny girl called Margaret, who was eager for company and soon had Doreen smiling with her tales and confident personality.

Doreen was happy to let her direct the conversation. She suspected she would always be a follower, never a leader, which was a shame considering her intelligence and creative mind. The work was hard but the company fun and she quickly got the hang of the routine. Wood Mill was old and one of three, with a combined loom count of some 250 machines. It was owned from early Edwardian times by Thomas Heap and Sons.

Standing on the slopes of the valley's steep walls the mill towered above everything. Running alongside, the narrow river was the only thing that separated it from the land the family's cottage stood on. The plus of its location being the shortness of time for Doreen to scurry home to the safety of Wood Mill Cottage and her mother. The downside being it was unlikely to widen the young girl's horizons, but it was a job and the girl needed to work.

The days passed quickly for the new employee and it was a relieved May that received the reply of, "Not so bad mum," to her questioning on how her week had been. There was little time for more as her brood was coming home from various jobs, all expecting to be fed. With Annie's growing frailty, the majority of the housework for the large family now fell to May. The old lady seldom moved from her chair by the fire nowadays, so it was not the time for idle conversation until everyone was fed.

Once all the girls were all home they pitched in to help, whilst the children were sent to fetch eggs from the chicken pen. May was eking out a paper-wrapped packet of sausages between them all and there was already an aroma of roast potatoes coming from the oven, whilst a pan of carrots was just coming to the boil. Soon Edward would be home and the kids needed to be fed and bathed still and as Edward always liked a little bit of time to listen to the radio whilst he soaked awhile. She had it down almost to a military operation. Only after that, they had a little peace as they all dispersed to whatever chores or interests they had and left the two women to the dishes and the radio. Life had its rhythm.

The pans were boiling on the stove as well as the water heater within the range and Lillian had dragged the old bath from the lean-to outside and placed it before the fire. The metal was warming slowly in readiness for the water and its weekly visitors. The younger children shared, usually followed by Edward who would be the dirtiest, although it was a close run thing with his youngest Graham who always had a knack of finding something earthy to roll in.

The girls would stay out of the kitchen on their mother's instruction, whilst Edward undressed behind the make-shift screen made of the wooden maiden with a draped sheet and he wouldease his aching bones into the welcome warmth of the warm water. May would dry the kids by the fire, readying them for bed whilst she chatted idly with her husband and then leaving him to relax as she put them to bed. Later the older girls would return to refill the bath for their own use and, now dressed, Edward would take his cue to vacate and wander down to the Top Bird to give them privacy on bath night. The house with five women in was not the most restful and he welcomed the excuse for a little respite from the chatter.

Within a couple of weeks May had grown used to just having one man around. Arthur was busy with his new wife and eager to progress in his job and was seen little. Of course it meant his previous chores had to be shared amongst the others, which didn't go down particularly well, but a week later they hardly noticed the changes and the protests had ceased.

Doreen had surprisingly settled into her new role and if anything it seemed to be bringing her out of her shell a little, which pleased May. Life progressed and her days were full with facilitating the social life of her daughters by keeping the few clothes they had washed and ready for an opportunity to enjoy their free time.

Much of her spare time was spent crocheting blankets from small skeins of wool picked up cheaply from the woollen mills. She had become quite an expert and it did pass the winter nights when there was little else to amuse a person. The cottage now had basic electricity but still no bathroom, yet for May the light and the radio was a luxury. Sometimes she would sit and write in her journal when all her brood had vacated or gone to bed and she grabbed that small time, which was all that was left to her after a busy day, to write down her thoughts.

In earlier years, crocheting by candlelight, whilst her hands felt their path along the wool, moving swiftly and calmly, allowed her to think her thoughts and she found the action quite meditative. It was the only thing she could do in the semi darkness. Even with the electric nowadays Annie's hands now were too crippled with arthritis take up her sewing often and she spent much of her time in the evenings dozing in and out of the radio programmes until May prompted her to retire. On the night Edward allowed himself a drink, the women would spend the evenings once the children were abed, in quiet companionship. At least the winter nights did not dictate their bedtimes these days, it was a huge leap forward.

Doreen had finally been given permission to go to Oldham on the train with her sisters to visit Hill Stores and her heart had been beating frantically with excitement ever since her mum had said she was allowed to go, under strict supervision of Rene of course, who at nearly twenty four, was a regular.

Saturday came and they walked down to the station with Edward. He gave them strict instructions on the time he expected them home. For Doreen, the train journey alone was enough to fill her with excitement. As they walked up the stairs into the ballroom and her hands grazed the smooth brown sculpted tiles as she walked at the sides of her sisters, she couldn't keep the sparkle out of her eyes.

She marvelled at the decor of the place, breathing in the sounds and smoky atmosphere. It was much nicer than she had thought it would be for the outskirts of Oldham. The noise of the clientele mingling with the band playing had her heart near bursting with the knowledge that she was finally attending her first grown up dance.

The soft pleats of her Sunday best skirt and blouse felt so much more glamorous in this setting and as the folds brushed against her calves like little frissons of excitement, she stepped into the lights of the huge room as the band played the closing strains of 'Moonlight Serenade'.

Drawing a long breath to calm her nerves she walked forward into the mass of movement in the surprisingly grand ballroom and then overwhelmed by the noise, dawdled in wonder behind her sisters at the sheer number of people all crammed into this place.

It had opened over forty years ago and survived the bombing to bring a fresh sense of romance to the post war generation. Hearts were light and hopeful for the future here and it was transmitted through the atmosphere of the room. She looked around at the stained glass windows and the beautiful curves of its ceiling and her eyes grew round with the wonder of it. For Doreen the building was the grandest she had ever seen.

"Come on Do, stop gawping, we're over here," shouted Lillian and Doreen jumped and moved forward with the momentum of the crowd. Rene walked in front with her usual elegance and Doreen noticed the attention she was receiving from several of the room's male occupants as they passed. Lillian following, hadn't the same aura, but what she lacked in grace, she made up for in confidence and she greeted several people as they made their way along the tables to a spot that they had obviously claimed previously near the stage. A large band played looking very smart. An attractive young man stepped out as they approached a crowded table and Rene smiled as he pulled out three chairs for them all. He was mid-twenties and despite the none too classy cut of what had obviously been his demob suit, he made a handsome figure with no shortage of confidence.

"Good evening Rene, Lillian…and I take it this is Doreen?"

Doreen blushed and looked down quickly to cover her embarrassment. Rene smiled graciously and offered him her hand and allowed him a turned cheek, which he immediately placed a kiss on. She really was a cool customer thought Doreen.

"Good evening Stan...Yes this is Doreen." She ushered her sister into a seat and Doreen watched in awe as Rene held court with all the occupants of the table. With her hair slicked back in a French pleat she looked so sophisticated that Doreen vowed that next time she came she would have that look. Her hand raised to her own black waves self-consciously feeling something was now lacking, despite the hours of preparation in comparison to her eldest sister.

Lillian plonked herself down and started a different conversation that soon had a burst of laughter from the table occupants. She had an acid tongue but delivered with a cutting humour that could be hilarious. It was clear the sisters were chalk and cheese. Rene was lady-like but straight talking and confident and Lillian was the more raucous, it was an interesting competition between the two.

The music struck up in a foxtrot and Stan stood to offer his hand to Rene. She raised up from her seat and he pulled her gently onto the dance floor and into his arms like they were one person. It looked so natural and Rene danced so elegantly that Doreen was transfixed. How she wanted to dance.

"Come on Do, this is easy, I'll show you," whispered Lillian and with it she pulled her sister from the chair and dragged her protesting onto the dance floor. Partnering her sister was not the first dance Doreen had imagined, but it was a start she supposed.

"Who is that man with Rene?" she whispered.

Lillian grinned and her reply of "It's her beau, Stan Hornby," sent Doreen's eyes as wide as gobstoppers. Dad would kill her!

When she voiced her thoughts her older sister's reply was wry. "He'll have to find out first… Come on concentrate!"

The evening flew by and Doreen soon found herself drawn into the dancing with the other young men in the group. She was so in awe of her eldest sister and so busy trying to dance without mistakes that she never even took notice of the compliments that she was getting.

A natural and graceful dancer and very pretty, which did not go unnoticed. Had she been old enough to realise how attractive she was, it would have gone to her head. Being young allowed her to glory in the romance of the evening without having to fend off unwelcome attention. The group around them took her into the fold and were very protective. It allowed Doreen to find her feet in the safety of family and friends and it was a tired but ecstatic girl who leaned her head on the glass of the train window as it clickety clacked its short journey back to Newhey. The odd flash of lights from houses near the track flickering past the windows were the only respite from a dark landscape.

Peering through the glass as her head rested wearily, she relived the glory of her first evening out as a young woman with a happy smile on her face.

"Come on Dopey Do!" nudged Lillian with a smile as the train slowed. They jumped up and Rene pulled down the brass window release and reached out to open the door to see Edward's lone figure, waiting on the platform to walk them up Huddersfield Road to home. He stepped forward from the waiting room door and hugged Doreen to him as she ran forward.

"Did you enjoy yourself lass?" He asked as she threw her arms round him.

"Oh Dad it was fabulous!" she breathed into his shoulder, her excitement spilling over.

"Come on then, tell me all about it." He caught her hand and linked it through his arm as the two older girls moved in front to exchange thoughts of their own. Lillian turned and shot her a warning look and Doreen knew she had to tell her father the potted version, which she did...all the way home. Edward smiled, his girls were growing up and Doreen, his timid little bird, was growing too.

Once through the door, the girls tiptoed passed their mothers and grandmother's room, so as not to disturb them and closing the bedroom door proceeded to discuss the night's events in a whisper.

Undressing quickly, they pulled on nightgowns old cardigans and bed-socks, making sure not to wake Maureen their younger sister who shared a bed with Doreen. The two younger boys had a rough partitioned area in the third bedroom with their grandmother. It was tight, but better now Arthur had vacated. The beds were strewn with coats as extra insulation from the cold in addition to their mothers crocheted blankets.

Jumping in to keep warm, Doreen was grateful her sister had already warmed the bed for her. Rene was already grumbling at Lillian for not putting a warming pan in earlier and reluctantly they moved closer to each other for warmth whilst the makeshift bedding heated from their bodies and did its work.

There was a moment or two of silence where you might have supposed they were drifting to sleep, but in reality, all three were full with their own thoughts and excitement. Rene, for the thoughts of her impending date with her new beau Stan. Lillian for the young man across the room whose eye she had caught with a brazen wink and Doreen, who in her youth had no particular fancy, just a head full of romance of the evening's dancing and more dancing. Life was becoming an adventure.

She quite liked this being considered grown up and when her wages came in she might be able to buy some new shoes...she loved shoes. As children, the one thing their mother had insisted on was good shoes. They might be poor but they were not having clogs like some of the other poor families. Doreen drifted with thoughts of Brussel's lace dance shoes like she had seen in some of the magazines her older sister sometimes bought. One of these days she would have lots of beautiful shoes, sparkling dance shoes, and the dresses to match. She so loved the dancing...her drowsy eyes were just starting to close in happy slumber when Lillian addressed Rene from the darkness.

"Did you kiss him then Re?" she asked shamelessly.

"None of your business," came the curt response.

"Well you were outside with him long enough, I saw you sneak out!"

"As I said, it's none of your business." There was shuffling as she turned on her side away from Lillian and the silence fell for a brief few seconds.

"Bet you did!" came the response.

"Well that's for me to know and you to find out."

Lillian's voice came out of the darkness once more.

"I'll just wait till you've gone to sleep and ask you then, you always tell me whatever I ask..."

"I do not!"

"Yes you do... sleep well!" said Lillian with a smirk as she turned over to sleep leaving the thought that she could get whatever she wanted out of Rene if she waited till she drifted off. She didn't know she was even answering. That was one thing the Duchess couldn't control, she talked in her sleep..you just had to wait for the right moment...

Chapter Fourteen - 1946

Arthur's boy was born just as Rene announced her engagement to Stan Hornby and was named Michael. May, his wife was not one for visiting and so they saw little of the new grandchild. Arthur seemed to be away more and more and apart from the odd pint in the Bird with his father, he was seen little. May had gone down the hill to visit her daughter-in-law on several occasions whilst she was pregnant but came home feeling rebuffed. The girl was not one for confidences but she sensed very quickly that all was not well between Arthur and her. It was a sadness and a disappointment that they could not be close, especially as this was her first grandchild.

When the baby came there was the obligatory get-together to wet the baby's head, but afterwards, Arthur's new wife never put herself out to bring the baby to see its new family. May worried that Arthur's wayward nature would not make it easy for him to settle into family life and this was possibly what was making his new wife unhappy and withdrawn. It would certainly explain her reticence to engage with her in-laws. Thinking perhaps the girl really needed a mother figure to give her support she decided to try once more to bring her into the fold.

It was eleven a.m. on a Monday when she knocked on the terraced house door. Her daughter in law opened it with the baby in her arms and nervously invited her in. May stepped over the threshold and she could see immediately that Arthur's money certainly wasn't going into the improvement of his home and little had changed since they had moved in. The girl herself seemed to be oblivious to her home. A bucket of dirty nappies were soaking by the back door of the kitchen she led her into and the smell was invading the atmosphere.

The baby was happy enough and May spent fifteen precious minutes holding her grandson, whilst her daughter-in-law boiled a kettle for tea. The conversation was limited and May worked hard to get a smile out of the girl with local gossip but she just didn't seem to have much of an interest in anything she had to say. When she asked of Arthur, all she received was a shrug of the shoulders and a curt reply tinged with something unhealthy and brooding saying, "I hardly see him, he's away a lot".

Her eyes didn't meet May's own and it was clear she didn't want to carry the conversation on. May's anger bubbled and she wasn't sure whether it was at this jaded young woman for not having more to say for herself or her son for treating his new wife so shamelessly. Regardless of her own opinions on Arthur's choice of wife, she deserved better than she was receiving and the babe certainly did.

"Where's he staying? And why does he need to be away so much?" she questioned.

"Don't know, he says his boss sends him all over and he has to go," was the only response she received.

"Does he indeed?" May looked around the kitchen. The larder was virtually bare. It was clear the girl either had no money for food other than the basics her rations allowed or she was too idle to make the effort to walk to the shops and provide for her child.

Whilst the baby boy seemed happy enough his clothes were badly washed and he looked unloved. The girl herself was listless and May pondered on whether she had a case of the baby blues. She made herself a promise to start him some garments and blankets poor mite and take more note of his mother's situation and welfare just in case.

She herself had had a couple of episodes of despair after her stillborns but never experienced it with healthy babies, but she had heard it was possible to fall into depression after a birth. She had been lucky to have her mother's support on those occasions. This girl was short of someone to fight her corner and she would make sure when Arthur showed his face next, he would get a piece of her mind.

As for her son, he was certainly a champagne Charlie with lemonade pockets that one. The first in the village to get a car when food was still subject to rationing. How he afforded it she didn't know but it was said hereabouts that only a bookie's runner could afford a car round here and Arthur played his cards close to his chest in respect of his dealings since becoming just that.

One week he would wave a wad of cash and another be tapping his dad up for a loan to tide him over the next few days. Edward said little to his wife but it was clear he was not happy with the direction his son had taken. She suspected there had been words more than once between them that Edward hadn't wanted to trouble her with.

A week later she marched into his house and told his wife to take the baby a walk whilst she had a word with Arthur and therein ensued an almighty row that half the street and his departing wife must have heard every word of.

May did not mince her words and it was clear by the end of it that her son had interests elsewhere. His excuses didn't stack up and she finally departed with the ultimatum that he, 'step up to the plate and do right by his family or he was no son of hers!'

His snarled response was enough to tell her that he had little care for what anyone thought of him. The shadowy company he was keeping was obviously having a bad influence and she felt at a loss to know what to do to bring him back. She flung her final words as she left of, "Get some decent clothes on your child's back and put some bloody food in these cupboards! You shame me and your Dad!" to a face that, full of bravado and anger, was nonetheless her son and it pained her to leave without anything resolved for the better.

He slammed the door in her wake and did she but know, it was to be the last she was to see of him for some time. When she called up a few days later with a parcel of things for the baby, the house looked empty and the girl and the child had gone. Knocking on the neighbours' door, she gleaned that the girl had gone back to her mother. The marriage had taken less than eighteen months to reach this rift.

Arthur had returned it seemed and Edward on hearing this from one of the pub regulars, in his quiet way, resolved to speak with his son. As he reached the front door of the small back to back, he heard laughter and for a moment he thought that his son and his wife had made their peace and reconciled.

He was soon disabused of that notion when the door was wrenched open and a strange woman was bundled out with Arthur pinching her backside. It was clear they were drunk and the two stopped short at the sight of Edward standing in the yard, his flat cap tipped over one eye and hands in his waistcoat as he surveyed the scene before him with a grim stare.

Arthur's grin faded at the sight of his father and the woman's giggling ceased and she had the grace at least to look embarrassed.

"What's this Arthur?" came the steely question.

Arthur flushed and his eyes dropped to the floor under his father's scrutiny. He breathed in deeply and raised his face to confront the older man.

"This is May!" was all he said. Edward's eyes flew open in disbelief.

"What the bloody hell do you mean boy? This isn't May. That poor lass has gone home to her mother with your kid. Have you no shame?"

"What am I supposed to do? she buggered off with Michael and they won't let me see him!" came the heated response.

"...and you wonder why?... and you girl, get yourself off home! Don't you know what they say about women with married men?"

The girl's jaw came up and she looked at Edward with a sneer. She was a hard-faced bint if ever he'd seen one. Dyed blond hair and over made up, with a dress that had a little too much on display.

"Actually, he was seeing me before May. He got her pregnant when we had a falling out. I'm the one he should have been with!" was her thoughtless response fuelled by too much ale.

Edward looked her up and down in a way that indicated just what his opinion was. He paused for a moment before giving his answer.

"Oh you think so, do you?" He turned to his son and spoke through gritted teeth his anger ready to spill over... "Well I'll tell you this Arthur your sister's wedding is next month. Turn up with your wife and kid in tow or don't come at all... and lose this trollop fast. There'll be no good end to be had here!" and with this Edward turned on his heel, pulled his cap down over his eye and walked away.

A couple of hours later a weary Edward pushed open the door to find a worried May waiting for him. Annie had taken herself off to bed with the rest of the household and May unused to her husband not coming home when expected, had waited for him, imagining what might have happened. Her relief was clear but distress made her angry.

"Edward where in heavens name have you been?"

Edward laid his cap on the table and glanced at his pocket watch. Shrugging out of his coat and hanging it by the door he turned sad eyes to his wife.

"I'm sorry luv...I went to see Arthur.." May crossed her arms awaiting the inevitable. From his demeanour it obviously hadn't gone well.

"And?"

"He had some woman with him. They'd been on the ale and she said she should have been with him but for him getting May pregnant, silly bitch!"

"So this has been going on all the time do you think"

"Aye lass. I think so.."

"There's no end to that lad's stupidity, who is she?" May sat down at the table and Edward sat opposite.

"She says she's called May. I didn't stick around for introductions. |It would have come to blows."

"May?" May questioned. "You must be kidding!"

"No luv, I wish I was" came the sad response. "I'm done with him."

Chapter Fifteen

Rene's wedding was soon upon them and as the day dawned there was a scurry of activity. Rene and Stan had bought a house just further up the hill in the village of Ogden for three hundred and fifty pounds. It was opposite the Bulls Head pub and close to Ogden Chapel. They had got it at a reduced price for its isolation; although Stan had joked that as it had a pub twenty yards away, he'd have paid more just for that.

They were having the wedding breakfast there, as it was bigger than the cottage. Stan was an engineer and he had just been promoted to supervisor. Rene was now working in the office at the mill and had a supplementary job behind the bar of the pub, which was convenient and allowed her to put money by to decorate their new home in readiness for moving in. It would be all the honeymoon they could afford for now, but Rene, being sensible preferred to put the money into the house and wait for Oldham Wakes to celebrate their union.

Doreen thought Stan was very handsome and suave but something in the way he spoke to her and Lillian unnerved her. He seemed a little too flirtatious. When she had mentioned to Lillian she had laughed at her saying, 'When had she become an expert in men?' and that he was just being friendly'.

Edward and May seemed to like him. He had bought a house for their daughter and seemed to have a bit about him. By comparison to their own eldest boy Arthur, who was frequently seen 'plaitin legs' from the pub to home more than a couple of times a week, he was a saint.

As May stood adjusting her daughter's veil that morning she marvelled on how serene and beautiful she looked, tall and slim with her sleek black hair and pale skin.

Although she was being married in the chapel and not the catholic church in Rochdale, her heart was bursting with pride that she had succeeded in bringing at least one of her children to an honourable marriage. The other two eldest girls stood as maids of honour in simple crepe de chine in white with chiffon sleeves and bands of silk flowers that all the women had a hand in producing. Doreen wore it well and was naturally excited and Lillian as always, shuffled uncomfortably at the entrapments of femininity she felt was not for her. She would always be a tomboy thought May fondly.

Maureen, the youngest of the girls had cried to be a bridesmaid and May had relented only in so much as giving her a headband the same as her sister's but funds weren't up to the full outfit so she had been appeased with that.

A strong-willed, but calm Rene, had insisted that her dress was bought and had saved up for it herself to prevent any interference in her choice. She had, however allowed her mother to embellish the simple gown with the seed pearls she had found on an old antique bag that had long since rotted, the pearls had been carefully saved for such an occasion as this.

Rene had style and the simple stately cut of the gown with this small addition took on a sophistication of its own. The curved silk headdress, trimmed with pearls and flowers was the perfect embellishment and set in Rene's sleek black waves, it enhanced her near perfect features, she was truly beautiful and May's eyes welled with the natural pride and equal grief of the loss of yet another of her children from the nest.

Edward waited to walk his daughter down the aisle of the small chapel in a suit that was a little big but nonetheless smart as May could make it with careful pressing. As he looked at his daughter she took his arm with a confident smile and he was the proudest father a girl could have. Walking slowly down the aisle to the grand sound of the beautiful organ that graced the side of the chapel, its pipes painted gold and soaring to the roof like the gates of heaven. He scanned the pews for any sign of his errant son as they progressed down the aisle. There was none and his heart fell. He had so hoped he would make the effort to come, wife or no and regretted his earlier ultimatum. May watched their approach with pride but noted Edwards suit was a little baggy on him, they were getting older and a little less strong.

By the time Edward had recovered his thoughts, he was at the altar and his eyes were watery with a combination of the pride of the moment and the disappointment that his eldest son could let his sister's wedding day go by without making an appearance. It stirred his anger once more.

He dutifully handed his daughter's hand to the man who waited for her and sent up a silent prayer that she would be happy and cared for. Rene looked to her beau and Edward stepped back. It was the hardest moment for a loving father.

May watched nearby and her thoughts were much the same. Doreen had cried the day before when Rene had packed her last bag, ready to move to her new home. Although it was only a short walk up the hill to the centre of the village. Doreen felt bereft at the loss of the sister she so admired. Lillian however rejoiced at the thought of being the eldest and having a bed to herself for the first time in her entire life.

Truth be known, she would also be glad of less competition socially now that Rene was marrying. There were few men around worth having and Lillian was eager to have some fun. Stan was good looking but thankfully not her type so she was grateful for him taking Rene out of the equation.

With her attractive sister and all her prudish airs and graces out of the way Lillian would now get a good crack at any available men without them mooning over Rene and Lillian having to play the clown to get any attention at all! Now she would be centre of things when they went out.

As she stood in the aisle alongside Doreen in the simple white gowns behind the bride clutching posies. They wore two completely different expressions. Doreen was tearful and demure. Lillian however, lifted her head and watched the proceedings with a small smile of triumph that a bystander would have mistaken for sisterly pride. 'Now that the duchess is out of the way' she thought... 'time for me.. and I won't be marrying the first man that comes calling! No sir!' she thought. She was looking forward to having a high old time.

The photos taken, the family adjourned to the back room of the Bull's Head for the wedding breakfast. May had threatened them all that they had to mind their manners in front of Rene's new in-laws and it was a fairly subdued gathering as they entered the pub. The younger three children particularly shy.

"We might be poor but we know how to behave...don't we?" she questioned them all with a raised eyebrow before they had set off to church with an implied threat to anyone who let her down. The younger children nodded dutifully as she slicked down Gary's thick black hair into some sort of order as the young boy squirmed under her attention.

Sitting at the top table, May couldn't help but ponder that in a way, Arthur's absence had probably given her one less potential embarrassment to worry about, for his sharp and reckless humour didn't sit well with her eldest daughter and there might well have been a clash once a few drinks had loosened his tongue... No, it was for the best.

Despite all the passing of the years she nonetheless had been raised to be a lady. Regardless of how life on the moors had roughened her manner through lack of more higher company, she still craved educated conversation and felt at home in the Hornby's company and as she sat at the table awaiting the meal and surveying her brood in their Sunday best, she knew she was equal in intelligence and breeding to anyone here despite their poor financial circumstances.

She couldn't help but think of her Aunt Anne, who had no doubt lived a lonely life after her swift departure with Edward. Three decades nearly since she had trodden on Irish soil and in this moment of celebration, she grieved for the Aunt who, in that fateful day had become her grandmother only to lose her before the day was out. 'What would she have thought of her now?' she pondered.

May had written to her once they had settled in England and received a brief but badly written letter in return. It was clear the Aunt was not at her best. Some weeks later a cart arrived with several large crates of all the contents of the cottage and whilst they had rejoiced at the comforts it had brought them. It also brought tears for the memories of their comfortable little home and the security of having a relative who cared for them had brought.

The last box was marked fragile and when she opened it, it was laden with straw. A letter sat atop it and as May opened it and read the contents, her heart broke for all that they had lost.

For her mother...living with the knowledge that her own mother, whilst still giving them her protection and support had denied her own daughter for all those years and the damage it had done to them both emotionally. The loss for May of the woman she admired as a girl and the loss for her Aunt Anne of the daughter and granddaughter she could have had if she had lived in a kinder world without fear of condemnation and retribution.

It was a heartache she would have to bear and she seethed as she read her aunt's words that day. Society and religion had a lot to answer for.

'Dear Anne and May,

I hope this finds you well and you are happy. I hope all your goods arrive safely with this letter. I have added some books that you always liked to read and some things that would have become yours eventually that I know you always admired May.

I don't know whether you will follow the faith in your new life England but I have enclosed the large brass crucifix that used to stand in the parlour. I hope Edward is providing for you both and that you and the child are well. There is a few pounds tucked away in a tin in this box. I hope you will buy something for the baby with it. I'd like to think I had had some input into its birth and welfare.

There has been much gossip here and I have had to let Susan go as she has brought much trouble to our door. It really is disappointing that some people cannot help but thrive on causing pain for others. However, it seems the worst of it is over now, but the house seems very quiet without you all. Ada and I bumble along, but alas the garden will suffer from Edward's absence and I was so looking forward to the spring. Take care of yourselves and let me know how you are.

Kindest Regards
Aunt Anne'

It was not what she said, but the sadness and loss that radiated out of the letter from the things she hadn't said and May had sobbed when she went carefully through the box and found the ruby lustres that she had so loved and a beautiful tea service that had graced the table on only the best occasions that she had once remarked upon. She cried mostly at the books that her aunt had sent and realised how much notice the old lady had taken of her likes and dislikes and each book she brought out gave May cause for more tears as she recognised the most favourite of the books that she had read repeatedly as a young girl.

Vanity Fair by William Makepeace Thackeray and Shakespeare's sonnets amongst others. Her aunt must have loved her very much to have known all of this and remembered. She noted that even now her aunt could not acknowledge her as a grandmother should and had signed the letter 'Aunt Anne' maintaining the pretence to the last.

May had written religiously once a month to her aunt for three years. It was a sad day when a letter came from Ada saying that the aunt was too frail to write anymore and that she had lost much of her faculties. Ada could hardly spell so the letter had been brief. May continued to write to the housekeeper and asked her to read it to the aunt and this continued until the day a letter arrived from a solicitors with a cheque for fifty pounds and a note saying her aunt had died leaving all but small bequests to the convent. Perhaps it was her way of making amends to her God. May certainly hadn't expected anything. Her aunt had said that the money she gave her on leaving Ireland would be her only inheritance and she had been true to her word.

May had tucked the cheque in her bag and banked it for the future, just as with the rest, for the day it might be needed. She wondered if her aunt would have been proud of the way they had made a life here from virtually nothing and she grieved that she had left the old lady to grow frail and old with no one to love and protect her. The reminiscences brought tears to her eyes and as she came back to the present in a room where the initial shyness was wearing off and people were chatting amiably, Doreen was leaning across the table concerned her hand outstretched and reaching for her mother's that rested on the white linen cloth.

"Mum, are you all right?" asked Doreen, noticing May's absence from the conversations. May patted her daughter's hand and gave thanks for all she had.

"Aye, I am love," she smiled. "Go get your mum another half of beer and tell him not to give the little ones any more ginger ale, they'll be piddling the bed."

***

Sunday morning came crisp and sunny and May opened the door to let some light and air into the kitchen and steam out from the dolly tub she was filling with water to do the wash.

As predicted the youngest child had wet the bed in the early hours and had wandered into her and Edward's room at four a.m. half-asleep and crying. She had stripped him, washed him and re dressing him in a new nightshirt, had tipped him in with his father to warm him. Luckily, the bed was largely unscathed, so she pulled the sheet out from under his sleeping older brother Gary without him even knowing and went about her business quietly.

Passed sleeping now, she decided to make an early start to the day. As she worked, her head was full of thoughts for her married daughter. Perhaps she should have talked more with her about marriage and sex. In all honesty, she felt she knew very little herself. She and Edward had always had a good relationship but it was a natural thing between them and she knew from village gossip that not all relationships fared as well as hers.

When the older girls had gone out for the first time, all she had managed in advice and true to her catholic background was to say, 'Don't you bring any trouble home!' The girls had looked at her bemused and when Doreen had asked Lillian later what her mum meant the only answer she received was a groan of frustration and one word, 'Babies!' Doreen's eyes had flown wide with horror and she had firmly believed for some time in the absence of any real advice, that all you had to do to get pregnant was to kiss someone. It was a terrifying prospect.

Lillian had smirked at her ignorance. She had eyes in her head and had seen enough animals breeding to get the gist. The rare films they got to see had filled in the romantic ideas. She just had to get her head round the physical.

May set back to her washing with a vengeance. The more delicate items she would hand wash in the sink, but the larger items went into the tub to be possed. It was not an easy task and soon May would feel it in her back as she pulled the waterlogged sheets out of the tub and fed them through the ringer. Still it was a nice day and good to blow the cobwebs of yesterday's ale away. Two less sets of washing now, she should be grateful, but somehow she felt bereft.

Chapter Sixteen

Doreen sat at her table in the cutting room at the mill, at home now amongst the other girls. A year had built her confidence threefold and now she chatted and laughed just like the rest of the mill workers.

She had taken to asking the foreman if she could take home some of the roll ends that had flaws and he had winked and given her the nod, as long as she didn't make a big thing of it. With a sack full of the flannel ends she hurried home and when questioned at the door by her mother she had hugged the sack to her with a smile and said, "I'm going to be a designer Mum and make my own clothes just like Dior. Can I use the table?"

May had smiled to cover her amusement. She had no idea who Dior was but obviously they had impressed her daughter and prompted her to action. It was no bad thing.

"You'll have to wait till after tea," she replied and Doreen beamed putting the bag behind the armchair her grandmother sat in.

Edward strode through the door waving his cap around his head. "Damn it! Those bastard midges are like Lancaster bombers.. they're swarming down by the brook and they followed me up the lane. I'm bitten to buggery!"

"Edward! Language please!" pleaded May as Doreen giggled.

"Ay lass... Doreen will have heard worse than that up in't mill, won't you love?" he grinned at Doreen and she ran for the bag to show her dad.

"See Dad! I'm going to start off with a simple kick pleat skirt and start selling them." She pulled the materials out and let it fall about her pretty calves swaying from side to side in her excitement.

"I've no doubt tha will love, but right now, how about coming with me to see to the horses?" said Edward and hugged his daughter to him affectionately.

"Okay Dad," she laughed, put her bag back behind the chair where Annie was peeling the potatoes for tea with gnarled hands. "Don't let Lillian pinch any Gran," she whispered to the old lady who snorted with humour, knowing Lillian well, it was a possibility.

Very soon Doreen was quite adept at cutting out the simple patterns she had made and her range was growing. She already had several requests from the village girls and was making a tidy profit and had invested in some material that was lighter and prettier to try out some dresses which she modelled herself at Hill Stores' dances. Taking swatches of materials with her to show prospective buyers when they admired her dress she often came home with two or three orders.

Edward had turned his hand to scrap and become a rag and bone man in his spare time between work on deliveries and Doreen returned home one evening to find her mum and dad stood in the kitchen on her return from work with a huge smile on their conspiratorial faces. They were obviously hiding something and when they stepped aside Doreen let out a shriek of delight.

"I got it cheap from this old tailor who was bringing in electric machines," he smiled as he revealed the little black and gold treadle machine. "Reckoned you showed enough gumption to deserve this," he said with quiet pride.

Doreen hugged her mum and dad not knowing whether to cry, laugh or dance, such was the delight that coursed through her at her present.

"Make sure I haven't wasted my hard earned brass lass," he smiled.

"Can you make me a rag doll Doreen?" asked Maureen who had come in from playing outside. "Look Gary..." she called to her twin. "Look what Mum and Dad have got Do!"

Gary and Gray ran in. Presents other than birthdays and Christmas weren't something that happened often in such a large family and the youngsters stood agog at this new technology as Edward demonstrated it and Doreen sat down on the stool to make the first sample stitches on the machine which she did with reverence.

***

Within a few weeks Doreen was turning the kitchen into a factory much to May's dismay and pride in equal amounts. Edward had created a monster, but a successful one and it was clear Doreen had a gift for style in the same way as her older sister and she had a quiet word with her husband about supporting her.

She couldn't produce much in her spare time but when she did, she gave half her profit to her mum as a thank you for the machine and to help now Rene and Arthur's contributions were no longer coming in. The other half she saved in a tin to buy new materials and scissors.

Edward, prompted by May, realised his daughter needed a space of her own and he set about building a workshop in the back of the barn for her, with a cutting table and makeshift rails and shelves from any old materials he picked up on his rag and bone round. He had even put in windows for natural light and rigged up an electric cable and bulb from the house for the dark nights. It wasn't the best but it allowed her to work without taking over the house.

Sometimes May and Annie would help in the small items of hand sewing that Doreen's design required and it brought a new camaraderie to the house as they sat sewing round the fire.

Doreen whitewashed the walls herself with the help of Lillian and they were quite proud of the area they had created. Edward had put a pot-bellied stove in one corner and they always had plenty of wood to burn from old furniture that Edward had collected but couldn't sell on. So they kept it warm so the materials wouldn't get damp. The main problem was keeping the mice out of the trims and cloth and everything had to be locked away in rodent proof boxes each night.

A few weeks later when the family were all sat down to Sunday lunch, Rene arrived with her husband. It seemed she had seen her sister's talents come to fruition and had ambitions of her own that included her sibling.

"How would it be if Stan and I rented a shop and sold some of Doreen's clothes with other things?" she said.

"Oh Dad please say yes," pleaded Doreen. "I'm earning nearly as much as at the mill now, think what I could do if I worked everyday?" It was clear Doreen had been privy to some earlier discussion and May looked to Edward with a wry expression. It was a risk and money wasn't exactly rolling in at the moment as Edward's work was diminishing. Motorised delivery was becoming more common, which had prompted his diversification into scrap.

"Please Mum." Doreen's face mirrored her desperation and May felt the old maternal pull that only Doreen could create in her.
"We need to know what she'd be earning Rene... It can't be done half-cocked," said May soberly.

Stan stepped forward. "We have saved up May and have the first year's rent on a premises in Rochdale. It's in a prime location and we have planned this for some time. It will be a great opportunity for us all, especially Doreen. I'm happy to sit down and take you both through our plans."

Edward looked to May. "No harm in hearing the lad out May," he said quietly. She looked once more to Doreen and nodded her agreement. Doreen's stomach leapt in excitement. Her future was hanging in the balance and dependent on the next few minutes and Stan's ability to sell the idea to her parents. She sat feeling both anxious and excited as the conversation went on. Stan was definitely a clever man and very smooth talking.

An hour later her face glowed with the thrill that she would be allowed a trial period of three months in which she would still have to stump up her keep. May would have a word with the mill manager and explain the opportunity in the hope he would allow her back if things went awry.

Rene had a good business head and would be doing the books so there was no way that Doreen would be taken for granted. The deal was that Rene took a third of any profit on the range. Doreen would work 4 days a week to supply and one day in the shop to help Rene and to get a feel for what customers liked.

Despite financial worry, May was secretly excited to see her two daughters heading into this venture. It had been her own dream as a girl, so in some way she could re-live this through her daughters and she resolved to give them as much support as she could. With a bit of luck she might even get the chance to earn a bob or two herself. As for Doreen working alongside her sister in the shop on a Saturday would build her confidence. She wasn't a girl to stand up for herself, unlike

Rene, who was nobody's fool and very polished. No, it would do the girl no end of good.

So a month later Doreen, May and Rene stood in the doorway of an old Victorian premises on prime shopping territory off Rochdale's Drake Street, hands full of bags of cleaning materials. The building was gracious and the windows curved with beautiful bevelled glass and polished wood. 'This was top class,' May thought to herself and although Rene was confident and not one given to demonstrations of affection, she nevertheless filled up when May clasped her to her and told her how proud she was. She then turned to the younger girl and hugged her also saying, "This is your big chance, don't let your sister down, she's placed a lot of faith in you."

"I won't Mum," beamed Doreen as they pushed the large glass door aside and breathed in the musty atmosphere of the old building. The counter was long and made of oak with wooden shelving with glass-fronted doors behind it. Open shelves graced the opposite wall and at the back was a room with the luxury of an indoor water closet and sink. There was room for rails and a small changing room. The décor was old but had been at one time lavish and was still graced with two large chandeliers hanging in the shop front. Rene had chosen well for her premises. It wouldn't take more than a lick of paint and some imagination to get this shop up to scratch.

"Right then!" said May. "Let's get to it girls, soonest done, soonest we can get this shop open and make a bit of brass."

Chapter Seventeen

It was a sunny, spring day when Rene opened the door of her shop to the public for its launch. Stan had managed to get a local dignitary to cut the ribbon and even put on food and tea. The Observer was there and there was a general hubbub of excitement at the opening of the new ladies outfitters.

She had named it 'Rene Couture' and when her mother had laughed at the over confident description, Rene had raised a severe eyebrow and told her in no uncertain terms not to underestimate her daughter's talents. People believed what they were sold and there was no way her shop was going to be ordinary!

May had nervously donated her inherited tea service to give the buffet an air of class and hoped no one was clumsy enough to break it. As she stood in her best black and white floral dress that Doreen had made with her, she beamed with genuine happiness that her life had finally taken a turn in a more genteel direction, surprisingly through the efforts of her children.

Rene stood tall and slim with her hair back in a French pleat and a beautiful cream pencil dress with a black satin stand up collar, graced with black satin shoes (from stock) to match on her long legs. She was the height of elegance and Doreen, similar in looks and build, was modelling a creation in silk with a full Dior-style skirt.

This style was currently thumbing the nose to the austerity of the war years when materials were scarce and May had to admit the two made an impressive pair. She served the teas whilst the girls chatted to the invited guests and May thought smugly to herself that you would have never guessed they had come from a cottage with only an outside lavvy and no bathroom. Perhaps she had done better than she had realised in teaching them that, poor or otherwise, they could still have manners and ambition.

May had been a bit taken aback when Rene had asked her to break the news that she didn't want Lillian or the other children in for the launch. "I'm not having Lillian shoot off her big mouth Mum and spoiling everything," she said. "This is a big thing for me and a lot of our savings are riding on it. She just can't behave like a lady and that's what we have to do, otherwise we'll lose the clientele on day one."

May saw the sense in that and got round it by asking Lillian to babysit the young ones. Lillian sniffed, her nose was definitely out of joint but she reluctantly complied. May couldn't help wonder if there would be revenge somewhere along the way for the implied snub. She hoped not.

Lillian in fact surprised them all by not taking the chance to make fun of her sisters' new venture. She was positively subdued the next few days and Lillian was not one to be subdued at the best of times.

Doreen was head down in the workshop during the day and at night when it went too cold to stay out in the barn, she would bring her small hand-stitched pieces in and sit with her mother and grandmother by the fire warming her fingers back to life as they put the world to rights. Rene was busy at home most nights working out the likely prices and profits of her wares. She had extended her range in the shop to handbags and it had meant the installation of a telephone both in her house and the shop, which caused quite a stir in the village, her reasoning being that she could make contact with the suppliers on her day off.

Tuesday was usually half day closing and so Rene would call Doreen in so that she could chase all the orders but be around should Doreen need help. Doreen had decided she wanted to be called 'Dene' as it was more up market for her new image as a designer and her skills and confidence was growing by the day. She had received some gentle ribbing from her younger siblings but they complied and soon it became the norm. May smothered down the hurt that the name she had given her daughter wasn't good enough with good grace understanding the need for an image.

It was on a warm evening in July when Lillian walked through the door and plonked herself down at the table with a satisfied smile and a letter in hand. Everyone was gathering for the evening meal and the room was full of the usual chatter. Rene had called in with Stan and asked if they could stay to tea so the table was crowded. When the meal had been served Lillian drew a deep long breath and announced she had some news. The table fell silent and Lillian opened up her envelope.

"I just wanted to tell you all I will be handing my notice in at the mill on Monday." She took out the sheet of ivory paper and everyone noted it was a typed letter, something they didn't often receive so it drew all their attention, even the younger ones took note.

"I've been accepted for nurses training at Oldham Infirmary and I start next month." She sat back with a satisfied expression.

"Nursing?" questioned Edward. "It's not something you've mentioned before love". Edward was concerned. His middle daughter was a wild one and he doubted she would handle the discipline required of nurses training well.

"I've been looking into it for a while now Dad. I can live on site while I train and its only two years till I qualify..."

There was the crux of the matter. Lillian was eager to fly the coop. May's eyes focused shrewdly on her daughter and Lillian's chin lifted stubbornly.

"I've accepted the position already," she said a little nervously but determinedly.

"Well..." said May, "It looks like you have it all worked out, but I'll tell you this my girl. You will not be living away from home. I know what goes on in those quarters. You'll live here and go on the bus and tip up your keep every week...If you stick it out for a year we'll consider you moving into nurses' quarters when you show me you can do the job. So you best get onto them first thing tomorrow and tell them you won't be taking up their kind offer of accommodation."

"But Mum..."

"No arguments!" May's tone brooked no defiance and the young woman looked down angrily knowing she dare not cross her mother. The table had fallen silent and Lillian quietly seethed that she had not got their wholehearted blessing. She thought they would have at least been proud. It hurt and Lillian didn't like to be thwarted. She had thought it would be fun to live at the hospital with all the freedoms of being away from home and the constraints placed on her by parents.

"Well...that's sorted," said May as she proceeded to serve the meal determindly. "I don't suppose anyone else has any earth shattering news for us whilst we're at it?" The sarcasm was evident and Rene looked to Stan with a grimace. Perhaps now wasn't the time after all, but hey ho, they had come specially.

"Actually Mum...we have," she said with a nervous smile and all eyes turned from Lillian to Rene.

"We're expecting a baby. It isn't ideal right now I know, but we can't plan these things sometimes can we?" she said quietly, with a proud smile.

"Congratulations love," said Edward with a huge smile in return. The mood around the table lightened and all the family joined in the celebration with the exception of two.

May heard herself speak her congratulations but after that she let the others take the conversation to talk of babies. Sitting quietly she smiled, but her heart couldn't help but sink at the thought that her daughter's new found business would suffer with the time required to bring a child into the world. She had so wanted one of her girls to follow her own childhood dreams and she had thought it was going to be Rene. Perhaps at least this one she would be allowed to be a grandmother to.

Across the table Lillian sat and seethed, her cheeks bright with temper. 'Trust the Duchess to steal her thunder as usual!'

Chapter Eighteen

René Couture was building itself quite a clientele from the more well-heeled of Rochdale and business was building steadily. Rene was almost grateful for the gradual build, as it allowed Doreen to get used to the way things had to be done to help Rene in her advancing pregnancy.

Her younger sister had blossomed under her tutelage and was soon happy to be left alone to run the shop whilst Rene rested at the back of the shop behind a curtained off area out of the clientele's eye, but near enough to listen in and chat with her younger sister from the comfort of an old armchair they had brought in.

Dene was young, but she was bright and friendly. The customers liked her and in some ways her youth made her less intimidating than Rene's more sophisticated persona. If she felt Doreen was out of her depth, Rene would put her morning sickness aside, pin on her best smile and glide through the curtain to assume command once more. It was almost seamless and the hapless troublemaker would normally be manoeuvred into a sale or through the door without knowing what had happened to her.

She had also allowed Doreen to bring small pieces in to stitch in exchange for her help and after lunch when she felt less nauseous, she would check the stock and takings whilst Doreen sat behind the curtain to catch up with her sewing. Rene knew she would really need Doreen to manage the business when the baby came and so this was a valuable time for her to learn all the skills required. She took to it like a duck to water and her intelligence, especially with accounts began to come to the fore. By the time Rene reached five months her sister was at home with most aspects of the business.

She paid Doreen a little for the couple of extra days which gave her the means to invest in more upmarket materials and the investment proved worthwhile. Soon the shop was full of 'Pink Lady' high-end evening wear, in addition to the daywear. Rene was secretly amazed at the light her sister had kept under a bushel and the work she produced delighted and inspired Rene. She would take the swatches that her sister was working on and ensure she had shoes and accessories to complete the look.

It was a winning combination. Soon Rene added a small selection of costume jewellery that went out the door like hot cakes and so between Doreen's flair for design and Rene's buying and selling skills they had it sewn up, literally. Soon Doreen couldn't produce fast enough to keep up with demand and so eventually May was brought in to stitch some of the basic pieces at home during the day. She found herself enjoying the time spent in the barn amongst the ever-increasing array of beautiful materials and haberdashery. It was becoming quite a cottage industry.

Glamour was definitely in after the constraints of post-war Britain and the favourite moment for the two sisters each day was on locking up. They would stand arm in arm and look at the windows they had dressed and congratulate themselves on their creativity. It certainly was a show-piece and they had heard that people in the area were remarking on the windows and had starting waiting for the new displays.

One last look and they would make the short walk to the station as they discussed new ideas. From there they would hop on the train to Milnrow, where Stan would be waiting to walk them home up the hill. Very soon he had enough to buy a small car and as Rene grew more bulky with the growing child, the transport up the hill at the end of the train journey, was a welcome addition. It was an old Austin and they had to balance their feet on the floor struts as the floor had rusted and was giving way, but they were grateful all the same, especially with the onset of autumn. Any car was a talking point in the area and it gave the owner a certain kudos in the poor community.

Lillian had replaced Rene behind the bar at the Bull's Head to supplement her small training income and it seemed she had fallen on her feet. Lillian's humour and cheek, normally found 'too much' in politer company, bounced happily off the clientele on the other side of the bar. She found herself looking forward to the evenings of flirting and banter with the mainly male drinkers. Here she could get away with talk that wouldn't be allowed at home and the safety of being behind the bar allowed her to flirt outrageously, but give them a gobful if they went too far or gave her any grief.

Perhaps she had found her calling after all and it wasn't in a hospital as she had thought. Still, no harm in doing both for now she would muse and it was a bob or two extra in her pocket. The tips were meagre, as no one had much money, but when she did come home with extra, she would hide it in a tin under the wardrobe. It was her escape money for the day she needed to move out of the confines of her family home. As much as she loved them, she craved the freedom of her own space. Things were too cramped here, even with Rene's departure. The rest of her wages she tipped up to May and was given what was thought appropriate back. That was the way it had always been and like it or not they complied.

As Lillian stood before the mirror she brushed her thick dark waves in readiness for her shift at the pub. It was much like her mother's had been at her age, almost unruly, but pretty nonetheless. As she applied her powder and lipstick, she mused on the close bond that her two sisters were making without her. They looked alike with their delicate features and sleek black hair and they both now had a shilling on themselves especially since Doreen had all this attention as well. It really rubbed Lillian up the wrong way. They were chalk and cheese, she and them, but a part of her could not help but sting at the snub, intended or otherwise.

She loved them both but Rene was no great loss to her socially as they had never really got on well. Doreen however, she had a soft spot for and now it hurt to see her younger sister hanging on Rene's every word with something akin to idolisation. She'd show them soon she was as good. Once she had qualified and had enough saved up, she was out of here. Mam was always on her back and she was too old to be tipping up all her pay. No it wouldn't be long, she would show them all.

Half an hour later she entered the pub with a lift of her chin, at least here she could be herself. Her nursing training was going better than anyone thought and although she was always getting reprimanded for her forward behaviour, she had a natural aptitude for lifting the spirits in her patients and she actually enjoyed the work. The poor buggers in there needed a laugh and she had enough sense to know when to keep her mouth shut and when to jolly someone round. She had taken to calling herself Lynne recently after finding Lillian old fashioned. May argued but couldn't press it as she has said nothing when Doreen had started calling herself Dene for business purposes.

She walked up the cobbled road into the village and breathed in the air. There was just a tinge of winter in its breath and the leaves that had fallen from the trees by the graveyard wall were making the rounded stones a little treacherous. She could hear the low hubbub of voices coming from the pub just up the way. The nights were drawing in and so most of the locals made for the Bull's Head taproom when they could no longer sit out in the sunshine.

The pub was particularly busy tonight and so she slipped off her coat and immediately popped under the bar and marched to the other end where the landlord was doing his best to serve the raucous crowd that was in tonight.

"Right then, who's next and don't all shout at once!" she shouted loud enough to be heard. Of course they were all 'next' so she made a swift decision and worked up and down the line till the grumblings subsided.

There were a few of the mill girls in a corner on some celebration or other. Unusual as it was to see women grouping here, it drew her attention and she noticed that a couple of the men nearby were trying their best to muscle in their conversation. Her eye strayed to one of the men in particular and her eyebrow lifted sarcastically.

Stan, Rene's husband was giving his best chat to a small blonde girl who obviously was susceptible to his charms. 'So...' she thought, 'Stan Hornby wasn't above a little game playing on the quiet', and as much as she clashed with her elder sister, she was family and she didn't like someone taking the Mick, even of the Duchess, poor cow was pregnant after all.

The blonde girl had turned back to her friends and Stan ambled to the bar obviously a little worse for wear and with his inhibitions turned loose because of it.

"Pint of bitter Lynne please," he smiled benignly as he leaned heavily across the bar. Lynne took his glass with a look that was reminiscent of her mother on a bad day.

"Don't you think you've had enough? You've got a wife at home could probably do with your company right now."

"Nah!" he grinned, "She's tired with the baby and going to bed early... You want one?" Lynne was tempted to say no, but her freedom tin would appreciate the visit so she nodded and took more than she should have for his cheek.

"I'll have it later," she said.

"I might have one with you then." The alcohol had obviously convinced him he was god's gift to women.

"No you won't, you'll get off home to your pregnant wife before I tell her about the interesting conversation you were having with that little blonde over there."

"Give over Lynne, I was only having a laugh." he grumbled and took up his pint and making his way back to the table he was sitting at with his mates. Plonking himself down sullenly, he kept his distance from the blonde. She had nipped that little flirtation in the bud hopefully.

"Sure Rene would appreciate the joke," she muttered wryly. That one was trouble if ever there was. Her clever sister had jumped too quick with him she thought. He might have a good job and a bit of brass but she reckoned he hadn't showed his true hand just yet and she hoped Rene wouldn't be regretting it.

"Excuse me Miss?" a sandy haired young man with glasses called from the other end of the bar.

"Hang on, I haven't two pairs of hands you know!" She was a little more sharp than she should have been and the man looked a bit taken aback at her abruptness.

"Sorry..." she said. "Bloody family, who'd have 'em, What can I get you?"

The young man smiled and she thought he had something about him. His looks didn't conform to the usual ideas of handsome, but when he smiled something about him caught her imagination and she felt he was worthy of her full attention. Pinning on her best smile she leaned across the bar to hear him above the noise.

"Pint of Guinness please," he asked politely and she winked at him in a bold response.

"Coming right up!" she grinned and picking up a glass, she moved over to the pump, pulling the dark brew with just the right amount of head. The young man had thought to move away from the crowd at the bar, but this feisty young woman persuaded him to pull up a tall stool and watch her as she bantered, throwing him the odd look with a smile in her eyes that told him she knew she had made an impression. He drank slowly to extend his evening and allow him the chance to talk to her when the older regulars ambled home.

By the end of the night they were chatting like old friends, a week later he asked her out and she said yes.

Chapter Nineteen

Saturday evening now had moved on from the local Hills Store. For the young women of the family, the lights of Manchester had beckoned and the glamour of the Ritz Ballroom with its ladies' room lined with ornate mirrors and bouncing dance floor beckoned. Rene was nearing her time and very conscious of her shape and had cried off, so Doreen had agreed to go with Lynne and her new man friend Derek, who seemed shy, but polite. She couldn't quite work out what her firebrand of a sister saw in him as he seemed the opposite of her personality. Maybe that was what appealed to Lynne... a place of calm in her personal storm.

They sat at the edge of the dance floor and watched the couples waltzing around. The floor was packed with a mix of stumblers and real dancers weaving in and out of each other's space. Doreen had a number of partners by now, who, appreciating her grace on the floor ensured she was rarely left sat for long.

Lynne and Derek seemed very much in love and were always deep in conversation when they weren't dancing and oblivious to her most of the time. Occasionally Derek would start up a conversation with Doreen, only to be whisked away by Lynne when a favourite tune came on and her enthusiasm spilled over.

From what conversation she had managed with him it appeared that he was a boiler man at Greenhalgh's, the dye works just up from their home. He spoke quietly and Doreen couldn't help but thinking he was far too gentle to keep up with her strong-willed sister. He wasn't particularly well educated and had a strong accent, but he was polite and would converse well when anyone approached them. Doreen thought that with a bit of luck he would rub off on Lynne and calm her sister down. Lynne looked to have taken to him so she was happy for her.

"May I have the next dance miss?" Doreen hadn't seen the tall young man with thick spectacles approach her. The cut of his suit and thick black hair combined with glasses gave him the look of a yank. She looked up in surprise as he bent nearer and repeated the request. He was actually English, with a northern accent that just wasn't quite from round here.

She nodded assent and he walked her onto the floor taking her into his arms. They made an elegant looking couple and though he wasn't the best dancer there, he moved well and confidently guiding her between the less talented couples that were hogging the edges and into the more open central space.

"I've been watching you all night and I just had to ask you to dance." He spoke as loud as he could, without shouting to be heard above the band.

"Oh really?" she was a little taken aback and lost for words.

"You're not from round here?" she questioned.

"Well I am and I'm not. My home is in Blackpool, but I manage a shoe shop in Rochdale.. I love this song... Red roses for a blue lady...don't you?" He changed direction and guided her easily.

"Well I'm a pink lady." she laughed at her own joke. I have my designs 'Pink Lady' in my sister's shop in Rochdale too."

He looked surprised, "Well what a coincidence, where?"

"René Couture on Drake Street."

"Well how strange, so am I...Timpson Shoes at the bottom."

"Oh my goodness, we're almost neighbours!" She paused dancing with surprise, "How have we never met?"

"I have no idea, perhaps we should rectify that? Do you get a lunch hour?"

"I could, but I don't normally bother."

"Could I take you for a coffee one day?"

"I don't even know you," she turned in his arms as he guided her into the centre of the floor.

"Well how about we say Friday next week and if you don't know me by then, you can say no, how about that?"

Doreen laughed wondering what on earth this friendly young man might have up his sleeve. They danced several times that night and when she started to gather her things he stepped up to where they sat once more and waved goodbye with a, "See you next week." She laughed and Lynne nudged her pointedly.

"Bit of all-right that one, but for the glasses!"

"I think he's very attractive," murmured Doreen following the direction the young man had taken.

"If you say so. Come on Derek, best get her home before she gets into trouble."

They gathered up their things and made for the cloakroom and as the young man raised his hand in farewell, Doreen felt her stomach give a little twist of excitement. It was her first physical reaction to a man and it brought a sparkle to her eyes and a glow to her cheeks. She explained it away as the affects of the cold wind as they made for Victoria Station and the journey home.

Doreen went through Sunday with a smile hovering around her lips. Lynne teased her constantly and her face was in a permanent blush most of the day. She wondered whether the young man whose name she didn't even know yet would make good on his promise.

She shouldn't have worried because one o'clock Monday the bell on the door jingled its warning and there he was, flowers in hand.

"I won't outstay my welcome," he said, handing her a small bunch of flowers. "These are for you, by the way my name is Dennis, have a lovely day."

Before Doreen had time to thank him, he was gone and Rene appeared through the curtain from her resting place curious at the presence of a male customer to find she only saw the back of him exiting the shop.

"Who was that?" she asked.

Doreen turned round blushing and Rene raised an eyebrow.

"Dennis," was all the answer her sister could give as her free hand flew to her cheek in embarrassment.

"Dennis indeed? Well you certainly have scored a hit there," she said eyeing the flowers. "We'd best get them in water."

Doreen looked down at the flowers and there was a card tucked inside.

'To the beautiful Pink Lady with my best wishes Dennis'

Each day until Thursday, he popped in with a small gift, nothing elaborate, but thoughtful, and each day the card had a little more information about him. Thursday's card finished with a question. 'Lunch tomorrow? May I pick you up at one?'

Rene, by then, was quite impressed by his determination. "Go on.." she said, "Can't do any harm."

"Don't tell Mum or Dad will you?" Doreen replied in a panic.

"Why not? You're nearly twenty. Big enough to stand on your own two feet if needs be."

Doreen's face paled in horror at the thought of May finding out and Rene relented. "Nothing to tell yet," she said with a grimace and then clutched her stomach.

"This baby's bound to be a boy, it's got a kick like Captain!"

Chapter Twenty

So it was that on Friday, Doreen, dressed in a simple pink dress with a full skirt and black suede belt she had matched with a soft suede neck tie and pink cardigan with recovered black buttons that she had fashioned from some scraps, waited as the clock ticked slowly onward.

After spending an hour in the back area modelling her dark hair into a neat French pleat she knew she looked very smart and modern, but her heart was beating like a frightened rabbit all morning and she found it hard to concentrate on the task Rene had given her.

Just as her nerves had reached a crescendo, the doorbell rang and Dennis came in. He was not quite so sure of himself as he had been earlier in the week now that it had come to the moment of reckoning. His face lit up as Doreen smiled shyly in welcome. Rene saw that her naive sister was struggling somewhat and walked forward confidently to greet the nervous young man.

Her gait was slightly less elegant with the pregnancy now heavy upon her, but nevertheless she looked beautiful in a tailored linen maternity dress in black which was a change from the norm. Pregnancy would not come between her and a business image and Rene would never give in to fatigue by allowing her personal appearance to slip in the way some expectant mothers would normally do. She was quite formidable in her own way and Doreen had absolute admiration for the way she carried herself at what must have been an exhausting time.

"Hello," she said holding out a hand. "I'm Rene, the older sister and you are Dennis I believe... I hope you won't keep her out too long, she's quite in demand with the clients, you know."

Dennis's face lit up with the realisation that he was being given the nod that his lunch date was on and he beamed, taking her hand to shake it amiably.

"Not at all. There's a little restaurant just down the way I thought we might go to...If that's alright with you?" He faltered at the realisation that in all his preparation, he hadn't actually remembered the object of his affection's name and he coloured with embarrassment as he spoke to her.

"Doreen." Rene interjected with a wry smile.

"Thank you," he smiled in relief and then looked to Doreen for affirmation.

"That would be lovely...Dennis, most people call me Dene now," she said with not a little humour and a grimace at her sister. "Shall we go?"

"Certainly..Dene!" he beamed and held open the front door with its bell jangling its celebration.

Once out on the street and into the daylight, Doreen's shyness overcame her, but once Dennis had put her at ease with his polite conversation, she found herself more confident by the time they entered the small restaurant. The staff were friendly and very soon they were chatting amicably over a simple lunch.

She told him all about the business that had followed on her new passion for all things fashion and that really, it was the business acumen of her sister that had allowed her to launch her skills and develop them.

Dennis, in turn, told her all about his family in Blackpool and how they had started the first charabanc coach trips along the promenade. How he had been raised to work on the family business and that when his grandfather had died all the coaches had been sold and they had found themselves career-less. His mother and he had often worked on them as conductors and for a while he had transferred over to the Blackpool trams as a natural progression.

His mother and father had divorced when he was a small child and when his grandfather's estate had been finalised, his mother found herself with a large inheritance. She had now the means to follow her dream of singing in the music halls without the need to go out and earn a living.

She had also bought a boarding house and took in permanent boarders which allowed her to pick and choose her venues and when and where she would sing and sing she did. With a beautiful soprano voice that always received rapturous applause, she was highly sought after.

Despite her success, she was overly careful with both her money and her affection. Whilst Dennis loved his mother, she rarely held him close for fear he would bring germs that would affect her voice. Dennis had grown up never being hugged or kissed and though, as a mother, Ivy had been caring in all other ways and he was never ill-treated, his upbringing had left him uncomfortable with displays of affection, never having been used to them.

Even though he was bowled over by Dene, he would find it hard to step over his boundaries from easy conversation, which he excelled at, to the physical. Fortunately for him this was Dene's first encounter with the opposite sex and having no benchmark by which to measure Dennis. She found him flattering and attentive and was quite captivated by his tall, slim looks, with a thick dark head of hair that was worthy of a film star.

Truth be known, she was dreading the moment when she would have to reveal that, far from being a middle-class business minded family, she had been brought up in near poverty on the Lancashire moors and that she had not had anywhere near the start in life that he had been privileged to have had.

Having a convent educated mother had its benefits and whilst a loving and boisterous family, May had still taught them all manners and the value of presentation. For the moment she could hold her own with this intelligent and sophisticated young man, He might only be a shoe shop manager but it was clear he had had a privileged upbringing. Her natural intelligence kicked in and combined with her sleek looks, near black hair and slim figure, made for a charming companion and Dennis was thanking his lucky stars for sending this beautiful young woman into his life.

When lunch was over, there was a moment of awkwardness as they made ready to leave. Dennis paid the bill and jumped up to help Dene on with her coat. She slipped her arms in and his hands brushed her shoulders and she felt a thrill of excitement run through her. Was this the beginnings of a love affair?...How exciting!

They walked almost in silence, each fearful that the other was not interested enough to continue the budding romance. Dennis was racking his brain to find something clever to say but all his wit had left him and he fell quiet.

He needn't have worried for when he finally plucked up the courage to ask her out again she smiled shyly holding out her hand and, to his delight, accepted. Parting with the handshake, both went in their respective directions with a new skip in their step and a flush of happy colour on both their cheeks.

Chapter Twenty One -1950

Christmas arrived amidst a cold winter where the snow was so high they had to walk atop the village dry stone walls to get anywhere. Thankfully the trains were still running and the roads were cleared better down the valley. The majority of the family found itself crowded around the kitchen table at Wood Mill Cottage once more. Dennis and Doreen or Dene as she now called herself, had been going out for three months and seemed happy enough. Rene was now heavily pregnant and the baby was expected anytime now.

Arthur still hadn't made an appearance and Lynne had settled into her training and her relationship with Derek. All in all it was a happy gathering and May looked about at the flushed faces of her extended family and considered herself in good company. The younger ones were excited at receiving more presents than usual, as their older siblings had wages to spend and spoiled them.

Annie had not been well with the onset of winter and it had left her frail, so she had a little table by her armchair and the fire where she surveyed the frivolity with a quiet smile, eating her Christmas dinner in as much comfort as an old arthritic woman could hope for. Never having been given to being openly emotional, she kept her own counsel, but there was a part of her that rejoiced in being the matriarch of this robust family. Her thoughts strayed back to the terror and heartbreak of their flight from Ireland and she considered that, all in all, they had come far.

The fire warmed her and eased the ache in her old bones. She was tired and the thought came upon her that she was not long for this world, but she was content. She had never known passion, but she had the blessings of a life in the embrace of her daughter's care and the casually given, but unfaltering love of her grandchildren...yes, she was content.

She caught a chill on New Year's Eve and by the second week of January, just as Rene went into labour, they had laid her tired bones to rest. Paul, a robust baby boy made his entrance into the world twelve hours later.

There was no time for grief in the passing of her life. May saved her tears for the early hours and during the day she was determined to rejoice in the birth of the grandson that she would be allowed to be a grandmother to. How she adored this black haired relentless child, who rarely slept but instead opened his blue eyes to survey his small world with quiet interest...until he was hungry.

Rene had not had an easy birth and therefore May had moved into their spare room and taken the babe to give her rest for a few days. When Rene had recovered she was eager to get back to work as soon as possible and so it seemed the most natural thing for May to take the child in the day, whilst her daughter resumed her work.

May ploughed all her emotion into this new generation and the baby thrived on the attention. She had little time to grieve the passing of her mother and very soon the promise of spring pushed the first green shoots of life into the bluebell woods nearby. March was here and daffodil yellow was the feature of Rene and Doreen's new window display and it created a stir.

May crocheted a beautiful spring blanket for the baby's pram decorated with daffodils and bluebells, she was an excellent craftswoman indeed. Rene who had a keen eye, thanked her mother profusely and asked her to start crocheting them and other designs for a baby line in the shop. Dene wasn't too keen as it drew her mother away from the fashion range, but Rene was a savvy business woman in ways Dene couldn't hope to compete in, so she bowed to her knowledge.

A few days later Dene ran through the back door of wood mill, eyes bright with excitement and eager to break the news that the Manchester Evening News was doing an article on her as a designer. All her newfound sophistication had fallen away and May smiled as her excited daughter recounted the phone call.

"I will have to make something really special to wear," she cried. "Oh Mum, I could be like Christian Dior!"

"That you might," laughed her mum as she set the table for tea and pushed the younger ones out from under her feet to play outside. Doreen ran out to the barn and came back with magazines to peruse for inspiration.

Further down the cobbled lane Teddy was coming back with a cart full of scrap and Graham and the twins had jumped up for the last few yards ride up to the house. The sky was staying lighter now and it felt good not to be coming home in the darkness of winter.

Graham sat at his dad's side and he passed him the reins. Captain stirred for a second and then resumed his trot towards home. The twins were dangling off the back trailing their shoes on the cobbles and there would be hell to pay when May caught a glimpse of the scuffs.

"Dad? Can I come with you on the cart tomorrow? I can drive it for you." Graham was eager to find an excuse to miss school. His dad pulled his cap from his head and plonked it atop of the boy's dark mop of hair, where it fell down over his eyes.

"When tha' gets big enough to fill that hat lad, you'll be big enough to come to work with me, but for now yer best off at school for.. Aye up! Mind the wall lad, pull the reins a little to the left." Edward smiled, but he knew his lad was struggling with his reading and writing and it was a sadness to him, he wanted better for his children. The boy pulled gently on the reins and Captain slowed to a stop just in front of the barn.

"Good lad," said Teddy to Graham and lifted the slight boy down from the cart. "Now go and get his oats ready and make sure his stall is clean for him while I take his reins off. Maureen, go and tell Mam I'm home and hungry as this horse!"

The twins jumped backwards off the cart and Maureen scurried in to impart the news that dad was home. Gary her twin now fourteen, started to uncouple the horse with Edward. He was short but a sturdy lad, unlike his older siblings, who were slim, His sister was the same and Edward occasionally wondered with a smile if May had strayed, as the twins had more of her and nothing he could see of him. Gary sang as he groomed the horse in his stable and Edward listened with pleasure, the boy had a talent. He couldn't wait to take his son down to the Bird in Hand. He'd certainly liven up the sing songs round the piano. No, all his children were all his and he loved them dearly.

Gary was due to start an apprenticeship at Greenhalgh's in a couple of weeks and Edward was looking forward to taking his son for his first pint, even if it wasn't alcoholic. Going with his dad to the pub was a symbol he was growing up and starting work was a cause for celebration. He was on his road to manhood.

***

Dene, featuring Rene Couture had a half page on the local news and Rene and Dene found themselves amongst a flurry of new activity as curious customers, who hadn't previously discovered them, came to investigate the latest novelty. Rene and Dene had to up their game as the clientele they were now getting were from monied backgrounds, eager to escape the austerity of the Second World War. Since Dior had created the full circular skirt, which was an extravagance of material and a thumbing to the nose of rationing had Dene working flat out to replicate the style.

Maureen, eager to avoid working in the mill pleaded to help Dene, but was turned down on the basis that she was too impatient with her stitching to create the standard of needlework that the range required. It did not go down well with the young girl and May found herself refereeing when instead Dene took on a local woman for the basic sewing. The atmosphere was strained for a couple of weeks until Maureen had been established in her new position and quite liked the banter with all the girls working there. Dene was eventually forgiven as Maureen wasn't one to hold grudges for long. The new woman worked well and could be trusted to work unsupervised.

A fabulous range of evening and cocktail wear graced the window and the full skirts and frivolity of net petticoats beneath couldn't help but attract the eye of passers by. The war years had passed to a new decade and the cotton mills and engineering works were in full throttle once more.

Even Edward was benefiting from the knock-on effects of the post-war boom and it seemed everyone wanted their lives full of material things to push old fears and restrictions into the past. The people with money bought new. Edward took the old and the poorer people bought from Edward. Things were looking up.

They had five wages coming in plus May's part time from sewing and the house itself was benefiting from Edward's rag and bone collection with better furniture and even a few luxuries.

The big event of 1949 had been the arrival of television into the Rochdale area despite the fact it was receiving its signal from the Sutton Coldfield transmitter twenty miles outside its range. The Holme Moss transmitter was in its planning stages and there would soon be more reliable coverage.

Stan had vowed over the Christmas meal that as soon as they could he would be the first person in Newhey with a television. Lynne, who made no bones about the fact she had no time for him, turned her by now, famous sneer towards him, muttering that of course Stan would have to be the big 'I am'. She had had her fill of him from across the bar and was happy she had her Derek and not this spiel merchant that her older sister had married.

"Who will be buying it?" she had asked, knowing that it was Rene and not him who was bringing the bigger share into the pot nowadays, despite his bragging in the pub. Stan had grimaced and carried on regardless and Lynne let it drop after a sideways glance from Edward that restrained any further retort.

Sure enough, some weeks later, there was a big hullabaloo as word spread that a television had indeed been delivered to the Hornby's house and the family were invited down to watch on the Saturday. Even the older ones gave up their night out and the living room at the terraced cottage was full to the brim with the younger ones jockeying for position on the floor directly in front.

Dennis and Derek were invited and there was quite a party atmosphere. The baby was in his pram and not short of admirers and Rene had made sandwiches for everyone. The men had brought bottled beer from the Bull's Head across the way and for the most part, the first hour had been spent mostly solidly watching the wonderful new invention and eating.

The only break in attention was when the majority realised that Dennis had just told them his mother had been asked to open the first ever test for the BBC broadcast in 1936 with a song, but she had turned them down, being too afraid to sing live in front of the cameras. Now Helen McKay would go down in history, having paintings of herself in galleries singing on that first magical moment of TV, whilst Ivy Barrie stayed at home tending her boarding house and never achieving the heights of fame her voice deserved.

Everyone stopped eating and looked to Dennis in awe, even Dene who had been seeing him for some months now, it was as if they viewed him in a new light.

"We really must go and watch your mother sing Dennis," said Dene, her eyes looking upon her polite young man with renewed interest. She had always been star-struck by the glamorous women who sang and danced in the movies and she often wished she had been blessed with a better voice as well as her ability to dance so gracefully. Young Gary had got that talent, although he insisted, as fourteen year old boys do in misusing it by squawking, but that didn't happen often. Gary was always acting the goat, but when he did sing seriously, it was a joy to hear, Gary was loud and boisterous, that was his nature, unstoppable energy.

"Mother's singing in a couple of weeks in Blackpool. Perhaps we can go up to visit and watch her," he replied with a smile.

Dene sat back in her chair. Visiting the mother was tantamount to a proposal and though the most she and Dennis had done was a few kisses, she felt a thrill run through her solar plexus at this new development.

"That would be lovely," she answered excitedly.

"Can I come?" asked Maureen, Gary's twin.

"Not this time, maybe another," said Dene already nervous at creating the right impression with a possible mother-in-law, without adding her loud family into the pot.

Chapter Twenty Two

The first warm days of spring were finally upon them when Edward took Gary to work for the first time and he felt the nerves for him. Gary on the other hand, unlike his sisters was happy to be out of school and ready to start work. He was a happy-go-lucky young man and Edward had no worries that he'd settle in, but as a father, he mourned on behalf of his boy for the loss of his childhood.

Derek, Lynne's fella, already worked there and Edward asked him to keep an eye on the boy. He wasn't the only apprentice starting there and would have company his own age. It would be good that he wouldn't be the only kid in a man's environment.

Edward needn't have worried, for Gary came home full of tales of his day and the other boys he was training with. May ruffled his thick, black hair and sent him off to help his dad with the horse first and then change out of his dirty clothes for tea. She laughed to herself that he was the only boy in her brood who had no concern with how he looked.

Even Gray, as young as he was, liked to be tidy. Gary was never happier than when he was covered in muck or oil. 'This job was just up his street,' she thought as he disappeared happily through the door and she turned back to her chores,

May loved spring, the doors were open and the house felt fresh. There wasn't the constant aroma of damp washing steaming by the fire and the house felt bigger and tidier for it. Edward had made a large wooden table and benches for the garden and the family loved to sit outside after work and break bread. It was always a happy atmosphere.

Edward would sit and repair the horse's tack. The girls would chatter and the boys would rough and tumble. Their little world was good.

The baby would be sat in his pram waiting for his mum to pick him up and May would put him underneath the washing line to amuse him. He would spend a happy hour kicking and burbling in the spring sunshine and May would motor through her chores, as she kept one eye on him through the window until it was time for his walk up the road to home.

The next morning she pushed her brood out of the doors with a slab of bread and gooseberry jam, eager to be on with her sewing tasks from Dene. She could still do these while she looked after the babe. Sometimes, the young woman Dene had employed to do the basic sewing would work alongside her and they would chat happily about life, each taking turns to amuse her young grandson or put the kettle on. The spring brought such joy and freedom from the confines of the house that you couldn't help but be happy.

...and so it was that this particular morning the two women were sitting laughing at some small gossip whilst cutting facings for a jacket design. The items had been spread on a clean white cloth that had been thrown over the garden table to keep the material clean and she was just picking up her second piece when she heard a shout from the road above. Looking up she was surprised to see Derek, Lynne's bloke, running full pelt towards them. The speed of his approach and his body language sent an instant bolt of fear right through to her solar plexus and she stood up and stepped away from the bench she had been sitting on, as he tumbled down the steps from the road to the level of the house below.

"May! You've got to come quick, there's been an accident!" His face was red from running, but it was clear he was in shock. May didn't need to ask who, Derek worked at Greenhalgh's and only one of her children worked there… her beloved boy Gary, with his quick smile and mop of black hair. Her legs nearly went from under her, her bladder nearly releasing.

"Look after the baby!" she told the woman now standing beside her desperately.

"I will...Go!" came the reply.

Greenhalgh's was a mere five hundred yards away, but as she ran behind Derek, her adrenalin kicked in and she found speed she never thought she would have at her age. She ran sweating but ashen-faced into the yard. It was clear there was something drastic occurring. One lad was crying and looked away as she ran past. The rest of the men were standing by the doors in quiet solemnity. There was the chill sound of nothing, no machinery noise, just an eerie quiet.

"Where is he?" she cried.

"Outside, round the back." Derek led her quickly onwards.

"Find Teddy and ring Rene at the shop... and get Maureen from Wood Mill," she screamed at a friend of her husband's. "Why is he round the back?" she cried to Derek as they ran.

"He went through the window May." Derek spoke almost dreading the words coming from his own mouth. "It's bad May, you need to be prepared."

May's heart near stopped with terror. The windows were a good twenty feet up, but there was worse to come. As she rounded the corner people were scurrying back and forth with blankets and sheets. One woman, who looked distraught, was ripping the cloth into strips close to a small group huddled around her boy on the floor. The manager, who was a good man, was leaning over the boy on the grass with his back to May, working on him. All she could see was the bloodied face of her boy and his beautiful, black hair sticky with it, where he wasn't hidden by the manager.

The man, grey with shock and the enormity of his task, looked to May with tears in his eyes as May followed the direction of his arms as he tended to the unconscious boy.
"I've got a tourniquet on it May, the ambulance is on its way. We can't do any more for now. I'm sorry... Give me them sheets!" he shouted to the woman nearby.

May fell to her knees with a scream that came up from the depths of her soul as she realised what the man was doing. He had the pressure on a spanner wrapped in his leather belt that was tight around her boy's thigh. Below was just a mass of tattered skin and extruding bone. His lower leg was completely gone. Fortunately for Gary, he was deeply unconscious and May crawled to his side and gently cradled his head in her arms as she sobbed and crooned, "Mum's here my darling.. mum's here, it's alright..." No one dared move the boy, he looked so broken.

A siren was heard in the distance and she whispered to her boy to hold on, they were coming. Her lower face was covered in his blood and by now she had seen the extent of his injuries. His head was bruised and cut, as were his fingers. His other leg was bent at a strange angle and surely broken. She was too paralysed with fear to do anything other than hold her lad.

"What happened?" she sobbed.

"The machine caught him by his sleeve and took him up through the framework. It threw him through the window May. I don't know much else for now..I'm so sorry"

The man's silent tears spilled with her own. He was sure her boy was going to die, how could he possibly survive this? He knew the mother saw it too. He stuffed the sheets below the boy's leg to keep him clean and catch the escaping blood for when he released the pressure her eyes flew open wide at the renewed flow and spurred her to action.

"Bring the ambulance round here!" she screamed... "Quickly!"

Even the ambulance man was stunned by the extent of the boy's injuries, but immediately got to work. May found strength she hadn't thought possible and fired instructions at people to tell the family where they were headed. Oldham Infirmary was quicker. They had little time to save this boy's life and speed was of the essence and as she sat at the back of the ambulance she prayed to the very core of her soul that her boy would be spared.

Two hours later as she sat ashen-faced in a waiting room, Stan brought Edward in. She had held herself together until now, but the sight of her husband's tortured face running into the ward was too much and her sobs howled out of her as Teddy held her to him.

Gary had lost his leg to above the knee. He had broken ribs and fingers. The other leg was broken and he was in theatre. That's all they knew. Stan was to go home and he and Rene must hold the family together until they knew what the outcome was.

Lynne flew in next. They had allowed her out of training and for once she sat quiet and still beside her mother and father in her nurse's uniform, holding her mother's hand firmly with a strength that belied the fear that churned around her belly.

The strangest of all things was Maureen. The girl had been carrying a bolt of material to another of the girls to load and was singing as she strode across the factory floor, when, for no reason whatsoever, at the time Gary had had the accident, his twin sister had fallen to the floor clutching her leg. Screaming shrilly she had passed out. They had taken her home only to find the women and the baby, full of fear with the news that her mother had gone to tend to her brother, who had been injured. No one would ever be able to explain it.

Doreen and Rene arrived home shortly after. Rene took the baby from the by now exhausted woman, sent her home and got everyone fed. Dene and Maureen sobbed brokenly the entire time and were not much use to anyone as she served the small group. Graham sat wide-eyed and terrified in the corner clutching his favourite pet chicken for comfort and refusing to eat. It was only when Stan returned did Rene let go her emotion and she cried with the rest for their younger brother.

Half an hour later Rene stood up, made sandwiches for Stan to take back to the hospital for her mum and dad and put on the water for them all to wash. "Gary was gravely ill but alive, that's all they knew, so they must hope for the best," was all she said, regaining her practical stance. Mum and dad would be home when they could and it fell to her and Stan to step up for now. Inside she howled for her brother. The sweet, noisy, irritating, brother, singing to the horse as he brushed him each night.

She went over to the pram where her young son, Paul slept and looked at him through renewed eyes. How precious a gift she had been given and she vowed there and then to keep him safe and to give him a life where he didn't have to work amongst factory machinery. No, not her boy!

She had told Stan she would stay at the cottage with her siblings and to call on his way back with an update. That night when they finally fell exhausted into bed, she held her baby close beside her and prayed for a long time.

They found out in the next few days that the lad May had seen sobbing in the yard had caused the accident. Boys would be boys apparently and the new group of apprentices had been playing practical jokes on each other. That fateful day Gary had turned off the machine to go underneath to retrieve something when the lad in question, not being the sharpest, had decided to give him a scare by turning the machine on. Gary's sleeve had been caught and it had dragged him across and up on the belts and up into the roof of the building, severing his lower leg in the process. Finally releasing him to throw him through the window to the bank below, which being grass, rather than the cobbled yard beneath some of the windows, had saved him from certain death. His leg was never found. It must have been thrown through the window onto the bank and rolled into the river to float away.

May and Edward were gone for several days, never leaving their boy's side. Praying for him to wake, but dreading the moment when he did. They were gone for over a week. He was out of danger for now they had said, but his progress would be slow, even without complications that may arise. During this time Rene left Dene in the shop whilst she stayed at home to look after her mum's house, the baby and the manufacturing end of their stock.

She would push the large coach pram up the road to her own house twice a day to ring the hospital and then ring the shop to pass on news to reassure her sister. Then she would do an hour of accounts whilst the baby slept and then return to Wood Mill Cottage to start tea for them all. It was a hard time enough for a young mother with a business to run, let alone run two houses, but she had the Handley grit and pushed on despite the fatigue of doing all this and being any kind of decent mother to her child.

Lynne would usually come in with an update, but her brother was mostly sleeping under sedation and there was little to tell. He had murmured in his sleep once or twice, but that was all. Once home, she would take over from Rene and shoo her home to rest. Maureen stepped up and would stalwartly take on all Gary's chores as well as her own. Once done, she and Lynne would tackle the washing and ironing.

Even Graham, young as he was, bore the burden well and tended the chickens and tidied the yard, so that when Stan finally fetched May home pale and weary a few days later, she was able just to sit in her chair whilst they quietly tended to her. No one dared ask much of her, as her eyes would fill with tears when questioned and they were all frightened of the answer. They had not seen their brother for two weeks now. His dad, when he came home the next day to allow May to go back, was so distracted and solemn that there was no time for affection and the young boy missed the precious times he had previously taken for granted, sitting at his dad's feet.

May and Edward took turns to stay at the hospital for the first two weeks, despite the matron stridently trying to usher them out. It was a battle of wills but May's Irish determination won out and the Matron relented, 'Seeing as the boy was so poorly.'

Gary moved little, May sitting quietly by his side with her hand on his arm, dozed mostly, and when she wasn't dozing, she would watch him closely, waiting for any sign that he might be making his way back to them. She sang 'Ave Maria' quietly and anything that might filter through the sedation to let him know she was there. She told him imaginary stories of what the family was doing and how they were preparing for him coming home… and then she would quietly weep when she had no response.

By fifteen days Edward had to return fully to work to put bread on the table and so she bore the brunt of the burden alone. Her dress hung limply and she had lost weight, with greasy hair tied into a plait for ease. She was mostly alone with her boy in a side room reserved for the critical. It was there she half lay with her head on her arms her fingers keeping contact with the unconscious boy. She stretched her back aching with the lack of movement when she heard a familiar voice from the door.

"Hello, Ma."

It took a few seconds for it to register but when it did, she raised her head and turned to see Arthur standing quietly in the doorway. His eyes filled with tears as he noted the flatness of the sheets where should have been his brother's leg.

"I didn't know.. I'm so sorry..I came straight away." His voice broke with emotion and despite the bad blood, he was her son once more.

May raised herself wearily from the hard chair and held out her arms to her errant son and he gathered her in and they cried together. No words were needed.

"I'm here now Ma, it'll be 'all reet', we'll get him back don't you worry." He hugged her to him tightly and then pushed her away fiddling in his jacket pocket.

"He's not woke up for days Arthur." She started to cry again and his heart nearly broke for her. He grabbed her hand and stuffed a note in it and closed her fingers around the paper.

"Here's ten bob Mam, now go and get us some grub from the cafe and have a walk outside...it's nice. I'll stay with him so don't hurry, get some fresh air, you'll feel better for it...Go on!."

May looked down at the money, "...but it's too much!"

"It's nowt, I've got it and I expect you need a few bob right now, so off you go." He gave her hand one last squeeze before aiming her for the door.

May hugged her eldest son once more and left to do as he suggested. He drew up the chair and sat down quietly by his brother and brushed his hair where it had spilled over his eyes. The swelling had gone down leaving a mass of yellowing bruises, his lips cracked and dehydrated.

"Now lad.." he said quietly. "You and me have got plenty to do, so thee'll have to shap thesen and wake up, do you hear?"

Gary's eyes flickered for a moment and then opened ever so slightly in recognition. It was more than he had done in two weeks.

"Mam?" the boy whimpered and Arthur leaned in taking his brothers hand.

"She's gone to bring us a butty... now my brave lad you and me need a chat and you're going to have to be a man about it, but it's not going to be the end of your world. We'll just have to make a slightly different world than we thought for you. Me and Ma and the rest. We'll do it together. Do you understand?"

"No.." The boys eyes opened a little more and he winced in pain.

"Tha's had an accident lad, but yer on the mend and we're all with you to help you get better. There's no better time to say this so you'll have to be brave."

He grasped the boy's hand, coming in close to his face. Rather he did this than Ma.. to tell her boy his leg was gone would break her, he saw that from the state of her as he'd walked in. Best he did the deed and let Ma comfort him afterwards.

By the time May came back, Gary had cried his tears until they dried into racking sobs and then silence. The doctor had been sent for. He had checked him over, given him words of reassurance and painkillers once more, with the promise of something tasty as soon as they could, but only a little as his stomach had been without food.

When she saw the boy half-awake but calm, she ran to him and kissed his face. His tears spilt over once more and mingled with those of his mother. Arthur stood quietly by, giving them time to grieve. When he felt the time was right, he produced a bar of chocolate and broke a piece off for each of them.

"The doc said its OK, but suck it slow." The boy raised a shaky hand to take the chocolate, but it was clear he had woken hungry and it was a joy to see him take it in his mouth and relish the taste. They might just have him back thought May as she popped the piece in her own mouth and she smiled at her boys as the chocolate melted and spread its love. Arthur pulled up a chair and sat down once more beside the mother who he thought he'd never speak to again and gave her hand a reassuring squeeze.

Chapter Twenty Three

The day, when it finally came, that Gary was carried through Wood Mill Cottage door by Arthur, was a mixture of joy and grief for May. Lynne, Arthur and Rene held anything they were feeling deep within and had Gary laughing within a few minutes. Dene, Maureen and Graham barely held their tears in check and hovered about him looking distraught. It was not doing the boy any good so in the end May shooed everyone else out to give her time and peace to settle her son back in. Edward had made him a sofa bed in the already crowded kitchen so he wouldn't be isolated in his bed upstairs for too long.

At the moment he was just about walking a few steps with crutches. There was talk of a false leg being fitted but that would take several weeks to arrange and for the stump to heal. For now May just rejoiced that he was alive and home. She kept her tears for bedtime.

Bath-times were particularly stressful as Gary didn't want anyone to see his stump but his mum and dad. It was hard work helping him in and out of the bath and Edward's health wasn't the best with his weak chest. Eventually seeing her parent's fatigue, Lynne took charge and naming herself his private nurse, took over bathing and wound dressing with a dismissive, "You've got nowt I haven't seen before boyo!" and it was a done deal.

It took a couple of weeks for Gary to settle back in, but eventually he was skipping agilely round the kitchen on his crutches and gaining strength by the day. The pain was hard and in those moments he fought the tears by being over-boisterous and the joker. If anything, his suffering had enlarged his already large personality and

May thanked God he had gone in a positive direction rather than given in to the pain.

True to his promise to himself Arthur turned up regular as clockwork each Saturday morning to take as many as could fit into his new car to Rochdale baths. As Gary loved to swim, it wasn't long before he faced his fears and embarrassment and was hopping up to the diving board. The sight created quite a stir amongst the onlookers below, who watched with bated breath as he slithered to the end and then balanced on one leg to take his dive.

May's heart missed a beat the first time he did it, but as he burst to the surface punching a hand victoriously in the air, her broken heart swelled with pride for him. Very soon he had become a local celebrity and everyone looked for the one-legged boy who now pulled himself up to the highest board and would fearlessly launch himself off. He was a sight to be seen.

After a couple of months he had been fitted with a metal leg, It clanked and was unwieldy, not to mention painful, but Gary was so excited to look 'normal' even with his loping gait to throw the leg into forward motion, that he didn't care. Doreen who by now had a regular cottage industry going in the barn and three girls employed, had enlisted the help of one of her more experienced staff to design him slightly wider pants, just enough to accommodate the leg being taken on an off.

Life seemed to settle back down once more and the siblings had gone into forward motion in their respective careers now that Gary was on the mend. Despite his disability, he was soon out tending the animals and going off with his dad on the cart to collect scrap.

Rene was now able to employ staff of her own also to mind the shop, allowing Dene to concentrate on her design and manufacture and herself on the books, the buying and her son. Dene was now receiving enquiries from Manchester stores for her designs and for the first time in their lives, money was not a worry. Each week the older girls would walk to the post office to deposit money in respective post office accounts and they delighted in watching the total growing.

Rene and Dene had also set up their first business bank accounts and the first time Dene wrote a cheque the whole family sat and watched in awe. Even May, used to doing the accounts for Aunt Anne in earlier years, was impressed at her previously shy and delicate daughter's business acumen. It was a surprise, Rene yes, but Dene she had always thought would cling to her apron strings and was too timid to make her own way. She had been wrong.

Lynne was happy in her training and out enjoying life more than she should with Derek, but they seemed happy enough. She still retained her barmaid role, in her words 'for entertainment' and the younger ones had reverted to normality, not even seeing Gary's disability as a problem now he was up and about.

They had missed Oldham Wakes because of Gary's accident but May was determined they would go late August to Butlin's as a celebration of all that they had achieved and overcome.

All of them, but Arthur, had agreed willingly. He had said work wouldn't allow him the time off. May let it go, knowing that it was more likely that her budding 'Champagne Charlie' was more used to the club life in Manchester for his entertainment. He was still with the woman he had been seeing when he split with his wife, but very little was said about his personal or business life, that way a kind of truce held.

He would arrive on Saturday, take the younger ones out with her and slip her a couple of quid for extras for the kids as he dropped them off. He was always tight-lipped on anything he did. She had found out he was managing to see his son every now and then and that he and May (his first wife) seemed to have gained some way of staying friends. More than that, she didn't know.

Edward kept his thoughts to himself, but truth be told, he had heard the rumours that Arthur had got himself in with the main Manchester Mafia crowd and really didn't want to consider what his eldest son was up to.

The day dawned and it was an excited family who queued for the coach to Pwllheli Butlin's. This particular camp was rated one of the best in the country and all the family were thrilled at the prospect of a week away in Wales.

Arthur had offered to stay at the house and look after the animals so that Edward could come. It was the first holiday the family had ever had. The sun beamed down in glorious approval and for the first time in many months life felt better and happy once more.

The consternation of the other travellers as the large, loud group boarded the coach for the three-hour journey brought a smile to Edward's face. This would be an interesting trip. He cuffed Graham affectionately once more to gee him up the coach and Gray beamed in excitement. His dad was happy again and back to his old self. It would be a fantastic adventure.

Gary struggled but refused help and by pulling up with his arms, he dragged the bad leg up the steps and hopped up the coach to his allocated seat.

The sun-coloured Yelloway's coach chugged its way through the outskirts of Manchester, mirroring the weather that was heading for heatwave territory. May handed out sandwiches and for the younger ones, sugar butties. It was considered a treat, but Gray wasn't sure whether he liked the feeling of the sugar grains crunching through the butter as he bit into the soft bread, but he was too hungry to argue. Sugar was still rationed so he didn't dare leave them, regardless.

The butter itself was an indulgence, but Edward refused margarine calling it 'wagon fat' and so May relented and stuck to the latter. It put a large dint in her purse with so many mouths to feed but she had to admit that it made all the difference as she sat savouring her cheese and onion sandwich and the passing scenery on the outskirts of Chester.

None of them had ever been to Butlin's before and as they drove through the gates and up to reception they all gasped at the outdoor swimming pool with its large four tier fountain. To their eyes, the whole place just looked like a fairyland, with its pastel colours and bright hedges of flowers.

The paths were festooned with fairy lights and the younger ones veered between having to be constrained or dragged along open-mouthed. It was like nothing they had ever seen before. When they reached the amusement park, on the way to their chalets they screamed with delight, and it took May all her time to prevent them from running to it, including Gary and she smiled.

The older ones followed behind with the suitcases as they made their way along the rows of chalets. Lynne and Dene, Rene and the baby had one. Stan had stayed home to work, so it made things easier. The youngest three bunked in with May and Edward and Derek and Dennis had opted to share. They had three chalets lined up next to each other so it was easy to organise themselves. May made a point of having the middle one so there would be no funny business between the unmarried girls and their young men.

When the two girls got together before bedtime and the discussion turned to romance and their respective beaus, it was clear that things were not at an intimate stage with either of them. Truth be known May had been so remiss in her education of her daughters on the physical side of relationships that for the first month after Dennis had kissed her Dene had fretted that she might have a baby until Lillan laughing scornfully, had put her right on the subject. With her new understanding borne of her nurses training she had become the expert on all things biological. Her amusement heightened still further at the horrified look on her sister's face as she went into all the gory details. Dene was young in her outlook, despite her acumen in business.

When Dene thought it over later, lying awake in the darkness, she considered wether she was doing something wrong, for Dennis hadn't tried any of those things. His behaviour had been impeccable. Did that mean she wasn't attractive then? Derek was always grabbing hold of Lynne and she was always shoving him off. Dennis was always so well-mannered, always attentive but never really physically confident. It worried her and she resolved to speak to Rene, who was more likely to tell her what she needed to know without drama or embellishment. Eventually her eyes grew heavy and she slept.

The morning sun streamed through the windows as the three young women stretched and woke. Paul was snuffling and stuffing his hands into his mouth that signalled the short time before he would be pulling himself up the bars of his cot and shouting for his morning milk. Rene threw the covers back and filled his bottle in readiness and then skipped quickly into the bathroom to wash, whilst Lynne and Dene brought him into bed to play whilst his milk warmed.

Already next door you could hear the laughter and excitement through the thin walls of the chalets as May chivvied up the twins and Graham in readiness to go over to the dining hall for breakfast. Lynne knocked up the men and before long they were headed across the lawns to the huge canteen the size of four schools halls and lined with tables.

Graham went for porridge, followed by boiled eggs, but grumbled when there was no evaporated milk for his oats and he had to make do with sugar and milk. They lined up at the serving bars and chattered to neighbours as they slowly moved along the queue. The whole room was a cacophony of happy chatter, which echoed and was made all the more loud because of the high ceilings. It was like being under water in a very busy sea. Everything was light-hearted and even Gary insisted on going for his own food, despite the risk of a trip on his leg and the embarrassment of spillage with his lopsided gait.

All fed, the children were released on the funfair and May and Edward watched happily as even the older girls and their men became children again in the thrill of the rides. May watched as she pushed Paul back and forwards in the new folding pushchair that Rene had bought to bring with them on the coach. It was the latest thing and thankfully, as unwieldy as it was, it enabled them to let the boy sleep without having to carry him everywhere. They certainly could not have got the huge grey coach pram on the coach. As May seemed to be falling to baby duty, she thanked her lucky stars that they had this expensive piece of equipment and that Rene had the means to buy it. Her back would certainly be grateful.

Next, they had lunch in the canteen once more and then straight out to the pools. Rene sat in the shallows with her son looking as elegant as a young mother could, whilst May and Edward snoozed in deckchairs with half an eye on the youngsters. Gary had caused a stir as he took his leg off, but as soon as he was in the water, he was no different to anyone else and May scowled at anyone who stared in sympathy, her boy was just fine. Water was his element and he would have stayed in for hours had she not ordered them out when they were starting to tire and squabble.

By a couple of days in, they were fully at home in their surroundings and every night the three young women turned heads as they wore Dene's latest creations. On the fourth night Lynne came across a poster for the beauty competition 'Miss Pink Lady' and Lynne ran across to Dene shouting, "Here Do! This is just up your street.. look! Miss Pink Lady, it's you!"

"Oh Dene... you've got to go in for this!" replied Rene.

"Think of the publicity if you win... Miss0 Pink Lady wins Miss Pink Lady!" They bustled her back to the chalet and rifled through her wardrobe for something pink, which was easily achieved as it was Dene's signature colour, She was paraded, made up and generally coiffed to within an inch of her life until they were satisfied that she had the right outfit and style to match.

When the family marched over to the main ballroom later that evening Dene was quaking in her shoes and Edward gave her a stiff brandy to loosen her up. The benefit of that was that alcohol went straight to her funny bone and produced giggles and a smile that could only be seen as dazzling.

The contestants were called up and asked to walk around the parameters of the ballroom as the band played 'Moonlight Serenade'. Doreen's natural grace to music kicked in and she walked like a model on a catwalk, showing off the pink and white chiffon dress with pink roses that floated outwards like a peony in the wind over the numerous net petticoats looking beautiful and to those that knew her, a little tipsy.

She was a delightful apparition with her almost black locks clipped up into a French pleat and diamanté clips sparkling in her glossy hair. Her shoes were pink satin with diamanté heels, just enough for classical elegance without too much of anything too showy.

May straightened with pride as she heard the 'oohs' and 'ahhs' of the people sitting nearby as her daughter glided past and she looked to her husband and saw his eyes glisten. He was a sentimental old thing. She reached out her hand and took his in hers and squeezed. This was a better life than had been for a while. His return look gave her reassurance and they laughed as Graham breathed in awe at his sister saying, "She's like a princess, Mam!"

"She certainly is love, she certainly is..."

Half an hour later Dene was crowned 'Miss Pink Lady' and posed for pictures, looking like she had modelled all her life. When they were put up on the board the next day, they were all amazed at how beautiful their previously-shy sister looked. May ordered three copies, Rene two, Dennis one and Doreen bought one for herself. Just in case.

"Right who's next then?" said Lynne as they walked to the ballroom the following night. Everyone looked at her perplexed and she continued as she now had all their attention.

"Next to win something. There's a talent show on tomorrow and a fancy dress competition," she replied, "We can't let Dene have all her own way or we'll never hear the last of it."

Everyone laughed out-loud.
"I don't think so," said Rene. "Who of us lot has got any talent?"

"Gary has! He has a great voice," said Maureen nudging her twin, who stumbled and grabbed for his dad to steady himself.

"I don't think your brother will want to go up on stage," said Edward glancing down at his son who by now had righted himself.

"I don't mind singing Da," he said. "I like singing!"

"Well bugger me!" said Edward as May slapped him playfully for his profanity. "Then my lad, if that's what you want, then you shall!"

"Edward...,"May said pulling on his arm. "Do you think that's a good idea? What if he falls or gets embarrassed?"

"If he can shimmy up to the top diving board one legged, he can get up a few steps and sing...it'll do him good. If he changes his mind, nay bother, but if the lad wants to do it, let him May," he muttered quietly so as not to be heard by the rest and May scowled her disapproval. She didn't want her boy ridiculed. Edward chose not to see. The boy had his life to live, it would be hard enough without the added burden of his disability.

Edward was determined to push Gary in any direction that made him happy and the boy looked pleased as punch at the thought of going up on stage. So, if he wanted it, he would let him have a go.

"I think you'll do grand lad, let's see where we sign you up!" He clapped Gary on the back and the boy's face lit up with excitement.

"Really Dad?"
"You've got a great voice Gary, but you'll have to decide what to sing and practise hard tomorrow."

"I will, I promise!"

Chapter Twenty Four

The theatre was full for the early evening talent show when the family had arrived in the foyer. Gary had signed on the evening before and when they held a quick audition, the redcoat in charge had been so impressed he had asked him back to have a quick rehearsal with the band in the afternoon. Edward had gone along with him on pain of death that he wasn't to tell anyone his song.

He had forgotten that the chalet walls were thin and the majority of his family already knew the song by heart as they listened to him repeatedly rehearse for the show from four until they were ready to walk across.

Everyone was excited, but the older ones were worried he would be viewed as a freak when he finally hobbled onto the stage. The redcoat, Sam had something about him and had really taken to Gary. He had made sure that he wouldn't be invited onto the stage like the rest, but instead had him come on behind the drapes and waited by the mic for them to open when he was announced.

Sam checked on him as the previous act was juggling in front of the curtains.

"You alright mate?," he asked a white-faced Gary.

"Nervous" was all he managed to get out. Sam clapped him on the shoulder and looked him right in the eye.

"I've given you top billing because you are that good! You'll be fab, give it everything you've got!" He gave his shoulder one last squeeze and left him with a final." Keep the mic close to your mouth...don't forget and pretend you're Elvis!"

He couldn't have said a better word. As the young teenager was announced with the words, "Here's a young man who knocked our socks off when we heard him...Give a big welcome to Gary Handley!" and the drapes parted. It could have gone either way. However, as Gary saw the haze of faces on the front row, smelt the heat of the lights and the wood and rope of the stage, something came over him and Gary brought a quiff of his thick black brill-creamed hair forward over his eyes and kicked out his bad leg as he stretched the mic to arm's length gripping it like his life depended on it.

The drummer kicked up the opening of the song and Gary started to twitch his bad leg which made his wide trousers dance hypnotically to the beat. May's mouth opened wide with delight that her son could stand there in the lights and not appear to have a moment's qualm about his ability. She all but laughed out loud and had to clap her hand over her mouth.

He cocked his head downwards and sideways to the mic and launched moodily into, "Well'a Bless my soul what'sa wrong with me, I'm itchin' like a man in a fuzzy tree..." The whole family sat in awe as the crowd responded to the young boy giving it his all in front of them. The band was spot on, or he was spot on, nobody knew, but whatever it was, they were completely in time with each other and Gary's voice was rich and full. No one could say it was an Elvis impression, it was something more.

By the end of it the crowd were on their feet clapping along with him and as he came to his last word he flung the mic and his leg out sideways in the way his hero Elvis would have done and dropped his head onto his chest, they erupted into applause and it was only then that Gary snapped back into reality and a huge grin spread across his face and he took a bow. Sam walked onto the stage and took the mic from the boy's hand as he stared transfixed at the audience in disbelief.

"Well, ladies and gentlemen, boys and girls...Mr Gary Handley!! a star in the making I think," He didn't need to ask for another round of applause. The audience carried on clapping as he loped to the side of the stage, the audience only then started to realise he was disabled and the applause renewed once again.

Sam guided him off the stage and told him to wait in the wings until he came for him. The band started up to fill the gap whilst the judges made their decision.

Meanwhile in the stalls the rest of his family burst into chatter as the emotion released at their brother's success.

"Oh my goodness, he was fabulous," said Dene to Lynne who responded in kind. Maureen and Graham were beaming with pride and Rene juggled the baby as she leaned into her mother with an excited "He's so good mum!" Edward sat quietly, he was too emotional to speak. To have seen his boy so close to death and now stood proud as punch on stage brought him near to tears of pride. That combined with thanks for whatever strength had been sent his boy to overcome his trauma and push on with his life.

"We have a special guest tonight to present the prizes tonight. Would you give a big Butlin's welcome to the big man himself Mr Billy Butlin!"

The audience leapt into applause. Billy Butlin was a big name and a big reputation. His genius had been spotting what people wanted and providing it for them. It had amassed himself a fortune since 1936 when he opened the first holiday camp. Even during the War he had fallen on his feet when he accommodated soldiers in them as training camps and then negotiated with the military to build another three over the duration of the war. At the end he negotiated to buy them back and his coup was complete.

People, eager to put the deprivation of the war behind them had flocked to the camps and Billy, who in fact was an old fairground man donning his larger than life entrepreneur mask, had excelled.

Butlins catered to over sixty thousand campers at its height and when he arrived at the camps with his entourage looking like a smooth gangster and his mob, he would terrify all the staff. Butlin had eyes like a hawk and he would have his network of spies checking undercover for anyone fiddling. As soon as they were found, they were out. He was just that hard. He was also a ladies man and his reputation in that area went before him also. His private life was a mess but to see him stride across the stage, very few of his audience would have thought he was anything other than his public persona.

He took the mic from the redcoat and launched into banter with the audience. Calling all the acts back onto the stage and congratulating them all on their various performances. The redcoat brought out the envelope and handed it over. It was the moment Gary realised that he desperately needed to win and minutes later, win he had as Billy announced "I think we have an undoubted winner here, our very own Elvis... GARY HANDLEY !"

Soon after Gary found himself clutching his prize of twenty pounds, which to him was a fortune. May and the family were on their feet with the crowd when it was announced and the younger ones were beside themselves with glee. Their brother had actually won and they raced backstage to greet him as he came off.

Gary was not alone, for when May came to collect him she found him talking animatedly with Billy Butlin himself. May walked over and Gary, overcome, flung himself into his mother's arms with a shout, "Mum! I won, I won!"

"You certainly did love." May looked at Billy Butlin. He was smiling broadly, but still a little scary to May and she found herself a little shy and subdued in his presence.

"You have a very talented lad here, Mrs Handley, I believe he's rallied from a very bad injury. I used to be a stretcher-bearer in the First World War and I saw some similar injuries and he's done very well to recover as he has."

"Yes he has," said May. "We're all very proud of him." She shook his outstretched hand and he shook hers firmly. He wasn't the biggest of men but she felt in awe of his large persona.

"I would like to have one of my team contact you Mrs Handley, I think we might be able to give this young man a leg up, so to speak. I think he deserves a chance to show what he can do. Would you be up for it?"

May cringed at his choice of words, but then saw the funny side. Gary's mouth had dropped open and was eagerly looking to his mum with every inch of pleading in his eyes.

"I would have to speak to my husband," was all she could think to say. He smiled and gave her a card.

"You do that, then give my office a call and ask for this man, he'll take it from there."

Before she knew it he had clasped Gary's hand followed by her own and was gone, followed swiftly by the several suits hovering nearby.

"Well done kid!" said Sam the redcoat. "Now go and enjoy the glory."

May and Gary made for the stage door amongst the hubbub of people and came out to where the family was waiting. He was surrounded by congratulations and it left him wondering which way to turn first. It was all happy banter.

"I met Billy Butlin after," he said to his dad.

"And what did he say son?" said Edward beaming.

"He gave mam his card, didn't he Mam?"

"He did." May looked at Edward, who looked puzzled.

"Why?" he asked.

May thought for a second or two and then she answered.

"I think he says he's going to promote him." May's eyes reflected her bemusement with recent occurrences. It was all too much, so she just raised her hands at a loss for words. Placing the card in her handbag, she decided it could wait. They were on holiday after all!

The rest of the week the family basked in their success and got lots of congratulations from other holidaymakers. Gary in particular got lots of attention, some good, some remarking on his talent despite his disability, which May gave short shrift to. By the end of the week the whole family had enjoyed themselves, but were ready for home.

Chapter Twenty Five

Dene couldn't wait to be home and the sun had hardly raised before she was out of the door on the first day back to make a phone call to the Manchester Evening News. Despite her natural nervousness she managed to charm the editor into publicising the coincidence of her new title and her business name. Two days later the photographers came to Rene's shop and Dene was posed in her sash against a very pink backdrop of her latest designs. Being attractive and in fashion was evidently a bonus for publicity purposes and she was in print by the following week, just a little disappointed that the picture was in black and white. Dennis said he liked the black and white, it was arty, so she was appeased.

The story was picked up by Vogue magazine and before Dene could gather her thoughts, she was invited down to London for a small photographic article. It was a daunting adventure for an inexperienced designer.

As Dennis had been very supportive, using his photography hobby, which he was passionate about, to produce a professional portfolio for her, she asked him to accompany her. He often posed her for shots and his presence made her feel comfortable. Whilst the upmarket photographers turned her this way and that, setting up for new shots as she changed outfits and hair, he smiled and nodded approval and gave her the thumbs up.

His portfolio was a hit with the Vogue people, which brought a smile to both their faces and Dennis came back from London equally as pleased as Dene and with a new glint of creativity in his eye.

A month later the orders were coming in thick and fast and Dene and Dennis found themselves invited to various upmarket events. Dene was very grateful that her boyfriend had been raised in a wealthy family and took the socialising quietly in his stride. His manners were impeccable and even though shy, he was articulate and friendly, which did them no end of good. Where she faltered he stepped in. His handsome bone structure and thick black hair gave him an air of sophistication. Even his thick black glasses gave him a style of his own.

Dene had been overwhelmed at first, but success has a way of bolstering the confidence and it wasn't long before she was holding her own without support. Dennis stepped back then, but his time moving in fashion circles, though brief, had inspired him and he had invested in more photographic equipment. With a small loan from his mother he set up a studio in Manchester, gave in his notice at the shoe shop and suggested that Dene moved her admin and production to share the same building. It would make her operation appear bigger, having her own 'in house' photographer. He, in turn, would benefit from the proximity to her.

She pondered on this for a few days before ambition kicked in and she took the decision to move. Keeping the barn workshop at home and the girls there working on small accessories appeased her mother, who would not have been happy if she had laid off local staff. Besides, she trusted these girls and until she had a staff established in Manchester that she was at ease with, she would leave it be and keep them as back up. Right now she knew that she would have to step up and upscale her operations to meet demand. Getting the right staff was always a risk for a new entrepreneur and she wasn't the most confident when it came to being an employer. Dennis stepped in once more and she had him manage the workroom staff and accounts, which brought him a wage and also allowed him time to concentrate on his own bookings which he diarised around the other duties.

The women they employed were less likely to challenge Dennis and allowed Dene to work in the design and manufacture freely, without having to get into wrangles with the staff over discipline. She in turn allowed them to think he was a partner. Life was much simpler that way. She was then free to take her samples out to the buyers and shop for her own materials. She employed three more women on a part-time basis; preferring to use young mothers as they had more to lose if they lost the job and were more likely to be reliable. Older women, she felt may sense her inexperience and dictate to her and that was something she didn't want happening.

She spent every Friday in the home workshop, working on designs and decoration and two days setting up any work for the week in the Manchester rooms. Dennis handled the other days whilst Dene went shopping and visited prospective buyers. It was a wonderful way to make a living and now the business was coming in steadily, she had a healthy bank balance. Whilst she dressed simply for working at home, she would step off the train at Victoria every Tuesday morning and turn heads as she strode confidently out across Piccadilly Gardens.

Dennis had got himself a flat in the same building as his studio as his own business was taking off on the portraiture side. They had little time to develop their romance. It was easy working alongside each other and life was pleasant. Dennis was very respectful and beyond a few exploring kisses, he had restrained himself. Dene still couldn't help but wonder if there should be something more, but having led a sheltered life in an old fashioned values family atmosphere, she knew not what 'more' was.

Dene was working frantically towards her first fashion show and for this she had chosen to use the Midland Hotel in the heart of Manchester. Following that, she was investigating the possibility of transferring the show to London. She had held back on this until now, choosing to assess the results of the first show before risking scorn and failure by heading for the capital unprepared.

She and Dennis had gone to London to recce the various venues. The aim was to keep it small and select, with an invited audience of buyers. They spent a pleasant day strolling between various venues and finally went for lunch at the Ritz as a treat. The atmosphere inside was elegance itself and Dene stared about her, absorbing the luxury of it all.

Dennis only had eyes for Dene as she sat there in a tweed linen suit in pale pink with a short tailored jacket and slim-line pencil skirt. She had topped it with a little pill box hat cocked to one side of her head. Her dark hair, sleek and elegant in a French pleat, with a little fringe peeping from under the brim was a perfect foil for her delicate face. Who would have thought the young woman sat here used to sleep with her sister in a bed piled with coats to keep the cold off in winter. She looked totally at home in this environment and Dennis was in awe of her.

They had just sat with a pot of tea to relax after the meal, when Dennis, looking nervously about him, suddenly got to his knees before her and produced a ring from his pocket with a small diamond.

"Dene," he said...,"I've been wanting to do this for some time, but it never seemed the right moment, but today, here, it seems right. Will you marry me?"

There was a moment of stunned silence whilst Dene took in what had been said and Dennis began to look uncomfortable on his knees. Her eyes had opened wide with shock as she truly had not seen this coming. For a moment she hesitated, not knowing why, but then her natural desire for romance kicked in and she reached for his hand. She smiled widely and gave him her answer, aware they were drawing the attention of the other diners, despite their secluded table.

"Yes, I will Dennis, I'd be honoured."

The relief was evident on his face and as he got to his feet and bent downwards to plant a kiss on her outstretched hand as he placed the ring on her finger. Conscious of the onlookers Dennis pulled her to her feet.

"Let's get out of here and have a walk down the Mall to Buckingham Palace." He placed some money on the plate the waiter had left earlier and they linked arms as they walked through the restaurant. The young beautiful woman and smart young man, with all their lives ahead of them to dream of.

Chapter Twenty Six - January 1952

Christmas had somehow come and gone that year and no one seemed to care as they all had their own particular projects to work on.

Young Gary had started his voice coaching in Manchester the year before and was signed to an agent that Billy Butlin had put him in touch with. May wasn't sure she liked the guy as all agents were pushy, weren't they? Nevertheless he soon had a couple of 'practice gigs' at small clubs lined up for him with a small combo to accompany him. Gary seemed to grow up overnight and, armed with his new stage suit that Dene had designed and made especially for him, he was was ready to go.

Stood still you would never have known he was missing a leg. His thick straight black hair was styled in a quiff and he looked quite the moody young singer. Dennis had treated him to a pair of new leather shoes discounted from his old shop and they adapted the shoe to fit on his new leg.

The only thing he insisted on was a venue with curtains so that he could set up behind with the band and no one would know of his disability until he had finished his slot and made his escape as unnoticed as he could. He wanted the response to be honest and not tinged with sympathy and so it was.. no curtains.. no booking.

Very soon he had gathered his confidence and standing on stage was as natural as breathing to him. The music was his love and it never occurred to him for a minute that there was any better out there for him. He had just received the news that Butlin's wanted him on a regular slot for the summer and so he had asked if it was alright to bring his mother for each of the weekend slots so May would get to live the high life for the few shorts weeks of his engagement. She was thrilled, not only for her boy's success but the escape from the mundane that it would bring.

Arthur would take them in his car whenever possible to the local bookings and seemed perfectly at ease in all the clubs that they visited, often knowing the owners. It seemed only natural that he became his minder and driver the majority of the time. May and Edward would sometimes go to watch him proudly from the audience and it did them both good to escape from the norm of work and bed that waited for them at home.

They eventually got used to the fact it was now his work, albeit the glamorous variety, and they allowed him to go on his own, with just his older brother and the band for company. Arthur was to be commended for his loyalty to his young brother, he had really stepped up since Gary's tragic accident.

Dennis had decided after the engagement that he and Dene would wait a couple of years to marry and planned for June 1953. To May it had seemed an awful long time for a young couple in love to wait, but they were in modern times now and careers seemed to take priority over home and family. Both Dennis and Dene were forging ahead in their respective careers, so much so that Dene had brought in a manager for the business to replace Dennis and allow him freedom to pursue his own work more intensely.

Often times they would go three of four days without setting eyes on each other as now Dennis was making a name for himself and travelling back and forth to London for contracts, his clientele being mainly in the fashion and accessory markets. Meanwhile Dene was working flat out on new lines for the new stores springing up everywhere in the post-war boom.

It was handy having Dennis working in the area he did, because a peek at his pictures as they dried gave her advance insight into the forthcoming trends from the big designers and she would often tweak her own designs to keep ahead of the local competition without telling him.

They endeavoured as much as possible to keep the weekends free for each other and all seemed well. Both were moving quietly upmarket, and whilst she was no Dior, she was getting a name in the industry for her medium price range, high quality design, which was perfectly placed for selling to the city based department stores. 'Pink Lady' was a name fast becoming well known and respected by its middle class customers. Dene produced, Dennis photographed and the catalogues went out in advance to all the major retailers for the next season and the orders came in before they had a chance to breath.

The business needed all the staff she had and now more. Selling was not a problem, but keeping up with demand was her greatest headache. She had brought Maureen in to man the phones and train as an invoice clerk and receptionist. It was not what Maureen had hoped for, but it was a start and she liked the fact that now she was working in a posh job in Manchester in her sister's company.

They were never short of new clothes as there was always spare material to be had and Maureen used to sit in her lunch break and work on a new blouse or skirt for herself out of left over materials that Dene would let her have. She had the same build as Gary, her twin, rounded and shorter in stature than her older sisters. It frustrated her that she couldn't seem to buy anything off the peg and so she had learned to serve herself with pleasing results. They weren't of quite the same quality as Dene's designs but they worked well enough on her and she was happy with her efforts.

She much preferred sitting at the reception desk by the window that looked down over Manchester's busy streets. The duties she had were much better than her previous job in the mill. She was gaining more knowledge by the day of running a business and handled the reception duties with confidence and capability, which, for her sister, was a pleasant surprise, as she was only used to the tomboy side of her.

After a few weeks, Maureen started to venture out in her break to the library and loved to devour romantic novels, each week taking a couple home to read before bed.

On the cold days of early spring she would often sit in the beautiful round library near St Anne's square only a couple of minutes walk from her office. There she would read for half an hour before returning to the workshop with her chosen books. She liked the quiet there, as opposed to the background clack of the women and machine in work. It was her escape and truth be known, warmer than her office. The boilers in the building that housed the business chose when they wanted to operate and heat was spasmodic. Chilblains weren't.

Manchester was not known for its tropical climate and so you needed to be hardy most of the time. The main library had a coal fire on a large wall that gave the rounded walls of the building a cosy atmosphere. Eventually, she tired of the romances and instead she would leaf through something a little more substantial. It was good for her as she gained a little knowledge of many things because of her proximity to this building and its contents and was surprising her family with her ability to discuss a variety of subjects with intelligence.

When she returned to work this particular day, Dene was accepting a delivery of rolls of the new materials and as she rolled out the different exquisite colours and textures across the worktable, the girls oohed and ah'd their approval. This next range was going to be something.

Maureen sat herself back at her desk and started to wade through the various receipts that had arrived with the goods and enter them in the ledgers for payment. She had another order ledger with individual pages for each customer and it seemed they were very quickly running out of pages to accommodate demand, which was good. Maureen liked a tidy desk, which was strange, because at home she was always being sent to her room to rediscover her bed amongst the chaos. Her sisters had permanently complained about her untidiness, yet here it seemed so natural to keep order here. Something which Dene had noticed and was thankful for.

Dene had to admit that she was really pleased now that she had bowed to pressure from her mother to give her young sister the chance, she really had stepped up. The most amusing thing was listening to her normally boisterous and talkative sister answer the phone. If Rene, her eldest sister was labelled 'the Duchess', Maureen was most definitely 'The Queen'.

She had been listening to too much radio and the twee way of speaking had rubbed off and was becoming the norm with the impressionable young girl, who had adopted that type of speech. Still, thought Dene, better than the broad northern manner of Lynne who would die rather than put on airs and graces, no, Maureen was doing just fine and they needed someone who sounded a little upmarket on the telephone anyway.

The girl had decided she would better herself and that was a good thing. No one would hold Maureen back if she chose a certain path. In that respect, nearly all of them, with the exception of Graham, had that level of determination. More so than Dene herself, who had to consider that her own confidence had had to be built rather than being something that was naturally within her. Where she quaked in her elegant stilettos at the prospect of any new challenge, Maureen seemed to relish it. For someone so young she was fast becoming an asset to the business. Any monies outstanding were soon rounded up and the cash flow was at healthy pace. 'Better in our bank than theirs,' was Maureen's motto.

Chapter Twenty Seven - February 1953

Soon, between them, Dennis and Dene had a healthy savings pot and nearer to the wedding date, started to look for a home. Dennis had wanted to buy closer Manchester, but Dene had insisted on staying close to home as she knew she might need her mother if and when babies arrived.

Reluctantly they agreed a compromise and put a deposit down on a new bungalow down the hill on a new development. Dennis liked minimalist and so the style suited him, Dene preferred older but as she had got her way on the siting of the house she bowed to his need for something modern.

Dennis moved in, vacated his flat in Manchester and took up residence in the new house to save money and to start to decorate, what was in effect a blank canvas, to their taste. Dene chose the drapes, as she had the eye for material, but Dennis set the design standard by insisting he be allowed to choose the wallcoverings and general decor. His taste was very dramatic and modern and whilst Dene would not have readily gone for that choice, she had to admit that the effect was dramatic and stylish. Combined with her sumptuous drapes, handmade in the studio and the minimalist pieces of furniture in grey and black bouclé, they had a home to be envied. They spent most of their spare time shopping and adding small touches and Dene would only go home about 9pm to fall into bed for propriety's sake, preferring the clean and spacious house she had now become accustomed to.

For Dene, the kitchen, fitted with the latest white formica units and an under counter twin tub, which could be pulled out and connected to the sink to fill and drain, was a dream come true. The family had been invited round when everything had been finished for a 'house warming' party, which apparently was the new thing and planned for the Sunday. Dene clucked all Saturday making sure everything was perfect. She wanted her mum and dad to be proud of all she had achieved.

On Sunday morning Rene came down to help her prepare and Dennis had gone out to buy drinks in the small Grey Morris Minor car he had bought. The family were expected at one and the two women set to work on the meal. Dene had given Rene the tour of the house and received glowing approval of their choices and after discussing business first, as was the norm for the two sisters, the talk turned to home and family.

"Have you heard what's happened with Gary?" questioned Rene.

"No. What?"

"He only came home and told mum he's got a TV slot!"

"You're kidding? That's amazing!"

"I know, just hope it doesn't go to his head. He's larger than life as it is!"

They laughed at the thought of their young brother, who, for all his challenges, had no shortage of confidence for a seventeen year old. How the couple of years since the accident had flown, but still the thought sent cold chills through them. 'Happier times now, thank God,' thought Dene.

"Arthur says he's having to fight the girls off him as it is," she said.

Rene sneered, "Arthur will be making sure he get his fair share of the pickings, if I know him". Time had obviously not softened Rene's opinion of her brother. Dene grimaced and the women worked on for a while in companionable silence.

"How's Paul doing at infant school?" asked Dene.

"Very well, he's enjoying it," Rene smiled, but something was missing behind the eyes. Dene knew her sister well and something was wrong.

"Any sign of another brother or sister?" At the question Rene fell silent for a minute and when she spoke at last, she chose her words carefully.

"Not the right time with all that's required of me at the moment". Dene noted that Rene had become subdued and waited for her sister to continue. After a moment's pause, she turned to her sister and her eyes held a great sadness that she wouldn't normally have shown to anyone else.

"He's playing away Dene." Rene bowed her head trying to control her emotions. Dene stopped stirring the pan and turned to her sister aghast.

"Rene! That is terrible, what are you going to do?"
"I'm going to stick it out till I've protected my business and saved some money and then I'm going to divorce him..."

Dene couldn't believe her ears, divorce was a shameful thing, even in the more modern times since the war. Her mum would go mad and it didn't bear thinking about.

Rene wiped a rogue tear aside with her fingers and straightened her apron to compose herself. "I've known for a while. He's always been a braggart. I used to find it attractive, but now I just despise him. He's not coming today. He's going to drop Paul off and make an excuse. I don't want him here."

Dene turned the cooker down and reached for her sister's hands. "Oh Rene, I'm so sorry, I don't know what to say, what can I do?" Rene's eyes welled once more and she squeezed Dene's hands.

"Say nothing please, promise me... I don't want anyone knowing yet. I don't want him profiting off my hard work if we split now, but I needed to tell someone, I'm so sorry to burden you."

Dene gathered her older sister close. "It's OK Rene, just talk to me, but maybe talk to dad when you know what you are going to do, he'll help you sort it." They hugged silently as Rene allowed herself to weep for just a moment and then she pushed herself from her sister's embrace, fumbling for a hanky in her pocket. It was already limp from many tears and Dene could have kicked herself that she had been so full of her own achievements that she had missed her sister's obvious pain.

"Anyway, enough for now, today's your day, let's crack on". Rene was a strong woman, but it took a few minutes for her to gain self-control once more and Dene let her work silently as she knew Dennis would be back soon. She would be embarrassed at being discovered weeping. It was not her style.

By the time Dennis pushed through the door with a box of ale and ginger beer, a strange normality had resumed. The day seemed less bright somehow and as the family arrived in dribs and drabs, both women pinned on a false smile and greeted them warmly. No one noticed, not even Dennis.

Graham came in shyly and perched himself uncomfortably on the low window ledge. He had the slight but gangly frame of the teenager he now was. The grandeur of this house made him ill at ease, but he was really proud of his big sister and had a special fondness for her above the others. Probably born of the fact that she had always been shy like him. He liked that she had made a success of herself despite that. Maybe there would be hope for him too. Lynne arrived next and piled in with Derek and a box of ale, heading straight for the kitchen to inspect all the mod cons she'd heard tell of.

"Ooh, look at you with all these fancy fine things!" It was spoken as a compliment, but as usual Lynne accompanied it with her famous bad smell sneer which her dad had laughingly referred to once as her 'resting bitch face' as though she was of the opinion that Dene had got too much of a shilling on herself. Lynne had no reason to be jealous as she had just made staff nurse and was doing really well in her nursing career. It was just her way.

Gary and Arthur were on their way back from a Saturday gig down south and had said they would call in if they got back in time and to save them a plate each.

Maureen arrived with May and Edward, and, as predicted Stan knocked on the door and just pushed Paul hastily through to Dene, saying he'd been called to the factory on an emergency repair and would she accept his apologies?

Dene nodded and smiled trying to remain friendly as Rene's warning, "Remember, not a word to anyone, especially Stan," was still ringing in her ears. She took the boy from his arms and did her best to look like she had accepted his excuse. He would just think she was annoyed at food wasted if he sensed something. When she returned in with her nephew Paul, he was immediately seized by his doting Grandma and Grandad, breaking the awkward explanation from Dene regarding his father's absence and no further questions were asked.

For most of the meal there was laughter, with enough good news going round the table to draw attention away from Rene's strained face. Just as the room hit a lull there was a knock at the door and in came Gary and Arthur, travel weary but full of tales to refresh the energy. Gary's TV slot was on a small talent show, but it was a start.

More beers were opened and passed around and Dene found herself getting giddy as the alcohol hit her system. It always had a transformative effect on her and her shyness dissipated, leaving a fun loving, joke telling comedienne in its place.

Just as Dennis was thinking what a successful job they'd done of entertaining and Dene had got up to make a pot of tea Lynne grabbed a tea spoon and tinkled it on her beer bottle, nudging Derek who had flushed, his fair skin and red hair doing nothing to hide his embarrassment.

"Go on...," Lynne nudged him and Derek looked terrified.

"Oh for goodness sake, I'll do it!... Listen up everybody, we have some news. Me and Derek... well we got wed yesterday!"

The room fell silent apart from Arthur snorting into his beer in surprise and amusement. All eyes went to the couple in the centre of the group and then to May whose features had turned to stone. She looked in silence at Edward first and then back to the young couple. Lynne's bravado was starting to wear off and she coloured also.

"Well we didn't want a fuss and we decided we'd rather put the money to a house deposit... so that's what we did," she blustered.

"...and what about respect for your family and your dad, did you stop to think about that?" questioned May, with a voice that rendered the room more silent than it already had become. They clearly hadn't and Derek and Lynne had the grace to look ashamed. Edward rose quietly.

"Would you mind if Derek and I used your dining room for a while Dennis?" Derek coloured more so and Dennis swallowed nervously and nodded his agreement. Somehow, in a few short seconds, his party had turned into something else and he looked at Lynne in annoyance for dropping this on them so inappropriately.

Dennis had a great regard and respect for Rene, but somehow he just couldn't warm to Lynne. It was not that she was unlikeable, because she had a kind heart equal to her forceful nature. It was just the erratic and loud behaviour that unnerved him. Thankfully, Dene exhibited none of this and he felt comforted by the thought that he had got the better deal.

"Why don't we go in the kitchen Dene and give Paul and Graham a ginger beer and some more cake and let your mum and Lynne have a talk?" His instruction was pointed and so the younger ones were conducted to the safety of the kitchen before May, who looked about to explode, lit the touch paper.

In comparison to the quiet coming from the dining room, the lounge was a cacophony of raised voices. Dennis sat the teenage boy and the tot down at the kitchen table and gave them pencils and paper for Graham to amuse Paul, It was a nice thought, but Graham still wasn't good with his writing and drawing skills and although he stoically tried to entertain the young child, all the time he had a nervous eye on the living room door. Dene started to wash the dishes and Dennis joined her.

"Might as well..," she whispered annoyed, "Party's ruined as usual, by Lillian of course!" she gave her proper name, knowing Lynne hated it, such was her feelings towards her sister at that moment. The argument had died down and a strained silence came from the living room as the dining room door opened and Edward led Derek into the living room once more.

"Get your coat May." May's eyes flew open in shock and the look she gave Edward was a question. Edward continued.

"Derek and Lynne are going to show us the new house they have rented in Milnrow and then we shall see what's what, apologies Dennis." His voice brooked no argument and five minutes later they were gone, leaving the rest to sit in stunned silence as the door closed behind the parents and a very subdued couple who followed them out. The remaining family looked at each other stunned as Dennis came through with a tray from the kitchen.

"More tea anyone?" he asked, trying his best to salvage the situation.

Chapter Twenty Eight – June 1953

Dene and Dennis's wedding day dawned bright and sunny and they had agreed that she would get ready at the bungalow, as it gave her and the bridesmaids more space and facilities. Dennis had been offered to stay at Rene's the night before and had happily agreed, still oblivious to the undercurrents going on there.

The bridal preparations were filled with laughter and teasing and Dene was happy, but very nervous. She sat in her pin curls in front of the dressing table whilst Rene applied her make-up, which was minimal. The dress, of her own design, hung on the door, a mass of cotton lace with a high pointed collar neck and full skirt that was very en vogue for the time. A simple lace and flower tiara sat in front of her and it seemed to emphasise her innocence. She had recently acquired a very experienced tailoress and the benefits were evident.

May had gone to round up Maureen and Lynne in the other bedroom. Lynne by now, was heavily pregnant, having conceived immediately had been excused bridesmaid duty, much to her relief. May asked her to make them all a light brunch. There would be no fainting on the bride's part if she could help it, although with the pallor of Dene's face, it would take more than toasted cheese to avert it. Back in the bedroom, Dene looked at Rene nervously.

"Rene, can I ask you something?"

"Course you can, fire away." Rene braced herself, she wasn't sure she could give an unbiased answer on the subject of wedded bliss right at this moment, but her sister was clearly fretting on something.

"Will it hurt? When we, you know..." Rene paused in the make-up application. This was a turn up thought Rene. They had been going out nearly three years, wasn't it?

"You mean you haven't actually done it?"

"No! I didn't want to get pregnant," Rene smiled. Her sister really was naive for all her business acumen and look of sophistication. She obviously hadn't discovered jonnies.

"What have you done then?" Dene flushed and looked down.

"Just kissing and stuff..."

"Have you ever got naked with him?" Dene's eyes flew open in shock at the forthright question.

"No! It wouldn't be right..and besides, Dennis has always been a gentleman."

Rene stood behind her sister and viewed her lovely frightened face through the mirror and smiled. Mum deserved a kick up the backside for her reticence to talk to her children about sex. She couldn't believe her sister had gone three years without getting past first base and what concerned her more was that Dennis hadn't tried. Although in retrospect, maybe that made him a better man than Stan, who she'd continuously fought off all through their courtship... and who now couldn't keep it in his pants.

"It will be fine. Have a couple of drinks an hour before you're due to leave the reception and it will relax you. Just let things happen naturally. It's tight when he puts himself inside of you for the first time but it's soon ok and you will enjoy it, so stop worrying.... You love him don't you?"

"Oh yes, he's a lovely man"

"Then enjoy your day and stop worrying!" She kissed her sister on top of the head. "Come on, put your dressing gown on and let's see what mum has made us." Dene smiled, but it was clear she was far from comforted.

The car and her dad arrived and there was a moment when Edward teared up at the sight of his beautiful daughter, resplendent in her lace gown and he held her hands with pride and pulled her close gently, fearful he would damage something on her gown or make-up.

"You look beautiful love... beautiful!"

"Thanks Dad". His proximity comforted her and whilst her own emotions welled, her tension eased and she started to feel the first excitement of this being her big day.

They had hired a car to make the journey to the church a big occasion and as she alighted the large black Austin at Ogden Chapel, her eyes sparkled and she looked as any other radiant bride. Edward thought his daughter looked the youngest he had seen her look for some time. The veil softened her face and all he saw was her large blue eyes and smile as she took his hand. Gone was the smartly dressed business woman he had become accustomed to and in her place a twenty three year old girl. Wide eyed and trembling in all her finery and still his child for a few more precious moments. He started to feel really old for the first time in his life.

"Alright, love?" His voice was gruff with emotion.

"I'm fine, Dad." she replied.

"Off we go then." He led her to the chapel gate where Maureen and another young cousin were waiting in their bridesmaids gowns.

Inside the church there was a low hum of conversation and the congregation was almost filling the church with family and wedding watchers. There wasn't much to do at the weekend for the women of the village and so a good wedding was always an occasion. It had filled the wooden pews to bursting in the charming old chapel and there was an air of expectation. Dene was of interest to any young woman in the area and they were all waiting to see what the up and coming fashion designer would be wearing.

Rene stood outside holding her son's hand. He was to be the page boy and she smiled at the approach of her sister, putting aside her own troubles for the moment. Rene hugged her to her, gave her last instructions to the young boy, adjusted Dene's veil and left them to take her place with the family inside.

As Dene stepped through the door she breathed in the old smell of the beautiful little chapel. The golden organ pipes struck up and she caught the sight of the beams of sunlight, coloured by the stained glass dancing off them. Little particles of dust kicked up by the congregation sparkled in the air as the sun warmed the church. It created a feeling that someone had sprinkled fairy dust. Her marriage would be blessed, she felt it in her bones.

Taking her first few steps down the aisle towards, she held tight to her father's arm. Dennis turned nervously and seeing her, he smiled before turning back to face the altar. Today was a good day, one to be remembered.

The wedding went smoothly and the sun shined its brightest for them all. Dene drank a couple of whiskies with a grimace at her sister's instructions and half an hour later she was vivacious and laughing all the way to the car and half the way home to the new bungalow, where she was suddenly overcome with shyness once more.

Dennis, true to tradition, carried her over the threshold and set her down gently in the hallway, equally shy. You would never have known they had been together as long as they had.

"Shall we have a cup of tea?" he asked.

"Yes, let's." She was thankful of the distraction.

"Do you want to use the bathroom first and I'll bring it to bed for you?"

Something in Dene saddened. Had she expected to be swept off her feet and taken to bed in some grand passion? She had hoped so. She should have known Dennis's caring nature would be considerate, but a small part of her wished he hadn't. As she changed into her nightwear she suddenly felt the urge to cry… was this natural? She didn't know. When Dennis finally came in he was wearing pyjamas and looked equally nervous.

"Shall I turn off the light?" he asked.

"Yes, do." It felt less exposed that way. She felt her new husband climb into bed and as her eyes grew accustomed to the dark, she saw his outline as he turned towards her to pull her close and kiss her tenderly.

"I do love you so much Dene," were his whispered words.

"I love you too Dennis," she responded.

As he drew her to him more intimately, it felt staged and clumsy and neither were at ease. Hopefully they would get better with practice she thought. There was some kissing and she tensed as his hand slid up her nightdress and his leg came across her, followed by a very brief lovemaking as nerves and excitement got the better of them.

Afterwards, he held her to him and they lay in silence, neither sure of what to say, so they remained quiet and Dene stared at the ceiling lit only by the cracks of moonlight filtering through her new drapes. She loved Dennis, he was a good man, but had she been blinkered and foolish? Wasn't it supposed to be like the movies...like in 'From here to Eternity?'

Dennis had whispered goodnight and appeared to have succumbed to sleep quickly. In reality, he was equally at a loss and wondering whether he should try to do more. Sensing his thoughts, Dene closed her eyes in the hope that it would feel better and more romantic next time. After all, it was their first time. Rene had been right, it didn't really hurt, but shouldn't she have felt better? Shouldn't there be something more than this anti-climax?

Dennis wasn't sleeping, he was feeling her disappointment and whilst he hadn't done anything particularly wrong, he felt he hadn't done anything particularly right. They both eventually slept with the identical thoughts of whether they were the ideally suited couple they had previously thought themselves.

Chapter Twenty- Nine 1957

Edward was stabling the horses with Graham as May appeared in the stable door impatiently. The sun was dipping and Edward was appreciative of the fine autumn day they had had, but the nights were drawing in and it would be cold later and he needed the animals in before dark. His chest wasn't good nowadays and he was always glad of the sunshine, the evening chill he avoided.

Graham was seventeen now and a great help, as he had an affinity with the animals and was never slow to do chores that involved working alongside them. The boy was still painfully shy until he took on the care of some sick animal and he would talk to it like a long lost friend. The animals usually responded well, as if knowing that in Graham's company they would be safe and cared for. He took after his father in that way.

Edward had been diagnosed with emphysema, a result of gassing in the war and the trauma of the cart crushing his chest in earlier years and so he was glad of his boy's enthusiasm. It took a load off.

When it came to striking up a conversation with a human, Graham struggled and often directed the conversation via whatever animal was present at the time. Those that knew him accepted it as his way. Those that didn't found it strange. Graham was really only comfortable in the embrace of his family and especially that of his mother, who knowing him to be her last-born, molly-coddled him, probably at the detriment of his need to become independent.

"Come on you two. We've only an hour to get ready and down there and I'm not missing it!" she shouted into the barn and stood, hands on hips until they showed signs of finishing.

Tonight they were all going to Dene and Dennis's as they had the biggest telly. Gary, who's career had been going from strength to strength, but with only a smattering of TV, had just received the biggest break likely in his entire life. Billy Butlin himself, through some manoeuvring on behalf of his protégé and the timely illness of a singer scheduled to perform that week, had played a blinder and Gary had rushed him down to London to make his debut appearance on Sunday Night at The London Palladium.

Around here, it didn't get any more famous than that! The haste of the booking hadn't given the family time to plan a trip themselves and so the television was the only chance to take part in his glory. The village was awash with the gossip about the boy from the poor family up the hill making it big. In truth, May had made a point of telling everyone she could, such was her pride and it would be a recluse who hadn't heard by now.

Gary had been touring the Butlin's sites at the time when Billy's entertainment officer had tracked him down. The first call he made was to Rene to pass the message on and to summon Arthur to go pick him up and get him down to London pronto. He would need a minder there. Arthur had packed two of his best suits and was on his way before May had a chance to gather herself and she had been so upset at the thought that she would not be present for his big moment.

A nervous Gary was thrown in the deep end of rehearsals on arrival and Arthur was pointedly told to make himself scarce. His services wouldn't be required backstage till later. It was obvious they were in the big league here and for the first time Arthur felt out of his depth and spoken down to by, 'these pompous bastards with a plum in their mouths,' as he put it none too diplomatically. Unfortunately, the remark was made within the earshot of the floor manager, who at that point requested that he was escorted politely but firmly to sit in the audience for the duration.

It didn't sit well with him. In Manchester he was something in the circles he moved in. Sometimes feared, but it was not something he shared with his family. In fact, he kept his own counsel on the subject of family. Manchester life was Manchester life and family was something he did not want to include in that. It made a person vulnerable. So Arthur, for all intents and purposes, once off the hill and into Salford, was a loner, with no family ties to anyone but his closest colleagues. He was a drinking buddy of Dougie Flood, a clubland bouncer, who had told him to separate his life totally from anything he did inside the City. Dougie was a hard man with a head on his shoulders and Arthur looked up to him.

He had married the new May quietly after his divorce from the previous May had come through, feeling he owed it to her for waiting for him all this time and whilst he took on his role of a new husband sincerely, part of him realised that the quieter of the two women and the mother of his child was more wife material. His thoughts strayed to his complicated marital circumstances and he was confused.

The current May was a party girl and whilst she adorned his arm in the pub and her fast wit made for hilarity. The same wild streak caused them many rows once the door to their home closed. She wasn't one for domesticity and children were definitely off her list. In fact, the only time they ever agreed was in bed or on the dance floor at the Ritz or one of Manchester's other clubs when the beer had been flowing and she was high on life. The fact that he still insisted on seeing his child and previous wife stuck in her throat, but Arthur refused to neglect them and in his own way was trying to make up for the unhappiness he had brought them.

The first May now had a little council house at Littleborough and a couple of times a month he would walk across the fields to take her money for the boy and spend a couple of hours with them.

At first she had been stand-offish, but took the money as she needed it, allowing him only the briefest glimpses of their son. Gradually, as he made the pilgrimage regularly, she started to soften and allowed him to take the boy to the park whilst she did her housework for a couple of hours. The third time she had a meal awaiting their return and the little boy sat babbling between them as a conversation without recriminations was attempted for the first time since he was a wee babe in arms.

She now worked part-time in a shop in the village and it brought her enough for the rent she told him, but little else. Arthur's money now filled the gap and even bought the odd luxury and whether or not she liked to admit it, his presence in their life brought them ease.

In the couple of years that had passed since their parting, she had overcome her depression and started to blossom into a fair young woman. Her house was neat and tidy and since Arthur's money had been coming in, she had started to add the odd home comfort.

Arthur saw this and inwardly kicked himself for the fool he'd been in destroying his own small family. Eventually she had become at ease with him once more and even welcoming on his visits. He had had to admit to himself that he much preferred her company and quiet humour than the sharper repartee of his current wife... still he'd made his bed and this was the best he could expect, all things considered. For once in his life Arthur restrained himself and took his fatherly duties seriously in the hope that one day May would forgive him. Hopefully, if he treated them kindly enough, she would see that he was genuinely sorry and allow him to remain close to his boy.

The band striking up brought him from his reverie and as the lights dimmed, he looked about him at the grandness of the theatre and silently whistled, 'phew, who would have thought his rumbustious younger brother would be performing on this giant stage in London to all these toffs whilst he was still in his late teens?'

Back at home, they all crowded nearer to the telly and settled just in time for the start of the programme. May sat centrally with Edward holding on to his hand in excitement. 'Their boy..on the telly!' The family pride was off the scale, not to mention the shock at the fee Gary had been told he would be receiving for his little slot.

Gary was on third, a slot for minor celebrities, but who cared? To the family, he was headlining and when the curtains went up on him they gasped as he had dancers with him and despite the fact that they could see he was clearly hanging onto the mic stand for balance, he managed to interact well with them all. The song he had chosen was another of his Elvis favourites, 'It's Now or Never', and it took some singing to do it credit.

To May, her boy was a hero but none of the family sat around the TV had reckoned on the standing ovation he would receive as he belted out the final note.

"Oh my goodness!" whispered May as her smile near split her face in two. "He's going to be a big star... our son!".

Edward placed his hand on May's and smiled. "You may just be right love. He'll have a head as big as one of your potato pies when he comes home!" She laughed, but her heart was so full she almost cried.

The whole family spent the evening on a high, Dennis was always a perfect host, but recently May had noticed he seemed a little impatient when all the family got together and she had started to feel that his quiet and polite nature was a little at odds with her, on the whole, raucous offspring.

They had grown up on these hills amongst farmers and mill workers, without the benefit of her convent education and they carried the accent and behaviour of the people they had grown up amongst, which was a far cry from the polite society Dennis had been reared in. Tonight they were on top form and Lynne and Derek had brought their tot Sharon, a sturdy little redhead with a mass of curls, and the child was a combination of her father and her Irish heritage no doubt and a live-wire to boot. Gray sat in the corner and amused her, it seemed he loved children as much as animals and they gravitated to him. Maureen was sitting at her mother's feet, full of pride for her brother and beyond excited.

The only one Dennis seemed to gel with, in a way that went above the requirements of good manners, was Rene. Probably down to her more serious nature and they were often to be found in quiet discussion whilst the others were laughing and bantering. Dene herself had been subdued in recent weeks and the thought occurred to May that something might be amiss and so she kept a quiet eye on the two of them, just in case.

This evening however was for celebration and May's doubts evaporated when Dene brought a cake through with a candle lit on it and they all turned to her wondering whose birthday they had missed. Dennis stood up to take it from her and they stood side by side.

"Just thought we'd celebrate the birth to come mum," was Dene's answer, when questioned.

"We have a baby on the way, due next June, its early days yet so we didn't want to tell the world, but Dene's not been feeling too good, so we might need some help," smiled Dennis.

"I can do more at work," answered Maureen excitedly.

"We'll all help," said Rene beaming. Her genuine pleasure as she hugged both Dennis and Dene quelled any doubts May had about Rene and Dennis becoming too friendly. Rene was rock solid and loved her sister, no, her thoughts were ridiculous. Rene was not one to be dishonourable.

Now they had a real party to have and the evening continued on until late, only interrupted by the obligatory phone call from Gary before he was rushed off to an after show party no less!

Everyone was on a high. The family celebrated at home and Gary was off with his brother to a London club at the invitation of one of the other Palladium guests. Arthur had already lined up a couple of girls from the dancers to have on their arm and as they exited the stage door to a London cab, the flashes popped and Arthur and Gary had the first taste of the life that success could bring.

Three hours later Gary was handing Arthur a cold compress for the black eye he had received for getting arsey with a punter in the club they had gone to. The younger brother's high was soon quelled with the realisation that his older brother could handle his drink and temper just about as well as he handled his women. Gary, instead of celebrating his glory, found himself picking his brother out of the gutter where the bouncers had thrown him and making their apologies for his embarrassing behaviour as he dragged him off to a cab. His leg was hurting and his brother's antics were the last thing he needed at that moment.

Gary spent the night as Arthur slept it off, worrying how he was going to tell his older brother that his services were no longer required as a driver, or as an assistant. He owed him such a lot for getting him back on his feet after the accident, but he was a loose cannon. This time Gary had been lucky, insomuch as the majority of the crew and the guests that had been with them, had made their excuses long before Arthur's alcohol limit had overridden his manners. It hadn't been the first time his brother had kicked off, and again tonight there was just no excuse.

As young as he was, Gary had already learned in the last couple of years that a shot at the big time was rare. He had his chance right now and nothing could come in its way, especially a brother who could not rein in his wild ways when it counted. No, he would have to find a way for Arthur and he to part company for the sake of his career. It was a decision that didn't sit well with the young man, but Arthur was not made for the circles he was now moving in and Gary had to admit to himself that he was ambitious enough not to want his brother damaging his chances.

The next morning May allowed herself the luxury of a lie in, which was rare. Lynne wasn't working today and she had been excused grandparent duty caring for her daughter, Sharon.

Edward had crept out early with a kiss on her forehead and left her to snuggle back down. When she finally rose, she found the parlour and kitchen fire lit to heat the little house from the autumn chill. He was a thoughtful man her husband and very dear to her.

She set to cleaning and as she paused for a moment before the living room mirror, it occurred to her that it had been a long time since she had paid attention to her looks. Her dark hair was still thick and wavy but it was more grey than dark nowadays. Where she had once been petite and buxom, she was matronly. What had happened to all those years where she had gone from a young woman to a grandmother? She and Edward would be the next ones to walk off the plank, it was a sobering thought.

Her thoughts strayed to Ireland and all her youthful dreams. The best she could expect now was to live them a little through the success of her children. What use had her education been in the end? She vowed she would start to put it to more use in future.

She hadn't read a book in months and then it had been some rubbish romance she had found by Maureen's bed. She was older, but somehow she felt that the years of motherhood and making do hadn't allowed her to develop her intellect as she would have wanted. Even her way of speaking had roughened over the years and her accent was more broad Lancashire than Irish now.

Gary would be home tomorrow and she looked forward to hearing about all his adventures. For now, she would finish her chores and have a walk down to the library in Milnrow. It would do her good and she deserved a day to herself occasionally. She might even get her hair done at the new salon on the way.

Wrapping up, she stepped outside into the crisp late October day and breathed in the scent of decaying vegetation. The leaves were gathering in golden brown piles and it would be soon time to batten down the hatches and keep the winter at bay. Here on the moors the winter ruled everything. Edward would be short of work and there would be little coming in apart from Maureen and Gary's contribution to the pot.

For the first time in decades, May had found herself visiting the bank to draw the odd pound or two from the money she had kept safe all these years. Edward himself had slowed down visibly. His cheeks looked gaunt nowadays and he was thinner. She said nothing, but she worried.

He no longer took the train to Appleby fair nowadays, preferring to stay close to home and potter around the barn polishing his horse brasses and livery. His rag and bone man round still brought him an income but people were reluctant to clear houses in winter and so there was always a seasonal decline. He was never still despite this.

It was the time of year when she got all the little repairs done around the house to appease his need for activity. Occasionally there might be a short flurry of trade when people made way for new items of furniture in time to impress visiting family for the Christmas celebrations. She certainly hoped so. If the snow hit hard this year, nothing would be moving and that was not good for anyone financially.

As she walked through the village the odd neighbour hailed her to talk about Gary's success. A couple were genuine, but village mentality encouraged gossip and not always for the right reasons and so she took the praise lightly. Knowing it was coming from a position of envy and curiosity, rather than real celebration she didn't give it much mind. Half of this lot would knife you in the back given the chance. She had long since learned that villagers were sometimes mistaken as friendly, when in reality many were just plain nosey and eager to pass on the latest gossip, malicious or otherwise. It was all the same here. You only told someone what you wanted everyone to know. There were a couple of women she knew that she thought she could trust, but on the whole she had been so consumed with bringing up her family that she hadn't really had time for friends.

Crossing behind the Bottom Bird, she took the short cut over the hill to Milnrow library. Up the cobbled lane, past St. John's Church with its tall spire that could be seen across the valley from Rochdale and down into the old village from the fields behind the park. It was a long but pleasant walk and soon she was ensconced in the library with a table full of books to peruse. She picked one to read to her grandchildren Sharon and Paul. Paul was old enough now to understand and Sharon would be happy just to listen to a story with a biscuit in her chubby hand. It would do them no harm to start learning from different books. The rest she chose carefully for the challenge of reading something more than fiction.

She borrowed several and it was only as she headed up the last leg of her mainly uphill journey home to Peppermint Bridge that she started to regret her enthusiasm. The bag of books, combined with her shopping, meant her arm was near pulling out of its socket as the weight took its toll. She had started to pant wearily, stopping every few minutes to swap the load over to the other arm.

'Mistake,' she had just began to think, as a car horn tooted loudly behind her.

Lucky for her, Arthur was driving Gary up the hill to drop him off and they pulled up to offer her a lift. Piling her shopping on the back seat she collapsed gratefully in and pulled the door closed excitedly exclaiming her pride at Gary's success. He smiled, but seemed subdued and as short as the journey was, the tension in the car wasn't lost on her, but she bided her time. Arthur was obviously anxious to be away, which heightened her suspicions even more. Gary offloaded his bag onto the kitchen table and sat down with cheeks flushed red as she passed him a mug of black tea.

"No milk, sorry, I forgot to buy some, but I gave you extra sugar. I'll get Gray to nip across to the farm later," she said.

"Thanks, mam." He kept his head down as he sipped the hot tea.

"You're welcome." She watched him in silence as she put her shopping away and then leaned against the sink picking up her own mug to drink.

"So, spill the beans, what's he done?" Her brow raised with a sarcastic arch. She loved her oldest boy but it was clear he was a right royal pain in the arse and much too old to not know better. She feared he would always bring trouble home. It was in his nature. She didn't know whether it was from hers or Edwards side, for neither of them had led anything more than a quiet family life. She could speak her mind a little too bluntly at times but she never sought out trouble. He must be a throwback somewhere along the line. Lynne had that capacity too...Fiery Irish temper, quick to rise, equally quick to subside.

Gary flushed more and he put his mug down and shook his head despondently. "I don't know what to do Mam. He's been so good to me, but he hasn't a clue how to behave. If anyone looks at him slantwise, he's ready to put up his fists. It doesn't help with that bloody glass eye cos he always looks like he's staring at someone. Mind you, he usually is!"

May had to smile at the eye reference. "I don't think he can help that, I'm blessed with sons that lose bits of themselves. But what's he done in particular this time?" She cupped his cheek affectionately to soften the joke.

"We got invited to this posh party in a club by this comedian and the producer and he only gets himself drunk, starts pawing the women and mouthing off to the blokes there. He only started a punch up with one of the producer's mates and the bouncers had to drag him off. I had to grovel to the guy to stop him having him arrested for assault. You should have heard him Mam, talking like he was the big 'I am' and some kind of gangster, it was humiliating!"

"What was the upshot?" asked May, a grim expression on her face.

"The producer took me to one side and said I'd better lose the ape before he ruined my chances, but he's my brother Mam. What can I do?"

May looked down at her son. He was clearly upset and torn between family loyalty and his own needs. She brushed a stray lock of hair that had escaped from his carefully bryl-creemed quiff.

"Get in touch with your manager and tell him you need a new, more professional driver, straight away. If they know what's best for them they'll get you one.. and leave the rest to me."

"Do you think?" Gary's tension lightened knowing he had his mum's backing. "I'm tired Mam, do you mind if I go up for a kip?"

"No, not at all love, off you go." May had noticed the travelling and multiple bookings had had its effect on her son. His stump was more inflamed recently with all the standing and although he looked after it as best he could, he needed a few hours a day without the friction from his false leg for it to recover.

"Get yourself up. I'll shout you for tea...and don't worry, it'll resolve itself." Gary raised himself up wearily from the table and made for the stairs, pulling himself up, one at a time.

"Thanks, Mam," he said dejectedly as May watch him labour upwards. Inwardly her blood boiled. She and Arthur would be having more words, that much was evident.

The following week the discussion exploded as Arthur finally showed his face. Gary had got an infection in his stump and had been ordered to get bed rest until the inflammation eased. His gig that week had to be cancelled, but fortunately it was a local club and they took news of his illness with good grace and rebooked him for eight weeks hence.

May had encountered Arthur as he walked up to the house, obviously unaware of Gary's illness. His wary look as she approached him demonstrated that he knew perfectly well that his mother would be aware of the previous week's circumstances by now and his chin came up defiantly. He was too old to take an ear bashing from May.

"Areeet mam?" His cocky question was all the trigger she required.

"Don't you come bloody swaggering up the hill playing the big man with me. Just remember I used to wipe your shitty arse. You and me will be settling something right now and you leave your brother out of this, It's between you and me!"

Arthur stood his ground against the onslaught, but he knew she was not one for backing down from a row. Unfortunately, in that respect he was a chip off the old block and twice as stubborn.

"If you've come to apologise to your brother for nearly ruining his chances, you're a week too late and he's ill and can't be doing with you shouting and bawling. So you can just turn round and go back to your cronies in Manchester because I'm telling you my lad, you won't be getting the chance to do it again!"

Arthur's temper flared and he flushed with resentment.

"It's nowt to do with you, it's between me and Gary!"

"Oh, you think so do you? Well, I'll tell you this for starters. I've spoken to his manager and he's replaced you."

Arthur's temper burst forth and for that moment he forgot he was talking to his mother and the aggression, that was the norm in the circles he now moved in burst forth and May flinched for a second as he stepped towards her, his one good eye staring as glassily as his false one.

"You interfering old bitch, what right have you got to put your two penneth in and get me fired?" The disrespect in his words was enough for May's Irish blood to respond in kind and she swung her arm and caught him with a fierce slap across his cheek. His own hand raised in response and for one moment she thought he was going to hit her back. Somewhere in him there must have been some restraint as he lowered it back to his side and he had the grace to look shamed.

"Get off with you..." snarled May through gritted teeth. "And don't come back this time, you're a bloody disgrace!" May's temper was beyond going back and she was stunned that he had dared to raise his hand to her. She watched as he turned and strode angrily down the cobbled lane until he rounded the bend and was out of sight.

Fighting down tears that were equally anger and sadness, she fought for control of her emotions. She absently rubbed the hand that had connected with him. The seven silver bracelets, one from Edward for each of her children, jangled in alarm as she rubbed the redness that was forming on the skin. Each child had been precious to her in their own way, until now. Arthur had taken a step too far this time and the reaction and bitterness was setting in deeply to May's heart. She started to shake and had to take a few deep breaths to stop the tears from flowing.

Walking back to the house she gathered herself as Edward came out from round the back of the barn. He had caught the end of the row and the noise had drawn him outside.

"What was that about?" he asked.

"What do you think?" answered May sadly.

"I take it you told him he's fired then?"

"Aye, I did and he told me what he thought about it, in no uncertain terms."

"Don't fret lass, you did the right thing. He's in with the wrong crowd and it's rubbing off. He's old enough to make his own mistakes and to face the consequences. Come on, put'th kettle on and we'll calm you down before you tell Gary. It'll do no good to upset him."

May sighed. "Expect so." and she turned towards the house with Edward's arm around her shoulder protectively. She went in with a heavy heart but as Gary came down the stairs gingerly on his inflamed leg, she pinned on a smile to greet him. Now was not the time to tell him of their bitter words.

"Hello love, how are you feeling?" she asked.

"Better Mam, thanks. I need to ring my manager." May rattled a few plates and placed some cake on one handing it to her son.

"It'll wait till tomorrow love, here you are and there's a brew on the table."

"Ta Mam." He walked unevenly to the table and undoing the catch on his false leg to bend the knee hinge, which it did with a whine, he slid into the chair, gathered the cake towards him and bit into it with gusto. 'No, now was not the time,' thought May.

"That leg needs oiling," was all she said.

***

Weeks went by and Arthur wasn't seen. Edward had heard he was back to working in the Manchester clubs, but that was as much as he knew. He also knew he was getting a name for hanging about with a few of the known Manchester villains and it worried him immensely. Still he wasn't a boy and he couldn't tell his son what to do any more. He would stand or fall on his own actions.

After that, they heard little. Gary got back into his rhythm and was back on the road. There was even talk of him cutting a record, which was all very exciting. Life moved on for some and stagnated for others.

Rene seemed obsessed with the shop lately. Lynne had decided she was going to become a landlady and give up nursing. True to her promise, Maureen had stepped up and was now running Dene's operation in Manchester, whilst her sister stayed close to home because of her delicate condition, but she couldn't help but worry that Dene was losing her edge by giving in to her morning sickness. Orders were falling with no one to woo the clients and for that they needed her there.

May took over temporary supervision of the workshop at home and Gray was now helping his dad on the rag and bone round and supplementing that with a bit of work for Freddie Bowmer, a local builder. They had taken to the shy boy and gradually he had come out of his shell with his workmates.

Yes life went on..

Chapter Thirty - 1958 June 20th

"Mam, come quick! Dennis has just rang and they've taken Dene to Oldham Infirmary, she's gone into labour." Maureen's flushed face was awash with excitement, but for a mother who had lost three babes in childbirth, it was always a time of fear. Once the baby was here safe, all would be well, but Dene had suffered badly with morning sickness and low blood pressure and it had not been a happy pregnancy. May needed to be with her daughter. It was as though the years had turned back and she was a sickly child once more, needing her mum.

"Take over tea and send Gray to meet your Dad, he'll be home in a few minutes." She piled a few things into her handbag and started cutting bread and cheese doorstops for her and Edward. There would be no evening meal for them tonight. Job done, she pulled on a cardigan and headed for the door, throwing one last comment over her shoulder as she left.

"If he comes home before I'm back tell him I've gone to the phone box to ring a taxi… and tell him to have a wash!" Maureen nodded and turned down the pan on the stove. Luckily it was 'tater hash' and would keep for later.

Many hours later, they were sitting in the cafe at the Infirmary with an over-brewed cup of tea to ease the fear and frustration. Dene was having a slow labour and after being allowed in at an early stage whilst it was still visiting hours, the matron had then shooed them off. It was just before breakfast the following morning that Dennis had approached flushed and smiling with the news that Dene and he had themselves a baby girl. They were tired and weary but elated. May finally breathed a sigh of relief. She took her husband's hand across the table.

"We can go home now love," she said with a stifled sigh. Edward smiled.

"Do you not want to see the baby?"

"We'll try, but I doubt they'll let us in till visiting and it's hours away."

"Let's give it a go at least." He raised himself stiffly from the hard chair, downed the last of his tea and pulled her to her feet as her ageing bones protested.

"Come on, old girl. Let's go look at our granddaughter."

Hand in hand they walked down the corridor. The grey, wiry-haired woman in the dark blue dress that was long since past its best and the gaunt faced man with his cap set jauntily over one eye and the suit that was a couple of sizes too big. It was almost the sixties... a new age of liberation and they were already beyond their time. The world was moving on and they were getting old.

Chapter Thirty One

Rene was in her kitchen preparing breakfast for Paul. Stan had not come home after leaving last night and as Rene moved around the kitchen clearing dishes, her head was full to bursting. She had just heard her sister was in labour and to top it all she and Stan had had a massive row the night before and there was no going back from the words that had been spoken. In the heat of the moment Stan had admitted that he had been unfaithful and that he had made a mistake in marrying so young.

Rene had looked at him and, instead of crying or shouting, she had paused, drawn a long breath and replied firmly, but quietly.

"I think you're right, you need to move out and we'll start divorce proceedings."

Stan had not expected this...something, but not this quiet determination and it had riled him. She had gotten too big for her breeches since she had started the business. The thought that he had been forced to carry on working whilst she swanned around like a princess stuck in his throat. He never once considered the work involved that had got her to that success.

"Oh you do, do you? And when did this occur?" he had snarled.

Rene had drawn herself up to her full height and looked him square in the eye.

"About five years ago actually, when I found out about that little blonde bint that worked at the mill.. oh and then followed by the woman you were seeing over in Rochdale when you were telling me you were doing overtime… and several in between I guess, although the names escape me now. So yes, I do think you getting married was a mistake, but not as much a mistake as I have made marrying a serial womaniser. So let's be done with it shall we, Stan? I'll have your bags packed ready for when you come home tomorrow. I expect someone will take you in. There's enough candidates to choose from."

Stan hadn't anticipated this cold cynical acceptance from her when he had thought about leaving previously. Tears maybe, recriminations definitely, but not this quiet strength. It threw him and his underlying selfish nature had come to the fore.

"Oh really? Well, you realise the business will have to be sold?" he had sneered at her. Rene's face became grim and she had leaned back against the kitchen counter where she had been preparing the evening meal. This was everything she had anticipated.

"What business?...The shop lease is now in my name when I renewed it last and the accounts are up to date, we're struggling and I've unpaid suppliers bills. So go ahead if you must, or leave me to try and bring the business back up to feed and house your son as I doubt you will!" She had been quaking inside at her own lies and whether she could carry them off, but she had defiantly matched his sneer with her own.

"You've been doing well, don't lie to me." His voice became a snarl and he had raised his hand to slap her. Anticipating this, she had felt for a carving knife left on the counter and she brought it swiftly forward to fend him off, as he would have struck her otherwise.

"Feel free to try by all means and if I don't stick you now. I might draw it to your attention that I have a brother who knocks about with the Quality Street Gang, who I'm sure would oblige if I asked." Her steely look had told Stan that she meant every word and Stan's mouth had opened and closed like a furious fish for several seconds before he turned and slammed out of the kitchen.

Rene's bravado had started to evaporate as fast as it had risen and she started to shake with reaction. Listening to him banging and thumping around the bedroom above her, she had surmised that he was throwing things into a case, she certainly hoped so. The thought had then occurred that her boy, Paul was alone and he might try to take him and she experienced a sudden cramp of fear that shot through her stomach. Years ago, he could have done, but the laws had changed in recent times and it was no longer the norm for men to have complete control over the children.

Nevertheless, she had kept the knife by her side and crept up the stairs, slipping into her son's room. Quietly closing the door and wedging a chair under the knob, she had remained quietly listening for what had seemed like hours, until she heard the front door slam, an engine started followed by an uneasy quiet as the roar of his engine had faded away leaving only her ragged breathing left to fill the void.

He hadn't even tried to see his son before he left, such was his lack of ability as a family man. Thank god she had filtered the shop's profits and kept them in a tin at Dene's. It was the most dishonest, but wisest thing she had ever done. 'No, let him sponge of someone else for a change and good riddance, he always spent more than his wage could afford every week and came to her for more. Let him see how he managed his extravagant ways alone!' had been her thoughts at the time.

The adrenalin stayed with her, preventing sleep, as she had listened for every noise, sleeping alongside her son until the morning had dawned and she was left facing the reality that her husband may actually have left for good and she was alone. He had rifled through the accounts cupboards and taken her purse, but she had been careful to transfer anything important to Dene's. A few quid was small change in relation to protecting her livelihood.

She readied Paul for school and made her way down to her mother's for news on Dene, only to be greeted by Graham, the only one left in the house. She told Graham to ask May to ring her urgently at the shop before picking Paul up for her, with a message not to leave it too late and on no account to let Stan pick him up and she would explain when May rang her.

She went to the shop and made her first phone call to a locksmith and had him come first to the shop, then arranged for another visit the next day from him at home. She gave her staff strict instructions that Stan was not allowed in the shop and to call the police if he arrived first and her second. The next day she had them cover whilst she erased all trace of her husband from their home. After she had bagged up the last of his things, she walked them to the pub and left them with the landlord to pass to Stan's friend. She then walked home, spread out her own clothes in the wardrobe and cleaned the house from top to bottom. It had been a cathartic move, but she felt better for it.

She hadn't yet seen her mother and in truth, as old as she was, she didn't relish it. Despite her absence from church, May remained a Catholic and divorce was a mortal sin for those of that persuasion. She definitely would not be happy with her.

Arriving at the house to pick Paul up as her mother prepared to visit Dene and the new baby, she risked a glance at her mother, who seemed not to notice. Paul was sitting at the table with soup and sandwiches and Rene walked in taking a deep breath for the onslaught to come. May looked up as she put her coat down.

"He's gone then?" was all May said.

"Yes, he has," replied her daughter. "News travels fast".

"Landlord bumped into your dad earlier." She buttoned her coat and continued. "Are you coming to see the baby and Dene then?"

"You're not angry mum?"

"At him love, not you. Him I never liked, but I said nowt...Too cocky by far. Paul can stay here with Gray and Maureen, you'll be all right won't you Paul, with Maureen?" the boy nodded and May continued, "You can tell me all about it on the train."

"Can I watch telly gran?"

"For a bit, if you're good for Maureen."

"I will be!"

"Good lad, give your mum a kiss." The boy slid off his chair and threw his arms round his mum's waist and it was almost the undoing of Rene. She hugged him to her. Later would be soon enough to tell the boy his father was gone.

***

The family made their way to the hospital maternity ward to find Dene sat in bed with the baby beside her. The tiny head poked just above the nursery blankets and could hardly be seen as Dennis's tall frame was peering over the crib in awe at his new daughter camera in hand.

Dene looked tired, but otherwise fine and May breathed a sigh of relief that her daughter had come through the birth more resilient than she had hoped. She went across and hugged her, followed swiftly by Edward. She followed suit kissing Dennis and then looked at the child tucked up snug and silent in the cot. Apart from a few stretches and snuffles the baby slept throughout the visit, even when Dene told her mum and dad they could hold her.

May picked up the little bundle gingerly and wondered why after all the children she had birthed before, that every new one seemed so tiny and breakable. Edward felt the same and preferred to let May do the holding, whilst he gazed on at the little face with its mass of black hair.

"What're you calling her?" she asked Dennis who smiled broadly saying.

"Deena… Its a combination of both our names, Deena, and then Carol for a middle name."

"Lovely, it's got Irish connotations," answered May.

"AND Danny Kaye named his daughter Deena and we like it!" added Dene. Danny Kaye was the movie star of the moment.

"Dene, Dennis and Deena... I expect we'll get ourselves knotted up in those three," Laughed Edward "..No, it's a lovely name pet.. lovely."
"Rene's waiting to come in, but she has some news so she might be upset," said May quietly. "So just bear with her"

Dene didn't like to say she had a good idea what it would be already, so stayed silent. Her mum might be upset that Rene had confided in her sister before her mother, so least said soonest mended. Shortly after Rene entered and they went through the usual pleasantries before Rene told Dene and Dennis the events of the day before. Dene held her hand as Rene struggled to maintain her dignity, but dignity was an important thing to Rene and she managed not to cry in the telling of it. When she finished, Dennis gave her his sympathies and stood up to busy himself with the baby and give the sisters a moment together.

"Have you got my money safe still?" she asked Dene whilst Dennis was putting the baby back in its crib.

"Yes, all fine," Dene answered. It's in a tin in the loft, safer."

"I might have a proposition for you when you're home," responded her sister quietly, "but you'll have to agree it with Dennis I expect."

"What's that then?" curiosity was raised.

"I've been thinking with the aggravation he might give me with the shop, that I need to cut my ties with anything past that includes him. So I'm thinking of moving, but I'm also thinking that your designs are too good to keep at Manchester level. What about taking my store to London and featuring your designs exclusively?"

Dene sat stunned for a minute, whilst the thought settled in. Her designs in an exclusive London premises. That would mean her favourite sister moving away and she didn't like the thought of that.

"But that's a big risk and I'll hardly ever see you?"

Rene sat back in the chair and shrugged with a smile.

"No silly, we'll see each other all the time, we'll have to! And as for risk, that's as maybe for me, but not for you, you already have a customer base other than me. I've made a success here, not that Stan thinks that as I've told him I'm all but bankrupt, so we would have to keep it quiet for now. But hey, I've got quite a bit of money stashed away that would fund my first year and a flat. If it fails, it fails, I know

I can come back here and start up again smaller, but I'm getting older and now is the time to try...It may be my only time. What do you think? I'll run and own the shop but I'll promote you, it could work very well and I know you wouldn't cheat me or let me down as a supplier."

Dene felt the excitement stirring in her belly, but she was tired and the baby had to be considered, she was a mother now after all, but it was very tempting.

"I'll have to discuss it with Dennis," she smiled as Dennis straightened up from the crib.

"Discuss what?" he asked.

"It can wait," said Rene. "Now let me have a look at this beautiful baby. She leaned over the crib to coo to the baby who shuffled a little and settled back to sleep.

"She's very calm," said Rene.

"Not like her mother then," laughed Denis and Dene tapped him playfully.

"She's a precious little thing, well done both of you. Anyway I'm hogging visiting, so here's some chocolates and biscuits for you and I'll see you soon." She kissed them both and with one last look at the babe, she took her leave.

Dennis looked to Dene "He's gone then?"

"Yes, such a shame. We'll have to help her best we can Dennis."

"Of course we will. Does she know I know?"

"No, I didn't like to tell her I'd broken a confidence."

"I'll keep mum then." he laughed and added "...I'll keep mum and you can be mum!"

They both laughed and turned their attention back to their daughter. They remained looking at the sleeping baby fascinated until the visiting bell rang time. 'How is it that babies drew you when they were newborn to the exclusion of everything else?' she wondered.

Chapter Thirty Two - June 1960

Maureen was almost 26 years old and today she had become
the sister of a pop star. As she walked through Manchester on a bright
summer's day, she couldn't help but think her life was on the up. She
had remained buxom and petite but it didn't seem to put the boys off.
The new shorter hairstyles flattered her, much to her mother's horror.
She was certainly a feisty one and armed with the knowledge born of
constant reading in a wide range of subject matter, she could hold a
conversation on most subjects and put you in your place if needed.
Boyfriends lasted a couple of weeks usually before being given the
heave-ho. The men around home were mainly mill workers and
farmers' sons and they were not for her. She had too much about her
to settle for ordinary.

She had spent the last couple of years virtually running the
workshop in Manchester whilst Dene ran between London and home
with the baby, only getting her head through the door two days a week.
Dennis was popping in when he could to oversee things, but his own
diary was full and in reality fashion photography and portraits were
his real interest, not manufacture.

Maureen had taken it all in her stride and now suppliers and
clients were happy to deal with her after an initial wariness. Things
were on the up for her at least and the business was benefiting from
her input.

Rene had spent a difficult couple of months transferring her
life and business idea to London, but was now back on track. The shop
was elegant and well run, but required Dene to have a presence at least
once a week to keep her profile in the industry building. They had also

started attending fashion and social events, which in reality took Dene away from home at least two days a week. She was tired and nervous and Maureen had naturally took the reins to alleviate the pressure on her. Dennis was often literally left holding the baby on the nights Dene was travelling. Still, things were starting to build and it would be worthwhile in the end and May was ever-present to help.

Today Gary's record had made it to No 23 in the single charts and she was so excited and had popped out to buy several copies from the music shop in Piccadilly. She had a bag full of his records, which she intended to hand to all the staff, in the hope it would boost him further up the charts and had just stopped at the library on the way back to exchange her books and have a quiet read.

Placing her bag on the floor she was soon engrossed in a history of the suffragette movement. When the young man on the table behind her pushed his chair back and stumbling, corrected his balance by standing squarely on her precious bag of vinyl. The crack was unmistakable and she jumped out of her skin, her eyes flying to the culprit.

He was already picking up the bag with a red face. A very good looking face, but red with embarrassment all the same. Smart in a suit and too tall for her petite frame really. His suave good looks distracted her almost enough to forgive him the disaster he had just brought upon them.

"Oh no! I'm so sorry! Have I broken something?" he asked and then realising he was in the library, respectfully lowered his voice to a whisper.

"I think so," she whispered back. Looking in the bag she cringed as at least two of the eight were broken, she brought them out despondently and they wobbled in the packets as only a broken record can. He grimaced, but there was a tinge of humour in it.

"Oh dear, I must replace them for you, I'm so sorry. Are you working nearby?"

"Just over the road a ways. I manage a design workshop for my sister near King Street."

"Have you time to go back to the shop with me to replace them?"

'Have I time?' she thought, as she looked at him and smelt a subtle aftershave. His collars were clean and crisp and he was stylish without being vain. She liked that.

"I think so, do you work nearby?"

"The university, I'm working on a recent invention. We are developing the first electronic stored programme computer". He said it like he wasn't expecting a positive response, but she smiled.

"I've read a bit about it in the news, it's ground-breaking isn't it?"

The young man smiled impressed at her response as they made their way along the bustling Manchester streets. By the time they were approaching the music shop once more they were chatting amiably.

"I'm Peter, by the way."

"Maureen," she responded. Sliding the duplicate records out on the shops counter with a comment. "Slight accident!" she inspected all the records and found that three were actually broken of the eight.

"You must like Gary Handley quite a bit," he noted with irony.

"I suppose so, he's my twin brother for my pains. Just trying to help him up the charts." She grinned and he smiled back. There was a moment and Maureen knew that this was the type of man she was looking for. He had brains, manners, good looks and was pleasant company to boot. Yes, she would be keeping this one.
She gave him her most dazzling smile as he paid for the records and he took the bait.

"Have you time for a coffee? There's a little jazz bar round the corner and they do a great sandwich," she invited with her eyes as much as her words.

"Certainly have!" he replied.

**

The romance bloomed much quicker than expected and whilst Maureen and Peter appeared total opposites in background. They had something that drew them inexplicably to each other's intelligence. Peter was an academic but with a good heart and Maureen was earthy with a good practical nature softened with a devilish wit and loving heart.

Her only vice was that she had taken up smoking in an attempt at sophistication. By the time she realised it made her look more like a docker's wife, she was enjoying it too much and refused to quit, despite groans of horror from her sisters every time she lit one up.

May struggled with the blossoming relationship, which was strange, as she told herself that she should be glad another of her daughters had found herself an upmarket boyfriend. Maybe she was jealous? She had posed that question to herself. That would then beg the question as to whether she had been happy in her life. This tiny house full of children on the sides of a small valley on the Lancashire moors and the husband that loved her unfailingly was hardly the life she had aspired to.

Yet, happy she was and she loved her husband for all that he was. A small part of her however admitted secretly that she was angry at herself for the mistakes of her girlhood. What could she have been if Edward had never walked up to her aunt's door all those years ago and she had not gotten herself with child?

The problem was definitely hers, she told herself. The past was the past and not to be undone, so no use fretting on it at an age where she could do nothing about it. She also had to examine her feelings towards Edward for all he was not. Was success and money valued above kindness and loyalty? Not at all! Then why was she so sad that her daughters had bettered themselves by their own endeavours whilst she had grown older and seen her childhood dreams evaporate in the cares and responsibilities of motherhood. She supposed it was because back then there was no choice. Unlike these times where apparently 'Free Love' was now fashionable. How the times were changing.

Perhaps Muareens beau Peter was all she had imagined for herself as a girl, hence her feelings were borne of her own lost dreams. Maybe, because here was a man she felt she should have had in her youth and now, with the years and hard work roughening her demeanour and taking her looks, she was merely aware of her own social shortcomings in finer company, that as a girl she would not have even considered.

The few occasions Peter had come to visit Maureen at her home had been strained and Peter had remarked to Maureen that he didn't feel May really liked him, but that he didn't know what could be done.

Maureen had laughed and told him that whilst her mum was an old battle-axe, she had a heart of gold and she always fought her corner for the family and wouldn't see any of them put down … With the exception of Arthur who had now gained the title of 'Black Sheep'.

If May had heard her daughter's description of her it would have made her feel as old as Methuselah. Peter had shrugged and hoped his future mother-in-law would feel the same when he proposed to Maureen at the weekend. He knew Maureen would accept, it was unspoken between them. May however, would be a different kettle of fish.

That weekend they went walking in the lakes and as they strolled back to the small B&B they had booked, Peter had stopped her as they walked along the banks of Ullswater and had gone down on one knee bringing out the ring he had been carrying around with him for days. The only response from Maureen was a beatific smile followed by the words...

"Silly boy, you didn't have to ask.. didn't you know it was a done deal?" Leaning forward, she took his cheeks in her hand and kissed him passionately.

"You and I will have loads of kids!" she said as she broke away and Peter smiled a huge wide smile that lit her day.

"I expect we will, my love," he winked. "Shall we go back and make a start?"

They were married soon after in Ogden Chapel as once more the family gathered round. Arthur was conspicuous by his absence, but it had become the norm by now and no one mentioned him by name.

Dene's toddler and Lynne's daughter were bridesmaids. The couple didn't want much fuss and so left after the wedding breakfast at the pub for a honeymoon in Scotland. They had put a deposit down on a house in Cheshire, which brought grumbles of 'getting above herself' from May. The benefits of 'Cheshire Life' were all too publicised. Deep down May was hurt, she had wanted her children and grandchildren close and this was a step too far after losing Rene to London. Gary was travelling mostly and Lynne was just moving into her first public house in Rochdale. Her family was finding its own way without her and dispersing.

That left Dene nearby and only Graham at home, all her chicks had flown the coop with the one exception. How would she fill her days? She couldn't conceive of the day her youngest boy left home, it didn't bear thinking about.

She decided to have a quiet cuppa and a read of the Oldham Chronicle. She became ensconced in an article that reported on the history of the Piethorne Valley and the navvies that had trodden the clay puddle core that was required to seal the dams on the reservoir with just sacking on their feet. Over and over again they trod the wet earth until the required height was reached. They called the navvies a 'Butty Gang'. Hence the question nowadays if there was 'a butty in it' when questioning likely profit.

Navvie was short for navigational engineers and the butty gang system whereby groups of navvies were paid on a fixed lump sum basis, leaving the workers to divide the money between them was the norm. They were well-paid, hard working and hard living . Some were lodged in the long shed at Kitcliffe. One woman, Betty Whitehead, a seventy year old local woman had said that the navvies spilt more beer than the locals ever drank and fights were common.

May sat reading interestedly and then it came to her, she needed a challenge. She would start writing to the newspapers on things that interested or annoyed her. So pulling out some paper and a fountain pen and a long since used bottle of ink, that was kept in the sideboard cupboard, she started to do a piece on the changes to the valley since then. How her family had arrived with nothing and yet thrived here on this hillside. The writing overcame her and when she had finished, she copied it out again more neatly this time. Setting off with a spring in her step, she walked all the way down to the post office in the village to buy more paper and with a silent prayer for recognition, she posted the article to the Chronicle editor. The intellectual activity made her feel better and Edward came home to a much more animated wife than he had been used to of late.

As he bent to pull off his boots, he started to cough and May had to get him a glass of water. His emphysema, now officially diagnosed had troubled him more of late, but he still wouldn't be told.

"You need to look after yourself more," she reprimanded him and he dismissed her with a wave.

"Don't cluck woman, I'm fine, besides, as long as I get them all to twenty one I don't care if I drop down the next day!" May scowled at him. She didn't like talk like that. It drew her attention to how old they were getting and it made her fearful of the future.

"Don't worry lass, I've a good few years in me yet. I mightn't be able to chase you round the bedroom no more, but I can still give you a good squeeze," and with it he hugged her to him and planted a large, loud kiss on both her cheeks as she leaned over the table to spread the tablecloth.

"Go on with you, she laughed and pushed him off… you'll be more use to me outside doing that painting you promised!"

"Nonsense woman it can wait a few days," he laughed.

"Yes.. and a few days become weeks!" He was not a fan of painting.

"We'll get Graham's birthday over and he can help me with it next week...I promise," he smiled a cheeky smile.

"I'll believe that when I see it," she laughed. "Look, have a read of my letter I've just sent to the Chron," she said.

Edward grimaced, he still was not a fan of reading and every so often she made him read something, just to keep him on track. She handed him the paper and he sat for a few moments with a brew as he slowly made his way down the script. She waited, watching his reaction as he read, but he was concentrating too much to show any. When he had finished, he put the paper on his lap and he looked up at her in admiration.

"Aye lass, you've missed your calling. You should have been a writer, it's bloody marvellous...almost like a poem!"

"Really?" she stood beaming with pride.

"I wouldn't say it if it weren't true lass"

"I know, thank you. That means a lot!"

Turning back to her preparations, she didn't see the look of sadness cross over her beloved husband's face. He was thinking of the bright young thing he had met and how perhaps loving him had changed her life onto a different path and maybe not for the better for her. For him yes, she was all he had ever wanted, even with that temper and habit of saying what she thought without the slightest hint of diplomacy. That blunt streak, coupled with intelligence meant you didn't mess with May Handley. She feared no one and never pulled her punches and if you crossed her, you found yourself facing a force to be reckoned with!

He smiled momentarily and she caught his eye and smiled back before returning to her chores. He had wished so much more for the woman that had lost a life of privilege to work alongside him, but life here was hard and his options limited. He wished he could have given all that she had wished for herself, but all that he had given her was roughened hands, children and little else, he sighed and stretching his toes, he noticed she had darned his socks...she must have been bored recently.

Chapter Thirty Three – July 1960

The little tot Deena was sat atop her grandad's knee as he drove the cart up Huddersfield Road. At two years old, it was to be one of her life's abiding memories, for in her little head she was driving the horse and cart herself, as he held the reins in her hands with his cupped around them. In truth, Captain knew his own way home and needed little steering, but the child was delighted and that was all that mattered.

May sat alongside smiling, just in case she needed to retrieve the little girl and she took a deep breath of the warm summer air. She glanced at her husband as he crooned to the baby in steady time to the horse's rhythm. 'What a beautiful day', she thought as they trotted slowly up the street.

On the back of the cart was her shopping jostling about in an orange crate, in preparation for the family gathering for Graham's twenty first tomorrow. She hoped the weather would stay good for them as the house was too small now to fit the extended family. Even Rene had come home from London with Paul and they were staying at Dene's for the duration because of the lack of space. How on earth did she ever manage when she had all seven at home and her mother?

The beer crates jangled happily to the clippity clop of the horse's hooves on the road and May went through endless internal lists to make sure she had forgotten nothing for the party. This would be no 'posh do', but it would be enough to mark the occasion.

She wondered where the years had gone between the affectionate young boy she had cuddled and the shy young man with a mop of curly hair who never quite seemed to grow up. He was the image of Arthur and his dad, but he was his mother's boy in affection and his dad's in admiration. She couldn't see him ever leaving home, let alone getting himself a wife. He adored his older sister Dene and it was often the only place, other than home, that he could be found. Dene knew she could leave the baby with him and he would guard her with his life, his natural affection for all things small drew animals and children to him in equal amounts. Probably because he himself was more at home in that kind of situation than in the company of adults. Nevertheless, tomorrow was the 18th July and his day. She was determined he would have the best day ever for him.

She had picked up a new suit for him and a shirt with the new shoestring tie he had been admiring. That had been as much as she could afford. Secretly, he aspired to look like Buddy Holly and was cultivating the mop of curls on top but a DA at the back. To the uninitiated that was a 'duck's arse', courtesy of the latest 'Teddy Boy' fashion.

Unbeknown to him, Gary, his now popular entertainer brother and the best earner at present, had bought him a gold signet ring that would start his love of jewellery. Despite his shyness, Gray loved to be smart. He took after Arthur in that respect, she was just grateful that it was only in that respect.

Between his work with Bowmer's and working to help his dad, he brought a decent amount of money home. It wasn't a lot, but he dutifully tipped most of it up to May and she dished him back out what she thought he needed and unlike the others, he never complained. Gray would give you his last penny if it was needed, it was just the way he was made. To May, he would always be her little boy and she dreaded ever losing his easy company. He was a good boy.

His birthday dawned and Rene and Dene had arrived early, leaving the baby and Paul with Dennis, to help their mum scrub and lay the outdoor table. The wind had kept away, which was a blessing and it enabled her to be a bit more ambitious with the decorations.

Gary was inside, having come home for a few days and she had set him to work peeling spuds for the roast dinner, pop star or not! Apple pies and custard were already made and set aside for later when Graham ambled downstairs in his pyjamas after the lads from work had took him for an early birthday drink the night before. He was slightly the worse for wear but managed a smile and blushed profusely when Edward, Dene, May and Gary all sang Happy Birthday to him.

They sat him down to open his cards at the kitchen table and May put him a brew down, which he sipped gingerly. His eyes lit up when May and Edward and Gary gave him their presents. The smile widened when he took off the paper and found the new clothes.

"Aw Mam...Dad thank you, this is fantastic! Can I wear them today?" he asked. May laughed happy that he liked the choice.

"Why do you think we gave them you now? Daft lad! Course you can, but you best open your brother's present now, you might like that as well."

Gray's eyes nearly popped out of his head at the sight of the ring encasing a single ruby. They had been a poor family and never had the luxury of jewellery. He looked at it in awe as he slipped it on. Dene handed him a Timex watch, which were all the rage. He felt overwhelmed with it all and was too emotional to speak his feelings. They all knew him and paid no mind to his diffidence, leaving him to finish his tea and examine his presents as they prepared for the onslaught of the rest of the family.

Lynne and Derek would be over soon. Maureen and Peter would scrape in at the last minute as they had just come back from holiday. Arthur hadn't been seen for some time.

Gary ambled around the table setting places and appreciating the chance to be in the fresh air. He had just come back from a stint at Butlin's and it had meant late nights and lie-ins that meant he didn't see much daylight time. He had had his first single go to number ten and another to five, but he never made the top slot. The last one barely made the top twenty and he had to face the reality that, despite his talent, he would never be a pop idol with one leg. It was a bitter blow, but he had gained enough popularity to make a good living and Gary being Gary, he had pinned on a smile and weathered it, grateful to be doing what he loved. May felt for him, who knows what it could have been had he not been disabled, but maybe the path chosen because of his accident had brought him to the notice of Billy Butlin where it may have not had he been any other lad. So all considered, it had maybe given him opportunities he would never have otherwise had. Small blessings.

The party was lively and happy, with children and babies toddling about. May surveyed her brood and was content. Graham, after a few beers always came out of his shell and was laughing and joking, absolutely delighted with each new present. As he was the youngest they had all gone to town and spoilt him. It was his best day ever.

At teatime, the men went off to the pub and the women cleared the table before the flies came out at dusk. It was a glorious still evening that held a scent of the river babbling below them and the smell of the hay in the nearby fields… Bliss.

All done, May and her girls sat with the children and a hot cuppa in the coming sunset and enjoyed the last of what had turned out to be a wonderful day. Edward left the younger men in the pub and came home to bed the horses down for the night and he joined them at the table, taking a swig from May's cup.

"Aye love, what a grand day," he said as he finished her cup. She tapped his hand, laughing at the knowledge that he was a bit tipsy. Edward was not a drinker, so God knows what state the boys would be in on their return. She held out her hand and he scooped it to his lips planting a large kiss in her palm.

"Lovely spread May, I'll go and make another pot, you sit yerself down a while longer and enjoy the peace...and sit she did... Idly listening to the chatter of her girls and the babble of her grandchildren. Edward came back and they sat side by side as the last rays of sunset created a halo above the trees on the crest of the hill that made the sides of this beautiful green valley.

"I'll start the barn tomorrow," he said with a smile.

"What about my kitchen?" she asked.

"All in good time," he smiled.

"You and your damn barn, them horses have better accommodation than I do!".

"Barn first, kitchen next woman... tha's no patience," he smiled and she smiled back as he reached to stir the pot.

Chapter Thirty Four - 1961

The next day dawned warm and clear and May and Edward rose early, each with their own list of chores on their mind. They spent an hour in happy companionship as Edward brought the water in to fill the tank on the stove and emptied the ashes in preparation for the new day's cooking. Other homes now had electric stoves, but May was quite happy to stay in her old routines.

She busied herself with breakfast and put a fresh batch of bread in the oven to be had with eggs. Gary and Graham were not likely to rise anytime soon and May preferred it that way, as getting them up before they had slept off the skinfull they had consumed on Saturday night, would not make for cheerful company. The night before she and Edward had just about given up on them and were readying themselves for bed when they had heard Gary and Graham return noisily and laughing.

She wasn't sure who was the drunkest, but it was definitely a close run thing. They smothered laughter as the two young men fought on who was supporting who up the stairs and the ensuing hilarity as Gary removed his false leg and tried to hop around the room drunkenly. It was music to their ears. Their boys were men now...job done. They had fallen asleep in a happy embrace smiling in the dark until sleep claimed them both.

May grumbled that Graham had been let off painting duty with his dad on the excuse that it was still his birthday weekend. Edward had smiled and said, "Let the lad have a day off, he's at work soon enough tomorrow and real life begins again."

Edward took the potty to empty and told her to bring him a butty about twelve as he was going to crack on with painting the barn. He'd been fortunate enough to be given a load of old gloss that was skinning over by the factory transport manager as a favour for taking away some scrap, and a split of the profit with him on the QT. The stuff stank to high heaven as paint did in those days but free was free and much appreciated.

May did her washing and hung it out to dry in the warm breeze. It was going to be a hot one, at least she could strip the beds and have it dry by afternoon if the weather held. Edward would have the barn done and dry in a few hours also and maybe they could go for a beer later, just the two of them to celebrate the end of parental responsibilities.

Gary was down first, but Graham had to be prized from his pit as his mother pulled the sheets from under him. He grumbled but got up regardless and staggered about looking for the missing potty.

For Gary, it was a welcome break from performing and he finished a slab of bread and lemon curd and clicking shut the catch on his metal leg he rose to give his mum the dishes.

"I'll go and see what me Da is up to Mam," he said, "I need the fresh air".

"That'll teach you for swigging too much ale...Tell your dad the kettle's on and I'll have a sandwich for him in ten minutes."

"OK." Gary ambled off with his loping gait. May filled the sink with warm water from the stove to wash the dishes and make ready for the next meal as Graham finally put in an appearance with his hair stood up comically atop his head and she smiled.

"You've finally made it down have you? Breakfast's over now, you'll have to have a cheese butty with your Dad as it's near lunchtime." Gray slumped into a chair and put his head on his arms.

"I don't think I can eat mum… and I had to wee out the window, where's the po?"

"You'd better not have!... Here have this, you'll be fine once you've got the first mouthful down. Here you are, a cup of tea." She ruffled his mop affectionately.

The door burst open and Gary stood in silhouette, the sun behind him. He was breathing heavy and it took a few seconds for her to realise there were tears streaming down his face.

"Mam, it's Dad! You need to come. I think he's dead!"

The words that came from him in a sob, were like a knife to the guts and fear shot through her body. Without thinking she threw down her tea towel and ran for the door with Graham and Gary in hot pursuit. Graham was the first to get there and when she rounded the corner he had already dropped to his knees where Edward lay prone. The paintbrush had fallen from his hand and the tin of green paint was knocked over and puddling around his feet.

Graham was shaking him in panic and sobbing and May pulled him aside. Edwards face was grey and his lips blue. His mouth was open as though he had died fighting for breath. There was no doubt he was lost to them and for some time. May howled her grief and only Gary stood silently crying with a pain in his chest that was nigh on unbearable. May cradled Edward to her and rocked back and forth whilst her boys looked on helplessly. There was no end to her pain and her soul screamed inwardly for the loss of the good man who had stood beside her unfailingly all these years.

When at last her tears abated, she looked up stricken and spoke to Graham who was also now in silent shock.

"Go to the phone and call an ambulance love," she told him and tell them it's too late to save him."

***

It was found that Edward had died through a bronchial attack brought on most likely by the strong paint fumes aggravating his emphysema and causing a heart attack. It was something none of them could have foreseen and, as they sat around the table for the wake, there was no celebration of his life. No laughter and stories of his exploits, the loss was just too costly for them all.

Only Lynne and Rene seemed to hold it together and Arthur, who had turned up at the funeral was himself stricken and without words for the first time in his life. Instead, he remained sitting on a chair outside the back door and just stared ahead. The fact that Arthur had been received back in the fold in this time of grief was the only good thing to come of it. All else was black depression.

Dene and Graham were inconsolable and Gary and Maureen sat forlornly on the sofa whilst Dennis and Peter took over kitchen duties and Derek escaped from the sad atmosphere to see to the animals. All May could do was sit at the table and every so often she would tell whoever was nearest that he had said, '...He didn't care if he dropped down the next day as long as he got them all to twenty-one.'

They were long and dark weeks ahead and May had decisions to make. The house and animals that had once been a happy part of their environment had become a burden to her. Each day she relied more and more on Graham to fill the huge hole in her life that her beloved Teddy had left behind in his passing.

Despite his age, Graham had cried once more when May said the horses would have to be sold as they couldn't afford to keep them, now that Edwards wage had gone. He was so distraught that she relented finally and said it could wait a while, she had some money for now.

The house that had once been so overcrowded now seemed hollow and empty. Even Gary was talking of buying a house and had surprisingly turned up one day with a willowy girl that stood a whole head taller than him and he introduced her to his mother as the woman he was going to marry. Irene had blushed and smiled shyly and May knew instantly he had chosen wisely. Here was no hanger-on, she was a genuine and naive young woman who looked to dote on Gary.

Shocked as she was, it was the only happy news recently and whilst she seized on it like a lifeline, another part of her knew the effect it would have on her finances with one less wage. She would have to find a solution before it became a real problem. 'Oh Teddy,' she cried inwardly. 'What will I do without your strength my love?' For a moment, she thought she heard him say, 'Nay lass, you're the strength around here!'

She found comfort in this and later she found herself writing a piece to The Observer about 'Benefits for Widows.' They published it a couple of weeks later and she felt heartened once more that they had found it worthy of publishing.

With little else in her life now but Graham, she threw herself into her writing and it wasn't long before she had gained a reputation for challenging the politicians on grass roots issues. May Handley always had the last word. She was particularly irked by Cyril Smith and had hammered home many a critique of his policies until he knew her by name. She just didn't like the man and made no bones about it.

Four months later, she was packing the last of her belongings and loading the cart to start the move from her beloved house in the valley to a smaller back-to-back cottage in the village, which was more affordable on their meagre income. By comparison, Wood Mill House was a mansion. Most of the family had come to help and as she opened the door to the tiny cottage and looking inside, she wanted to weep for all that she had lost.

The new cottage stood on a small green, with a pub to the side of her and a tiny shop nearby. The main thing that had motivated her to take on such a small dwelling, other than the savings, was the fact that she had sold the horses to the farmer opposite and Captain the Shire could be seen reaching over the wire fence for the sweet long grass on the other side. Graham would just be a minute's walk from his beloved horse and his memories of time with Edward. It was a small blessing in an otherwise dark time.

To her surprise as she entered her new home there was now a large rug on the newly-scrubbed stone floor, and in pride of place in the miniscule kitchen stood an electric cooker which her offspring unveiled with a 'tada!' The living room only had enough for a small settee and a chair. 'So, no family gatherings here,' she thought sadly. A table with two bentwood chairs stood by the window and a sideboard next to the fireplace. She had scarce gotten over the shock of the cooker when she spotted the small television in the corner that she almost missed in the chaos of having the majority of her children in this small space.

"We all clubbed together Mum," said Dene and she nearly wept at the gesture.

"We thought the telly could keep you company in the evenings," said another. May smiled and gave her heartfelt thanks but she knew there would be nothing that could fill the void of Edward's loss. Her days as a woman were gone and from now on the best she could hope for was the role of mother and grandmother. She suddenly felt tired and lost. The tears came and they all cried with her until she blew her nose and then looking at the new cooker said... "Right then, someone show me how to use this bloody contraption and I'll put the kettle on, then we can get cracking."

They soon had the small cottage in order and as the last of her children left, it was looking cosier, but it was not her home... Just some strange alien place that had no memories of her beloved Teddy. She looked at Graham who was stoking the fire and she could see he felt the same, but was trying his best not to let it show.

The new cottage had one downstairs room with the kitchen and pantry running off it and just a curtain for separation. From the narrow kitchen led a door to the cellar, which was little more than a coalhole and a place to store a dolly tub and mangle and a few bits and bats. There was an outside toilet and an outhouse at the side where they stored the tin bath. No garden as they were back to back. Not much of anything really. The only blessing was that it was still pretty rural and she offered up silent thanks that she hadn't been forced to live in one of the dismal back streets of Rochdale or Oldham. That, she didn't think she could have borne.

Up the small stairs were two tiny rooms fitting little more than a bed and a large chest of drawers in May's and a wardrobe in Graham's. How they had struggled getting it all up the stairs, but May had insisted. It had been the same chest that every new babe of hers had been lain in the bottom drawer of and she was not about to be living without it, or a wardrobe for that matter. As a trace of her Irish accent came in, they all knew she wouldn't budge and so with some scraping of wood on walls, the task was achieved. The beds were metal framed and could be taken apart, but the heavy flock mattresses were another challenge. The one redeeming factor was that the house had electricity installed and it would allow her to write in the evenings.

By the time her over helpful brood had left. The beds were made with warming bottles in, curtains hung, clothes away and pantry stocked. Even the step had been stoned and all that was left for her to do was arrange her few ornaments. She lovingly drew the ruby coloured lustres from the safety of their padding and placed them on the sideboard. She would keep her door closed tight until she knew the calibre of her new neighbours or they would be the first to go if anyone was light fingered!

As she put her late husband's horse brasses above the fireplace, Graham had plugged in the TV and was trying to adjust the aerial. He was not a technical or patient young man and as he bloody'd and buggered his way through his chosen task, she smiled, daring not to show him her amusement as it would make him all the more frustrated. 'Bless him', she thought, 'he's trying to be the man of the house and it's not going well'. A lump formed in her throat and she held back her tears once more.

One bright sunny morning a few months ago they had all before them and, suddenly, here she was in a strange part of the village wrenched from all that was precious to her. Her moors, the river and the frugal but happy life with all her children around her. The husband that she had expected to grow old in the company of, along with her dreams of their retirement, were now a thing of the past. This tiny house and struggle was all the future she could look to for now. God help her if Gray found himself a girl, she would be destitute. Her emotions and anxiety were about to consume her one more when Gray gave a shout.

"I've done it Mum! Look! Coronation Street's coming on, everyone's talking about it." Gray was triumphant.

"Good lad, let's have a brew and some toast eh and we'll watch it."

So there they were, the widow and the young man sat side by side immersed in someone else's life as a means to escape the present. A blanket over their lap in the flickering monochrome light, finding a way to face a different day dawning and Christmas just appearing on the horizon.

Chapter Thirty Five - 1962

Christmas came and went and it was as though everyone had played it down for May's sake. Christmas Day was spent with Dene and Dennis and the tot Deena. Graham was happy enough as always, in his older sister's company and Dennis was polite and welcoming. Truth be known, he would have much rather preferred to be on their own. Still it was early days for May and Graham and they had to do the best to help her recover from all they had lost. Dennis was a kind man and as such he tried to make life a little better for them.

On Christmas Eve they had a wander up to the Bull's Head at Ogden and the company was merry. The family came together there and were welcomed in by Frank Mills the current landlord. May put on her bravest face. Especially when she learnt at the last minute that Dennis's mother and step-father would be staying over for Christmas also.

Ivy Barrie (as was her stage name) was a lovely woman, but had not been the most maternal mother to Dennis, but she seemed genuinely taken by her granddaughter and May felt eclipsed as she came in for Christmas dinner with her black hair crimped still in the style of a thirties movie star. With a royal blue lurex cocktail dress and the most stunning costume jewellery, she was a picture of sophistication.

Pop, as he was called, her husband, was a pleasant man. Bald and tall, but with a kindly face. Ivy, after a disappointing first marriage had taken the shock route of divorce and shortly after inherited her fortune. She vowed the next time she married that the man would look after her and that is exactly what he did. It was a team that seemed to work. Pop never seemed fazed by her theatrical stance and when she would have drifted, he grounded her gently. She in turn gave him a life of ease and the pleasure of her effervescent company.

By comparison, May felt dowdy in her best dress and as she realised it was the same one she had worn for her daughter's wedding a flush of embarrassment coloured her face. The child Deena, who she previously had first affection from, seemed fascinated by the glamorous new Nana with the beautiful smile. May had to swallow down a lump of pique as she watched Ivy dangle the child on her knee and turn her into a ventriloquist's dummy. The child laughed and complied, revelling in the attention and applause.

Only recently the child had been on a visit to her new Nana in Blackpool and had gone to see her sing in a theatre on Dixon Rd. When Nana had held her hand and taken her on for a bow at the end of her set, the child was enthralled by the smell of the rope and wood and the glow from the lights just as Gary had been on his first experience of fame. When the dimly lit audience behind them, almost like a sea of glowing faces and all smiling widely, had applauded even louder as Ivy introduced the latest starlet in her family, it was a moment the little girl would never forget and she was captivated as she did her best curtsey.

How could May compare with that? She pinned on a polite smile, but deep within, the jealousy for all that Ivy had been brought up to expect and indeed still had, burned deep. It was the life that she had been brought up to expect, and lost. Ivy would never know hardship and the fear of falling on hard times that she was now experiencing. The catholic part of her could not help but condemn the actions of a woman who could be so blasé as to rid herself of one husband and almost immediately take another...shameless!

The fact that Ivy seemed very happy with her husband brought home all the more the loneliness she felt without Edward.

As soon as she was able she made her excuses and made to leave, calling Graham to get his coat. Dene gave her a look and Dennis looked put out. Gray moaned all the way home that he was just starting to enjoy himself, but she paid him no mind and refused the offer of a lift from Dennis, saying the walk would do them good. It was an anti-climax to what should have been a pleasant day.

Later, as she lay in her bed, she cried for Teddy out of loneliness and not a little guilt for her mean-spiritedness to people who had only shown her friendship.

***

New Year came in mild and clear, which was a blessing. Coal was expensive and they had no ready supply of wood as they once had all around them on the moors above Newhey. It was a cost she hadn't anticipated and so she remained frugal on the strength of fire she made. The new electric oven was another cost over her old-fashioned stove, which used to heat the room, boil her water and cook their food. This new-fangled stuff was wonderful, but it came with an extra cost.

She had just got the house warm, when there was a knock on the door. The family would normally march on in, so she pulled off her apron and went to see who was calling at such an early hour of the day. She fair dropped with surprise when she encountered the old Catholic priest, stood hesitantly on her doorstep, bearing his best parish smile.

Father Brown had been a younger, over pious man when she had last encountered him many years previously. It was not a happy memory, as he had made it plainly clear on that occasion that she would not be welcome in church whilst she was married to a protestant. As if Edward had ever followed a religion in the first place... although that had probably made things worse and he would have been considered a total heathen. Had she been in Ireland she would have suffered for her choice, but in England the Catholic Church did not have the same dominance over society.

Her mouth dropped open in surprise for a moment before setting grimly again, teeth grating against teeth. The last time he had turned up was ten years ago at Wood Mill House and they had all been playing cards for money. It had caused some hilarity as seeing him pass the window, May had guiltily snatched all the cards and scooped the money into her apron and run upstairs embarrassed at being seen gambling. Edward had opened the door in her stead whilst she hovered on the landing. The priest had said he would come back when May was home...he never did. Edward had smiled wryly as May returned sheepishly with, "Still a good catholic girl then?"

"What can I do for you Father Brown?" she enquired as politely as she could.

"I heard you had been recently widowed May... Yes... and I felt I should come to offer you some comfort at this sad time. The Lord takes care of all his children, even the lost lambs, and I wondered that, perhaps now your husband is no longer with us, you might like to come and receive communion once more?"

May's mouth set into a firm line and she felt a cold anger start to bubble up from the pit of her stomach, by the time the priest had finished the majority of his 'all is forgiven' speech, she could stomach no more and she raised the flat of her hand to silence his patronising delivery.

"My husband may no longer be with you, but I assure you, he is very much with me! You have the bloody barefaced cheek to stand on my doorstep when you've shunned me for nigh on forty years and expect I'll be grateful? You hypocritical old bastard!"

There, she had said it...and so far no lightning strike had been forthcoming. The priest's face reddened with outrage as he fought stammering to find the words to convey it.

"May God forgive you May Handley!" he blustered, never having had the experience of a tongue-lashing from one of his flock before, but May hadn't finished and she continued with gusto.

"Aye, that's what I am...May Handley!... You remember it and if I wasn't good enough with that name before, I'm definitely not good enough now... Although actually, you're not good enough for me. I hear how you preach piety to all those fools that would listen. As I hear tell, it's all you can do to make it through a sermon with all the whisky you're supping!...Oh yes, I hear the gossip. Only last week someone told me how you married their cousin three times because you had to keep starting again you were so drunk!. Go on with you, clear off! I don't want your kind dirtying my doorstep!"

The priest stepped back in shock and nearly fell off the narrow pavement. Graham chose that moment to round the corner and stopped dead in his track at the sight of his mother chasing off the old man in his black robes.

"Go on... piss off! And say a few Hail Mary's for yourself on the way... and mind you go fast now, you wouldn't want my foot up your fecking arse!"

May's Irish accent, long since gone, came back with a vengeance in that moment and Gray started to howl with laughter at the sight. His mother rarely said anything above bloody, but it was clear this was an exceptional circumstance. The priest scuttled away unsteadily and May brushed her skirt straight in the need for something to do with her hands, lest she be tempted to pick something up and hurl it at the old man's departing back. Graham staggered up to his mum, trying to control his mirth and she turned her aggression on him for a brief second.

"What you laughing at boy?"

"Aw Mam, you're a star!" he wheezed, and for a moment she saw the funny side of it and a smile hovered around her face.

"Well, if I wasn't ex-communicated before, I'm sure as damnation am now! Come on, let's go have a half in this new pub...I may as well be hanged for a sheep as a lamb, lad!"

"This lot will have a field day with it when they hear what their new neighbour has done, Mam!"

She smiled grimly at her son's words and quickly grabbed her purse from the table, not giving him time to change his mind. Linking his arm affectionately, she steered him back towards the door, glad to have at least one of her children for comfort at a moment that could have sent her downhill, had she been alone. The thoughts of the lack of respect for her Teddy brought a lump to her throat but she would not let that old fool bring her down.

"Aye... but they'll think twice round here before they mess with May Handley and her family." She grinned in defiance and Graham returned the smile as they walked to the pub on the green.

Chapter Thirty Six 1964

It was spring and May had settled into her new home, as small as it was. Close proximity to neighbours always had to be managed, but on the whole, it wasn't an unpleasant place to live.

The sixties had brought with it a craze for all things crocheted as long as it was with knee length boots or white tights. Rene was keeping her mum busy in creating designer wedding dresses. Dene also had a link into a shop in Carnaby Street, where the wealthy elite would pay exorbitant prices just to appear non-conformist and had sold them on her mother's skills. Soon May was making a tidy sum copying and producing the designs supplied and life seemed a little less worrying as her bank balance started to creep back up to a healthy level once more. Her fingers were often cramped, but the peace of mind was worth the pain.

Rene was doing just fine, business wise, but May sensed that Rene was lonely for home and Dene was equally frustrated with home life. She had noticed there was often an atmosphere between Dennis and Dene when she called up unannounced. On one occasion she had found Dennis out and Dene sobbing hysterically. It had been a row over decorating and May couldn't help but think her daughter was reverting back to a tendency towards hysteria in her dissatisfaction. Dennis was always polite, but she could see there was strain behind his eyes. Though he said nothing in particular, she felt he was starting to regret marrying into a class beneath him and May couldn't help but resent the implication not openly voiced.

Perhaps it was her own lack of self-esteem or the knowledge that where she once had status, she had over time lost her etiquette and confidence in society and had instead just turned into a rough and poor

Irish immigrant. The only place she felt completely at home was in the pages of her latest article on regional politics or history. Here she was incisive, fearless and had quite a reputation.

When questioned about homelife, Dene would just say, "We're just not getting on mum, nobody's done anything, it's just not what I expected from my life." Other than that she was close lipped. May thought her daughter was too much of a romantic and unless life was all hearts and flowers, it would always be a disappointment. She didn't handle reality very well and perhaps May had to shoulder some of the blame in the spoiling of her as a youngster. She was still very proud of all Dene had achieved and couldn't help but be protective of her despite her concerns.

It seemed that all of her daughters but one, were not the best at relationships and she had already started to hear tales that Lynne was making a name for herself as one of the most fiery landladies in the area. Her customers knew if they spoke out of turn they would likely receive the unwelcome launching of an ashtray that would smash above their heads and shower the offender with glass. She had a good aim Lynne, but no common sense when it came to business. It was either howling raucous laughter or a vicious tongue-lashing with her. There was simply no in between. Maureen was the only girl who seemed blissfully happy and for that she was thankful. Gary and Irene were happy breeding children and this was the third in quick succession.

Summer was approaching and May decided it would be nice if they revisited a few old memories for Oldham Wakes and booked a holiday at Butlin's once more. Graham was game for it, but Rene couldn't get away from London.

Dennis and Derek both cried off, citing work commitments so it left Lynne, Dene, May, the two grandchildren and Graham. A good enough number to manage. Gary was at home with a pregnant Irene who was too far on to travel, but he had managed to get them a little discount on the holiday even though his star as a performer seemed to be on the decline.

There were no foreign holidays except for the very rich, so Butlin's it was. As they walked through the grassy avenues between the pastel painted chalets a few weeks later, May felt her heart lighten and fall at the same time. Edward would have loved this time with the little ones. Sharon was eleven and Deena six and May had saved a little money to treat them all, so very soon the children were excited with the purchase of a Basil Brush hand puppet and a gonk.

Graham was content to follow in the wake of his sisters and was happy as long has he had a couple of pints to bolster his social courage. By the end of the holidays he had even allowed them to teach him the basic steps of the waltz. He hadn't managed to get off with a girl, but he had hovered around the dance floor, so that was a step in the right direction and just being in Dene's company, who he idolised, was enough.

The days were spent by the pool or on the cable cars to the beach and the kids were having the best of times. The early evenings after tea were spent in the chalets with Dene and Lynne preparing for the evening's entertainment. May had offered to bring the kids home at nine p.m. and leave Graham and the girls to enjoy the dancing. She found she was more tired these days and glad of an early night after a full day. She had to acknowledge for the first time in her life that her bones were getting old. Too many years in the cold, damp environment of Wood Mill House were taking their toll.

The girls were out to the death and by the third day May cottoned on that both of them were enjoying the male attention just a little too much and were particularly concerned with looking the best they could. Butlin's had entered the swinging sixties and to the less naive, it was now known for sun, sea and sex. By the sixth evening of the first week a dark- haired male with a goatee beard called Wes would appear at Dene's side the minute she entered the ballroom and likewise Lynne with a big brash fella who went by the name of Kevin. May said nothing, but she noticed much and was not best pleased.

By the beginning of week two her daughters had given up the pretence that there was no romance in the air and May had lectured them both on their behaviour to be rebuked with, "Mum, it's just a bit of fun, there's no harm in it," from Lynne.

"...And what are these kids seeing and how will you explain that when they talk to their fathers when we get home?" was her retort.

"Deena's too little to see anything Mum and I've not done anything, he's just nice company and someone to dance with," answered an embarrassed Dene, with just a little too much colour.

"Aye, that's how it starts like enough, but I'll tell you now my girl, it stops here and you can look after your own children tonight, I'm not being your muggins!" Dene had the grace to look shamed but Lynne stuck out a stubborn chin.

"Aw Mam, don't be mean. Sharon won't say anything, I've promised her a new teddy if she keeps her gob shut, there's nothing serious going on with me and Kevin, we're just having a laugh!"

"Well tonight you can have a laugh with your kids in tow, because I'm going out for a drink with a couple of people I've met from Ireland."

Neither daughter looked pleased, but they had no choice but to comply and true to her threat, May took up with a couple of brothers, Paddy and Michael from County Cork and could be found downing the odd Guinness in the Gaiety Bar every night till the holiday ended, reminiscing on life in the 'old country'. The kids were trailed behind their mothers, but had a whale of a time regardless, as both the men courted the mothers through the child and they were spoilt rotten.

As they boarded the coach to depart for home, May noticed a particularly tearful exchange between Dene and her admirer, Wes. Apparently, he worked for Shell Oil in management and May was silently fuming as Dene had let slip he was also married, '...though unhappily', she had added and drawn a snort of derision from her mother and the retort of, "Aren't they all?"

Lynne seemed unperturbed at leaving her beau behind and gave him a hearty kiss of defiance on the cheek, knowing her mother to be watching and then left him without a backward glance. The two young girls trotted up to the coach, both in possession of an expensive teddy.

When they reached the Yelloways station in Rochdale Derek and Dennis were waiting to collect the baggage and ferry them all home. The kids were excited to see their daddies and, as Dennis swung Deena up into his arms, May heard Derek say to Sharon, "That's a lovely teddy, what's his name?"

"Kevin," came the little girl's response, "...after mummy's friend who bought it me."

May felt Lynne stiffen, rather than saw it, and Derek's face went puce as realisation dawned. Lynne scowled at the child and responded to her husband's glare with, "Don't get your knickers in a twist, it's not what you think!"

May hoped she had a good explanation ready and felt it best to ride in the car with Dennis and Dene who had fortunately missed the exchange, hoping for a little light relief. There was none to be found. Instead of recounting all they had done, Dene sat silently, leaving the child to chatter happily to her father all the way home. 'Yes, the times are changing and not for the good,' observed May grimly, as she sat quietly in the back with the excited child on her knee and sandwiched between Gray and the suitcases piled beside her and let the little girl ease the tension.

An hour later she was back in the small house and turning on the television to settle for the night. Graham was up in his room with a new record to add to the collection he now had, after finding an old wind-up gramophone in a house renovation that had been thrown out some weeks ago.

She lit the fire and put the kettle on when the noise on the television attracted her attention. There was a wrestling programme and Mick McManus was currently throwing some hapless opponent across the ropes. May had never seen anything like it before and she brought her cup into the living room and sat down to watch. She was getting to like this television more and more.

Ten minutes later Graham came running downstairs. "Mam! Are you all right?" Graham had heard her cries and mistaken it for distress. She sat before the television transfixed.

"Ooh you bugger! Get him! Get him you big Jesse!" It appeared May had found a new passion and she was hooked. Graham shrugged, made himself a brew and went back upstairs to the relative peace of the new Beatles single, 'I Feel Fine'.

Chapter Thirty Seven - 1965

Dene looked out of her office window across the Manchester skyline and chewed her nails. Wes hadn't given her his usual call from work today, usually posing as a buyer. She fretted at the thought he was losing interest.

The affair, as some would call it, was little more than a few passionate kisses on snatched lunches here and there when Wes was on business in town. It was all that they had managed, but the longing to be together had over-ridden propriety and she felt it wouldn't be long before they stepped over boundaries into a fully-fledged affair.

Dennis and she barely kissed nowadays and all the romance that she had dreamed of as a bride had never materialised. Their relationship sexually had never really started. When Dennis had approached her it was polite and perfunctory and Dene was always glad when it was over and she could turn away and dream her dreams of another life. Sometimes with a movie star or others a top fashion designer and more recently, Wes.

There just wasn't the chemistry and after Deena's birth, their further attempts at conceiving had resulted in two miscarriages. Dene had been warned that there would likely be no chance of conceiving after the last ectopic pregnancy had resulted in sepsis when the tube had ruptured. That had been the greatest sadness and the final nail in the coffin of their family plans. Recently, she had used her predisposition to losing babies as a shield from sex and Dennis had gradually ceased to try.

They both loved their little girl, but beyond that it was becoming a business relationship for survival's sake. They had recently had a downturn in Dene's trade. Elegance wasn't required as much nowadays and Dene, born in a time when it was a requirement, could not understand this new generation with their brightly coloured pants and floppy hats and mini-skirts that showed nearly everything they had got. She was mid-thirties and apparently already past it. She simply refused to copy the new styles and therefore had become a victim of her own reluctance to change with the times.

When you had the likes of Mary Quant and Biba on the high street and young, aspiring women took their business there, it wasn't long before the big stores followed. They were starting to include these new lines in-house and often this was at Pink Lady's expense.

They had eventually found it difficult to keep up the payments on the bungalow, despite Dennis's best efforts to take on extra work and they had reluctantly sold it, buying a small cottage in front of the row that May was in. It was sweet and overlooked Fletcher's Farmhouse but compared to the previous property, it was a come-down and Dennis had taken it particularly hard, blaming himself for not successfully promoting his own work enough to keep them afloat.

In truth, Dennis was earning enough to manage but it was Dene's business debts that had been sucking them dry. She refused to accept that this wasn't just a 'lean period' that would soon end and that they just had to ride out, but in fact the demise of her business.

Dennis had considered approaching his mother for a loan on Dene's persuasion, but he was too proud and when he had refused, it had just brought further rows between them. Life in the Elsworth household was tense at best and sour on the whole, each retreating into their own personal hell or, in Dene's case, heaven, where Wes was the main feature and her husband took second billing. It was her escape from life's disappointments.

Dennis hadn't liked the idea of being too close to his mother-in- law, but Dene had sold the idea that having mum a minute's walk away was a blessing rather than a curse. May could have the little girl before going to school and take her and pick her up whilst they were at work in Manchester. 'It would be such a help,' Dene had said and she had campaigned until Dennis had caved in to the pressure for the sake of peace.

Within a few short weeks he had already started to regret his decision as, 'May being May' and a strong character, was starting to get on his nerves with her constant calling in with Graham in tow and making 'suggestions' that impacted on his previous peaceful free time. All in all, his life in general had taken a turn for the worse and he was deeply unhappy. Dene was equally so, but for her it was the pain and frustration of her heart and imagination being engaged elsewhere, whilst responsibility held her captive here.

The phone rang and brought Dene back to reality and she picked it up quickly before her sister Maureen could answer. Maureen knew all the buyers and was quick witted enough to recognise an impersonator. Wes, being in oil sales would hardly pass for a Lewis's buyer under Maureen's questioning.

"Dene speaking." Her voice was breathy and betrayed her underlying nerves.

"Good morning, my darling, how are you today...are you alone?" He spoke quietly, so as not to be heard if anyone was close by.

Dene started to relax back into her chair, her relief evident to anyone who chanced to walk by her office window on the way to the cutting room, but no one did.

"Yes...I was starting to worry when you didn't call, are you alright?"

At the other end of the phone Wes's tone was weary. He also was in a marriage that had lost its love and the result for him was a wife who refused to do anything but keep his house, serve him and the children dinner and then retreat to her own room to watch the television. When she did venture out, it was to harangue him for the loss of her freedom to a man she couldn't bear to be with. It had resulted in them living separate lives, in all but name, nowadays.

This morning had been such an occasion and the resulting row had delayed him getting to work and he had spent most of his time since arriving at the office, desperately cramming for an important meeting and a presentation he had to deliver after lunch. He sounded strained and said he couldn't talk now, but he was on his way to Manchester next Tuesday and could they meet?

"I have something on, but I will re arrange it," she said "...I love you Wes," she said.

"I love you too, my darling." The phone clicked and Dene sat at her desk revelling in the little frisson's of excitement running through her solar plexus. She was a creature of imagination and the thought of the two of them, just seven days apart, was enough to keep her going through another worrying week of trying to balance the books and addressing the very real problems in her business.

At the other end of the phone Wes sat dejected at his desk. He hadn't said much to Dene, but his row with Margaret this morning had gone further than he had anticipated. It seemed she had somehow got wind that he was seeing someone and had made it perfectly clear that she was on to him.

Wes was a staunch catholic and had a family around him that would not appreciate his deviation into sin. He was totally bowled over by Dene and she had become his addiction, but leaving his wife and children for another woman? However much in love he was, it sent an arrow of despair to his heart. What was he to do? The implications to his life were huge.

Back in Manchester, Maureen had come into Dene's office with a worried look. She placed a stack of letters on the desk in front of Dene.

"We've got three reminders and a threat to put us on stop, what shall I do with them?" Dene looked up from her reverie slightly dazed and then she realised what her sister had said.

"You'd better pay them, we need them for the next range."

"Okay...Are we in real trouble Dene?" asked Maureen.

"I think we are," responded Dene sadly, "...but who do I choose to lay off?" Maureen pulled up a chair and sat down.

"How about me?" Maureen's matter-of-fact tone belied her excitement.

"No! I couldn't do that!" Dene cried out and her eyes filled with tears.

"You could if I was pregnant and needed a break," said Maureen with a mischievous smile. "Peter's on a good wage, so I was only staying because I like the work, but now I have to admit, with the last few days of feeling sick, I'd rather be at home over my own toilet bowl!"

Dene, looked at her sister with eyes wide. "Oh my god Mo, you finally managed it!"

"Not as if we haven't been trying hard enough!" she laughed. "The doc had said I might have problem conceiving, something to do with my tubes, but hey ho! Job done!." She raised her hands victoriously and gave Dene her best reassuring smile.

Dene rose and made her way round the desk to hug her sister. In her heart she knew it would take more than Maureen falling on her sword to save them, but it might give her breathing room to make some vital changes.

Maureen left swiftly to throw up and Dene realised how distracted she must have been to miss her sister's symptoms. She reached for the invoices once more and scanning them, picked up the phone to schmooze the companies and buy them some more time.

Chapter Thirty Eight - 1965

Lynne poured herself a drink as she prepared for opening time. The last year since their return from holiday had been difficult, with accusations and explanations and then more accusations. The atmosphere was thick with it.

Derek wasn't buying her story that she had just been friendly with her daughter's benefactor and he wasn't letting it go. Lynne herself, had to admit that she didn't actually sound plausible to herself and his attitude was understandable. As the first week had gone on the rows had become more heated until, standing her ground for the umpteenth time, she had let go of her temper and spat her responses straight back at him with no restraint.

"If you weren't so bloody boring, I wouldn't have to have looked for a bit of fun somewhere else!" The words were out before she could halt her mouth and the resounding slap she got across her face knocked her sideways. Since when had Derek ever laid a finger on her? It was a shock to both of them and for a few seconds she stood fazed and silent. The shock only lasted a moment and then she reached for a dining chair and threw it at him with all her strength.

"Don't think you are going to start that with me, you bastard, I'll bloody have you!"

Derek had dodged the chair but got a grip of her arm and twisted her wrist viciously up her back. She was grateful for the fashion being stiletto's and she scored a track down his shin that made him yelp and release her.

As they stood facing each other across the flat above the pub, it was clear that battle lines had been drawn. On that occasion Derek had slammed out and not come back until the early hours, surly and withdrawing from any conversation. She spent several hours mulling over her feelings and had to come to the conclusion that something had broken. It had been a few years coming, but she had to acknowledge that the fault, to some extent, was hers. Derek had never been a party animal and although he was pleasant and efficient, he wasn't geared up to a landlord's life as she was. It was long hours and high energy and he just wasn't the type. He would have much preferred to be back in his old job with its set hours and routine.

The behaviour had gradually deteriorated from them both. Derek had started leaving her to tend the bar alone once the heavy jobs were done and truth be known, she preferred it that way. By now, she was well known for her temper and humour equally and it tended to attract characters, as the more timid types shied away. The bar was noisy, brash and lively but not because of aggression. There were rarely fights and if there were, they were quickly over and the idiot stupid enough to start them was despatched through the doors by the seat of his pants. Derek seldom came down at night and the months turned to a year and no real reconciliation was evident. Lynne didn't miss the sex and she could find all the social company she needed on the other side of the bar and particularly in the form of an attractive fireman called Bob, who always got her laughing. For now, it was enough.

The appearance of her brother, Arthur and a few of his mates from Manchester was enough to deter anyone with half a brain and whilst they sat and drank and laughed like normal punters, you didn't mess with them, neither did you interrupt their conversations by starting a ruckus. The word had gone out that this was the Rochdale haunt of a couple of the Quality Street Gang, when they bothered to venture out of the Manchester limits. Only those with half a brain would start trouble in Lynne's establishment. She was connected now and a force to be reckoned with. The last few months of violent rows with Derek had taught her a few tricks of her own and she had toughened up.

The marriage, she felt, was over in all but the shouting...and shout they did, and often. The only time there was peace was when their daughter was home and for appearance's sake they both restrained their feelings most of the time and made nice in front of the young girl.

Sharon was a fiery redhead, inherited from her father, but her quick wit and feisty personality was definitely her mothers. Strong-willed and intelligent, she could give as good as she got, and by twelve she could out argue them both. Neither was she blind and could clearly see that her mum and dad weren't happy. By fourteen she was mature for her age and under no illusions that her parents needed to separate.

***

Dene hurried across Manchester to get the train to Wilmslow, telling her staff she had a meeting with a potential new buyer. There was a little hotel that had a restaurant that was quiet enough to give them privacy and it had become the regular place for her and Wes to meet. As usual, the train journey seemed endless and she felt that all eyes must be upon her flushed cheeks, though it was only minutes in reality.

Every step of this journey she knew as it took her to Wes and she committed it to memory for a time in the future when memories may be all she had. It was a combination of fear and exhilaration that propelled her onward and despite the recklessness of her actions she couldn't help herself. Leaving the train it was a short walk to the hotel, but nevertheless she scanned the pavement ahead of her, just in case she had the misfortune to bump into someone she knew.

Wes was in the reception when she arrived and as always, he stood and shook her hand as though it were a business meeting they were attending. If the reception suspected anything other, they did not show it as they made their way into the restaurant to be seated by the Maître D'.

Once alone, he grasped her hand across the table and kissed it passionately and the thrills that she had felt, all too rarely recently shuddered through her stomach once more at his caress.

"I've missed you so much darling, it's been too long," he whispered.

"I know, I can hardly bear it, Wes! I'm so lonely when I don't see you for this long." Her eyes filled with tears, part of it self-pity for her own plight financially and the feeling that Dennis didn't appreciate what it all meant to her and part genuine in her feelings for the man sat before her. Wes saw the tears sparkling in her eyes and mirrored her distress. He squeezed her hand tightly, unable to give her comfort in any other way.

"I'm sorry it's been so difficult lately, my wife is not the easiest woman and I have the children to consider." He placed his hand back in his lap as the waitress approached to leave the menu and only took her hand once more when he was sure they were unobserved.

"Can't we find a way to be together Wes? I can't go on like this with nothing but these lunches. I want to be proud to stand on your arm, not hide away like this!" It was clear by her voice she was at the end of her tether.

"My wife is a strong catholic, Dene, she would never let me go easily. I'm racking my brains for a solution for both of us. There is no easy way out and we would have to give them grounds for divorce, otherwise it's such a long wait. My worry is she would stop me seeing the children and my own family would disown me if I got divorced...It's just so hard." His own voice was thick with emotion and Dene sat back in her chair with a determined expression.

"So what happens to us, Wes? We can't keep meeting like this for ever. I want to be with you...in every way." Dene was past caring what people thought and never having religion as a strong influence in her life, it was only propriety that was holding her back.

Wes kissed her hand and held it to his cheek once more. His eyes told her his thoughts and the passion flared once more between them.

"I have a room here and a meeting tomorrow, I..."

"Let's go there!" she silenced him quickly and bent to pick up her bag. Gone was her doubt, the longing for something to give her life meaning once more had overcome it and she stood up to see him sitting there dazed.

"Are you sure?" he whispered looking around guiltily.

"More than I ever have been." Her eyes gave her away and he rose from the table and waved the waitress away, giving his apologies for their change of mind.

The journey up the stairs was a mix of terror and desire. Every step felt to Dene like a caress as he walked just behind her. She sensed every breath on her neck as he looked sideways to watch her. It was a heady and intoxicating feeling, knowing that they were about to be lovers for the first time.

When they reached his room door, he fumbled for the key and as he closed the door behind him, they just stood for what seemed like an age, paralysed with a passion that had them shaking with some previously unknown reaction.

"This is wrong on every level," he whispered and reached for her.

"Kiss me," was her only answer.

***

May had picked Dene's daughter up from school. The little girl had cried the first few days, but had settled as the week had gone on, regaling her horrified grandmother all the way home with the tale that one boy had brought his pet grass snake in and how she had stroked it. Dene would fair pass out if her daughter repeated it to her mother later, so she warned the child not to tell mummy as she didn't like snakes.

The afternoon was warm and May instructed Deena to sit on the step and draw whilst she made tea for her. In that respect the child followed her mother in so much as she was content to sit for hours crayoning mermaids and stories and was very little trouble. The little girl adored her grandmother and she, in return was adored. It was an easy companionship.

"Grandma, will you help me make a rag doll?" she asked.

"If you want...here, eat your sandwich and I'll find some scraps for after and we'll have a go."

The child looked in distaste at the bread sprinkled with sugar.

"Ugh...sugar! I don't like the way it crunches on your teeth." She moaned, following in her uncle's footsteps.

"Be still child and if you're good we'll go to the shop for a twopenny jubbly," the child's eyes lit up.

"Afternoon, Mrs Handley," came a voice from the road. It was the workmen from nearby that May had been keeping in a supply of tea all week. "We're just going to the pub for a pint. Do you want us to bring you a bottle back?"

May stepped over Deena, sat eating her sandwich reluctantly on the doorstep, as she wiped her hands on her pinny to go speak to the men.

"That's very kind of you, I'll have a milk stout," she smiled.

"Right oh!... What will the little girl have?" Deena looked up from her sandwich to the workmen.

"I'll have a milk stout as well, please," she said, quite matter of factly.

The men exploded with laughter and May smiled.

"No, she actually will...she's quite used to it...good for the bones."

"Why were those men laughing Grandma?" asked the seven year old.

"They're not Irish, they don't understand". May smiled.

***

Dene barely made it back home in time that evening and May saw that she was distracted. Dennis would be home within the hour and she would have to pull herself together by then. The shakes began again as she got off the train and made her way home. She was in love, deeply, for the first time in her life and it felt like nothing she had ever felt before.

The brief two hours they had snatched together had been heaven and heartbreak rolled into one. It was as though you could not tell where one body ended and the other began and the eroticism of their lovemaking had overwhelmed her. It had come so naturally that she was bemused as to why she was capable of feeling and sharing such intimacy with Wes that she could not feel for Dennis. Was it because she was older now?... it was beyond her. Wes had unlocked some hidden woman that had lain dormant all these years and her adrenalin was pumping fit to burst her heart. Frisson's of her orgasm were still echoing through her and she flushed at the memory.

Overheated, she took off her jacket and lay it across her arm seeking something to cool and calm herself before she got home. The breeze had done its trick to some extent, but not enough to deflect May's keen eye.

"You alright, love?" she had asked, knowing that times were difficult at the moment with work.

"Just hectic Mum. I'd best get home and sort out tea," she said gathering Deena's things quickly with her head down.

"But Grandma said she'd help me make a dolly!" wailed the child in protest.

"Leave her be, get home and sort your chores and I'll bring her round in a bit," said May, sensing that Dene was a bag of nerves and putting it down to financial pressures. Dene seized the opportunity to go home and re-live her afternoon and make some sense of the situation without her daughter underfoot. She gave the little girl a kiss and was gone with a swift thanks. By the time Dennis arrived she had claimed some of her equilibrium back and tea and normality was on on the table once more.

There were bills to open on his arrival and a discussion ensued about money, which was never good. Dennis was worried.

"What about selling your car?" she had said.

"That's all I've got for myself, everything else goes to support you," he had responded outraged.

"Well, that's good for you, but when do you ever take me out for a drive in it?" she upped the level somewhat with a sarcastic tone.

"You're always too bloody busy," he snarled back, exasperated. It wasn't going well, as Dennis was feeling aggrieved and discussion turned to row. Dene had a tendency to become hysterical when an argument ensued and would not be calmed down easily. Dennis wasn't to know there was a whole other reason for her dissatisfaction with life and assumed she was being a drama queen and told her as much.

This did not go down well and as May walked towards the cottage with the little girl sat atop Gray's shoulders walking beside her. The row was in full flow and could be heard up the street. Not just heard, but seen, as Dene was currently stood with a stray brick from a loose section of the garden wall in her hand, poised over the bonnet of the grey Morris Minor parked on the front drive. May shouted and broke into a run as Dennis's arm wrestled with her daughter, but it was too late and she launched the brick, but with less power than she'd hoped due to Dennis's restraint on her arm. Gray dropped the child to her feet and ran after his mother holding the little girl's hand.

By the time they reached the couple, the brick was sat atop the car bonnet and Dennis's face was a mask of horror. Dene was sobbing and shouting incoherently and May waded in.

"You! Inside!" she ordered Dene. "Gray, take the little one to the park!" She looked at Dennis, who had gingerly lifted the brick to assess the damage as Dene fled inside.

"What's this about?" she asked him.

"I'm buggered if I know, she's off her head!" He was close to tears and May felt sorry for him. He was a nice enough bloke, just not right for Dene, he had given in to her too much and he was probably just too nice for her highly-strung daughter. She looked at the car and smiled sadly.

"Looks like miraculously it's escaped injury... I suggest you get in it and take yourself off awhile. I'll see what's up with her."

Dennis stood for a moment and thought better of telling his mother-in-law to 'bugger off'. Yet maybe she could talk some sense into his wife. The thought kept him silent and right now he was heartily sick of this family and putting his own feelings and needs aside for them. He was not a drinker but probably better that he took himself off in the car to find the peace of a quiet pint and preserve it and himself from further assault. May walked inside to find Dene sobbing hysterically still with her head in her hands on the sofa.

"You are going to have to sort yourself out, girl. This can't go on..."

"Oh, Mum!" she wailed. "I'm so unhappy!" and she commenced sobbing once more.

May let her cry it out and went into the kitchen to put on the kettle. By the time she had brought in a cup of sweet tea for them both Dene had drained her emotions and was relatively calm once more. Handing her a hanky, she sat across from her and waited for complete silence before speaking.

"You need to tell me what's going on here, Doreen". She used her proper name, something she rarely did nowadays.

Dene lifted stricken eyes towards her mother. "I don't want to be in this marriage any more, Mum...I hate it!" She started to cry again.

"Does he hit you?" she asked grimly.

"No!"

"Treat you badly?"

"No...its not like that...It's just never been right...from the beginning. There's nothing between us...Nothing!" The tears spilled over once more. "Everything's such a mess and the business is going under...I don't know what to do."

May sat quietly whilst her daughter's words spilled over each other, a mixture of fear for her career and dissatisfaction with the life that hadn't turned out as she had hoped. When she had run down to silence once more, May leaned forward in her chair and spoke quietly.

"I'll tell you, love. When I first came over here with your dad, I had very little left in me and there felt like there was nothing left to give. It took a while, but gradually I felt my feelings grow once more. Times can be hard and there are moments when you might feel you have made the wrong choices. I left a life of wealth and comfort behind, that I felt I should have had, to live this simple and poor life here. There were times when I resented what I had potentially lost, but I had you all and there was nothing I could change about the road life had taken me on, so I embraced it. Now you might not be having the best time, at the moment, but you have that beautiful little girl. Your business may go under, but you can learn from it and start again if you have to... and for that child's sake you must learn to mend what is broken in your marriage. Dennis isn't a bad man Dene. He may be the best you have on offer and he is your husband who you made a commitment to. You should try to do your best to honour that, otherwise you will bring down a whole heap of unhappiness on both your heads."

Dene's eyes fell to her lap and she sighed, "What if I don't want to mend it mum? We're both so unhappy and I know he feels the same."

"Then you both need to sort it out and do what's right for your daughter...whatever it is!" Her voice held a hint of steel and Dene flinched at the rebuke. She knew her mother was right but she was too far gone with her feelings for Wes to think of anything other than the possibility of a life with him. The rest of her obligations paled into insignificance beside it. She and Wes had taken an irrevocable step and now all Dene could think of was beating a path to him, regardless of the consequences. She might even be pregnant by him. There was just too much of the romantic in her to assess the situation from a realistic stance, so she chose to hide her real situation, knowing her mother would not approve. Besides Rene managed well enough alone, so could she.

"I'll try my best...," was her answer, but deep down Dene knew they were just words. Her heart was set on Wes, and naively she had pushed any thought of the pain that she could cause safely to the back of her mind and set her heart on a course of action that demonstrated she had no intention of following her mother's advice.

Later that evening, Dennis came home to a sullen and quiet wife. Deena, the child, was tucked up in bed and fortunately had not been unduly traumatised by the scene she had caught a glimpse of.

"I'm sorry if I came across too heavy earlier Dene. I didn't mean to upset you, but we have to talk about this." Dennis knew that to argue would only cause more histrionics, but the situation was serious and the financial difficulties had to be addressed.

"You don't need to worry. I'm running down the business and I will close it once the current orders are met. I'll get a job...so you have got your way!" She sat with a monotone voice tinged with sarcasm. It really was unfair on Dennis, but in her head she had started to form a plan to free her to be with Wes and she was manufacturing a subconscious blame to excuse her adultery.

Whether it was right or fair right now didn't matter. Besides the business would hamper being a wife to Wes, he travelled abroad to America and she would want to go with him. Reality, in the throes of passion, was taking a back seat.

"It isn't 'my way' at all Dene, that's so unfair!" Dennis was appalled but Dene didn't care right now. She had seen a chink of light through the door and her fingers were on the wood, ready to prise it fully open and run through to whatever she thought may be on the other side.

***

A couple of months later, Dene was closing the doors on her business for the last time and cried brokenly in the hallway. All her dreams had been in Pink Lady for so many years and here she was reduced to accepting a job in a local carpet shop until she was back on an even keel financially. Her staff had been leaving in dribs and drabs as she had told them early on to give them chance to find other work without a break in employment, but it was still a sad last day for the few left.

Wes had been so understanding when she told him the business had to be closed and even offered to loan her money, but her pride wouldn't allow her to take it. She had felt a little ashamed that she had laid a lot of the blame on Dennis' shoulders, citing his lack of support. She didn't want Wes thinking she was a bad business woman and so it seemed the only way to justify the losses. In truth, she recognised that it was her own reluctance to move with the times that had been her downfall, she knew that now and she wouldn't make that mistake should there be a next time.

Time was ticking and Dene was completely excluding Dennis from her life and playing the victim to justify her actions. She was not a naturally cruel person, but it was the only way to achieve the freedom she wanted so badly. Her conversations when required were clipped and cold.

Dennis she could see, was so very unhappy and she felt bad for him. After weeks of Dene's constant rebuffs he had become equally cold and clipped in return and it started to spark a few sarcastic comments. Before long, they had started to deteriorate into full-blown rows once more. Dene, it seemed, was getting her way and driving Dennis to distraction and a decision.

There wasn't really any concrete final straw, but it was a Saturday morning and from nowhere the row had blown up, just as she had made a tray of tea and biscuits for her mother and Graham, who were on the way round.

"Not your mother, again?. It's ten o'clock in the morning at the weekend for God's sake! Does she need to be here all the time? And does she have to trail Graham on her apron strings everywhere?" Dennis hadn't even the chance to feel bad about his comments when something in Dene snapped and she launched the tray upwards and then back down over his head, as he sat with a clatter. The teapot had flown upwards and shattered on the low ceiling spewing its contents across them both.

May and Graham chose that moment to make their entrance unannounced to find Dennis spattered with tea leaves and cursing as the water scalded where it caught him. The ceiling took the brunt and was carrying the 'one for the pot' share of tea leaves. Dennis carried the majority of the remainder.

Graham stood open mouthed, but then seeing Dennis in such a state, saw the funny side in his youthful lack of wisdom and started to laugh. May just uttered two words, 'Bugger me!' This was enough for Dennis, his humiliation was complete and his anger long held in, erupted.

"That's it!" he yelled. "I've just about had enough of you and this family!" He would have carried on had he not seen the little girl sat peering through the bamboo poles on the stairs. The poles he had put in as a modern touch to the old cottage that wasn't really his taste, framed the face of his stricken child and it was enough. He ran to Deena and cuddled her on the stairs.

"It's all right darling, mummy and daddy didn't mean it, you go up to your room awhile and play whilst we clear this mess, ok? And then maybe Grandma will take you to the shop for some sweeties?"

"Ok, Daddy," the child sniffed, a single tear spilling from her eyes. It damn near broke his heart and he knew the rows could not go on any longer. He gave the child one last kiss and took her back to her room and spent a few minutes going through the motions of playing with the sweet shop she had had for Christmas to reassure her, whilst his thoughts hammered through his head.

When he felt she was okay, he left her with another kiss and went into the other room. After standing with his hands over his face for a minute to draw a few broken breaths, he silently packed a case, washed himself off as best he could and walked down the stairs past a sobbing Dene and her mother, glowered at Graham and walked out the door.

The Morris Minor departed slowly and Dennis turned the car in the direction of his old home, Blackpool, and his mother. It wasn't until many years later that he would tell his daughter how he had cried every night for the loss of his child in the first few painful days after he took his decision to leave.

Back at the cottage, as the noise of the car subsided, everyone sat stunned. May sat on the edge of the sofa and put her arm around Dene.

"Perhaps it's for the best, love," she said. "Graham, clean this up and make us another pot of tea, love."

"But the pot's smashed Mam," he said.

"Use your loaf lad! There's a pan over there... and check on Deena."

Graham ran up the stairs and looked in on the little girl. She was sitting on the floor with her toys around her, but she was very subdued.

"Do you want a drink our smelly?" He called her by the nickname he had given her for her first proud effort with her potty and it had stuck.

"Has Daddy gone?" was all she said, but it was clear the child hadn't missed much. Graham struggled for words for a minute as events hit home and the fact that this little girl might have to live without the daddy who loved her, close by.

"Aye love, he's had to go visit his mum for a few days."

"Why couldn't I go with him?"

"Because you've got school on Monday and you don't want the Headmaster knocking on our door now, do you? He'll be back soon enough… Milk?" The little girl's lip quivered but she bravely held back. She was an intelligent child and it was clear she could hear her mums crying from below.

"…and biscuits?" It was enough to appease the little girl for the moment and as Graham descended the stairs he vowed he would be the best uncle that little girl could have.

Chapter Thirty Nine 1965

Rene smoothed her taffeta dress as she walked through the hotel doors looking serene and confident. The fashion show was the last she would attend before moving her business back to Manchester.

Paul, her son was about to start secondary school. Thinking it would be the best time to make the move, she had timed it so he could start with all the others at the new year's first term. This way he would just be like all the rest and not be so much the 'comer inner', to use an old northern term. Especially as he had acquired a soft southern twang. He would have enough to combat on his return, without being subjected to the class bully if he stood out.

London had been exciting at first for Rene, but within a couple of years she had realised that city life wasn't all she had thought it would be and, truth be known, she missed being able to look up and see the moors. London had some beautiful areas, but they were beyond her budget and she was confined to the less affluent areas and a flat without a garden. She missed having neighbours that chatted on the street. In short, she missed home and her siblings, especially Dene. She even missed Lynne, which surprised her most of all.

She had been asked out on several occasions by attractive men and had accepted, but never let anyone too close. Her heart was set on being her own person and her experience with Stan had made her reluctant to put her trust in anyone else. She had Paul and he was a bright boy, but it was an isolated life. The success seemed hollow without her family close to share it with and having made enough money to invest back home she took the decision to return.

Once the thought settled she felt happier. Paul wasn't so happy as he had friends nearby, but she convinced him that he would have lots of new friends at the Bluecoat School she had managed to get him into, which was considered the best in the area.

She had rented a gracious looking shop on Union Street, which was the more affluent part of the town. She didn't want to be working at the current pace for much longer and was looking forward to moving into the little house at Uppermill she had purchased outright with the equity from her London flat, such was the difference in north and south property prices.

Uppermill was picturesque and up and coming and had a station to Manchester down the road, so she had thought it a sound investment. She also bought another small cottage in Mossley nearby as a rental to supplement her income. She could always sell it then and realise the capital if times got hard.

The fashion show was a necessity for business and as glamorous as it looked, it was just work. It required her to get a sitter for Paul, as she didn't like leaving him alone at home in the heart of London till late, which he resented. At fourteen he was mature for his age, with the thick black 'Handley' hair that, combined with his father's looks, made him a handsome boy. He would not be short of girls when he got older and with his friendly, outgoing and kind personality it wouldn't take him long to resettle back home. His sitter was a nice woman who lived next door and as Rene came in late and weary, the woman was just making herself a pot of tea.

"How was the show?" she enquired.

"The usual, all psychedelic and loud music" she grimaced.
"What happened to Glen Miller and the crooners for goodness sake?. Much easier on my head!"

The woman laughed, "Well I hate to add to your pain, but Paul has discovered 'The Animals'. He's been playing that 'House of the Rising Sun' he found in a second hand record shop on the way home from school constantly, it's nearly driven me mad..."

"Oh good God! I knew I shouldn't have bought him that Dansette record player last Christmas!" She laughed with her.

"It gets worse..."

"Could it?" Rene asked smiling widely.

"Oh yes...I asked him what he wanted to do when he left school and he told me he was going to be a DJ and call himself Prince Paul and his Go Go Girls."

"Good lord, there's no hope." and both the women laughed out loud once more.

***

Dene had been to the extravagance of having a telephone installed within a week of Dennis's departure, using the excuse that Deena would be able to talk to her daddy more often. There was some truth in that as Dene had noticed that the child was looking pale, with dark shadows under her eyes and it had occurred that, despite everyone's reassurances, her daughter was grieving for her father. In truth, it was she who had been on the phone to Wes constantly.

Now that she and Dennis had split, it was even harder to make ends meet and Dennis himself had taken temporary accommodation in a back room at his mother's and was far from happy. Until he could get a job and some money, he was dependent on his mother's generosity.

It certainly wasn't the most glorious time for a proud man. The room was long and narrow and to Dennis it was the final insult in his decline from an affluent life and his own stylish home to a miserable bedsit. The room was vacant for the simple reason that it didn't rent often in his mother's full house because it was so depressing. Dene and he hadn't sorted out maintenance because, as yet they hadn't spoken personally, such was the resentment and anger between them.

His mother had uncomfortably become the go-between as she had always been fond of Dene and was best placed to keep the peace. Right now Dene had only her own income from the part-time job at the carpet store to pay the bills and she was constantly frightened. Luckily, there had been few debts to pay on the closure of her business but neither were there any savings. She would have to make an official approach soon if Dennis didn't send something to them.

The first week after the split she had rung Wes to be met with stunned silence when she told him the news and that she was free to be with him.

"Dene, it's not that simple, these things take time and I have my children to think of." Dene had started to cry, saying that it was, 'ok for her to upset her child for him, but he wasn't prepared to make the same sacrifice'. He had comforted her and sent her twenty pounds in an envelope to help her for a couple of weeks whilst he got his head round things. It pacified her for a week or so, but very soon she was again questioning him as to when he would make the break with his wife.

"Let me come and see you and we'll talk things through Dene. This is all so sudden and we had never really discussed you making the break from your husband...you have to give me time to get my head round things," he had said, and Dene and he had arranged a day the next week.

Wes had replaced the phone with a heavy heart. It really wasn't that simple. Every day he looked at his wife and children with renewed guilt. It was all very well being madly in love with someone, but when that someone wasn't your wife you carried a heavy heart at the pain you were inflicting on the ones who deserved your loyalty first and foremost. If you were a decent man, it lay heavier still.

Wes had spent several sleepless nights running different scenarios through his head. Dene wasn't about to be kept in the background and he would have to make his decision and live with it. Every day of that week he sleepwalked through work carrying a burden he felt would break him.

His marriage was no bed of roses but he had committed to it before God and divorce was a sin. Not to mention the hell and fury that would be rained down upon him from his wife and her family, let alone his own. He loved Dene so much, but was it enough to exchange for the potential loss of his children and family? He couldn't come to any conclusion, so he put it off, hoping to find some miracle solution when they met the following week.

Dene became ever more agitated as the week went on and May began to worry about her daughter's frame of mind, unaware as she was of the real cause, she thought the stress of the break up was having an effect. She took the little girl as much as possible to give her a break.

Poor Graham bore the brunt as Deena insisted on giving him a hairstyle every day. He patiently tolerated hours of her repeatedly soaking him through as the little girl stood behind him on the sofa with a comb and a cup of water to style his DA (Duck's Arse) into a place she was happy with in her child's mind. He was a diffident young man, but he set that aside and came into his own with children. May had thought what a lovely father he could make one day.

Thursday was the day and Dene had planned to be ill from work, but hadn't told her mother. She took Deena to school as normal and then snuck home instead of catching the bus to her employment in Shaw. She had pondered on what was the greater risk and decided home was preferable to meeting him nearby and risking discovery by someone that knew her employer. She needed the job right now and 'skiving off' did not come naturally.

She rushed home to bathe and prepare, just in case talking turned to lovemaking and she wanted to look her best for Wes. The day was dull, but she didn't dare risk turning the lights on, on the chance her mother or Graham might come past and discover she had stayed off work.

Her nerves were jangling and she could barely stand with the adrenalin rushing through her. Surely Wes would have to make a move soon, they couldn't keep putting it off. As for herself, she was quite prepared to take the role of guilty party in any divorce, as long as the end result was a new life for her and the man she adored.

His deep green Austin Healey 3000 was not a car easily missed in a small village as it pulled up across from the cottage. Dene hovered in the window having had a warning call ten minutes before from a phone box nearby asking if was okay to come now. She opened the door quickly and ushered him in, shaking and smiling and close to tears all at once.

Once the door was closed, he hugged her to him but didn't go to kiss her. Instead, he beckoned her to come and sit down.

"Don't you want some tea or anything?" she asked nervously. It all felt wrong and not at all the atmosphere she had imagined and she became more jittery.

"No thank you my love...please come and talk to me and tell me how you are". He patted the seat beside him.

"We have to be careful, mum isn't far away, perhaps we should go out to lunch after all?" she carried on distractedly.

"Dene...come and sit please...and when we've talked we can go to lunch if you want to?" he said solemnly. She complied and sat down, tears ready to spill. He took her hand in his and kissed it affectionately.

"I love you very much Dene, you must know that, but these past months have been the hardest for me, and you, to bear. My wife is not a happy woman, neither does she have any affection for me. I don't know why...it just is that way. Maybe we married too soon. I expect you feel that way yourself. She is a strong personality and I know right now if I tell her I'm leaving her and then set up house with another woman, she would stop me seeing my children and I don't want a day when I can't be the first and the last person they see...Can you understand that?"

Dene sat silently, a cold pit of fear lodging in her stomach. What a fool she had been. He was giving her the brush off, she knew it! He took her silence for understanding and continued.

"This has developed so suddenly that I have hardly had time to think things through. I never thought you and your husband were so close to splitting up, so it's all moved a bit too fast for me to prepare... What I suggest is we keep things as they are and I'll help you financially...baby don't cry!" He stopped, appalled as her tears spilled over silently and went to hug her to him, but she resisted and pushed him away.

"I thought you loved me...What an idiot I've been!" Wes was stricken by the venom in her voice.

"I do love you!... but it's not as easy as you seem to believe."

"It was easy for me! All I've done is make life hell for Dennis because I believed that was the only way for us to be together." Her anger started to rise and she moved away from him, her body language telling its own story. He grasped her hand and tried to turn her back to him but she shrugged him off.

"You have your daughter. It's nearly always that way," he continued, "but the men never really get the children in a divorce. The mothers always win on that score nowadays. I'd have to live without them and I can't do that Dene. If you loved me you wouldn't ask me to!...I'm just asking for time."

His distress was clear, but to Dene, the realisation that he was not about to immediately come to her had broken all her romantic dreams apart. She rose up suddenly from the sofa, tears ceased and her mouth so dry she feared she couldn't even swallow, let alone speak. He saw how shocked she was and stood to gather her to him once more. This time she threw him off violently.

"Get out!" she screamed.

"Dene, please!"

"GET OUT!"

The door opened suddenly as May and Graham appeared. They really had a knack for choosing the most inappropriate times.

May had gone to Shaw Market and called into the carpet shop to see her daughter, only to be told she was ill and she had come round to see if she was alright. Clearly, she wasn't, but not for the reasons May had thought and her mouth set in a grim line as she recognised Wes from Butlin's and saw her daughter's distress. She had only caught a few seconds conversation, but it was enough.

"What the bloody hell is going on here?" Her angry words brought her both their attention. Wes was the first to recover.

"I'm sorry, Mrs Handley, I didn't mean to upset her...I care a great deal for her...," he stammered, shaken by the interruption in the middle of everything.

"But not enough eh?...I know your type, you're ten a penny, big shiny car and your flash suits and you think you're God's gift to women!"

"Make him go, Mum", sobbed Dene, crying once more.

"You heard her." Graham had become a man and found his voice.

"I just want to speak to her for a few minutes...please." His eyes flew to Dene as he pleaded and she started to weaken and would have relented, but May was having none of it.

"Out! Graham... get him out and if he won't go, throw him out! And I'll make sure his wife knows what he's been up to!" May's tone brooked no argument and Graham didn't need any second bidding. He grabbed Wes by the scruff of the neck as Dene protested and launched him through the open door and in the direction of his car. He tried to turn to speak to Dene as she followed them through the door crying, but he was being pushed across the road, aggressively. May stood between Dene and the scuffling pair, keeping one eye on them both, but it seemed Graham was holding his own and she turned on Dene who was now crying out to Wes.

"Get inside!" she growled. "Haven't you embarrassed yourself enough you stupid girl?" She was hardly a girl, but at that moment she felt like a sixteen year old experiencing her first broken heart.

"It's none of your business, Mum...I love him!" she howled at her mother. By now, Wes had climbed in his car and Graham had kicked at the door as he fumbled to start the sleek machine and take it out of harms way.

"Go on...Begger off and don't come back unless you want some more!" he shouted triumphantly. No man was messing about with his sister.

"You don't know what love is, by God or you wouldn't have put your child through all this, for what? Some married man, who won't leave his wife...oh yes, I heard! Here was me thinking it was all Dennis' doing and it's you all along! I'm ashamed of you, ashamed!" shouted May.

Graham came in proud as a peacock and expecting praise to be turned on by his sister.

"You had no right to treat him like that! How dare you interfere in my life!" Gray's mouth opened and closed like a codfish. He wasn't expecting that his sister, having never raised her voice to him in all these years would attack him so verbally after she asked them to throw Wes out. It was a bitter blow and Graham did not take well to criticism.

"Well what was he bloody doing here anyway?... and why weren't you at work? Mam says you were off sick. That's a likely story by the look of you!" He stomped off through the door leaving May to finish the discussion.

"I'm done with you, my girl. All this time I felt sorry for you and you were behaving like a bloody harlot. I'll look after Deena for you while you work, but don't ask me for anything else in future!"

She was gone so quick that the silence left behind after half an hour of chaos was ominous and Dene sat stunned, too stricken to cry another tear. The ticking of the clock was her only company. She was separated, with no money and a child, having lost the only man she had ever felt anything real for and who could have given them a good life. For what? Pride? The hatred her family had shown him would surely keep him away forever. She was alone...

She hadn't even the ability to move and she sat paralysed for what seemed like hours. Her eyes felt stiff and when she finally went to the mirror to check, she saw that they had ballooned in some kind of strange reaction with unshed tears. There was a dullness that couldn't be broken as she went to the school for Deena in a daze not daring to trust that her mother would collect her after today. May was at the gate, but clearly not for talking other than to say that she would keep the child overnight, but by tomorrow she had best pull herself together and look to her own. She walked away silently and went home to bed. It was 4pm. She stayed in bed the next day and only got up in time to receive her daughter home.

May kissed the child and said little else as she pushed her through the door. Graham was nowhere to be seen and he could sulk for England. At that point, Dene was so past caring she didn't even feel anything beyond her own self-pity.

She had just given her daughter tea when the door rapped and opened. In walked Lynne with Sharon reluctantly in tow.

"She's only gone and got bloody nits our Do, will you help me get them out?" Sharon came through the door looking as though she was about to be shot and Dene sat her niece down to reassure her it would be ok. It was what she needed. Lynne said nothing but Dene knew.

"News travels fast then?" she looked at her sister who was pouring some noxious fluid onto Sharon's scalp.

"Did you think it wouldn't? By heck you're a dark horse!"

"Mum's not speaking to me..."

"Take no mind, the cantankerous old bat has no room to talk. Our Rene was nearly born a bastard but for a few weeks grace!"

"Lynne!" whispered Dene in horror, glancing towards the children.

"Well she was! We call Rene the duchess, but out of all of us she has least right to the name...our Mam saw to that." She grinned at Dene and it brought the first chink of light back into the darkness.

"I'm glad she's coming back from London...I miss her," said Dene.

"Well I don't! She'd best not come lording over me when she gets back, stuck up bitch!" she replied and rubbed the nit solution harshly into her daughter's head whilst she squirmed.

"Lynne! That's awful of you," cried Dene.

"Well...she is a stuck up bitch!" came the retort. They never had seen eye to eye, but she had the grace to look a little shamed. She loved her sister really.

"What am I going to do for money Lynne? Dennis hasn't given me any maintenance yet and Wes was helping me and now that's all blown to pieces. I don't know what to do!" She welled up with tears.

"Stop worrying over nothing Do," she said. "You can have a couple of bar shifts at the weekend at mine and bring Deena with you. Our Sharon will look after her. That'll bring you a few quid and you'll get tips, the pretty ones always do."

"Thanks Lynne, that could help," She sniffed and blew her nose, thinking, 'How the mighty are fallen', but beggars couldn't be choosers and she needed the money.

***

A week later Rene returned home and was busy setting up the new shop with new suppliers, sensing Dene was not up to restarting her business just now. She'd offered Dene a job, but Oldham was a longer journey than the ten minutes bus ride to the carpet shop in Shaw, so she thanked her and turned it down reluctantly. There was a part of her that baulked against becoming Rene's assistant again, when she once had status as a partner. It would be the last straw for her pride to see some other designs other than her own featured, but she couldn't promise to deliver working on her own and so they agreed it was best for Rene to find her stock elsewhere for now. She had lost her confidence along with her heart and she hadn't the strength to rebuild on her own.

Working for Lynne was almost social once she got her head around pulling a good pint quickly and she could cope with that. So on Saturday, as low as she felt, she knew she had to get up, get dressed and put on her make-up and make for the Bowl and Onion. Wes hadn't rung and she was too hurt and proud to ring him. No, that part of her life was over. She would never allow any man into her heart again.

As she trudged to the bus stop with Deena in tow, every step felt like she was wading through mud. The little girl sensed her mood and was quiet too. That didn't last long, for as soon as she reached Lynne's pub Deena and Sharon were given the task of polishing the tables and putting out the ashtrays. Derek kept to the kitchen and Lynne fronted operations, showing Dene how to pull the perfect pint.

As soon as the doors opened Lynne shooed the girls upstairs and Sharon took her cousin to play all her new records. Deena thought her cousin was very grown up. She particularly liking the one by 'Twinkle' and, although it was very sad, it appealed. Another romantic in the making.

Three hours later, Dene was in the thick of the hubbub that was Lynne's establishment. She hadn't time to be sad and the one thing you could say for Lynne was that she was a force to be reckoned with. Whether it was in producing hilarity or sending a few sarcastic words in the right direction that left the receiver in no uncertain terms that the wrong behaviour wouldn't be tolerated in her pub.

Dene was doing the lunchtime shift and as she left at 4pm with Deena skipping alongside, she realised that despite it being full-on work, she had found herself smiling. Perhaps she would survive this heartbreak after all.

Chapter Forty - 1967

Sharon was just fourteen and a half as she wandered through Rochdale on her way home from school. Hearing her name called, she turned. Scanning the street ahead, she realised her uncle Arthur was standing ahead of her with a couple of shady looking men. The pair who turned out to be the local booky's 'collectors'. She waved and walked over. Arthur stood, smartly dressed as always and with his glass eye staring back wildly at anyone who glanced his way. He threw his arm round her shoulder.

"Hiya our kid, what you up to?" he greeted her affectionately.

"Nothing really, just going to pop into 'Woolies' to buy myself a record. Isn't it hot? I'm fair melting."

"That it is, come on, shap thesen, we're going for a drink in Yates's. I'll buy you a shandy, but you'll have to take your tie off or we'll be done for buying you a drink under age. If you want I'll give you a lift home, but for God's sake don't tell yer mam you've been in Yates's or she'll have my guts for garters!" Even though he moved more in Manchester circles nowadays, he still delighted in using his strong rural dialect.

This was a bit grown up thought Sharon, not one to shy away from a bit of mischief. Uncle Arthur was always good for a laugh and she followed on gladly. Yates's Wine Lodge beckoned as they crossed the road facing the gracious Rochdale Town Hall that Adolf Hitler had admired so much for its architecture that he had aspired to dismantle and rebuild it in his new elite capital city of the Third Reich, Germania. Had the Nazi invasion been successful, it would have flown a different flag. Sharon had learned that in her history lesson and she looked on the building now in a new light and she wondered how scared her parents must have been as children watching the Manchester Blitz from the hills and wondering if the bogeyman was coming for them at any time.

"Sit in the corner while I go to the bar and behave yourself till I get back." Sharon nodded and scurried over to the booth that hid her from view. Arthur always looked the part in his smart suits and Sharon had heard he was a bit of a gangster, but to the young girl it just made him a bit exciting to hang about with. Arthur and his mates went to the bar with the exception of one who sat down beside her.

"So what's yer name then?" he asked.

"Sharon..." She eyed the newcomer, who was quite good looking and about thirty. Just starting to reach an age where she was curious about boys, he was young enough to be interesting to her, but old enough to know better.

The others came over just as he was into his chat up routine and becoming a little too forward. Sharon, despite her normal confidence, was aware she was trapped in her seat by him and her body language must have been showing her discomfort. Arthur tapped the man on the shoulder and motioned to him to vacate the seat and let him in. His drinking buddy obviously fancied his chances and was not happy to move easily.

"What's up?" he said, "I didn't know it was your bird, did |I?" Arthur grabbed his shoulder and hoicked him up quickly and with his one good eye boring into the man, he made it plain he was not appreciative of the comment.

"This is my bloody niece! And she's fourteen, I think it's time you were off, don't you?" The words through gritted teeth didn't bear contradiction and the man shuffled off grumbling that he wasn't to know.

"Sorry kid," said Arthur, "You sup this and I'll give you a lift home in a few minutes."

"Cheers, Uncle Arthur." she said.

Arthur looked at the other two who had joined them saying…

"You two best mind yer manners as well. This is my niece and I don't want her upset."

The two thought it wise to concur regardless of any inner feelings and Sharon settled back into her seat comfortable once more. Used to the banter around her parents' pub, she was soon giving as good as she got. The time flew by and she realised with a shock that she was late.

"I've got to go Uncle Arthur, my mum will kill me!"

"What about your record?"

"Leave that. Can we go now?"

"Aye lass, don't fret." He swilled the rest of his pint and stood up saying his goodbyes to the other two. His car was round the corner and in ten minutes he pulled up outside the Bowl and Onion pub.

"I'll come in. I want a word with your mam." He slammed the car door and strolled to the back gate with Sharon chatting away. He even gave her two bob, which was a fortune to a fourteen year old.

Their timing was great as Lynne and Derek had chosen that very moment to escalate a battle of words into the physical. Derek had hit her and Lynne had hit back. Being stronger in physique, Derek had a grip of Lynne by the hair when the two walked in and stopped open mouthed by the back door.

"Bloody hell!" was all Arthur said and immediately threw his arm round Derek's neck and got him in a headlock. Lynne was still kicking out and managed to land one on Arthur's foot, who howled in pain. Had it not been so frightening, Sharon might have thought it funny in someone else, but this was her parents. She grabbed a tray of glasses and slammed them to the floor. The glass smashed far and wide and was enough to halt the fight.

"That's enough! I'm sick of it!" Her shrill cry echoed around the pub kitchen and brought them all to a stop. Derek let go, Arthur let go and Lynne raised her hand to her cheek where the blow had landed and a red welt was appearing.

"I'm sorry luv," said Derek, as Sharon's eyes welled with tears.

"You two need to be apart!" was all she said. "Permanently!"

Derek silently picked up his coat and walked out. Arthur would have gripped him but Lynne raised a hand to halt him and nodded towards Sharon who looked stricken. Instead, Arthur brought Lynne through to the bar and set her on a high stool whilst he wrung cold water out of a bar towel and handed it to his shaking sister. Sharon's tears had spilled over by now and the reaction of what she had witnessed set in. Putting his arm round his niece's shoulder, he gave her a quick hug.

"Get yer mum a brandy luv, in fact, get us all one while you're there," he said. Looking at Lynne he gave her a solemn stare. "She's right you know?"

"I know," came the sad response from his sister. She didn't like to admit her defeat but it was time her marriage was over.

"...And here was me coming to see if I could hire your room out back for my wedding buffet." Lynne's eyes flew wide and it broke a very tense moment.

"Who the hell are you marrying now? Your divorce from May has only just come through!" she said in disbelief.

Arthur grinned sheepishly, "I thought I'd marry May again..."

"May?...The first May, your first wife?" Lynne was all but speechless. "Our mam will kill you!"

"Expect she will," he laughed and placed the cold cloth on her cheek.

Chapter Forty One – 1967

The radio played Andy Williams as May scrubbed Graham's collar. She paused for a moment, deep in thought and sighed. Three daughters divorced and she a Catholic. Back in Ireland she couldn't have borne the shame, but here she buried it deep and was allowed a normal life in spite of it. That left four kids she thought. Gray was too shy to even get himself a girl and Arthur! Well, he was another disgrace. Not content with ruining his first marriage, to divorce and set up with another woman and then buggering off back to the first one with intentions to marry her twice! Well he'd be one guest short that one! She'd die before she'd go and celebrate any further stupidity. It seemed the only two capable of having a happy married life were the twins. Thank God that at least two of her children had what it takes!

She realised she was grinding her teeth and Graham's collar was in danger of wearing away and she pulled herself back to the present. Throwing the collar to one side she stretched her aching back. Sixty-nine going on seventy and she was still washing her son's shirts! Her bones definitely felt old now and she seemed to have lost all the fire in her belly for life. The years had passed quickly since Edward had passed, but the worst of it was, she had never felt old before, not whilst he was by her side. Now all she craved was peace and her family.

Her pension was small, but with Graham's money they were managing and she no longer felt she had to work as long as they lived frugally. Graham showed no signs of picking up with anyone and when on the rare occasion his eye turned on a woman, May seldom approved and had seen them off. If she were honest with herself, she knew without him it would be a lonely life.

He was a good son, but unlike Edward, not the most patient when it came to decorating and repairs. Why use a screw when a four-inch nail would do was Graham's motto and he would 'bloody' and 'bugger' his way through any task until something resembling the job she had asked for was done. Yet give him a sick or injured animal and he was there. Last year he had taken on a small-holding with the intention of getting a pony. A friend had brought him a goat he'd found wandering and he penned it up. Next came the chickens. A few weeks later he was given a sheep that had been ill-treated and he spent hours feeding and caring for it until it was back to full health.

One spring morning he went to the pen to find the sheep had had a lamb and an incestuous relationship later, he was on his way to a flock! Still, May had thought. At least he wasn't carousing and up to all sorts of mischief like that older brother of his. For that, she was grateful. Deena, Dene's child, was always at his heels nowadays, following him round the pen asking limitless questions. For all his short fuse in other ways, with the child he had infinite patience and she was proud of him.

As for the rest, it seemed to her that her offspring were doing the best to finish her off with worry. Dene and she had not so much as made friends but ceased battle. Her daughter was too tired and strained, trying to make a living with the small amount of maintenance Dennis had been sending, to continue the argument. Still, at least he was sending something, which was more than some women had the benefit of.

It seemed to May that the world seemed to have lost its family values in this new 'Permissive Society' and Mary Whitehouse had good cause to campaign for greater censure on the TV. There was all sorts on after nine o'clock now. They didn't even care about being seen naked, some of these new actors and she was shocked to the core. Everything was violence and sex nowadays. No wonder the youngsters were going wild. Now in America, they were prancing round naked with flowers in their hair preaching free love. There was no end to it.

May walked into her small living room and paused for a second. It had been a while since she had written anything to The Observer. Perhaps she should write about how the times had changed over her lifetime and not for the good.

Getting to her knees slowly, she rooted around in the lower sideboard cupboard and brought out her old notebook. It had seen better days but as she grabbed some paper and a fountain pen and ink, the mood took her. Sitting down at the table, she leafed through her old letter copies and her head was full once more with those first old days when she had put pen to paper in the house at Wood Mill. She wrote, 'As I approach my seventieth year...'

The writing brought her closer to all that she had seen and lost. Even the best memory forgot some things and it was a lovely hour spent leafing through old times. There were moments where a memory brought her tears and others a smile of humour. Refining her words, she copied her final piece to paper and popped it in an envelope. Addressing it with a flourish she sealed the envelope and called the dog to heel.

"Come on Lucky, let's have a wander to the postbox," she said and the large black Dulux dog's ears pricked and his tail started to wag slowly. Lucky was another one of Graham's rescues. He had been working for a few years now on the new motorway maintenance team. Whilst the new road had brought him a good living, it had decimated the heart of the old village and ploughed its way through Fletcher's Farm just a hundred yards from their house. Instead of the green fields and tranquillity, there was now the constant hum of the M62, soon to become one of the busiest motorways in England.

Whilst cutting the verges underneath Scammonden Bridge one morning he had found a rubbish bag that some lowlife had dumped on the side of the road. All the puppies but one had been killed. Graham had picked him up, run home with him in his coat and warmed him up by the fire, giving him meat gravy and water to revive him. When May had questioned what he was going to do, Graham had said that if he made it through the night he would be lucky. Next morning he was up in his box, still with them and whimpering for food, so Lucky he became.

Graham loved that dog so much and a more intelligent dog couldn't be found. Now at the pen he had two followers, equally loyal. A small girl and the large dog, hanging on his every word. If Graham was lonely, he never showed it. All he seemed to need was the company of his sister and her child, his mum and his animals and the occasional embrace of the whole family.

Once a week he would head off to The Free Trade Inn and sit with a couple of mates and then would quietly stagger home, 'a bit giddy', as May would put it with a wry smile. She was thankful he didn't choose to head to Lynne's place and Arthur's cronies, very often. She'd rather he avoided his brother's influence. Physically there was no doubting they were brothers, but in nature, it was a whole other matter.

Chapter Forty Two – 1968

Knocking at the door always worried May. Most neighbours and family would call and enter. Knocking signified something else...formality, worry and bad tidings. She had been recovering from a cold and had recently been diagnosed with diabetes, so she was slow to move and reluctant to answer. When she did, she was greeted by a stranger with a broad smile. 'Selling something', she thought cynically and was ready to send him off with a flea in his ear, but apparently this salesman knew her name.

"May Handley?" he questioned cheerfully.

"It is," she answered, "...and who might you be?"

"Dan Pheelan, local reporter for the Observer," he replied. "Might I come in?"

"Do you need to?" May was wary. Couldn't trust anyone nowadays.

"If you wouldn't mind, only we got your last letter and we'd like to do a piece on you for your seventieth birthday, seeing as you have been one of the paper's longest contributors." His smiled widened and he stepped forward as May's mouth dropped open and she faltered.

"May I?" he asked again and she complied, taken completely by surprise. Still dumbstruck she pulled out a chair at the small table for him and signalled him to join her.

"I didn't realise anyone had noticed," she said quietly.

"Well, my editor has and that's why he sent me. Seems you've been writing some pretty powerful letters and articles for a lot of years and he'd like to feature you and your article in our next edition, Mrs Handley.

It took a few moments to dawn, but as it did, May's face lit up with pride. 'All these years Edward', she thought to herself. 'People were listening to what I had to say and I never realised...I should have done more!' From somewhere she heard him reply, 'Aye lass, you should and I'm fair proud of you.' The reporter continued, but May was so far away she had to ask him to repeat himself.

"As I said, Mrs Handley. We are going to send someone to pick you up and we'll take you up to Ogden for a couple of pictures, if that's OK?"

"Oh yes, that would be lovely, thank you."

The reporter took his leave after giving her a name and contact if she had any difficulties, otherwise they would collect her next Tuesday. She closed the door as he left and stood behind it for a few seconds before chuckling quietly to herself.

"Well I'll be blowed," was all she could say.

***

Gary slid himself out of his car and hobbled with a swinging gait up to his mum's door with the kids in tow. His stump was sore today and the kids were playing up. It was the school holidays and Irene had gone to town to buy them uniforms, preferring to do it alone rather than direct three boisterous kids and make any kind of sensible purchase. He had finished his ice cream round early and taken the van back to the yard ready for tomorrow. They were the only kids who could not be placated by ice cream so he had thought a trip to his mam's would sort them out.

Gary's pain had left him larger than life to overcome it and nothing he did was quiet. He was always jolly and if life had thrown him a few disappointments, then he had weathered them well, finding a happy family life. Without his disability he might well have had his name in lights and who was to say what would have been the better option. His bookings had slowed and it meant travelling further to earn enough. That in turn meant he saw less of his wife and kids, not to mention the fatigue. Eventually he made the choice of what was his greater priority and chose home and family. His kids loved him, and Irene, his wife, often exasperated with the chaos of being the only quiet member of a large rumbustious family, loved him too. What else could a man need?

"Hiya Mam, I've brought you some wafers, stick them in your freezer compartment." May had little time to argue as he bundled a newspaper into her hands that was insulating the quickly melting ice cream. May's new luxury had been a small fridge, which Graham had bought from the Co-op on hire purchase and had been shoved none too firmly into the only space left in the small kitchen under the stairs. It just about had room to squeeze the wafers in, mainly due to the fact that she was wary of freezing anything, for chance they got food poisoning. Gary and Graham had laughed at her for her old-fashioned ways, but she had refused to put anything in it until now.

"Right kids, tell your gran what we've been doing."

The kids clambered onto the settee together, and Susan, the eldest started to tell her gran they been to the cinema to see 'Dr Who and the Daleks'. May nodded and 'oohed and ah'd' in all the right places, but frankly hadn't a clue what they were babbling about. Clearly, they were excited and the volume rose in the small room.

Looking at them, May couldn't help but be proud of all Gary had overcome and achieved. Who would have thought of all her children he would have produced the biggest family? Susan was the spit of her as a girl with the beautiful 'Handley' eyes and the two boys were definitely boys and a handful. They were lively, happy kids and that was all that mattered.

"Right you three, off you go to the corner shop and go and get us one of them bottles of cream soda." They didn't need any second bidding and she turned to put the kettle on as Gary hitched his good leg onto a chair.

"How's things, Mam?" he asked.

"Good, very good...I'm about to have an article done on me in the newspaper." Her proud expression had Gary laughing.

"Ooh, bloody hell, hark at you!"

"Don't be cheeky," she smiled. "Have you heard from Maureen lately?"

"Aye," he said a little sadly, "You know they are thinking of adopting."

May sat down with a cuppa and handed it to him. "No I didn't, but I know the doctors had said she was unlikely to conceive...I thought they were happy just to have Mandy?"

"Apparently not. Peter's got a promotion and Maureen wanted to fill their new big house with kids. I suppose it's their business, but it's a big thing to take on a child that's not your own."

"I expect so, but she's like you… she's got a big heart and for all Peter and I don't seem to see eye to eye, he's a good man. The child couldn't want for better parents if they go ahead," replied May.

"They've signed up to foster for now, with a view to adopting."

"Best way forward I expect for them...Now tell me have you seen our Arthur since he's got himself wed again?"

"No, Lynne sees him, but I don't like the look of the company he keeps, so I keep myself out of it." May's smile faded as Gary spoke.

"I hear tell he's still knocking about with a couple of the Quality Street gang, have you heard what he's up to?...I worry."

"Our Arthur will do what he wants Mam. You should know that by now."

"Well regardless, that lot won't get one over on Lynne," she said grimly and Gary frowned.

"I wouldn't be too sure Mam, there are a few hard cases amongst that lot. I wouldn't want to cross them, you might find yourself hanging upside down off the edge of a Manchester car park!...she needs to have a care if they're making her pub their stomping ground."

May spooned sugar in his cup, he always liked it sweet and he had lost his lean bones and acquired a chubby face with age and appetite. He still had his ready smile that started in his eyes despite the pain he must have been enduring daily. He had a good heart, May thought as he played with the dog.

"Our Lynne's as hard work as Arthur. I'm hard pressed to decide which one of the two of them is the most trouble," said his mother.

"She talks big, but she'd be no match for them if she gets involved with any of their antics. They're already running a few of the Manchester clubs. Can't you have a word with her?" Gary pressed his mum's hand as he spoke and that told her there was more than he was saying.

"We're going next week for my birthday, so I'll see her then, I'll have a word."

"Good..." He was about to continue when the door banged on its hinges. They were back, the boys fighting over who was carrying the pop and Susan rolling her eyes heavenwards for her nine years and handing back the change.

Chapter Forty Three- 1968

May refused to have her hair done into the new shorter styles for the photographs and instead swept its length back into her usual plait. Donning her best wool coat, she pinned on a brooch and that was the only concession to the occasion she would make.

True to his word, Dan Feelan arrived with a photographer and she was whizzed up to the site of Ogden Chapel and posed for a picture. As it was lunchtime, they took her in the Bull's Head for a milk stout whilst they did an interview and, sitting by the window, she looked around at the changes that had been made. They had removed the tap room and opened up the ground floor into what had once been part of the Landlord's quarters. It seemed nothing stayed the same for long nowadays. Before she knew it, she was home and Graham's tea would be required very soon, so there was no room to sit and become big headed over her newfound fame.

Soon enough Gray was home, but not happy. He came in sullen faced and quiet, throwing his jacket over the back of the settee. Something was troubling him.

"What's up then? I know you and something is?" she asked.

"The bastards are making me redundant, they say I will get a few grand, but I want my job. I like it!"

Graham had worked enough years to earn himself a decent payout, but he didn't understand money and forms, so it was only when May read the notice and settlement with eyes as big as saucers, that he realised his misfortune in one respect was the pot of gold at the end of the rainbow.

"My good God!" she whispered in shock. "You'll get enough to buy this house AND do it up if you wanted." Gray's eyes mirrored her shock.

"Are you sure, Mam?" He was finding it hard to believe.

"Aye lad, if this is to be believed!"

Gray grinned from ear to ear. Never having had money, the prospect of owning his house was addictive.

"Then that's what we'll do! Bloody Hell Mam, we're going shopping!"

"Hold your horses laddie...Let's get the money in your pocket before you spend it shall we?" She laughed out loud with delight.

Graham was so excited, he forgot his normal reticence and danced his mother round the room. It was a time when jobs were plentiful, and he could always get work with Freddie Bowmer if he was struggling. A place that 'he' owned. How good was that? He would be as good as the rest of his siblings now!

***

"Right you lot, who wants serving?...and don't all shout at once". Lynne's voice rang out against the bar and there was a moment's pause before the hubbub started again.

"I give up!... Oh thank God you're here Dene, I'm going under with this lot. They're drinking me dry!"

"You know you like it!" shouted Sid, a regular across the bar. "Anyway, put another in here Dene, your sister's slowing down in her old age!" He thrust his empty glass through the sea of faces and into Dene's hands before she'd had time even to wash them.

Lynne, never missing anything, retorted, "You're a cheeky bugger Sid Walsh, I'll go twice as slow next time!"

Dene started to pull the pint, she was a popular barmaid but her air of gentility and elegance, in comparison to Lynne's robust nature, deterred even the most confident. She was friendly, but aloof and it preserved her from unwanted advances. Lynne on the other hand deterred all but the most confident also. Mainly because she was too fiery. Yet overall it was the knowledge that both the women were Arthur's sisters, that kept them from fighting off the men.

Lynne had even asked Rene to help on the odd occasion, such was the need. Truth be known, She and her elder sister would never get on completely. Their natures were just too different and Rene was perfectly aware that behind her back Lynne still referred to her as 'the duchess' to punters. Rene took it with good grace, better than having a nickname less regal.

Paul was now well settled in school and already popular with his peers. True to form he had soon started DJing at his school disco and the occasional event for Lynne. Rene had no doubt that in a couple of years he would be working the Manchester clubs with his promised Go Go Girls! Arthur had said he would get him some contacts but Rene wasn't sure she was happy with that prospect and thanked him politely but ignored taking the offer forward.

Tonight all three women were required, mainly because it was a family occasion and the family were gathering to celebrate May's 70th birthday. Gary and Irene had arrived, but Maureen and Peter were unable to make it until the weekend, when the whole family were booked for a meal in a local restaurant. Tonight was just a drink to mark the day with the real party awaiting in a few days.

May arrived with Graham in a taxi, a rare treat and she was sporting a new dress from Graham for the occasion. Lynne whispered to Dene as May showed off her present.

"She'll expect you to fork out for the bag and me the shoes, then she'll tell the Duchess she needs a new coat. You watch that one play us all off against each other..." Lynne grinned wickedly and Dene giggled.

Graham looked very pleased with himself, for a man about to be out of work for the first time in his life. Once he made them privy to his financial windfall, they realised that Graham for the first time in his life was proud of himself and it warmed their heart.

"Sit down Mam, I'll send the drinks over...Here Graham," shouted Lynne, "I've done some butties in the kitchen for you all, go get them." The happy group took over one corner of the pub and soon the atmosphere was infectious. They had all had a couple by the time the doors rolled open and Arthur arrived with a cigar hanging out of his mouth, with a bunch of flowers in one hand and a small package and card in the other.

May stiffened initially, but the alcohol had softened her resolve and she smiled unusually graciously towards her son who plonked the goods on the table in front of her with a, "Happy Birthday you old bugger! Don't say I never buy you nothing." May managed to retain her smile. It clearly wasn't his first stop of the night, but she wouldn't rise to the bait. She took the parcels and card, but it was actually the flowers that touched her the most. For all his bravado, he had made a real effort. Her surprise grew as she opened the small box and found an exquisite silver rosary and she was quite moved.

"Thank you, son," she said as her eyes welled. Why did he always make her love him again when she disapproved of everything he was? If he noticed, he didn't show it. He was already off to the bar, flashing his cash and ordering champagne.

"Don't be bloody silly!" Lynne laughed "Do you think my clientèle's the type for Champers? You'll have Guinness and like it!"

The pub by ten was rowdy and rammed now with family and regulars, when the door opened and what looked like a couple of Arthur's mates walked in. Rene was first to notice and raised an eyebrow to Dene who went to greet them politely. They weren't his regular crowd, but they clearly knew him and walked over to him. For once, Arthur wasn't his usual welcoming self but he intervened as Dene took their order and he paid for their drinks taking them over to a table away from the family group to talk.

Gary took a sideways glance at the newcomers and decided he was best staying put rather than going to talk to his brother, but Graham, having had a couple and on a high, went to sit with them. Arthur looked sideways with his one good eye, but didn't send him away. There was no mistaking they were brothers, and that the younger one idolised his older brother.

The two acknowledged him briefly and carried on with their previous conversation. It wasn't long before Graham started to look uneasy and got up to leave them.

"Aren't you getting them in again, lad?" one of the men said.

"Leave him be Witty, he's out celebrating my mam's birthday." Somehow, the tone had changed and Graham was out of his depth.

"I'd best see if she wants another drink." Graham came back to the family and sat down.

"Not keen on them buggers, I don't think Arthur is either," he muttered.

"Well, you stay here mate," said Gary. "He'll be back whenever he's finished whatever business he's conducting, but before you do, get our Irene a port and lemon will you. Irene smiled her thanks and carried on talking to May. The bar had quieted somewhat and Lynne had told Dene and Rene to join the family and they squeezed out from under the bar and through the remaining punters. Gray was just on his way to order as they approached him.

Rene was first to pass Arthur's table and the one called Witty saw her out of the corner of his eye and a hand snaked out to imprison her wrist in a grip that was a little too strong for politeness.

"Hey, you're a Bobby Dazzler love, aren't you? Fancy coming out to a club after with me and my mates?" Arthur's eyes narrowed. He didn't like these two much but there was business to be done, reluctant as he was.

Rene stood stock-still and looked down at her captive wrist with a look of quiet distaste.

"I don't think so, thank you all the same...Do you mind?" She looked again pointedly at her hand and waited. Witty got the message and let go dramatically.

"Oh get her! Sorry and all that...What about you love? I don't mind which one of you, you're both a bit of all right!" Dene finding his attention was on her, coloured up and tried to stay out of arm's length, but he caught the back of her full skirt and yanked her back.

"That's enough, leave her be!" Arthur growled quietly looking up from his pint with his one good eye meaning business.

"What's up with you? I'm only having a fucking laugh...it's just a bit of skirt!" Dene took her opportunity to wriggle away from the sleaze and Arthur continued.

"Watch your mouth in here! It's a family pub and they don't want to be hearing your potty mouth! If you can't take your drink then go home! We'll talk another time."

"Who the fuck do you think you are? I'll do what I like!"

"Not with my sister you don't." The Handley temper had come to the fore swiftly and May and the family heard the loud scrape of the chair as it tumbled and fell, rather than sensing anything was wrong. Other punters nearby had paused in their drinking, sensing trouble, but Arthur was fast and before anyone could react, he had kicked the man's chair backwards and sent him sprawling. Before he had chance to go in the other man gripped Arthur from behind allowing Witty to recover and get to his feet.

All attention was drawn and May had risen seeing the trouble start. Gary jumped up as quickly as his leg would allow.

"Get Mam out of the way Irene," he said grimly and went to hobble over to do what he could. Graham had already jumped across a table and waded in and Lynne had swung out from under the bar seeing her family were involved. Rene and Dene stood horrified as it was hard to tell who was beating who.

It wasn't your normal brawl. These two were dirty fighters and weren't averse to causing real damage and right now Arthur was their target. Graham was trying his best to drag the other one off and allow Arthur to get to his feet, which he did and the odds were a little more even for a moment.

Lynne was bawling over the top of them and for once her voice was unheard and did nothing to deter any further violence. Arthur was bloody but raging and Gary had had his good leg kicked from under him and had fallen badly. Seeing it Gray shouted, "You bastard!" and launched himself with renewed vigour at the guy who was clearly bigger and stronger. The man turned and pushed him off.

"Back off, if you know what's good for you," he said menacingly, but Gray wasn't hearing. The Handleys were known for their temper, though rarely exhibited when they blew, they blew. Graham went back in yet again and this time the man turned on him and delivered several low blows.

From the floor where he had fallen and was stranded with nothing to pull himself back up on, Gary caught the flash of a blade and tried desperately to roll back up onto his feet as he shouted a warning to his brothers, but his pot leg prevented him. He saw Graham go down as Lynne smashed a heavy glass ashtray over his opponent's head. The man went down like a ton of bricks on top of Gray as Arthur laid Witty out with a punch to the jaw.

May waded through the crowd free of Irene's attempts at restraint and pulled the man off her son with every bit of strength she had. There was blood running down the man's face onto Graham's jacket, but it somehow seemed too much for the small cut he had sustained. Graham staggered to his feet dazed.

"Thanks Mam," he said clearly shaken. May looked at Lynne.

"Ring the police..." she shouted, "and an ambulance, now!"

"Not for these buggers I'm not!" said Arthur wiping a cut on his lips with the back of his hand.

"No... for your brother, quickly!" she shouted and the onlookers followed her eyes to where the knife protruded from Graham's side. As Gray also started to feel the pain of his injury he looked down and his face went ashen with the realisation he had been stabbed. There was a cry from Dene and Rene in unison as he fell to the floor, unconscious.

The rest was a blur, someone went to pull the knife out, but Lynne knocked their hand aside before they did any damage.

"Get me clean bar towels and get on that phone NOW!"

Her years of nursing came to the fore and she took over with an efficiency and seriousness that no one had ever seen before. Gone was the loud joker and in its place was something new. People scurried in all directions. Some to direct the police and ambulance. Others restrained the two perpetrators. Some with less stomach and something to hide skulked off quietly avoiding attention and any possible retribution. Soon after the first distant sounds of the ambulance started to be heard, Gray's eyes flickered open and he lifted his head not really with it.

"Stay still our kid," said Lynne as she compressed around the wound and thanked her lucky stars the pub was so close to the hospital.

"I want to get up," muttered Graham in his disorientation.

"Stay down or I'll lamp you myself," she threatened.

"Where's me mam?" he asked weakly.

"I'm here love, do as Lynne says," said May as she lowered herself awkwardly to the floor and grabbed his hand. He started to shake with reaction and someone put a jacket under his head. She had been stood frozen in fear whilst Lynne had worked on him. He was still her boy and it was like Gary all over again. She couldn't bear it a second time. As the hand pressed his head gently back onto the makeshift pillow, May looked up to thank them and found the tortured eyes of her eldest son.

"This is your doing!" The words left her mouth like venom and Arthur visibly recoiled.

"It weren't his fault Mam," Graham said, his teeth chattering now.

"Not bloody much it wasn't!...this was you and the foul company you keep, your nothing but a twopenny gangster, get out of my sight, you disgust me!" May would have said more but Rene's hand on her shoulder stopped her.

"Not now Mum eh?...the ambulance is here...and the police."

Gary had managed to get his leg unlocked and had gone outside to hurry the medics in. The arrival of the police soon had everyone rounded up to one corner of the pub to take statements.

"Can our Dene come to the hospital with us Mam?" Gray asked as they were loading him on a stretcher. Dene had been sitting on the other side of him, terrified and crying quietly.

"If you want love." May threw one last look at Arthur. "You mind you make these two pay or there'll be trouble. Don't you be ducking out when the police's backs are turned or you'll have me to deal with!" Arthur nodded grimly but said nothing.

As Dene and May left with Graham in the ambulance, the other family members gave their names as witnesses and left Lynne and Arthur to make sure the culprits were arrested. Lynne looked at Arthur.

"Who the hell were they for Christ's sake? You could have got our brother killed."

"I'm sorry Lynne...I don't know them well. Tommy Dearden put them onto me for a bit of business and just sent them here to find me. I didn't know they were nutters!" His good eye glistened with unshed tears and despite his bravado, he was clearly heartbroken.

"Well I'll tell you this for free. Don't you bring your cronies in my pub ever again! In fact, I don't want you here again. You best make these two suffer or I'll want to know why and when you've done that I'll consider us quits!" She turned to Gary as he walked away from speaking to the police.

"Gary, get Irene home and go round to the babysitter's for Deena and bring her here, our Sharon will be home from her dad's soon and can look after her while I go up to the hospital with Rene and then come up yourself...and you better use the phone and ring our Maureen as soon as you can..."

"Ok, sis." It seemed for once Lynne had took the lead over Rene as Rene stood stock still, watching the departure of the ambulance. Her silence demonstrating that she was in shock.

The police were bundling Witty and his psychopathic mate into a Black Mariah. Arthur watched them leave as the copper waited to put him in a second car and the exchange in looks was enough to know the day's business was not yet settled. There would be consequences. Gary loped up behind Rene and she jumped as he spoke.

"Rene..." Gary prompted her. "Are you going with Lynne? You've got your car?"

"Yes, yes I'll do that," she said as she grabbed for her handbag and rifled through it for a hanky as tears quietly spilled over.

"Get a grip Rene." Lynne's none too sympathetic voice came over her shoulder. "Right everyone out!...This pub is closed!" She bundled the last two stragglers out and closed the door behind them. She drew a deep breath and handed Rene a hanky.

"He'll be all right," she said.

"Will he?" Rene asked.

"He's a Handley isn't he? We don't quit easy."

Rene dabbed the tears from her eyes. "He's still a kid!"

"He's a grown man, he's just been mollycoddled by mam that's all, but when it counted he stood up, so he'll be alright. Blow your nose, put that hanky away and get that car door open". Lynne watched as her sister fiddled for the keys and her composure. 'She's not a bad old stick for all her posh airs,' she thought. Turning to her as she sat down beside her, she gave Rene the first genuine smile in years and Rene after a second's hesitation, smiled back.

Chapter Forty Four - 1968

Dene and May were sitting silently in the corridor when all Graham's siblings arrived at the hospital in dribs and drabs. Maureen rushed in about eleven p.m. and burst into tears and was inconsolable. The only one missing was Arthur, who was still at the police station.

At present, Gray was in the operating theatre, that was all they knew, and it was a sombre group that stood waiting. As the gathering group grew in size, a nurse was sent to usher them to a side room. May sat down wearily and the rest followed and for a while there was total silence. Maureen was the first to speak.

"What happened, Mum?"

"Arthur happened, that's what!" May was still burning with fear and anger.

"Where is he?" Maureen hadn't had much of a story from her twin and was at a loss to understand how her younger brother had got himself stabbed, as shy in nature as he normally was.

"I don't know, probably at the cop shop," said Lynne.

Rene finally came out of her silence and took up the baton. "It's what he's always done, mixing with the wrong people. Is it any surprise something like this has happened?. Always wanting easy money is Arthur. He's an accident waiting to happen."

"That's not fair Rene. He's a good man and a good brother, he wasn't to know that was going to happen. It could have been anyone.

Those two were just trouble!" Lynne jumped to his defence despite her earlier verbal attack on him.

"Of course it's fair! If you knock about with scum like that, something always happens. He's never done a hard day's work in his life. God knows what he's responsible for and you should know better than to let those types on your premises!" Rene's back was up and Lynne bristled at the implication.

"Look at Miss Bloody High and Mighty here! I couldn't see you dealing with them any better than I did. You stood there wailing when our Gray and Gary were getting seven colours of shit knocked out of them. At least I intervened!"

"I'm sorry if I can't use my fists like you, but I wouldn't have a premises that invited that kind of trouble in, in the first place!" The voices were raising in the heat of the exchange and Dene started to well up with tears. Gary put his hand up in the air.

"That's enough, all of you. Let's leave the recriminations untll we know he's all right shall we?" His words echoed round the ugly painted walls and they fell to order once more. It was clear that emotions were running high and at times like these, you either held together, or fractured and now was not a time to fracture.

May got up from her seat. The waiting and not knowing was overcoming her once more and she walked to the door and looked out and up the corridor. The room they had given them was far away from any main activity.

"Quite frankly, right now that boy is the only one I'm thinking of, so you can all put your petty squabbles aside. For God's sake, he might be dying right now!" It was enough to bring them to heel and as May started to walk up corridor Dene followed her out.

"Mum, where are you going?" she said.

"I'm going to see if I still have a son and get away from all of you. You bring me nothing but worry and that lad's never done anything in his life to deserve this, so you can all bugger off...I've had enough!" May marched up the corridor and as she rounded the corner she came face to face with Arthur.

"Mam...I'm sorry, really I didn't..." She slapped him hard across the cheek and would have hit him again had he not stayed her hand.

"Now I'll take the first, but I don't deserve the second!" he said with a low growl.

"You beggar off!" she hissed back at him. "There's nothing for you here. I never want to set eyes on you again! Look what your dirty business has done to my boy!" Arthur took a deep breath as she fell silent and for a moment he looked about to cry and then just as quickly his face hardened and he looked her square in the eye.

"Your beloved boy's alright by the way, I've just spoke to the doctor...I'm alright too, just a few cuts and bruises if you're interested, but you're not, are you?" He said it with a hint of venom and turned and walked away up the corridor, pulling a packet of cigs out of his pocket for something to do with his hands.

May burst into tears of relief and all she could think of was getting to Graham. This thing with Arthur had started many years ago and it would likely continue for many more. Right now, Graham needed her. It never occurred that for all his bravado, her eldest son needed her also and her rebuff had been the final nail in the coffin of her relationship with him.

Arthur walked out of the main door and headed across to a bench where he slumped in the dark and lit a cigarette. Blowing out the blue smoke, he swallowed down his emotions but they fought right back up again and putting his head in his hands, he wept brokenly.

"I'm sorry our kid," he cried as he whispered the words. "I'm sorry...I'll make the bastard pay!"

***

Graham had had a lucky escape, the doctor had said, and the knife had missed any vital organs. He would be fine in a few days, barring infection. The news was good, but May was not placated. As far as she was concerned, Arthur may as well have stuck the knife in himself. She sat by Graham's bedside until the next morning with Dene, when he woke up and asked for breakfast. Only then did she allow herself a break.

As she sat in the canteen, she pondered on motherhood and how the worry never seemed to leave her, however old they got. Could she have done better? She guessed all mothers ask themselves that question at some time in their life. Re-running the decades of her life from the moment she became a thinking rational adult she wondered if there had been any time in her life when she had just been May, pure and simple, no-one's wife, mother or grandmother. She concluded there had probably been only one moment in recent years that had been truly hers. The moment she sat in the Bull's Head at Ogden discussing her article.

Apart from that, she had been too bogged down in family life to take any more than a few snatched hours for her writing. Was this all life was meant to be, an endless jumping from one stepping-stone of worry to the next of disaster. Surely, some women had full lives without needing to surround themselves with responsibility?

Here she was at seventy with her family in tatters once more, on a day that was supposed to be a celebration of her life. Her special day...Couldn't the fates at least have let her have had that? Her lips set into a bitter line and at that moment something in her turned old and she decided that this was it, enough. Time to rest and let them all get on with it, she was done.

Chapter Forty Five

Of course, she wasn't done... Graham came home fully
recovered, bought his house and had it done up. In those few weeks,
Dene helped wherever she could and bridges were rebuilt a little more
and old wounds healed. On the day Graham had started the rebuild
with Freddy Bowmer and his boys, May had been told to move out to
Dene's and not come back until it was done.

She spent six weeks forbidden to enter. The most she saw was
the coming and goings of the builders and the hammering and
occasional cloud of dust billowing from the open front door as she
peaked through Dene's kitchen window that overlooked Graham's
house. When finally it was ready, Graham strung a ribbon across the
new front door of Stott Street and had raised a plaque above the lintel
in brass, which read 'On the 6th Day God created man and then he
rested. On the 7th Day God created woman and no bugger ever rested
again..'

Despite his intended micky take, all Graham's unspoken love
for his mother was woven into the walls of that small cottage and as
she cut the ribbon, Dene and her daughter standing nearby saw his
heart full with pride that it was he that had provided his mother with a
home in her old age. That was all it meant to him, he had achieved.
From the boy who couldn't read or add up, this had been a long journey.

There was mention that the man Arthur had fought with and
who had stabbed Graham that fateful night had disappeared. No one
dared think what had been the cause and if they thought, they didn't
ask. No one saw Arthur again for years. It was heard he was about on
the odd occasion, but even Lynne had not seen him or any his cronies.

They heard of the inevitable second divorce from May and Michael, his son never sought out his father's family, but other than that, his life going forward had been a mystery.

Shortly after, Lynne met and married her second husband Bob and they took over the running of a pub in Royton and the link was broken. If Arthur had ever come back to the old pub in Rochdale, he would not have found her there. There was no social media to track someone down, no mobiles. You had to physically walk to question whoever and so the gulf widened and Arthur was lost to them. Lynne broke the odd ashtray but otherwise mellowed to as much as Lynne ever would.

Maureen and Peter adopted a boy, Jamie and, shortly after they went to watch an event with Billy Graham and so very suddenly Peter and his family flew to start a new life in Switzerland with Peter training as a priest in the Presbyterian church. Following on from that they spent many years in Scotland and Peter was later awarded a CBE for his relief work in Africa. May saw little of them and the children and was sad. She was too old to travel that distance comfortably now and they were so tied to his Parish and work that it made it difficult to make the journey to her. She kept in touch by letter as was her preference and if she felt the need to call any of her children, she had voiced that the call box around the corner was close enough and no need for a phone at home. It was her way.

Gary remained his same steadfast self and life for him went on as normal. His kids grew and flourished and had kids of their own. His leg was a trouble and his heart had started to be affected, but he could still belt out a fabulous tune and was always the life and soul of any gathering.

Rene met a kind and gentle man named Jack and they lived happily, transferring her dress business to a corner shop. There was no glory in this new enterprise, but she didn't mind. Paul took to his new stepdad well and pursued a life as President Paul and his Go Go Girls, a slight name change from his aspirations as a teenager. Nothing was less than Rene had expected of him and she was proud. She still graced her small shop as elegantly as she had walked the fashion shows of London. It didn't matter where she was, she had found peace in the person she was with. She and Lynne never really breached the distance created in that hospital waiting room but they stayed in touch, just about...

Dene tried a reconciliation with Dennis, but it was doomed to failure. Never again being able to find the love that she had thought she had found in Wes, she settled for something else. Wes had never come back and so she impatient for love she had moved on in an effort to mend her heart but never quite found her dream. She ploughed her love into the two grandchildren Deena gave her instead, having married twice more, widowed once and was on her way to another divorce. Yet, ever still the romantic, wishing for something more. She remained beautiful but disappointed with life. Eventually, she found herself back in Milnrow and close to her mother.

This is the way life goes for most of humanity. Big dreams, not so big realities. The family had fractured a little that night and it they were never quite the same afterwards. Factions were made, sides were taken, loyalties were demanded and, although some refused to take sides and stayed in the middle, trying to please all, something was lost. Life moved on, time moved on and dreams faded, as did bitterness. Day to day life took over and the norm resumed and truces were called.

If we examine our lives, we would see that ninety percent of us 'almost' make it big, but very few of us actually achieve our dreams. Even as we bask briefly in those precious moments of glory, we know they are fleeting. When all is done, it boils down to love and family and the closeness of good friends being the real measure of our success in life. For when we lose those that undertake the journey with us, what else is left?

May watched it all through tired eyes and wished it had been different. Short of banging her middle-aged children's heads together, what could she do?. So she did nothing. She let it be, as only one learns to do with great age and emotional fatigue. The years passed by and she watched them all grow, taking pleasure in the little ones and letting her children lead their own lives and protect the world of the children they had themselves born.

***

Arthur emerged some years later and lived frugally on what money and from where?, no one questioned. He still had the roving eye and still only the one, Emphasized now by bottle stop glasses that magnified his stationary glass eye stare. He was still quick with a dry joke when the occasion demanded and gradually one by one he encountered his siblings and they forgave him for the past. Perhaps they were all getting wiser with age.

It never seemed quite the same though and there didn't seem to be the big family gatherings now that they had experienced in earlier days. The pace of life was speeding up and people had little time for each other. Each intent on pursuing their own small nucleus of immediate family and subject to the pressures and division that the pace of modern times brought about, the closeness was lost. It was a sadness.

Occasionally there would be a flurry of activity and cousins of the new generations met up at a wedding or birthday and some would form friendships and others kept their distance. Beneath it all though, there was still a sense of family, despite them being scattered to the wind and often miles apart. May watched and grieved for the days at Wood Mill around the cramped but happy table in the kitchen that the family threatened to overwhelm. What she would give to be back there once more. Those had been simple times where people needed very little to be happy. Nowadays it all seemed to depend on what you had materialistically. She would have given anything to have revisited the nights she and Edward had lain the latest babe in the bottom drawer and snuggled down beneath the covers listening to the bairns shuffling and noises ,with the intention to make more...

Chapter Forty Six - 1982

Today May was tired, but excited, the Pope was coming to
Heaton Park! Pope Jean-Paul was coming to Heaton Park! And she
was beside herself. It was 1982 and she was in her eighty-fourth year.
The weather had been very warm for the month of May and May had
so wanted to go, but her blood pressure had been up. She had been
advised by the doctor to take things easy and was very frustrated that
they were treating her like an invalid.

May had been remarking recently that she wouldn't be long for
this world, as old people do and Graham had laughed at her saying,
"You'll outlive us all you old bugger". Deep down he was aware that
she was slowing up and no longer the force to be reckoned with for
some time now. Perhaps she was depressed because she couldn't go to
see the Pope. They could tell she was more than disappointed and
Graham had said Dene and Deena would pick them up and they would
go out for lunch instead, would that please her?

May had agreed when Graham had said there were over quarter
of a million people expected at the park and it would be too much for
her. Besides, they wouldn't get close for all the drunken Polish people
that would be falling about celebrating, and she would be lucky if she
got to see anything. So, they had deterred her and she had accepted it
would be unwise in this heat. So instead, they were heading up to
Ogden for a look at the reservoirs and a bite to eat in the Bull's Head
and May thought this was second best by far, but a nice one
nevertheless.

Dene and Deena arrived and May gathered her scarf and bag
and took a coat, just in case it got cooler later. They had just stepped

out onto the path outside the cottage, when the sound of a helicopter flying overhead and low made them look up instinctively. It had the Pope's livery on and it was the time he was due to arrive at Heaton Park. There was no doubt it was him.

To say she was delighted was an understatement. She considered it a personal blessing that he had flown over her head. 'Who needed to fight the crowds at Heaton Park?' Flushed with excitement and eyes aglow she had said, "That's it. I can go tomorrow now if I want and die happy." Her children smiled that she had kept her faith despite everything.

They had a lovely meal and May had remained enthralled with her blessing. It was a glorious afternoon and May wanted to walk to the end of the road to where Ogden Chapel had once stood and the graveyard where Edward used be found tending the grounds in their younger days. The reservoirs were still and blue from the sky and people were fishing peacefully on the banks. May breathed in the warm air with all its sweet scents and memories.

"Another few weeks and the winberries will be out and then we'll have a pie to remember," she said. Sitting on a bench that overlooked the valley, she sat and looked about her at the moors that had adopted the young pregnant woman from Ireland and brought a kind of peace to her life. "Aye, there's nothing like this place, I wish I was still up here."

"I love it here too Gran," said Deena. She sat with her gran whilst Dene and Graham wandered further, where May was too unsteady on her feet to follow and May envied them. She thanked the Lord her children were all safe and said a prayer that they would remain so. She spent the time that Gray and Dene were walking pointing out all the places that her brood had played and worked to her granddaughter, and for the briefest of moments the young woman felt the memory of being a babe in the kitchen at the Wood Mill house and her grandad holding her small fingers around the reins, as she steered the horse and cart up the Huddersfield Road. This place had a magic of its own. She laid her hand on May's and they sat in quiet companionship till the others returned.

Dropping her off at the house with Graham, Dene and her daughter headed home happy after a lovely afternoon. May kicked off her shoes and sat down in the armchair with a groan and massaged her swollen feet marked by her cramped shoes.

'What a grand day,' she thought as Gray put the kettle on and called the dog to walk with him to the corner shop for milk. She snoozed for awhile in the chair with the front door open for air and the cat on her lap. The motorway's peak time hum had quieted enough to let her sleep and the clock's tick was all that held her attention until she drifted off.

In her dreams, she was a young woman again, walking with Edward across the moors. She awoke still feeling his hand on hers and she looked down at the silver bracelets, one for every child he had given her.

"Are you coming for me soon, my love?" she half whispered.

***

At 11p.m. Deena took an anxious call from her mother to say her grandmother had had a heart attack and the ambulance was on the way. The word went round and by the early hours they were all headed for the hospital. She was unconscious, which was a blessing and Graham, Dene and Deena sat by her bed in silence, as one by one the others arrived.

They knew it was bad, as no one on duty stopped them and the whole family was allowed in the small side room. Graham hardly spoke, the likely loss of his beloved mother so hard to bear that speech was beyond him. The rest waited for the inevitable, each with their own thoughts.

True to her words as the Pope had flown over her, May waited for the next day and with her family around her and Arthur's hand on the door as her breathing grew more shallow. She took a long last breath and allowed her son to come in before passing peacefully as he reached her side with a soft, "Hiya Mam." No one said anything, there was nothing to say. She was gone and in her leaving, a part of each of them had gone with her.

To some, her passing was hardly noticed as they just passed on the news that Old Ma Handley had died. To others close to her, it was searing pain and a void that would never be filled.

Our time on earth is often only valued by the few that are really close to us. May Handley had her dreams of a grand life but little opportunity to achieve her potential in a world of inequality for women that was taken for granted and to some degree still is. She had lost those dreams by taking one small diversion from her dreams, hardly noticed at the time. The evening Edward had helped her up onto the back of Lady and she had been lost in the romance of it all and it had changed her path. She had exchanged life for love.

Instead of a lady with prospects, she became a mother and a grandmother, something that holds increasingly less value in today's material society. Yet to those that had experienced her love and care, she had been a force of nature and her value immeasurable...

Chapter Forty - Seven

It was a cool autumn day when the woman and her husband walked slowly to the centre of the small stone bridge. She stood a while looking at, and listening to the river that bubbled over the fallen millstones beneath its surface. As she watched it it meander downwards through the valley, she breathed in the mild sweet air full of earth and the seasons decay and turned to look about her.

The quarry, where Lynne had once dangled from the end of Trotter's tail was to her right. To her left were the trees on the side of the hill where the mill had once stood with its looms clacking joyously.

Bluebell Wood and the reservoirs rose up on the moors above Ogden in a clear autumn sky. Greenhalgh's, where Gary had his leg torn from him at just fourteen, still remained in a modern incarnation at the top of the valley. She was fifty-nine years old and had just lost her mother.

Opening the small container, she paused to quietly say her goodbyes and for a moment when the lid came away, it was as though she could hear the clatter of the cart wheels where once they had skimmed the edge of the narrow bridge and barely missed slipping off into the water below. The ruts of the carts wheels were still in the stone of the bridge and would only remain for a brief few years more before it would eventually collapse into the river, gone forever.

Her children, Sarah and Alex, wouldn't even remember it. For they had never lived on these moors. It had never grown into their hearts as it had hers, and she knew she would be the last of her line to love this place. Perhaps she should write it down so that one day when they had come to know and treasure their own families, they might also read her words and appreciate the family that had been the route to the people that they now were.

Her grandmother had never seen her great grandson, but she had adored her firstborn daughter. How May, on having had a small stroke whilst she had been pregnant with her first child, had insisted that her granddaughter sat beside her and learned the crotchet stitch to finish the christening shawl that she had been making for the new bairn, just in case 'she popped her clogs'. She didn't of course and made a swift recovery, living on for a further four years. Yet how that tradition would now continue taking the pattern her grandmother had taught her down to the next generation. Each of her own grandchildren had been given the same shawl crocheted with the same love.

This woman stood silently with her memories had, after divorcing young, retrained and become a stage and costume designer and more recently and artist and writer. It had been a hard road, juggling the roles of single parent and a career, but a rewarding one. All the things that May might have aspired to had she followed a different path, in a more forgiving time.

The world had moved on and women were now 'expected' to have a career and also maintain the family unit. After many years of chasing equality and never quite catching it up, she had just found out that the government had stolen six years of her pension and she would now be too old by the time she was allowed to rest and concentrate on her hard earned dreams to write. It had been a devastating blow to what little future she had left... Maybe just this one important book then.

Perhaps the combination of her two grandmothers love of performance and writing and her own mothers love of design had had an impact that had brought her to this point. Those small moments in our childhood often set something in motion that we do not acknowledge until later in life. Here in this place, with a head full of memories, it all seemed so clear. She was a product of all their past dreams and ambitions.

Hanging over Peppermint Bridge the trees whispered in the wind and she sensed the voices of the past still calling to her from the open windows of the mill that had once towered above them... but that had been gone for many years now.

All that remained of Wood Mill Cottage, itself, were a few stones in the hillside. They were the only testament to it ever having ever existed. The rest of the foundations having been covered and levelled to make a woodland campsite.

A few cobbles remained of the path up to the where the mill had stood, pointing the way to a history that was now long gone. Any clues of its presence were now disguised by the undergrowth on the banks of the valley. She tried to conjure it as it had once been, but the memories were fading and she felt sad that she would never again experience the joy of being a child in that time and this place.

Carefully tipping the ashes towards the water she hoped that at some point they would find and merge with the ashes of her uncle Gray's that had been scattered here just a few years before. For this was the place of their happiness as children. As young as she had been herself when she first walked this path with her mother, it was forever in her memories.

Where Edward had frightened her with his Guy Fawkes mask. Where he had held her on his lap and let her hold Captain's reins as a toddler. Small, but precious and vivid memories. Here, where as a babe she had been safe in the arms of this poor but proud family, who carried their babies in baskets over Captain's back. Who fought, laughed and protected each other and then fought again, but always there was love, unspoken, but constant.

The ashes she scattered, were those of the last of May's children to leave this earth...Dene. She had been born the weakest and yet had outlived all her siblings. Her daughter, Deena, who scattered them, knew she would always be a product of the love and character that had run through the veins of her family before her. She was just a small part of them all. These hills, so very far from where she now lived, still claimed her heart and her soul. How swiftly time had flown since she was a child and here she was, a mere step away from old age herself.

She pondered on the last words she had spoken to her mother in her final moments...How she had told her it was ok to go now. All she had to do was walk across Peppermint Bridge and open the gate to Wood Mill Cottage and they would all be waiting for her. Dene had asked often in her dementia when her mum and dad would be coming for her and her daughter had prayed that she would finally get her wish. A single tear had then slipped from her mothers eye and as Deena dried it told her not to cry, that it would be all right, she had quietly passed.

It had been almost a hundred years since May had first set eyes on Edward in her aunt's parlour and it had sent her forth on a journey away from her beloved Ireland. The Ireland that she never saw again. Those years had been filled with what treasures?... The biggest treasure of all... family. For life is fleeting, but the spirits of all those who had lived on these moors were strong in the soil, the water, trees and in the smell of the vegetation. Whilst there was still a descendent who remembered them, they would never be lost. For here had lived the Handleys. They were as much a part of the history and energy of this place as the moors themselves.

As the last of the ashes filtered through her fingers and drifted down to the water to be claimed by the banks and the roots of the trees she knew they would never be gone from her. It was because she herself was a child of May... and that very strength of her grandmother's spirit was running through her blood and that of her children's. Whilst May had lived and beyond, part of her would always be with them.

As she brushed away her tears for the loss of her mother and turned from the bridge to take her husband's outstretched hand, a breath of wind brushed her face and she thought she heard a young boy shout... "Come on our Doreen! Mam is calling you! There'll be hell to pay, you're late!

THE END

Lightning Source UK Ltd.
Milton Keynes UK
UKHW020958130720
366454UK00017B/1481

9 781916 390027